The Other Woman

By Joy Fielding

THE BEST OF FRIENDS
TRANCE
THE TRANSFORMATION
KISS MOMMY GOODBYE
THE OTHER WOMAN

The Other Woman

JOY FIELDING

Doubleday & Company, Garden City, New York
Doubleday Canada Limited, Toronto, Ontario
1983

Library of Congress Cataloging in Publication Data

Fielding, Joy.
The other woman.

I. Title.
PR9199.3.F51808   1982   813'.54
AACR2
ISBN: 0-385-17811-5
Library of Congress Catalog Card Number 81-43548
Copyright © 1983 by Joy Fielding, Inc.

To Warren

The Other Woman

Chapter 1

"Excuse me, Mrs. Plumley?"

The girl was young and pretty, with large breasts and a surprisingly husky voice. Jill Plumley shifted uncomfortably, the heels of her shoes making fresh holes in the uneven knoll of newly manicured grass. She had wanted to wear flat shoes—it was an outdoor picnic, after all, even if it *was* being held at the chic Rosedale Country Club—but David had insisted that all the other wives would be more formally dressed, and he was right. Except for this girl, who wore a casual red T-shirt and a pair of defiantly non-designer jeans pulled tight across her equally defiant young bottom. Whose wife was she anyway?

Jill smiled, quickly taking in the girl's violet eyes and flawless skin, artfully made up to look as if she wore no makeup at all. Her discomfort increased when she realized she was being similarly inspected. She felt instantly self-conscious about her hair—it always looked as if she were just about to comb it—and her height—five foot nine inches. This girl had silky black hair and stood a more reasonable five foot six, or so Jill quickly estimated, feeling her own shoulders slump instinctively to com-

pensate for the difference in eye level, feeling generally awkward and too large, the bull in the china shop confronted by
the porcelain doll.

"Yes?" It was half-statement, half-question. Yes, I am Mrs.
Plumley; yes, what is it you want? Jill was surprised at how
husky her own voice had suddenly become.

The girl's face lit into a broad, perfect smile. "I'm Nicole
Clark," she said, extending her hand. "I'm going to marry your
husband."

Everything stopped. Like a movie which suddenly snaps in
mid-reel, the annual firm picnic of Weatherby, Ross jerked violently out of sync and was abruptly pulled from view.

It was one of those days. She'd known it from the minute her
stomach had catapulted her out of bed toward the bathroom at
not quite seven that morning to rebel against the shrimp dinner
of the night before. David had followed her with his spray can
of Lysol and there they had remained, alternately heaving and
spraying, until Jill was able to sustain sufficient breath to yell at
David to kindly stop that damn spraying—the smell was making
her sick. He, in turn, wished her a happy anniversary—their
fourth—and got back into bed, leaving her to contend with the
final arrangements for picking up the two children from his previous marriage and bringing them to the picnic, an event they
looked forward to with almost as much anticipation as a trip to
the dentist's. Or a visit with their stepmother. On top of all
that, Her Royal Highness, the first Mrs. Plumley, had greeted
Jill at the door to David's palatial former home—looking just
past her as if she really wasn't there—to request that David and
Jill also feed the children supper—she had a date.

An anniversary, an upset stomach, two hostile stepchildren,
her husband's ex-wife, and now this. Jill stared wordlessly at
the girl, this Nicole Clark, who stared back as directly and
pleasantly as if she'd just asked her for the correct time. Slowly,
the scene around her began to re-form, regain its shape and
colors, impose its reality on the absurdity of the situation. She
was standing in the middle of some one hundred lawyers, all
members of one of Chicago's largest and most prestigious law
firms, their various spouses and offspring. It was a white-hot
day in the middle of June; her sundress was sticking to her back
and underarms; her white shoes were slowly burying themselves

into the soft earth beneath her, and she was talking to a girl at least a decade younger than herself, with perfect skin and hair that didn't frizz up with the humidity, who had just informed her that she was going to marry her husband.

It had to be a joke. Someone—possibly even David—had put the girl up to it as a gag on their anniversary. Jill allowed her mouth to relax into a friendly grin, feeling a little foolish at having taken so long to catch on to what was happening.

"This isn't a joke," the girl said, reading Jill's mind. "I'm very serious." Jill's grin stretched even farther across her face. This girl was good, whoever she was. Maybe even a professional actress brought in especially for the occasion. Or possibly she was a client of David's. That thought made Jill vaguely uncomfortable, recalling as it did a remark her mother had made to her once long ago and one she had confronted David with on their first memorable meeting. Then she had appeared in her role of brash young television producer and he as the ever-cocky, potential interviewee, one of the city's most successful divorce attorneys and quite probably the most gorgeous hunk of legal training she had ever seen. Without seeming to move her eyes, she had taken in his artistic face, his athletic body and his plain gold wedding band, and thought of her mother's caustic observance when her cousin Ruth had begun dating the divorced divorce attorney who had handled Ruth's own recent separation. Is it true, Jill had asked David almost six years previously, wishing that her mother's casual observations weren't so frequently uncannily astute, that divorce lawyers who are themselves divorced often fool around with their clients? I couldn't answer that, he had stated, a wicked half-smile slowly curling the corners of his mouth, I've never been divorced. How long have you been married? she pushed, knowing the question was irrelevant, not anywhere in her notes. Fifteen years, he said, his face suddenly without expression.

Jill continued grinning at Nicole, hoping nevertheless that she wasn't a client. She had also had enough of the gag and wished fervently that the girl, whoever she was, would just take her magenta fingernails and go home.

"I thought it was only fair to warn you," Nicole continued, about to say more.

"That's enough," Jill said, cutting her off abruptly, surprising them both with the sudden fierceness of her tone, the soft huskiness having disappeared altogether from her voice.

"I mean," she continued, softening, "you had me going a bit there, I admit it. So it was a cute gag and I'll get a good laugh out of it when I tell my friends, but the trick is to leave 'em laughing—"

"This isn't a joke," the girl repeated.

Jill's mouth closed tight. Her voice turned low, barely audible against the sound of her heart pumping fresh blood past her ears. "Then I think you better get the hell away from me." Jill drew her body up to its full height, pushing her shoulders back as proudly as if she had just been named this year's Posture Queen, and stared down at Nicole Clark. I am not afraid of you, she shouted wordlessly. I am not afraid of you or your youth or your threats.

Nicole Clark shrugged, her smile undisturbed. With almost deliberate slowness, she turned in a half circle and disappeared into the well-dressed crowd.

Where was David? Jill suddenly wondered, spinning around quickly, feeling her body shaking with sudden indignation as she searched the crowd, recognizing that despite her earlier self-assurances, she had never been so afraid in all her thirty-four years. Her eyes narrowed as she caught sight of Nicole snaking her way languorously through the crowd, smiling comfortably at those she passed, obviously headed in a specific direction. Where? Jill watched her with fresh intensity.

"Jill Plumley!" The voice was male and carried with it a recognizable insistence. Reluctantly, Jill turned in its direction. "I said to Harve, if anyone knows the answer to this one, it's Jill Plumley. Jill knows *trivia*."

Jill smiled at Al Weatherby, the firm's original founding father, though he hardly looked the role with his wiry boy's body and wavy brown hair, and subtly angled her glance back toward the crowd. She couldn't find Nicole.

"Who's the girl who starred with Dick Benjamin in *The Marriage of a Young Stockbroker?*" he asked, his broad smile filling his face. "I bet Harve Prescott fifty dollars you'd know the answer." Harve Prescott hovered anxiously nearby.

"Joanna Shimkus," Jill answered absently, her body shifting slightly.

"No, not the wife. The other one—you know, the other woman, the real sexy one who sprawled out on the bed and lifted her skirt—"

"Tiffany Bolling," she answered, feeling her body being pulled like a magnet toward the crowd.

"Right!" she heard him call after her as she moved away. "You're terrific! I knew you'd know! Did you hear that, Harve?"

Jill hoped she hadn't been too noticeably rude as she pushed herself farther into the crowd. Al Weatherby was more than just the kingpin of a successful law firm who had single-handedly built his own legal empire from its humble beginnings over a drycleaner's shop. He was the man most responsible for her husband's own rapid rise to prominence, the one who had recognized David's early potential and first brought him into the growing firm, nurturing and guiding him along the way, and in the process becoming a close personal friend. He had even taught the two wary novices to play bridge, displaying at all times the legendary patience he was most noted for. She heard him laugh, turned in his direction in time to catch his playful wink, and realized she needn't have worried. Al Weatherby was not a man who took easy offense. Her mind returned quickly to the girl in the red T-shirt.

Nicole Clark had disappeared. Maybe she went home, Jill hoped, taking a deep breath and doing a quick turn. She caught sight of David's daughter, Laurie, sulking over by the dessert table (though she would never touch a bite of anything on it), and his son Jason halfheartedly deigning to participate in an impromptu game of hide-and-seek with some of the other, more animated youngsters. Were all teenagers this sullen? Jill found herself suddenly smiling, the thought of Nicole having to contend with these two delights making her feel instantly better. Laurie's younger brother, though not yet into his teens, bore an uncomfortable resemblance to his mother, and was almost unbearably shy. If either youngster smiled at all, especially in her presence, it was usually to the accompaniment of news that their mother was going back to court to ask for an increase in alimony payments or that she was about to recarpet the entire house in white plush because she was feeling a little low since her return from her holdiay in Europe and was in need of perking up. For a man of David's considerable reputation, he'd certainly been taken for a royal ride when it came to his own divorce. Judges were always toughest on members of the legal profession, David had explained, quickly bypassing seventeen years of marriage, two children and an undisclosed number of illicit liaisons, their own included.

Laurie looked directly at her, shooting her a look filled with such perfect disdain that Jill almost had to admire the skinny child's skill, for it told her in a glance that not only was she still considered a homewrecker six years after the fact, an interloper, an outsider, a temporary inconvenience who would surely be discarded when their father came to his senses—in short, a total yuck—but she was also weird, dumb, gross and all those other peculiar adjectives fourteen-year-olds seem so drawn to.

I did not break up your parents' marriage, Jill tried to communicate to the young girl with her eyes, recalling Elizabeth Taylor's choice remark when Eddie Fisher left Debbie Reynolds to her diaper pins and pigtails—you can't break up a happy marriage. Laurie turned away from Jill's gaze. Sure, she thought, expect a fourteen-year-old girl to buy that one! Did Debbie Reynolds buy it?

Jason appeared, accidentally brushing up against her side, the heel of his shoe jamming into her exposed toes. "Oh," he said, recognizing her. "S-sorry. Did—did I step on you?"

"It's all right," Jill told him, trying subtly to extricate her right foot from the earth which now covered it. "I have another one." Jason looked close to tears. "Sorry, old joke," she continued, forcing a chuckle. "So—are you having a good time?" Why was she asking that? Any idiot could see the answer.

"It's okay," he answered slowly, so as not to stutter, a stutter which Elaine had been quick to point out had only developed *after* his father had left home, and which served as a constant reminder to David of his failure as a parent. The boy had lately taken to talking more slowly in an effort to control it. If only David's guilt could be as easily controlled, Jill thought, watching Jason, who always appeared so much older than his years. She could almost hear his mother's voice—you're the man of the house now, Jason.

For an instant, Jill felt the overwhelming urge to throw her arms around the young boy, but the look in Jason's eyes suddenly hardened and Jill felt herself pull back as Jason shuffled away, his growing boredom reflected in his walk. Maybe he'd find his father, persuade him to leave the picnic early.

Where was David?

Jill found him posed beneath a monstrous weeping willow—an appropriately dramatic setting, she thought—engaged in what even from this distance she could recognize was an earnest, and therefore, probably long, conversation with one of his partners, a conversation nobody would dare to interrupt. She felt her body relax a little, the acid in her stomach gamely trying to return to its normal level, admittedly never low.

Just looking at him made her feel good. People were always telling her he looked like Robert Redford, but even with his wheat-blond hair falling carelessly across his forehead and his mischievous pale green eyes, she thought that was stretching things a bit. What he was, however, was absolutely, unquestionably handsome, and if he lacked the singular presence that went into the making of a major movie idol, well, so what? She doubted that Robert Redford knew the difference between a tort and a tart. She only hoped David would remember, thinking unwillingly of Nicole Clark.

Undoubtedly, if you were going to be objective about it, they made the more appropriate-looking couple, her husband and this other woman. They complemented each other well, both sculpted from the same mold of casual perfection. Even her black hair co-ordinated with his blondness, each accenting and highlighting the other. The hell with being obejctive, Jill suddenly decided, shaking her own reddish mane, feeling several stray hairs sticking spitefully to her back. In happier moods, she told herself she looked like Carly Simon, but as no one else had ever commented on the resemblance, she had concluded that it must be somewhat subtle. At any rate, it didn't really matter. *She* was the one David had married—and he'd left one conventionally attractive woman in order to do so. Somehow the thought of her husband's earlier infidelity and divorce didn't make her feel any better. She wanted to go home. Perhaps she could plead illness—her stomach, the heat—

"So, how's university life?"

The voice startled her and she visibly jumped, turning to confront Beth Weatherby, wife of Al and one of the few office wives with whom she felt any sort of kinship at all.

"Fine," Jill lied, seeing instantly that Beth didn't believe her.

"The hell it is," laughed Beth, who was, at forty-five, twelve years younger than her husband. They had been married twenty-seven years, a fact which constantly amazed Jill: to know what it was you wanted when you were eighteen and to still want the same thing almost three decades later. "I saw Al trying to corner you before," Beth said, as if recognizing Jill's sudden change of thought. "Honestly, a grown man and he's just like a kid. He sat up half the night trying to think up movie trivia that would stump you." Jill laughed. "You really miss it, don't you?" she asked suddenly.

"Miss what?" Jill asked, although she already knew the answer to the question.

"Television," came the expected response.

"Yes," Jill said simply, her attention suddenly diverted anew by the sight of Nicole Clark re-emerging and maneuvering her way toward David. Jill watched as her husband moved to include the newcomer easily in the conversation.

"Who is that?" she asked Beth Weatherby.

Beth looked toward the towering weeping willow. "The girl talking to your husband? I can't remember her name, but she's new. One of the law students, I think, working at Weatherby, Ross for the summer."

"She's going to be a lawyer?"

"Al says she's very good. Very smart. In fact, now that I remember it, he hasn't spoken as highly of anyone since he met David and asked him to join the firm. He says she has an absolutely brilliant future ahead of her. Wouldn't you know she'd be absolutely gorgeous to boot!"

Jill felt her stomach beginning to turn over. "Excuse me, I'm not feeling very well." She retreated to an unoccupied corner of grass. She felt her heels submerge, locking her in place. Beth Weatherby was instantly at her side, pulling some large white pills from out of her yellow straw bag.

"Antacid," she explained before Jill could ask. "Take a couple."

Jill did as she was told and put the two tablets in her mouth. "Chew them."

Jill began to chew, her face reflecting growing displeasure.

"I know, they're terrible. Taste just like chalk. But they work. I've been taking them for more years than I can remember. Ulcers," she said, again not waiting for the obvious question.

"Why do you have ulcers?" Jill asked, genuinely surprised.

"Occupational hazard," Beth said, smiling. "Lawyer's wife."

Not to mention having raised three children, Jill thought, remembering that David had recently told her that the youngest, a boy of seventeen, had dropped out of school to join the Hare Krishnas. At the same time David was telling her this, he had given Jill permission to shoot his own son should a similar insanity ever overtake the boy.

"Here, *this* should make you feel better," Beth announced, pulling what Jill assumed was another pill out of her purse, and putting it into her outstretched hand. Jill looked at her palm. Not pills. Instead she saw a plain white envelope addressed to herself in Beth Weatherby's backhand scrawl. "I thought you'd appreciate it," Beth said, giving her a sly smile and then moving over to join a small cluster of other wives who promptly shifted their bodies to admit her. Like an amoeba swallowing its prey, Jill thought, seeing Beth virtually disappear, and turned her attention to the letter in her hand. She tore open the envelope and pulled out its contents.

The letter was to the point and neatly typed. Only her name had been written in by hand. She read it quickly and then read it again.

Dear *Jill*,

Are you bored in bed? Tired of waking up every morning to the same assortment of grunts and smells and complaints? Do you miss the excitement of those bygone days when his heart was bigger than his bald spot?

We know how you feel. We feel the same way. So
we have devised a plan. Simply send your husband to
the first name on the list below, cross that name off
the list, and then add your own name to the bottom.
Then make copies of this letter and send it to five of
your friends. Within six months, you will receive
40,000 husbands.

But be careful—YOU MUST NOT BREAK THE
CHAIN! Two years ago, Barbie Feldman broke the
chain and not only has she been stuck with poor old
Freddie ever since, but her GE toaster-oven broke
down and she was raped by her Maytag repairman!
We don't want this to happen to you!

Why take a chance on misfortune? Come on—it
beats ironing shirts. Just send your husband and add
your name. Then do a favor for five of your friends.
DO NOT BREAK THE CHAIN!

It was followed by a list of five names, Beth Weatherby's
being the new addition at the bottom.

She laughed out loud, feeling instantly better. Leave it to
Beth, she thought, looking toward the weeping willow, seeing
her husband now alone in conversation with Nicole, feeling instantly worse.

She watched them talking, unaware of her attention. David
seemed relaxed and happy. Even from this distance she could
make out the roguish twinkle in his eyes. Suddenly, he threw
his head back in laughter, undoubtedly the result of a hopelessly clever remark Nicole Clark had made. He caught her
eye as he turned his head to push back the hair that had fallen
out of place. Immediately, he smiled warmly, lifting his wine-
glass in her direction for a silent toast. As she watched, he lowered his head toward Nicole, whispering something while the
girl nodded acknowledgment. Jill's eyes traveled immediately to
Nicole, who quickly trapped her gaze and returned it, lifting her
own glass into the air in a toast exactly like David's. Her lips
moved silently. "Happy anniversary," she said.

Chapter 2

The offices of Weatherby, Ross occupied two full floors of the ninety-four-story John Hancock center, and they were everything a Hollywood set designer could imagine—thick beige Berber carpeting against caramel suede walls covered with modern lithographs and tapestries, and corridors which wound their way lovingly in all directions, stopping at suitably spaced intervals for spacious offices with floor-to-ceiling windows and views appropriate to the rank and stature of the various inhabitants.

David Plumley's office was located just past the wide, interior, circular stairway and almost directly across the hall from the boardroom. His view—from the fifty-eighth floor—was spectacular. The office itself was a mess.

Jill Listerwoll had been ushered in politely and told that David Plumley would be in to see her momentarily. That had been almost twenty minutes ago, but Jill didn't mind, using the time to go over her notes and reread the information she had gathered from those lawyers she had already interviewed. Of all the offices she had been in that afternoon, this was by far the most disorganized. She had never seen so many papers or law books scattered about in so seemingly chaotic a fashion. The large oak desk was completely swamped, as were the bookcases, filled to bursting. Even the visitors' area—two blue-and-green-striped chairs hugging a round glass table—was piled high with legalese, and stacks of papers grew like ivy from the base of the walls. The artwork was interesting, detached in its blatant modernity. The only hint of a sense of humor lay in one of the lithos—a stark recreation of a parking meter registering "Expired," which hung directly behind the desk and which, she surmised, was meant to serve as a subtle reminder to tardy clients that their time was up. There were no family portraits—appropriate, she thought, for one of the winningest divorce lawyers in town.

David Plumley walked into his office and sat down behind his desk. Jill took quick note of his blond hair, green eyes and boyish I-know-I'm-a-handsome-devil grin, felt the meter ticking behind him, and plunged right away into her first question, the one she had told her mother, with just the proper degree of disdain, that she had absolutely no intention of asking.

"Is it true that divorce lawyers who are themselves divorced often fool around with their clients?"

His mischievous grin grew wider. "I couldn't answer that," he said simply. "I've never been divorced."

"How long have you been married?" she continued, aware of the antique gold band on the appropriate finger of his left hand. It was an unnecessary ornament, she felt—everyone knew that the ones who looked like he did were invariably married.

"Fifteen years," he said. His face and voice were suddenly flat. "I'm sorry I kept you waiting."

"Waiting?" For one crazy second, Jill felt he was in some way still referring to his marriage.

"I got tied up in the boardroom." The mischievous grin was back on his face. Almost as if he could read her thoughts, as if he could sense the confusion into which her whole body had suddenly been thrust. "Can I get you a cup of coffee?"

"No, thank you," she said, looking around, hoping to avoid his eyes. "I've had three cups already."

"Then I'm not your first—interview, that is," he continued coyly as her eyes crept slowly back in his direction.

"No, you're not," she answered sharply. Surely they were both too old to be this cute. "Is your office always such a mess?"

His voice was equally sharp, his answer as precise as her question. He needed no second hints. "Yes," he said. "Now, what exactly can I do for you?"

She told him, slipping comfortably back into the role of TV producer, distancing herself from his cool green eyes. She was doing a news show on the elite of the Chicago legal profession, interviewing the three top firms (he questioned the other two choices) and trying to gain some insight into the way a firm of the size and scope of Weatherby, Ross functioned on a daily basis. Al Weatherby, whom she had interviewed first, had taken her on a general tour of the offices, had explained that the eventual goal of the large firm was to be even larger still, indeed the largest law firm in the city. There were eighty-five lawyers on staff, he had proudly explained, predicting an increase to one hundred within five years, and beyond as the firm expanded with time. Of the eighty-five lawyers, almost thirty were senior partners, the remainder consisting of juniors and associates. Each lawyer employed one full-time secretary, and there was an additional coterie of general office staff and law clerks. In addition to the individual offices and boardroom, there was a library, a cafeteria and two staff lounges. Al Weatherby had estimated their annual rental at around one million dollars.

The lawyers themselves fell into different categories. Basically, in decidedly non-legal terms, if there was a problem, there was also a lawyer to solve it. Corporate, criminal, tax, family, litigation, real estate—*et al.* They were all here. And doing very well, thank you.

"How much money do you make a year?" Jill asked David Plumley, trying to catch him off guard.

"Is that relevant?" he asked.

"I think so," she said, looking directly at him. "Considering that this *is* a show about the highest-paid members of your profession. I like to know roughly what I'm talking about."

"Don't we all," he mused, almost to himself. "Six figures."

"Over a hundred thousand dollars a year?"

"Six figures," he repeated.

"Do you work on a contingency basis? The higher the settlement, the larger your share of the profits?"

"No, that's not my style."

"Why not? What is your style?"

"I prefer to charge according to the amount of work I do, the time I spend. Contingency fees aren't always fair, in my opinion, although there are a great many highly reputable lawyers who would give you a good argument on that point."

"But you don't like that system—"

"I prefer another method."

"Moral ethics?"

"Possibly. We lawyers do have them, you know." He smiled for the first time in several minutes. "I feel like I'm being cross-examined."

"What sort of day do you put in?" she asked, suddenly switching gears.

He shrugged, a touch of irony creeping into his voice. "Oh, just your average fifteen-hour day—in by 8 A.M., home by 10 P.M."

"That's only fourteen hours."

Again he smiled.

"Do you feel it's 'fair'—your word—to be making so much money from other people's misery?" she brushed on.

"I like to feel I'm putting an end to the misery. And yes, I think it's eminently fair. I work very hard."

"What do you think of the charge that's been made by many parties involved in divorce actions that everything goes along fine until the lawyers get involved?"

"I think you've been talking to a lot of losers."

Jill tried not to smile. "You don't think it's true, then," she began, shaking her head back, throwing off the temporary invasion of his charm, "that a lot of women are really out for blood and that they often try and take the poor guy for everything he's got—"

"It may well be true," he answered honestly. "It's also true that a lot of men will try any number of dirty tricks to get away without paying their wives what they rightfully owe. And that's

one of the problems. I think that a lot of women still don't understand all their rights under the law, despite the advent of
women's liberation, and they don't realize just what they're entitled to. I *tell* them what they're entitled to." He paused. "And
then I get it for them."

"Are most of your clients women?"

"About two thirds."

"What first interested you in the law?"

"I like to give advice."

"And family law?"

He paused. "I'm not really sure." He shrugged. "I tried out
the various alternatives, didn't like real estate or criminal law,
hated corporate and tax law although I was very good at it. I
guess I just kind of drifted over to divorce. Are you married?"

"No."

"Divorced?" An engaging tilt of his head.

"Single," she stated with a touch of defiance. "Never married. Spinster. Old maid."

Her eyes challenged his—okay, buster, you started this.
Where are you headed?

For his part, David Plumley saw a woman with large brown
eyes and frantic reddish hair who took almost a perverse
delight in downplaying how attractive she really was, hiding
behind baggy pants, a shapeless shirt and a rough, even abra-
sive manner. He saw an independent, slightly fey kind of
woman with an important, even glamorous, job who was trying
very hard not to be attracted to him, and despite the fact that
she was far from the prettiest woman he'd had in his office that
day, she was as appealing to him at that moment as any woman
he'd ever met.

The knock at the door interrupted their thoughts. Al Weatherby popped in to whisper that Warren Marcus was getting a
little hot under the collar about everyone's tardiness and kindly
requested that he please have all his dockets in by five o'clock.

"What are dockets?" Jill asked as soon as the door closed
again, feeling grateful for the interruption, her pencil poised.

His answer was precise and well thought out, as if he were
used to explaining things to novices, and enjoyed doing so.
"Dockets are time records that every lawyer keeps which set

out, one, how long he worked on a particular matter, and two, what that matter was about. It's what I was mentioning briefly before when you asked about my style. Say, you come to me for a divorce and we spend two hours discussing it. When you leave, I get out my file marked Listerwoll, Jill, and I fill in 'Two hours: discussed divorce petition.' A few days later, you call me on the phone, you're worried your husband's going to sue for custody of the children. We talk for thirty minutes. When we're through, I get out your file and fill in 'Thirty minutes: talk re custody.' At the end of three months, I take your file and add up all the hours I've spent on your messy little marriage and multiply them by my hourly rate, so I can then send you a bill which also lets you know exactly what I've done. That is a docket."

Jill smiled widely, immensely pleased he had remembered her whole name. "You're cute," she said, feeling herself suddenly relax, and they both laughed, Jill aware that this extraordinary-looking man could be had for the asking, feeling inexplicably very sorry for his wife. I wouldn't want to be married to a man like this, she found herself thinking. A man you'd have to share with the world.

"What are you thinking about?" he asked.

She looked into his eyes and said nothing. He knows, she thought.

"Oh, you smell good," he said, coming up behind her in the small bathroom and kissing the nape of her neck. Jill's back moved up against him instinctively, hoping for more. "You almost finished in here?" he asked.

Jill put down the mascara she had been holding and looked at his reflection in the mirror. "You know what my idea of luxury is?" she asked, not waiting for him to answer. "Two bathrooms."

He turned her around and kissed her on the mouth. "You almost finished?" he asked again, smiling.

She groaned playfully. "I guess I can brush my hair in the bedroom."

He looked at her quizzically. "I thought it was brushed," he said.

"Thanks a lot." She grabbed the brush and headed out into the hall.

"That was a compliment," he called after her.

"Sure it was," she said, plopping down on their queen-size bed and staring at herself in the mirror over the dresser. What had ever possessed her to paint the walls yellow? It was definitely the wrong color for her complexion, not to mention her hair. She ran an indifferent brush through the tangles, then got up from the bed and moved toward her image, stroking her hair with greater concentration and determination. When she was satisfied, she put the brush down and returned to the bed, trying to decide on what to wear. She'd narrowed her choice down to two outfits—a pink sundress or white pants with a lime-green halter top. She decided on the pants since it was foolish to wrinkle an expensive new dress on three hours of bridge. I've become so practical, she minced, thinking that the dress was, in fact, a year old. David walked into the room looking appealingly disheveled. Could this man never look less than gorgeous? she wondered. And what on earth did he see in her? It was a question she knew was in the minds of whoever saw the two of them together, of all the office wives, excepting Beth, who could never understand why he had discarded Elaine (why, Jill isn't even pretty, she had once overheard). Undoubtedly, Nicole Clark had asked herself that very question.

"Where's the brush?" David asked.

"On the dresser." She pointed. "Go ahead. Take it."

"That's all right," he said, good-naturedly, "I'll wait until after you've used it."

"Great."

"What's the matter?"

"I just used it, you turkey!" she said, jumping up, the belt on her bathrobe coming loose to expose the naked body beneath it.

In a flash he had thrown her back across the bed and was scrambling on top of her, the two of them laughing so hard it was impossible to do anything else.

"I was just teasing you," he said, throwing her arms up behind her head and pinning them there. "You look magnificent. I think you are absolutely terrific-looking." He started kissing her in earnest now and their laughter ceased as his hands moved expertly down her body.

The phone rang.

"It's for you," she said. "Guess who?"

"What makes you so sure it's Elaine?" he asked, stretching his arm across her to the telephone, without moving the rest of his body.

"Because she always calls at moments like this and besides, the dear thing only phoned twice today already. I take it you didn't return her calls?"

"I never return her calls." He picked up the phone. "You could be wrong, you know. Hello." Jill waited for the inevitable, oh yes, hello, Elaine, and it followed immediately. She gazed up at the cracks in the ceiling while her husband, still lying on top of her, talked with obvious exasperation to his first wife.

"Yes, I saw your messages; no, I didn't bother returning your calls. I didn't have the time for another argument about nothing." He looked down at Jill, kissing her nose. "I don't have the time now." He paused long enough for Jill to catch the whine in the other woman's voice. The passion had left her, she realized with only a modest degree of surprise. The woman must have a television camera hidden somewhere in the room, Jill thought, so she knows each time exactly when to call. Pushing David aside gently, she maneuvered her body free of his and moved toward the walk-in closet, opened it, stepped inside and pulled out her white pants and green halter top.

"Of course I know Jason is going to camp at the end of next week. Who do you think is paying for it?!"

Jill went to the dresser and took out a pair of white panties.

"Why does he need a new sleeping bag? He has a perfectly good sleeping bag. So what if it's five years old? The parts don't stop working!"

Jill stepped into her panties and slipped into her lime-green halter top. She stared in the mirror. Who was she kidding? If you wanted to wear halter tops, you needed boobs. She thought of Nicole Clark, who'd have no trouble holding the damn thing up. She looked over at David. She hadn't told him of her conversation with the younger woman. What was the point? If anything, it would only perk his interest. What man wouldn't be intrigued by the sheer audacity of such an unprovoked declaration? Especially when the declaree looked like Nicole Clark. Especially when the man was David. She discarded the green halter top and returned to the closet.

"I don't care if the damn thing is ripped to kingdom come, I am not paying for a new sleeping bag. It's a thousand dollars a month at this camp you're sending him to—don't they have any beds?"

Jill selected a hot pink oversized shirt and threw it over her head, poking her arms through the wide sleeves.

"Look, Elaine, I'm not going to discuss it further. You think the kid needs a new sleeping bag, *you* buy him one—with the seventy-five hundred dollars a month I'm already paying you!"

Jill looked in the mirror. She looked pregnant, she thought, feeling suddenly light-headed at the prospect. Maybe, she hoped, silently calculating the number of days till her next period. She looked over at David, a shiver running through her.

He shook his head, covering the receiver with his hand. "You look pregnant," he whispered, obviously displeased by the notion. Of late, she had noticed his increasing reluctance to start a new family or even to discuss the possibility. Quickly she removed the pink shirt and returned it to the closet. David's voice brought her running back.

"What?" he yelled, raising his voice for the first time in the conversation. "You're crazy, Elaine. Do what you want! You want to go back to court? Fine. We'll go back to court!" He slammed the receiver.

"She's going back to court?"

"She's making threatening noises."

"What for this time? My God, don't tell me she heard I saved enough money to buy a new sweater?!" Jill was only half-joking. Alimony, child support and taxes depleted the lion's share of David's income, making her job at the university not only one of convenience, but one of necessity. You're a kept man, she would sometimes tease her husband, trying to mitigate her hostility by laughing at what was eating at her, namely that all David's money seemed to go to his ex-wife and kids while all her money went to support the two of them.

She'd been paying the rent on their downtown apartment since their marriage four years ago, despite the fact that the arrangement had supposedly been temporary. Not quite the life-style she'd envisioned.

"She says that she's thinking of asking for a cost-of-living clause because, well, you know, inflation." Jill stared at her husband with blank eyes. She couldn't speak without risking anger, and what was the point of getting angry at David? It certainly wouldn't help matters. "Is that what you're going to wear?" he asked. She looked down at her naked breasts and white slacks. "Why the hell doesn't she get married again?" he asked, throwing up his hands.

Jill found herself back at the closet. "Are you kidding?" she asked scornfully. "That woman will *never* get married again. She's having much too good a time pulling the strings—purse and otherwise."

David laughed ruefully. "It would have to be a pretty special kind of guy—one who only likes to screw twice a year."

Jill ran a hasty hand through her blouses, seeing prominent stains on the few she would have considered, wondering why she had ever bought the others to begin with. They were awful. "Wear the green halter," David said, squeezing past her to get at his own clothes. "It looked cute."

Jill grabbed the skimpy top, her thoughts immediately back on Nicole. She lowered it and turned to David. "What do you think," she asked, "do we have time to finish what we started before?"

He checked his watch. "We're due at the Weatherbys' in exactly thirty-five minutes and Lake Forest isn't exactly around the corner."

She dragged the green halter top down over her hair—what difference did it make?—and firmly closed the closet door.

"We'll finish when we get home," he called after her. She nodded though she knew he wasn't looking. What made people live in the suburbs? Jill wondered, feeling frustrated and annoyed as she plopped on the bed and waited for David to finish dressing. She looked over at the phone. She always knows just when to call, Jill thought. Somehow, she knows.

Chapter 3

"One no trump."

"Pass."

"Two hearts."

"Pass."

"Pass."

"Pass."

"Two hearts it is and my beautiful partner is playing," said Al Weatherby, looking across the table at his wife of twenty-seven years. David led the king of spades and Al Weatherby laid down his hand as dummy. "Eighteen beautiful points. Too bad you don't have anything to go with it, honey," he said, walking around the table to see what Beth had in her hand.

"Oh, Al, I'm so sorry," Beth said, paling noticeably. "I don't know where my mind was." She laid her cards against her chest, hoping Al would choose not to look, and when he chose otherwise, she reluctantly brought her hand forward for him to see. "I forgot everything!" she moaned.

"My God, look at what you've got here," he said, his voice registering more shock than anger.

"I know. I know." Beth's voice was barely audible.

"We've got at least a small slam between us and we're playing two hearts! Where are you tonight, honey?" Beth's eyes filled with tears. "Oh, please don't cry, sweetie," he said quickly. "It's only a card game! I'm not angry. In fact, now that I see your cards better, I can see that two hearts is the perfect bid. I would have said exactly the same thing."

Both David and Jill laughed and Beth tried to laugh too, but couldn't. Jill felt so sorry for Beth—she'd been playing very badly all night despite her years of experience at the game. At least Al was the kind of partner who never lost his temper. It was, as he had said, just a game.

"Just play it, honey," Al said, returning to his seat. "You can't go wrong."

Beth played out the hand in silence, missing only one trick and easily making the small slam she should have bid. She smiled over at Al sheepishly at the hand's conclusion.

"You should have finessed the king at trick three," he said patiently, gathering up the cards. "That way you would have had them all—you had nothing to lose."

"Let's have some coffee," Beth said, getting up from the table and bumping into Jill's chair. She let out a short, involuntary gasp.

"Are you okay?" Jill asked, concerned.

Beth nodded. "Just that I keep hitting the same spot all the time. You know what they say about open wounds." She stopped. "Do they say anything about open wounds?" she asked and everybody laughed. Jill's offer of assistance in the kitchen was turned down as they moved from the card room to the large and comfortable living area, filled to overflowing with expensive antiques.

"I'll help Beth," Al volunteered, making sure his guests were comfortable first. "That was a real cute chain letter Beth sent out, wasn't it? God, I had such a good laugh about it. By the way, Jill," he said suddenly, a mysterious glint creeping into his eyes, "who were the three women who starred in *A Letter to Three Wives?*"

"Jeanne Crain, Ann Sothern, and Linda Darnell," Jill answered without a moment's hesitation. "You want the men's names, too?"

"Are you kidding? A good lawyer always knows when to quit. Isn't that right, David?"

David nodded. "She's the champ."

"Thought it might be before her time."

"I watch a lot of old movies," Jill said, remembering the days when it had not been uncommon for her to watch a whole string of late-night features only to stumble in to work on an hour's sleep, fresh images of Joan Crawford rolling around in her brain.

She didn't stay up all night watching old movies anymore. David started his day at six-fifteen in the morning. He liked to be in bed early, and he claimed he couldn't get to sleep if she wasn't in bed beside him.

"Let's see, David, you like cream, no sugar, right?" Al Weatherby asked, already heading toward the large hallway. Jill thought that you could pick up their whole apartment and plop it right in the middle of that hallway and still have lots of room to move around.

David nodded. "And Jill, you like yours black." It was a statement, not a question.

"Please."

"I think Beth made an extraordinary blueberry flan," he said. "If you'll excuse me, I'll go help her and be right back."

Jill watched Al Weatherby leave the room. He was only minimally taller than herself, an elf-like man of seemingly boundless energy and patience, his thin body made surprisingly muscular because of an early and deep interest in lifting weights. It was said he could survive on virtually two hours' sleep a night, and David had once commented that in the fifteen years he had been with the firm (the last eight as a senior partner) he had never seen Al Weatherby lose his temper. Al also made a point of ferreting out as much information as he could about the spouses of the lawyers in his corporation. When he'd learned that Jill was as addicted to trivia and the Classified Ads section of the morning paper as he was, she'd become his special favorite. His acceptance of her had made her acceptance by the other lawyers and their spouses (especially those who had known and liked Elaine) infinitely easier.

"What letter is he talking about?" David asked, settling back comfortably into the soft velvet of the old Victorian sofa. For an instant, Jill thought he must be talking to someone else.

"Oh, the chain letter—about the husbands. You know—didn't I show it to you?" He shook his head. "Oh, well, I still have it —somewhere. Beth gave it to me at the picnic." Her voice faded away.

"The picnic," David repeated ominously. "Are you going to tell me what happened at the picnic?"

"What are you talking about?"

"Something happened at that picnic that you won't tell me about, and every time I mention it, your face goes kind of funny and your eyes get this curious kind of dazed look about them—there, they've got it right now." Jill blushed. "And you're blushing! You never blush."

"I'm not blushing," Jill said, trying to laugh away the truth of his words. "You're crazy." She looked around. "Such a huge house for just the two of them."

"A not very subtle attempt at trying to change the subject," he winked.

"They have such gorgeous kids," she continued, ignoring him and concentrating on a beautifully framed portrait of the three Weatherby offspring which hung above the large marble fireplace.

"Not exactly kids anymore," David reminded her. "The youngest is seventeen." David shook his head in obvious dismay, his mouth opening again to speak.

"I know," Jill interrupted. "If Jason ever starts reciting the Moonie alphabet, I have your permission to shoot him."

"Is that what they recite?" he asked. Jill shrugged playfully. "Smart-ass," David said, pulling her closer beside him, about to kiss her.

The scream from the kitchen sent them scrambling to their feet. Jill made it to the kitchen door only seconds before her husband, and both rushed immediately to Beth Weatherby's side when they saw the blood.

If anything, Al Weatherby was even whiter than his wife. "What the hell happened, Beth?" he was saying, his voice almost icily calm. "Christ, I turn my back for two seconds and you almost kill yourself—" He turned on the cold water tap and grabbed Beth's arm, thrusting her blood-covered hand under the flow. She screamed again at the sudden impact of water on flesh, the force of the spray quickly washing the blood away to reveal a deep cut that ran almost like a second lifeline across the width of her hand, just below the base of her fingers.

"I don't know how I did it," Beth was saying, holding back the tears. "I was cutting the flan and I must have made the crust too hard because—ow!—the knife kind of caught, and so I jiggled it, and the next thing I knew, wham, right across my hand. Jesus, that hurts!"

"Hold still," Al Weatherby said calmly, the color returning to his face. "There's a lot of blood. I don't know. Maybe we should take you to the hospital."

"No," his wife insisted. "Please, I'll be all right. There's some gauze upstairs—"

"I'll get it," David offered, already out of the room.

"First bathroom on the right," Al called after him. "It's that damn phone call from Lisa, isn't it?" he stated more than asked. Then he turned to Jill. "Having a bit of trouble with our daughter," he explained, still keeping his eye on his wife's bleeding hand. "Seems she's gotten herself involved with some musician—married, naturally."

Naturally, Jill thought.

"Little children, little problems," David said in the car on the long drive home. "Big children, big problems. It's not worth it, Jill, believe me. It's just not worth it."

They'd been driving for some twenty minutes.

"It's just around the corner—there, that house on the left, number 90."

David pulled the car into the first available space. The street was narrow and dark, lined on both sides with semi-detached homes which had probably been quite elegant in their day but which were now showing definite signs of neglect and the decay wrought by the onslaught of the Chicago weather. "It doesn't look very safe," he said, bringing the car to a halt.

Jill smiled. "Oh, it's safe. I'm on the second floor and my landlady lives down below with her two pets—a Doberman and a shotgun."

"The American way," David laughed.

Jill was about to open the car door when she hesitated, realizing how reluctant she was to leave this man. "I want to thank you," she began.

"Don't thank me," he interrupted. "It was a purely selfish gesture on my part. I'm only sorry you don't live farther away; then I'd get to enjoy your company a little longer."

Jill smiled, thinking back over the afternoon in his office. She had finally stopped acting so belligerent, and had listened to what David Plumley was saying, allowing his humor and his personality to temper her hostility, a hostility which she knew had only developed when she felt herself so instantly attracted to him, when she realized he knew exactly what she was feeling, and she was embarrassed and afraid. She'd accepted his offer of a cup of coffee, and listened to him hold court on everything she could hope to know about the legal profession and the people who practiced it. One hour quickly became another, as all calls and other appointments were put on hold or canceled. It was close to 6 P.M. when she realized with some disappointment that any further questions she might ask would have absolutely nothing to do with law and everything to do with his wife and family and the obvious possibility of other women. He, in turn, offered to drive her home, and she readily accepted, despite the fact that her car was parked in the underground parking lot. What the hell, she'd go back for it the next day.

She pushed open the heavy car door. "Well—thanks again— for everything." She stopped, once more turning in his direction. "I feel kind of guilty about having taken up so much of your time," she lied, deciding that having come so far, she might as well push ahead all the way. "If you weren't married, I'd invite you inside for dinner."

His answer was simple. "I'm separated," he said, neglecting only to mention that by separated, he meant his wife was at home with his children while he was here in his car with Jill.

"I'm sorry," he said, abruptly sitting up in bed. "I know I'm keeping you up. I just can't seem to get comfortable."

Jill sat up beside her husband and peered over at the clock. It was almost three-thirty in the morning. "We shouldn't have had all that coffee," she said, thinking back to the large pot they had brewed and drunk as soon as they walked through the door of their apartment. They had left the Weatherby house when Beth's bleeding had stopped and her hand was safely bandaged up. Al had suggested his wife go right up to bed, and though Beth protested, Jill and David had thought it best that they leave. The blood had made Jill vaguely queasy herself, and David's vehemence in the car about not fathering any more children had upset her further. Coffee seemed the only viable solution. They had finished the pot, gotten undressed and into bed, and drifted into a restless and unsatisfying sleep, forgetful of their earlier desires, wanting only to disappear into their pillows until morning.

"Do you want anything to eat?" she offered.

"What is there?" he asked, straightening his shoulders.

"Some cheesecake—" He shook his head. "Some of that rice pudding I made from the other night—"

"No."

"Do you want to call in for a pizza?"

He laughed quietly. "No—food's not the answer."

"Ginger ale? Juice?"

"No." He peered into the darkness. "Shit," he muttered with frustration.

"You want me to rub your back?"

He tilted his head. "Yeah, that's what I want," he smiled, flipping over. Jill immediately climbed on top of him, her hands working on his shoulders.

"How's that?" she asked after several minutes, her hands tiring.

"Awful," he said gently. "You always did give the world's worst backrubs."

"Oh, is that so?" she asked, suddenly pounding on his back. "Well, how's this?"

"Better," he laughed, flipping her over and crawling on top of her, quickly entering her and starting to thrust. "Much better."

Later they lay very still, side by side, their breathing even, their eyes open, relaxed but still not sleepy.

"So," he said suddenly, "are you going to tell me what happened at the picnic?"

"What do you mean?" she asked, startled.

"Jill," he said, patiently, "you haven't been yourself the last few days. You're as bad as Beth Weatherby—walking into walls, changing your clothes fifty times a day—"

"I am not. I haven't been—"

"How many times did you change tonight?"

"I don't know what you're getting at. The picnic was fine. Nothing unusual happened." She felt herself beginning to blush. "Why do I feel like if I tell one more lie my nose will fall off?"

David laughed. "Because you're as transparent as Pinocchio, that's why. Now, tell me what happened."

Jill sat up, bringing her knees to her chest and leaning her head against them. "I don't understand how you always know what I'm thinking."

"I don't know *what* you're thinking—only that you *are* thinking. Come on, you know you can never keep anything from me. Are you going to tell me?" He waited, saying nothing.

Jill tried to choose her words carefully. What could she say? How could she tell him without maximizing the inherent appeal her words would carry? Listen, David, you know that brilliant and beautiful law student that's working for the summer in your office—the one with the big tits and the flawless complexion— well, she wants to marry you. She tossed the words around in her head a few more times, trying to make them sound funny, casual, non-threatening. Guess what? she tried silently, there's another woman in love with you—

"Well?" he asked.

"This is going to give your ego a real boost," she began nervously, wondering why she was so afraid of telling him. "I'm just telling you this because I trust you so much—"

He laughed. "Oh, lay on the old guilt," he bellowed. "Make me feel so guilty in advance, I won't be able to enjoy it—whatever it is! Are you going to tell me?"

"It's about Nicole Clark," she stated directly, plunging right in.

"Who?" he asked earnestly.

"Nicole Clark," she repeated.

He looked genuinely puzzled. "Who's Nicole Clark?"

Jill's face broke into a wide grin; she felt instantly better. "You really don't know? She works in your office. Or at least,

she's there this summer—she's a student. Dark hair, young—
pretty, if you like that perfect kind of type—you were talking to
her for quite a while at the picnic—"

David's eyes reflected his confusion. She could actually see
him trying to piece together the various parts of the invisible
puzzle, trying to put a face to the name Nicole Clark. Pretty
. . . dark hair . . . student . . . "Oh, Jeez, Nicki, of course.
Nicole Clark! You made her sound so formal. Pretty, you said?
She's gorgeous!"

He obviously liked that perfect sort of type. Jill felt her face
muscles tense. "So, you know who I mean," she said unnecessarily.

"Of course. Bright, *bright* girl. Nice, too. Very sensitive."

"I'm sure," Jill said, flopping backward onto her pillow, her
back rigid.

"What's the matter?"

"Oh, nothing. Just that that gorgeous, bright, nice, sensitive
person informed me at the picnic that she intends to marry
you."

For several seconds, David said absolutely nothing. Then he
started to laugh.

"I'm not sure I see what's so funny," Jill said quietly, trying
not to pout.

David kept laughing. "Well, it was a *joke,* for heaven's
sake." He laughed even louder. "That's very funny. I didn't realize she had such a sense of humor."

"Now she has a sense of humor too. Wonderful," Jill muttered.

"Jill, come on, you're not really upset, are you?"

Jill's voice was louder than she had intended. "Why
shouldn't I be upset? Some girl tells me she's going to marry my
husband and my husband makes me feel much better by telling
me she's a) gorgeous, b) smart, c) sweet and d) sensitive. Oh,
and I almost forgot e) she has a wonderful sense of humor."

David was suddenly all over her, kissing her face and neck,
tickling her sides. "Come on, you silly goose. What are you
upset about, huh? You know I love you. Well, don't you?" Reluctantly, she found herself nodding. "So, why do you let a
silly little joke upset you?"

"Because it wasn't a joke. She told me that. She made it very clear."

David sat up. "Tell me exactly what she said." Jill related the Sunday afternoon conversation to the best of her ability, trying to keep her voice as flat as possible.

"Still think it's all a joke?" she asked.

David's voice was suddenly very serious. He looked directly at his wife. "I love you," he began. "I love you very much. It's why I married you. And I have absolutely no intention of marrying anyone else. Do you understand? Or even looking at anyone else. You are the only one I want or need or will ever want or need. In other words, you, lady, are stuck with me. For keeps. If Nicole Clark was serious, she's a very foolish girl and I'm extremely disappointed in her behavior."

Jill felt her eyes fill up with tears of love and gratitude. She repeated his words over and over in her mind, trying to stop herself from wondering if he had ever said anything similar to Elaine, trying to stifle the sound of her mother's initial warning when she had told her she was involved with a married man: "If he'll do it to one woman," she had said plainly, "he'll do it to you."

"Go away, Mother," she muttered.

"What?"

Jill laughed. "Nothing."

"Why are you crying?"

She shook her head. "I love you," she said as he kissed away her tears.

"Well, then, do me a favor," he said, kissing her nose. "Keep remembering that *I* love *you,* and that you're as beautiful as any woman I've ever known."

He kissed her mouth. "Now hold me," he commanded gently, turning over and feeling her crawl into the space around him, their limbs resting comfortably against each other. She was almost asleep when he started to laugh. "I can't believe Nicki actually said that!"

Jill said nothing, feigning sleep. Instinctively, her body moved closer, hugged him tighter to her. Damn him, she thought sullenly, any hopes she'd had for sleep vanishing, he's interested.

Chapter 4

Jill tossed restlessly, vaguely aware that it was morning and probably time to get up. She wasn't ready yet—her eyes were still unwilling to open themselves to the light she knew was trying to crawl beneath the bedroom curtains, and her body was tense and sore from lying in all the wrong ways. If only she'd been able to sleep for a few hours, she thought as she reluctantly opened her eyes, swallowing the nausea that always developed when she didn't get enough rest, and looking over at the clock radio which was mysteriously sitting on the end table beside her. What was it doing there? she wondered, feeling suddenly disoriented. It was always on David's side of the bed. At precisely 6 A.M. every weekday morning, David's hand would blindly reach for the right button, his face remaining submerged beneath the blankets, and abruptly silence whoever was rocking them awake. With no need for further alarms, David would sit up in bed fifteen minutes later, and head for the bathroom. Whatever it was he did in there took exactly one hour. (She had once timed his activities—five minutes in the shower, ten minutes to shave, thirty seconds to brush his teeth, and another

five minutes to blow-dry his hair. That left thirty-nine minutes
and thirty seconds unaccounted for, and when she once asked
him "What is it that you *do* in there for so long?!," he had
winked and said, "Ask my mother. She trained me.") Men put
such a premium on their precious bowels, Jill thought, closing
her eyes again. Every morning like clockwork or you'd think
the world was coming to an end. Jill thought quickly of the
large container of Metamucil on the bottom shelf of the medicine cabinet. It was there for just such an emergency. She
laughed silently. She was the one who should be taking it, with
her regular irregularity. She often went as long as three or four
days without— Her eyes opened suddenly, shooting back at the
clock. It was after eight! David was usually long-gone by this
hour. Perhaps he had already left, having completed his morning rituals in absolute silence. Had he come in to wake her up
at seven-thirty the way he always did? She couldn't remember
his mouth grazing the side of her cheek the way he did to say
good morning and have a good day. She couldn't remember
anything having happened at all.

And if it hadn't—if the alarm hadn't gone off for the first time
in four years (probably because whoever moved it had loused
up something inside)—that meant that they had overslept and
David would be late for court that morning. She remembered
he had to be in court by nine o'clock. Frantically, she turned
toward her husband.

"David—" She stopped short at what she saw.

They were lying together beside her, wrapped up in each
other's arms, their legs encircling each other's hips which were
rotating grotesquely, their hair falling across each other's faces,
so that at first she couldn't make out who exactly they were. Jill
sat up in bed and moved closer to the couple who were obviously ignorant or unmindful of her presence. She pulled back
the blanket and watched in wonderment as their bodies slapped
against each other, flapping like fish at the bottom of a row-
boat, colliding and retreating in endless repetition. She saw the
woman's ample bosom squashed beneath the light blond hairs
of her husband's chest, heard her husky voice whisper something in David's ear. "She's watching," she knew the girl had
said, wondering why she was able to hear so clearly. David

laughed and swung their bodies around so that the girl was now on top. His hands reached up and suddenly pushed the girl's body away, so that the large breasts and effortlessly flat stomach were thrown back, arching up toward the ceiling. They remained locked together as her black hair fell away from her face. She was laughing. Slowly, she turned her head to stare directly at Jill. It was her mother!

Jill sat up in bed with a start, a loud gasp escaping her mouth, her eyes fully open and on the alert. In the next instant, David was awake beside her.

"My God, Jill, what's the matter? Are you going to be sick?" Jill's eyes moved immediately to her husband's startled face. He looked terrified.

"Jill?" he asked. "Answer me—are you going to be sick?"

It took a minute for Jill to come to terms with the fact that she and David were alone in the bed and that what had transpired had all been a peculiar dream. It had felt so real.

"I had the most ridiculous dream," she said slowly, in amazement.

"Jesus," David muttered, falling back against his pillow. "Jesus."

"Well, I didn't do it on purpose," Jill said in her defense. "Wow, was it strange! And in such detail."

"What time is it?" David asked, retreating under the covers.

Jill looked over at the end table beside her. The clock radio was gone.

"Where's the radio?" she asked in alarm.

Once again, David shot up in the bed, looking at the table to his right. "What's the matter with you? It's right here. Where it always is." Jill looked over in his direction. "And it's five to six, for God's sake. I could have slept five more minutes." He looked anxiously at his wife. "Is there any point in my trying to lie down again?"

"I should have known it was a dream when the clock was on the wrong side of the bed," she said, watching David lie back and roll over. "That was the tip-off." She lay down beside her husband, hugging his back to her stomach. "Not to mention my mother."

"What are you muttering about?" he asked, his voice muffled against the pillow.

It was a question that required no answer. Indeed, it was a question that precluded any answers, that almost dared her to try. She recognized the tone. It meant be quiet and let me get some sleep. Jill felt herself going over the events of her dream, losing them as they ran to get away from her conscious self. By the time David's hand reached up to silence the musical alarm (Barbra Streisand and Barry Gibb doing "Guilty"), all but the image of her mother's face on Nicole's body—she knew it was Nicole's body welded to David's groin—had disappeared.

David sat up in bed and stretched. Jill waited for the feel of the bed emptying as his body moved quickly out, but instead she felt cold, a draft, like her blanket, reaching up and covering her from her feet to her shoulders.

"Out of bed," he said, playfully, pulling at her arms, her completely exposed body curling into itself against his sudden invasion. "Come on, you cost me five minutes of sleep. Time to pay the penalty." He let go of her hands and began pulling at her feet.

"What are you doing?" she laughed, kicking at him. "Go away. You know I have another hour and a half! What are you doing?" She screamed, laughing helplessly, as she felt herself being tugged onto the floor. He grabbed her ankles. "What are you doing? Where are you taking me?"

She opened her eyes, tears of laughter running down her cheeks, and watched his nude body (magnificent, she told herself, even at six in the morning) dragging her nude body (less than magnificent, she thought, trying to cover the slight rounding at her belly) across the bedroom carpet. "Watch my head!" she shrieked, as they rounded the corner and moved out into the hall. "Where are you taking me?"

"You need a shower," he said.

"Oh, no!" Jill screamed, starting to struggle in earnest. "Not at six in the morning, I don't need a shower! No!" She yelled again as David pulled her into the small washroom.

"You're lucky this floor is carpeted," he said over her squeals, one hand holding firmly onto her foot, as he reached up and, leaning over the tub, turned on the shower. Jill kicked at him frantically with her free leg before she felt his arms grab her around the waist, lift her struggling body up into the air and deposit her with seemingly no effort at all under the forceful spray of the shower.

"Shit," she screamed. "It's freezing!"

"Sorry," he said, quickly adjusting the taps and climbing in after her.

"You're getting my hair all wet," she yelled, starting to laugh again.

"It needs washing."

"I just washed it!" She squirmed along the side of the tub.

Again David picked her up and deposited her directly under the flow. Every time she tried to protest, her mouth filled up with water, so she stopped trying to speak and recognized that she was actually enjoying the water and the sheer force of it as it pelted her body. She was aware of his hands now on her breasts, soaping them with a gentle massage, moving down to her stomach. In another few seconds, he was inside her, pounding her back against the tile, moving her up and down against the taps. If this is another dream, she thought, it sure beats the last one.

Her mind flashed back to almost five years ago, the night he had come to her door at two in the morning, drunker than she had ever remembered seeing anybody—the only time during their illicit romance that he had stayed till the morning. Abruptly, she was back in the present, the water stopping as David maneuvered his wet body away from her own, kissing her sweetly on the lips. "Get out of here," he whispered. "I have work to do."

She laughed. "You always were terrific under water," she said, confident he would understand her reference. He gave her backside an affectionate pat as she struggled out of the tub and into a waiting towel. "I'll make some breakfast," she said.

"I'll be a while," he answered.

"Yes, I know," she said, backing out of the room, closing the door behind her and heading down the familiar hallway.

It was six thirty-five. She had an extra hour before she really had to be up. David would be in the bathroom for another forty minutes. She could crawl back into bed and try to get some

more sleep. Or she could do some exercises, she thought, drying herself off and dropping the towel to stare at herself nude in
front of the mirror. Definitely some exercises, she decided, lying
on the floor and bringing her knees to her chest, rolling them
back and forth from side to side. Beth had told her about an
exercise class and suggested that the two of them join. She'd
have to call Beth and ask her about it. She'd definitely like to
start. Her body was falling apart. Had David noticed?

Jill kept her knees bent and put the bottoms of her feet on
the floor. Cupping her hands behind her head, she tried to sit
up. "Oh, my God," she said, "this is ridiculous." She managed
to get herself in a sitting position. Beth, she thought, visions of
Beth's bleeding hand before her eyes. She wondered how she
was this morning, if the bleeding had stopped. The cut had
been deep, very unpleasant-looking. She'd call Beth after her
nine o'clock class.

The thought of her morning class made her instantly depressed, all those bright, young faces waiting eagerly for her to
unleash the vast secrets of her experience and expertise. She
hadn't even thought about today's lecture, what she was going
to say to these youngsters who still thought that all you needed
was a college degree and a love of film to be able to walk up on
the stage and collect your Academy Award. They would all be
in her classroom at the sound of the bell, waiting for her words
of wisdom. What could she tell them? That she was bored to
tears and wished she were anywhere else? What was she doing
stuck in a classroom? She was meant to be out there in the real
world, directing its violent outbursts and capturing history as it
stumbled forward in all its trivial displays. She was meant to be
moving!

What was she doing here on the floor? she wondered suddenly, pushing her body up with her elbows. This isn't going to
work, she told herself, standing up. She needed the discipline of
the very classroom she hated if she was going to get her body
back in shape. She selected a mauve cotton dress from her
closet and put it on, wrapping the towel around her head as she
moved from the bedroom, down the hall to the front door.

The morning paper was waiting. The paper boy was always
very prompt—he must get up at dawn, Jill thought, bringing the

paper into the kitchen and laying it on the counter as she poured some coffee into the percolator. The headlines were as depressing as usual—the economy was going all to hell; they were in the midst of a recession which was in all probability leading them toward a depression; the arms race was back in bloom; the I.R.A. and the P.L.O. were doing business as usual. Wonderful, she thought.

"Do you want some eggs?" she called toward the bathroom.

"No thanks," David yelled back. "Just toast and coffee."

Jill reached for the bread basket and took out several pieces of white bread. David was always telling her to buy whole wheat, but she hated the taste, and stuck stubbornly to the Wonder Bread she had known since childhood. Leaving the coffee to perk and the bread to sit until David was ready to toast it, she picked up the paper and went into the den.

The large leather chair beckoned invitingly and she plopped herself down, flipping quickly through the paper. She felt strangely assured to note that in addition to the latest in floods, fires and other natural disasters, Chicago could still be counted on to produce its share of murders, rapes and robberies. Jill moved directly to the Classified Ads and Companions Wanted columns. She settled comfortably back and began to read.

The ad caught her eye immediately:

WANTED

Black, attractive man, 6'1", professional baker, separated, no ties, from upper middle class family, planning to return home to West Indies in December, seeks attractive, exuberant, intelligent, plump, sensuous Caucasian female accountant.

Now, that's telling them, Jill thought, laughing out loud. No room for error here. It was all spelled out perfectly clearly. Exactly what the man desired. Her eyes quickly ran down the rest of the Companions Wanted columns. It seemed that all sorts of gorgeous, intelligent, successful people were out there looking for friends. Friends? she asked herself. An interesting choice of words.

Sensuous, caring professional man desires to meet
beautiful, shapely sylph with warmth and rhythm.

Rhythm this one wanted, not friendship. What motivated
these people? she wondered. Who were the faces behind the
often bizarre requests? More to the point, did they really get
everything they seemed to want? Do any of us? she wondered
skeptically, flipping over the page to the Birth and Death Notices. All she needed was one really gross announcement to
make her day. She found it.

Frey, Joel and Joan (nee Sampson) are thrilled to
announce that Joel wasn't just shooting blanks all
those cold winter nights! Twins Gordon and Marsha
greeted the new day at a very respectable 6 lbs. and 5
lbs. 10 oz. respectively, shrieking their approval of
the pains to which their parents had gone. (Especially Mom!) We thank Dr. Pearlman and the entire
staff of Women's College Hospital.

Jill closed the paper, hearing her coffee beginning to perk in
the kitchen.

The phone rang just as she finished pouring herself a cup. Jill
glanced automatically at the clock. It was barely 7 A.M. Even
Elaine wouldn't have the nerve to call this early. Unless it was
an emergency. Jill reached anxiously for the phone.

"Hello?"

"Is David there, please?"

The voice was dark and husky and definitely not Elaine's.
Jill recognized it immediately. "Who is this?" she asked anyway.

"It's Nicole Clark," came the reply. "I hope I'm not disturbing you."

I'm sure, Jill said silently. "Is something wrong?" Jill
asked.

"No," the voice replied quietly. "I just wanted to make sure
I talked to David before he left. I know he leaves very early in
the mornings."

"Well, he's in the bathroom," Jill said in distinctly businesslike tones, trying not to sound too territorial. "He can't come to the phone right now." *Your fiancé is taking a shit,* she wanted to yell. Instead she said, "Can I take a message?"

There was a moment's hesitation. Then Nicole's soft tones floated gently to Jill's ears. Each word stuck against her scalp like a pin on a paper donkey's tail. "It's kind of a complicated message. Maybe he better call me back."

I'm not exactly an idiot, Jill told the other woman wordlessly. *I know how to take a message.* Aloud she said, "As you like. What's your number?"

Nicole Clark began to recite her phone number as Jill looked frantically by the phone for a pencil. "Just a minute," she interrupted. "I can't find a pencil."

"Who is it?" David shouted from the bathroom.

Jill paused. "Nicole Clark," she called in his direction, wishing she could see the look on his face.

It was David's turn to pause. "What does she want?"

"She wants you to call her back."

"Okay. Get her number."

Good idea, Jill decided, rummaging through a drawer and finally locating a pencil that wasn't broken.

"All right, I have one," she said into the phone. "531—?"

"1-7-4-1," Nicole completed.

"He'll call you," Jill said.

"Thank you," the other woman purred.

Jill replaced the receiver and growled at the telephone. "Keep your legal little fingers away from my husband," she whispered, picturing Nicole's long purple nails and comparing them to her own short, chewed and tattered ones. Her embarrassed fingers, the obvious loser in any contest, encircled her coffee cup, and she quickly lifted it to her mouth.

Why had Nicole called? Did she really need some early-morning information or was it all a ploy, a simple part of her master plan to capture her husband and ferret him away? *Keep the little wifey nice and edgy,* she thought.

Jill took a long, slow sip of her coffee and opened the pantry door, coming face to face with at least half a dozen stale donuts. She reached up and grabbed two of them. *Just what I need,* she thought, trying to figure out exactly what it was that

Nicole was doing. "Enough of this," she said aloud, then finished the rest of the thought in silence. *If I'm going to worry about every little number who looks lustingly after my husband, I'm going to drive myself nuts.* Probably exactly what she has in mind, Jill decided, taking a big bite out of one of the donuts, thinking at the same time that Nicole Clark—Nicki to her intimates—had done more than just look. She had brazenly announced her intentions. Jill swallowed the rest of the donut. *The hell with it,* she thought. *That's her problem, not mine.* She took a bite out of the second donut. She'd definitely have to phone Beth later about that exercise class.

She heard the bathroom door open and once again looked up at the clock. David couldn't be finished in there already—it was too early. He appeared in the doorway draped in a towel.

"She wouldn't say what she wanted?" David asked, carefully avoiding the mention of her name.

"Apparently she doesn't trust me to take a message," Jill answered, automatically pouring David a cup of coffee and adjusting it to his specifications. "There's the number," she said, pointing to a piece of scrap paper. "You're finished early today," she noted.

"She probably wants to know what courtroom," he said, almost absently. "She asked yesterday if she could sit in this morning, you know, to observe."

"Of course," Jill said, finishing off her donut and walking toward the den. "I'll leave you two alone."

David laughed and picked up the phone. Jill heard him dialing as she walked into the den and sat back down in the leather chair. The morning paper was where she had left it. She retrieved it and began perusing the real estate section. From the kitchen, she heard David's voice. "Hello, Nicki. It's David Plumley." Both names, she noted. He's keeping it formal. "What can I do for you?" *I'll tell you what you can do for me,* Jill said silently, and then shook her head to free herself of the thought. The towel that had been wrapped around her hair fell to the floor. "Great," she said, bending over to pick it up, and dropping the newspaper in the process. "This is starting to feel like a bad comedy," she muttered, grabbing the newspaper and watching it come apart in her hands, loose pages all over the floor. She got down on her hands and knees and began noisily piecing the pages together again, folding one inside the other. She realized as she was doing this that she couldn't hear anything that David was saying, and decided that was probably why she was doing it, so she wouldn't have to.

"What is all the rustling going on in here?" David asked from the doorway.

"I dropped the paper."

"So I see."

"What did Snow White want?" Jill asked, getting awkwardly to her feet.

"What I thought. She wanted to know what courtroom to meet me in."

"And you told her, of course."

David smiled indulgently. "What choice did I have?" He moved toward Jill. "If you had told me yesterday what she'd said to you at the picnic, I could have thought of some excuse to tell her not to come. But it's too late today." He kissed her. "That'll teach you to keep things from me." He started toward the bedroom and then stopped. "Do you want me to say anything to her?" he asked.

Jill shook her head. "What can you say? No, just ignore it." She smiled. "Besides, she'll be gone at the end of the summer anyway." David said nothing. "Won't she? I mean, Beth told me that she's just there for the summer."

David lowered his head. "There's a good chance she'll be joining the firm after she's called to the bar in September," he said. "A few of the partners have talked about asking her."

Jill nodded. "I understand Al Weatherby thinks she's pretty terrific."

"She is," he said. "Legally speaking."

"I always speak legal," Jill joked, stepping into David's outstretched arms.

"I love you."

"I know you do."

"Do you want me to say something to her?" he asked again. "I will, if you want."

"Actions speak louder than words," she told him.

He smiled. "Right you are." He kissed her nose, signaling

the end of the discussion, and Jill watched him move down the hall before she went quickly into the bathroom to dry her hair and brush her teeth. She had just closed the bathroom door when she was aware David was speaking.

"What did you say?" she called, opening the door.

"I said why don't you come down to court this morning and watch me too?"

"I have a class."

"Only at nine o'clock. Then you're free till two. Isn't that Thursday's schedule?"

"Yeah," she said, mulling over his suggestion.

"So, come after ten and watch me, then we'll go to Winston's for lunch. How does that sound?"

"Sounds fantastic. You got yourself a deal." She retreated into the bathroom and plugged in the hair dryer, immediately feeling the hot air as it blew against her skin. What would Nicole think of her suddenly showing up at the courtroom? Would she interpret it as a sign of insecurity, a show of weakness? The mother hen protecting her chick, making sure he didn't stray too far from the fold?

The hell with what Nicole thinks, she told herself, watching her hair curl stubbornly away from the style she was intending. She can think whatever she wants to think. Nicole Clark was simply not one of her concerns.

Jill looked down at what she was wearing. Just the same, she thought, maybe she'd change her dress.

Chapter 5

"Just when was it you discovered your ex-wife had a lover?"

"Six—eight months ago, maybe."

"Maybe? You're not sure?"

The witness—a good-looking man approximately the same age as David Plumley, who was conducting the cross-examination—squirmed uneasily in his seat.

"I'm sure she has a lover," the man said evenly. "If you want, I'm sure I can pinpoint the exact time of my discovering this fact."

"That would be nice," David remarked obligingly, moving back from the witness stand and closer to the table and chairs he occupied when not questioning a witness. From her seat in the courtroom, Jill watched her husband as he moved, conscious, as the witness was not, that by seeming to back away, David was, in fact, only playing with his prey, the deadly panther seeking merely to improve his position before rushing in for the final, killing stroke.

The witness paused for several seconds, his eyes obviously retracing time, finally locating the date he sought. "October

17," he said, not without a touch of smugness. "I remember the exact date because it was a surprise birthday party for a friend of mine."

David paused for precisely the same length of time as had the witness. Then he spoke. "October 17? That's nine months ago, almost ten."

"Yes," the witness agreed. Then he smiled. "I guess it's been going on even longer than I realized."

David returned the man's smile. "You don't feel your ex-wife is entitled to have a lover?"

"Not that I have to support," the man shot back sharply.

"Tell me, just as a matter of interest," David asked almost lazily, "did you have a date for this surprise party?"

"Yes," the man answered. "Aren't *I* entitled?"

"Is it fair to say that in the five years you and Patty Arnold have been divorced you have had a substantial number of 'dates'?" David asked, ignoring the man's question and putting a noticeable stress on his final word.

"As you already noted," the man replied, "I've been divorced for five years. I thought that gave me the legal right to 'date' anyone I wanted to."

"Exactly so," David said, brushing up against the table, where Nicole Clark sat beside his empty chair, observing him intently. "You don't feel your wife is entitled to the same privileges?" Jill watched as David moved away from the table. She could feel Nicole's eyes riveted on his back. He must feel like he's back in high school, Jill thought, trying to impress the girl in the last row. Was that why he was coming down so hard on this man, this man who on more than just a superficial level so closely resembled himself? And which girl was he trying so hard to impress?

"My *ex*-wife," the witness spat back defiantly, the words suddenly pouring out of his mouth like spilt milk from a pitcher, "and she's entitled to do any goddamn thing she wants as long as I don't have to support her!" The judge banged his gavel, reminding the witness that such language would not be tolerated in a court of law and cautioning him to refrain from further outbursts. From her seat several rows behind the rectangular table, Jill Plumley knew the man had already lost, for as good as such histrionic outbursts looked in the movies, as bad did they appear in front of a judge. A good lawyer, David had once told her, always impressed upon his witnesses the importance of staying calm. On the other hand, if you could provoke the other side to anger, it greatly improved your own chances of success. The man on the witness stand looked helplessly around the room and finally brought his eyes to rest on Nicole, speaking his next words as if directly, and only, to her. "Look, I'm not saying that she's not entitled to have any friends or lovers. I'm just saying that for the past five years I've been busting my —— working very hard to try and live a reasonably decent life and still keep up with all my alimony payments. She got the house, the furniture, the car, the kids, everything. I walked out with the suit on my back and my briefcase. For the past five years I've been paying her a thousand dollars a month in alimony and a thousand in child support. Now, I have no objection to the child support—I'll support my kids for as long as they need me—but why should I have to pay for my wife to set up house with some other guy and give this jerk my hard-earned money so that he can start a new business?"

Again David ignored the man's question. "How long were you married, Mr. Arnold?"

"Twelve years."

"Two children?"

"Two boys."

"So, what you've just told me is that after twelve years of marriage and two sons you just walked out!" He paused. "With the suit on your back and your briefcase, of course."

The man wasn't sure he liked the way the facts had been restated but he answered in the affirmative.

"What was in the briefcase?" David asked suddenly. Jill found herself smiling. "Stocks, as I recall," David continued, answering for him. "A few mortgages, wasn't it? The deed to some property up in Canada?" The man said nothing. "So, you weren't quite as empty-handed as you'd have this court believe."

"That was five years ago," the man said, resuming his squirming. "I'm talking about today."

David nodded. "And today you say your ex-wife is living with another man and has been for the last ten months—"

"Well, I heard about their affair ten months ago at this party—"

"October 17—"

"Yes—October 17." He stopped. "I'm not sure exactly when they started living together."

David returned to his table. "What makes you so sure your ex-wife is living with this man?"

"I followed them on numerous occasions. His car was parked there day and night."

Jill listened as intently as she knew Nicole was listening, as the witness parried with the lawyer, exchanging thrusts along with information, hearing as David produced evidence that the lover in question continued to pay rent on his own apartment—indeed to visit it daily—to explain that Mrs. Arnold was entitled to spend her money in any way she saw fit and that if she chose to invest in her lover's business as a way of potentially increasing her own capital, she was as entitled as the witness himself with regard to his own investments. Then she stopped listening, knowing David had won his case, that the man squirming uncomfortably on the chair would get no reduction in the amount of his monthly alimony payments and that it was unlikely Patty Arnold would be threatened in this manner again. The world was once again safe for ex-wives and lovers.

He was a brilliant lawyer, she thought, always knowing just how far he could go, when he had to stop and pull back, when he could plunge full-scale ahead. She'd forgotten how impressive he was in a court of law, not just the way he looked which was glorious, but how he moved, the way he spoke, his choice of words. In the early days of their affair, she'd come often to watch him work. He obviously loved what he was doing, his eyes sparkling with the excitement of the challenge and the ultimate certainty of conquest. Her schedule, erratic as it had been, had filled certain of her weeks to overflowing, and left her at other times with virtually hours to spare. She had spent as many as she could watching this man. Any chance at all to be with him.

David walked past the rectangular table where Nicole sat

watching, and winked—his victory wink, he had once told her. Except that this time, the wink had been for Nicole. Jill wondered if David even remembered at this moment that she was there, feeling suddenly very much the outsider, knowing that as close as she usually felt to him, as close as he professed to be to her, she could never completely understand the sense of victory he must be feeling at this time, she could never fully share in moments like this one. The way Nicole undoubtedly could.

Jill watched as her husband crossed back in front of the table, his deep voice dismissing the man on the stand, his body lean and striking in his dark navy suit. He suddenly caught her stare and smiled widely before returning to his table and sitting down beside Nicole. The other woman leaned toward him and whispered something in his ear. Congratulations, no doubt, on a job well done. You were wonderful, David. Really wonderful. David smiled guardedly, undoubtedly realizing Jill was watching him.

She couldn't blame David if he did find himself attracted to Nicole, Jill realized, feeling the same sudden intrusion of objectivity she had felt at the firm picnic just last weekend. Aside from the younger woman's obvious physical beauty, she was bright—no, bright, David had stressed the night before—and she was glamorous and held down a challenging job, or would very soon anyway. And they had the law in common. They could probably sit for hours and discuss their various cases. Her own job at the university rarely provided anything worth talking about anymore. They'd given up the pretense.

It had been interesting at first, something new, something different. She had told herself it would be challenging to try and train new minds. She pictured herself as Miss Jean Brodie in her prime. Or more precisely, Maggie Smith as Miss Jean Brodie in her prime. "Give me a girl at an impressionable age and she's mine for life," she whispered. Something like that. Except that her students turned out to be long past impressing, and she'd discovered all too quickly that she hated teaching. Beth Weatherby had been right—she missed television, its excitement, its deadlines, its danger.

What she didn't miss were the problems it had created in her marriage. At least most of those had been solved when she had informed the network she was leaving. David was right—it was crazy for her to keep putting her life in jeopardy, leaving him to expose herself to bullets and disease all over the globe. Besides, he missed her when she was gone, and he worried about her. His worry interfered with his work. He needed her support. He couldn't feel it when she was half a world away. Didn't she think she could find something more sedentary, something closer to home? Didn't she want to start a family? Yes, she did. She didn't like the separations any more than he did. She missed him terribly. And a man like David needed a lot of ego gratification. If she wasn't there to provide it, she knew there were many who would be only too delighted.

Still, it didn't seem fair. His life, despite a change in wives and the reduced time with his children, had remained remarkably unchanged to all outward appearances. True, he'd exchanged a large house for a small apartment, but it was still a prestige building in a prime location and there was still someone waiting with a hot meal when he finally walked through the door at the end of the day, some nights as late as ten o'clock. Most importantly, he was still doing the work he loved.

Her life, on the other hand, had undergone a total transformation, from her surroundings to her marital status to her job. Instead of doing the work she loved, she was teaching others how to do it. TV journalism, the course proclaimed. Jill Plumley, professor. Her world was now confined to a classroom and she could invariably jump off in time to prepare dinner. Why, she'd become a regular little Betty Crocker in the kitchen. How had it all come about, she wondered, trying to get a fix on the subtle shifts that time had wrought. Temporarily forgetful of her surroundings, Jill pictured a David of approximately five years ago pacing angrily back and forth in front of her. That long ago, she marveled as his image became increasingly clear, his words gaining resonance and conviction. For several minutes, as the past overtook the present, the courtroom disappeared altogether.

She was obviously excited and he was just as obviously upset by her excitement.

"Why shouldn't I be happy? I've never been to Ireland before!"

"We're not talking about a sunny little vacation trip to Dublin—we're talking about bombs and snipers in Belfast."

"I survived the Vietnam war," she reminded him, trying not to sound too cute.

"I don't know why the network has to send you!"

"Because I happen to be a first-rate producer, that's why. And because I asked for this assignment."

"You what?"

"I like to travel, you know that. And this is the kind of project I do very well. Besides," she said softly, "I don't think it would be such a terrible thing for us to take a two-week breather."

"What do you mean?"

"You know what I mean."

It seemed lately that's how all their conversations ended up. What do you mean? You know what I mean. It all means the same thing—you're a married man.

"All right," he said, "you want to go off for a few weeks, fine. Go to Los Angeles. Go to Bermuda, for Christ's sake. There's no civil war in Bermuda."

"There's nothing in Bermuda."

"You could get killed!"

"I'm not going to get killed."

"Oh, you have that in writing, do you?"

She smiled and kissed him gently. "Only a lawyer would ask a question like that."

"Then do a show on lawyers."

"I already did. That's why I'm in this mess. Remember?"

He sat down on the bed and watched her take out her suitcase and start to pack.

"This is the fourth trip you've taken in the last six months," he said.

"You can't call a two-day stopover in Buffalo a trip!"

"You were away."

He watched her throw a few cotton shirts and several pairs of jeans into the suitcase.

"You like it that I go away," she said jokingly, before she realized that she really wasn't kidding at all.

"What are you talking about?"

"It's part of my mystique," she told him. "It's what sets me apart."

"Apart from what?"

"From the others," she said, knowing instinctively there had been. "From your wife."

He laughed. "My wife's idea of an exciting holiday is two weeks in Las Vegas so that she can play the nickel slot machines and listen to Robert Goulet."

"I was in Las Vegas," Jill told him, "a few years back. We did a story on those wedding chapels that are open twenty-four hours a day."

"Is there anywhere you haven't been?" he asked her. "Aside from Ireland, that is."

Her face lit into a broad smile. "China," she said. "Parts of Africa. But I'm working on it."

"China, huh? I'd like to see China."

"Well, you can come with me."

"I love you, you know," he said, his voice suddenly soft and serious.

Jill sat on David's lap and let her arms encircle his neck. "Why do you love me?" she asked with genuine interest. "Why does a man who looks the way you do fall in love with a woman who looks the way I do?"

"First of all because you're smart."

"Oh, thanks. You're supposed to say there's absolutely nothing wrong with the way I look, that you think I'm pretty gorgeous."

"I do, that's exactly right, and I love you because you're smart enough to know it."

She laughed. "Yes, okay, what else?"

"I don't know," he shrugged. "You're bright, sensitive, you know what's going on in the world, you do interesting things. You're smart."

"You said that." He nodded. "Not smart enough to tell you to get lost when I found out your definition of marital separation."

"I just couldn't let you walk out of that car," he said, remembering.

She got up off his lap. "I hate this situation. I hate the whole idea of it. I like women too much to be involved with a married man. I don't want to hurt your wife and I certainly don't want to get hurt myself."

"What do you think I want?" he asked.

"I don't know."

He exhaled a deep breath of air. "Neither do I," he said. "I was hoping you could tell me." He looked down at her suitcase. "Is that all you're going to take?"

She went to the bathroom and opened the medicine cabinet, tossing a few items into a small kit.

"You're taking your birth control pills?" he asked, watching her.

He could see her smiling at him indulgently from the reflection of the bathroom mirror. "You don't stop taking them, you know, because you're not going to be doing anything for a few weeks." She came back into the room.

"How long have you been on them?" he asked.

"Eight years," she answered.

"Isn't that a long time?"

"It's eight years."

"Ever think about stopping?"

"All the time. But I don't think this is a particularly appropriate time in my life to conceive, do you? Much as I would very much like to have a child."

"You should. You'd make a really good mother."

"Yes. I think I would."

The conversation halted abruptly. They were back at square one—she was going to Ireland and he was a married man.

"Will you call me as soon as you get back?" he asked.

("What do you mean you're involved with a married man? How could you let yourself do anything so stupid? You're a smart girl, Jill, how can you be so dumb? You think he loves you? Well, maybe he does. You think his wife doesn't understand him? Well, maybe she doesn't. You think he's going to leave her to marry you? Don't kid yourself, my darling daughter, it'll never happen. And if it does, if he does leave her for you, think about it for a minute—what kind of prize are you getting? A man who walks out on one woman when he finds one he likes better. A man who trades a slightly used family for a newer set. Is this someone you'll be able to trust? Believe me, Jill, if he'll do it once, he'll do it again. What do you need it for? Think about it, darling. Do you really need this kind of aggravation?")

"Will you call me as soon as you get back?" he repeated.

"Yes," she answered.

There was a great flurry of movement around her, snapping Jill back into the reality of the present.

"Excuse me," said a voice beside her, as a woman pushed her way past Jill and toward the middle aisle. Jill looked up at the clock on the wall. It was noon. Her eyes tried to find David and finally located him in a conference with several other men. The judge was gone. Obviously, court had been dismissed. And she'd missed the final verdict although she was sure she knew what it was. Still, if David should ask—

"Wonderful, wasn't he?" the voice asked huskily.

Jill looked to her right. Nicole Clark, her hair pulled back into a French braid, was smiling attractively at her, as if it was only natural that she do so. Maybe it was. Maybe she *had* been joking at the picnic. "Yes, he was," Jill answered, determined to be pleasant. "It's been a while since I've had the chance to watch him. I forgot how impressive he can be."

"That's not very smart," Nicole said, her smile as bright as ever. "It's something I never forget."

Nicole turned and walked toward the rear door. Jill was about to go after her, put an end to the cruel joke once and for all with a simple blow to the head. Would anyone actually have the nerve to charge her? But David was suddenly at her side, his face flushed with victory, his arm around her waist.

"Ready for lunch?" he asked. Before she could answer, he was holding her tight against him and leading her out of the courtroom.

Chapter 6

"I felt a little sorry for that guy on the stand," Jill said, taking a large shrimp from her bowl and covering it in sauce before lifting it to her mouth.

"Don't," David said simply. "Guy's a jerk. He's making three times what he was making five years ago and even then, he tried to get out of everything he could. He got off easy, I assure you." He shook his head. "Jerk. Doesn't even hire a private detective, he's so damn cheap. Follows them himself in his car for a few weeks. That's his idea of evidence. He's lucky the judge didn't *increase* his payments." She laughed, helping herself to another shrimp. "So, did you enjoy yourself this morning?"

Jill smiled widely. "It was terrific. I'd forgotten how good you look in court." She paused, recalling Nicole's words. "Anyway," she said, recovering quickly, "I want to thank you for suggesting that I come. It was a good idea. You were really wonderful."

David smiled. "My pleasure. Very routine stuff."

"Well," she demurred, knowing his ego was searching for a

few more strokes, "you make it seem like it's all very routine, but I know how hard you work. And I know that behind that seemingly casual facade is a man with a map of his every move. And you're terrific, so what else can I say?"

"More of the same would be nice," he smiled.

"And you look absolutely gorgeous," Jill continued, not missing a beat. "Actually, it was very interesting the way you let the poor sucker relax, then—pounce. Very exciting."

"I'm glad you enjoyed yourself."

"I enjoyed *you*," she stated, finishing off the last of her shrimp, and smiling with her open mouth.

"You have sauce on your teeth," he said.

Jill quickly brought her lips together. "Wonderful," she said. "Someday, I'm going to learn how to eat these things properly." She licked at her teeth without opening her mouth. "Gone?" she asked timidly. David nodded. "What can you expect from a girl raised on well-done roast beef and mashed potatoes?" she asked. "So—what did Nicole think of your performance?" She tried to sound as unthreatened as possible.

"She didn't say much. Congratulations. Well done, that sort of thing. She thanked me, of course."

"Of course."

"I noticed the two of you were talking," he broached. "Anything interesting?"

"Very interesting."

"Did she apologize for what she said at the picnic?"

"Not exactly."

"What then? Tell you it was all a joke?"

"Not quite."

"Jill—" he said, a touch of exasperation creeping into his voice.

"She said she thought you were wonderful. Well, no, actually her precise words were 'wonderful, wasn't he?'"

David shifted uncomfortably in his seat. "Well, she meant the way I cross-examined the poor bugger—"

"I agreed with her," Jill continued. "Then I said I'd forgotten how impressive you could be, and she said—" Jill paused, lowering her voice and trying to capture the other woman's tone. " 'That's not very smart. It's something I never forget.' "

Jill stared directly into David's eyes. There was a second's silence and then he started to laugh. "You're really enjoying all
this, aren't you?" Jill accused him, trying to keep from laughing
herself.

"No, of course not," he chuckled.

"Oh, sure. You look like the cat who swallowed the canary."

He shook his head. "Well, you have to admit it *is* pretty
funny."

"To you, maybe."

"Well, it's not often a man has two beautiful women fighting
over him."

"You've had it all your life," she reminded him. "And I'm
not sure if I'm more flattered that you think I'm beautiful or
more angry that you think she is!" David opened his mouth to
speak, but said nothing. "Anyway, let's change the subject. I
spoke to Beth this morning."

"Oh, how is she?"

"Well, she was apologizing all over the place, of course, for
ruining our evening."

"That's ridiculous."

"That's what I told her. It's the last thing she has to worry
about. But she apologized anyway. She said her hand finally
stopped bleeding around three in the morning, so she didn't get
a whole lot of sleep."

"That's too bad. But it's all right now?"

"Apparently. I suggested she have a doctor take a look at it,
but she said it's okay. I'm going to see her next week. We've
decided to take an exercise class together every Wednesday."

"That's a good idea."

"You're supposed to say, what do *you* need to exercise for?"

"Everybody needs exercise," he said.

"You never do."

"I should."

"When was the last time you played squash?" she asked.

"February," he answered. "And it's racquetball, not
squash."

"What difference does it make if you don't play?"

"I'm thinking of starting again."

"You should. The club's right in your building. Do you still belong?"

He nodded. "At seventeen hundred dollars a year," he calculated, "that was probably the most expensive racquetball game in history."

"One thousand, seven hundred dollars a year?" Jill repeated. "David, what we could be doing with that money—"

"I'll start using it again," he promised. "How was your class this morning?"

"You're changing the subject."

"A good lawyer always knows when to change the subject."

"And a good husband?"

"Especially a good husband." He paused, reaching across the table and covering her hand with his own. "So, tell me, were you brilliant as usual?"

"I was awful, as usual," she said. "I'm a rotten teacher, David. I know it and they know it. I'm bored to tears and so are they. One kid was actually reading the morning paper while I was talking."

"What were you talking about?"

"How to conduct an interview."

"Sounds interesting."

"It's not. At least not talking about it. What's interesting is doing it."

"You have to know how first."

"I *do* know how," Jill said, surprising them both with the passion in her voice. "That's just the point. I should be out there, not stuck in some classroom. I feel sometimes when I'm talking that I'm going to burst wide open with—"

"With what?"

"Resentment," she said quietly. "I really resent those kids wanting to be what I was, knowing that a few of them will probably do well, become producers, filmmakers. Knowing that they think I'm a teacher because I couldn't make it—"

"That's not true. You know it's not."

"*They* don't. They're all firm believers in the old adage: 'Them that can, do. Them that can't—teach.'"

There was a second's pause before David spoke. "And me?" he asked. "Do you resent me, too?"

She lowered her head, prepared to lie. "Sometimes," she finally admitted, truthfully. "I know it's not your fault, David. Honestly, I know that. It was an impossible situation. I was away too much. We hardly got a chance to see each other. Not that we see that much of each other lately, anyway."

"Things will slow down again, Jill. It just got very hectic all of a sudden," he apologized.

"Summer's usually the slow time, I thought," Jill said quietly.

"Another few weeks," he said. "It should calm down a bit by then." He looked around. It was obvious to Jill that this was not turning out to be quite the victory luncheon David had had in mind. "What is it you want, Jill?" he asked. "You want to quit work at the university? You want to go back into television?"

Jill recalled the early crises in her marriage. They had all revolved around her job. "I don't know what I want," she said at last.

"I don't want to be the heavy in all this," David was saying. "God knows I have nothing against your working. You know that. I don't even mind that you work in television. Christ, that's how I met you. And you were wonderful—you had such spark."

"That's just it, David, I'm *losing* my spark."

"No," he argued sincerely. "No. You're just hiding it temporarily." He smiled at her and waited until she reluctantly returned his smile. "Look, why don't you call the network, call Ernie whatever-his-name-was—"

"Irving," she corrected. "Irving Saunders."

"Call Irving and see if he doesn't have something that wouldn't involve any traveling—"

"I asked him that two years ago when I left. There just isn't anything. Not in my field. I mean, there might be a few shows out of Chicago, but nobody's going to guarantee I won't have to do some traveling, or that I can finish up by five o'clock every night or won't have to work weekends or even all night sometimes."

"So, what are you saying?"

"I don't know. I don't know what I'm saying."

"You don't think it's worth a try?"

"David, what would you say to a potential lawyer, say Nicole Clark, for instance," she offered, and immediately wished she hadn't. "Anyway," she continued, "say she told you she'd be delighted to join your firm but she wanted it understood up front that she wouldn't work past 5 P.M., and that weekends were out of the question."

"I'd tell her to find herself another law firm."

"Exactly."

"What can I tell you, Jill? I can't make up your mind for you."

"I know."

"Maybe you're getting your period."

"What's that got to do with anything?"

"Well, you know how you sometimes get depressed when—"

"Everybody gets depressed from time to time! Don't start on my hormones—"

"I don't want to argue with you. I've made my suggstion. You can decide to act on it or not."

"You wouldn't mind if I got my old job back?" she asked timidly.

"I didn't say that," he answered. "I'd probably mind it very much. As far as I'm concerned, all the old objections are still valid. But I also have to recognize that it's your life and your decision." He shook his head. "I don't happen to think that you're giving the teaching a fair shake. You decided almost at the outset that you hated it—although I think you hate the idea of it more than you actually hate the teaching itself—and you won't allow yourself to enjoy it. You feel it would be some kind of betrayal. To what, I don't know."

"You're way off base, counselor."

"Maybe," he said. "If I am, I apologize. I was just trying to give you my opinion."

"You don't give opinions," she said, sullenly. "You give lectures."

"Maybe I should be the teacher," he said, smiling, his hand back on hers.

"Damn it," Jill said, allowing a small smile to crease her lips.

"Why'd you have to be so charming? I'm sorry, David. I'm acting like a spoiled brat."

"And I was probably lecturing. You're right. Sometimes I
get awfully impressed by the sound of my own voice."

"I love you," she said.

David signaled the waiter for the bill. "What do you think
we should do with the kids this weekend?" he asked.

"I don't know. A movie, maybe?"

"Think about it," he said. "Jason leaves for camp in less
than a week. Maybe you could make a special dinner for him."
Jill shrugged, thinking that all Jason ever ate was hamburgers
and that Laurie never ate anything at all. David gave the waiter
his gold American Express card. "Come on back to the office
for a few minutes," he said. "You've got time." She looked
skeptical. "Come on," he coaxed. "We've made a few changes.
It'll do you good."

"Okay," Jill agreed, thinking maybe David was right about
her attitude toward teaching. Maybe she'd never given it the
proper chance. She decided to try extra hard for her two
o'clock class. No matter what she did, she knew, watching her
husband sign the tab and tear off his portion of the receipt, anything was better than risking the loss of this man. He was better
than a daily dose of Vitamin C. There was no way she ever
wanted to live without him. It was as simple as that.

"Good afternoon, Mrs. Plumley," Diane greeted her pleasantly.
"How are you today?"

"Just fine, thank you," Jill told her husband's secretary.

"Good. Been looking around?" Jill nodded. "They made
some nice improvements to the staff lounge," Diane continued.
"And your husband chose all the new paintings."

"He told me. They're lovely."

The secretary smiled, turning her attention to her employer.

"Mrs. Whittaker has been calling you all morning," she announced as David walked past her toward his office. "And Julie
Rickerd has called twice. She says it's very important. And a
Mr. Powadiuk—I think that's how you pronounce it—he says
could you call him, he came home from a fishing trip yesterday

to find his wife had left and cleaned out their entire apartment. Didn't even leave him the paper plates."

David thanked her, taking the messages from her outstretched hand and motioning for Jill to follow him inside. He closed the door behind them, sitting down immediately at his paper-strewn desk. Jill went to the window and gazed out at the tops of the city buildings. "It's so beautiful up here," she said. "Like being in a different world."

David smiled in agreement and pressed the buzzer for his secretary. "Diane, get me the files on Julie Rickerd and Sheila Whittaker, please. And call this Mr. Powa—whatever-his-name-is." He flipped off the intercom. "What's this?" he asked, sifting through the clutter of his desk and retrieving a delicate bud vase containing a single red rose.

Diane brought the requested files in immediately, somehow finding room for them amid the general clutter of his desk. "I'll call Mr. Powad—whatever," she said, going out again.

David flipped absently through the files, then looked back at the flower.

"Is there a card?" Jill asked, a queasy feeling building in the pit of her stomach.

David searched the top of his desk. "I don't see one," he said. "Probably Diane put it there."

Jill walked over to his desk and reached into the stack of papers, pulling out a small lavender envelope. She handed it to David.

"Didn't see it," he said, reluctantly taking it from her and tearing it open. He read it quickly and handed it to Jill. "I'll talk to her," he said.

Jill read the note aloud. "Thank you again for a most interesting morning." She lowered the note to the table. "Nicki," she said, repeating the signature out loud.

"I'll call her right now if you'd like. You can be here while I talk to her."

"No. No," Jill protested, "let's just leave it alone, okay? If you bring her in here, it'll only embarrass everybody. It's just a thank-you note. A very nice touch, actually. Just ignore it. Maybe if she sees she's the only one playing this silly game, she'll get tired of it and go home."

"That's fine by me. You're the one I don't want to see upset," he said.

"I'm not," she lied. "If I can survive Elaine, I'm sure I can outlive Nicole. Nicki," she minced. David laughed but the laugh stuck in his throat.

"Maybe we're reading too much into all this," David offered. "We're liable to get paranoid if we're not careful. She's really a first-class lawyer."

David's buzzer sounded. "I have Mr. Powa—he's on the phone," Diane said.

"I'll go," Jill whispered as David picked up the receiver. She bent over and kissed his forehead, her nose immediately catching the subtle scent of the rose.

He waved goodbye as she closed the door behind her.

On the other side, her heart was pounding wildly. She stood for a minute at the doorway and tried to catch her breath.

"Are you all right, Mrs. Plumley?" Diane asked.

Jill looked over at her husband's secretary, a pretty girl with dark brown hair and large blue eyes. David had always surrounded himself with attractive women. During his marriage to Elaine, he had often succumbed to their attractions. He lied easily and well, he had once told her. And often, she knew, when he was married to Elaine. Had he ever lied to her? Jill wondered, then threw the thought away with a toss of her head. It was something she preferred not to think about. Nicole might have grand designs, Jill decided, but that was all they would ever be.

"I'm fine," Jill told Diane. "I'll see you again." She started down the long, winding corridor.

You had to give the girl high marks for trying, Jill thought. She was very clever. No doubt she would make a first-rate attorney. She was so bold, so brazen. Coming right out and stating her intentions. Putting the wife on immediate guard, on constant edge. Forcing her to imagine hidden meanings where none existed, perhaps causing unnecessary friction at home, laying the groundwork for small doubts to bloom into large ones. Bloom, Jill thought. Like a rose.

The best solution, short of murder, was simple indifference. She would not allow herself to get upset; she wouldn't even

allow herself the luxury of sarcasm. Not in front of David, anyway. There would be no fights because of this girl.

And David would be extra cautious, she knew. But also very
intrigued. How could he be anything less? Annoyed? Maybe.
Indignant? Possibly. But definitely intrigued. All part of the
master plan: the insecure and suspicious wife at home, the in-
triguing other woman at the office.

She was almost at the end of the hall when the voice stopped
her.

"Jilly? Jilly, is that you?"

She stopped and turned around. There were only two men in
the world who called her Jilly. One was her gynecologist. The
other was one of David's partners, a highly esteemed criminal
lawyer with a fondness for outrageous clothes and irritating
nicknames.

His name was Don Eliot and he stood before her in blue
jeans and a brown corduroy jacket. She was surprised to see he
was wearing a tie until she saw that the figure embroidered at
its base was Mickey Mouse. Hello, Donny, she wanted to say,
but thought better of it.

"Hello, Don," she said instead. "How are you?"

"Just wonderful," he said, taking hold of both her hands.
"How's Adeline?"

"Oh, fine. Great. The kids are driving her nuts, of course,
but that's not unusual." He looked her over. "You look good,"
he said, as if commenting on the quality of a sweater. "A little
tired, maybe. You getting enough sleep, Jilly?"

Thanks a lot for the compliment, Donny, she thought. His
remarks were the last thing she needed to hear. "Do we ever
get enough sleep?" she questioned in response.

"No, I guess not," he said. "Certainly not around our house.
Can you believe we had two of them up running around the
bedrooms last night at four in the morning—the two-year-old,
who's just learned how to climb out of his crib, and the four-
year-old, who wanted to see what all the commotion was about.
I tell you, Jilly, you and David have probably made the right
decision not to have kids. It changes your whole life, I tell you.
Of course, David already has two. That's plenty. We should
have stopped at two. Five is crazy!"

Jill tried to smile, grateful that Don Eliot obviously required no comments from her end. She was afraid that if she did speak, she might cry. So David had discussed his intentions (or lack of them) with regard to future children with others. Indeed, had told them the decision had already been made.

"Well," she said, finally. "Few decisions are carved in stone. You never know."

"Thatta girl, Jilly," he said, patting her shoulder and starting to move away. "Oh, by the way, now that I've got you here—Adeline's been after me for weeks to invite you two for dinner. How about a week this Saturday?"

Jill could think of nothing to say, so she nodded her head.

"Good," he said. "I'll have Adeline call you, set up a time."

"Sounds good," Jill lied.

"See you then." He disappeared behind a curve in the wall.

Jill stood for a few seconds in the corridor, trying to collect her thoughts. Since that lovely episode in the shower, early that morning, the day had taken a distinct downhill turn.

"Looking for a way out?" the husky voice asked with just the hint of a smile.

Nicole Clark stood only six feet away. Jill stared at her with a look of what she hoped was calm superiority. "Thank you," she said. "But I know my way around." Gathering herself up to her full height, hoping desperately that she wouldn't trip over her own feet, she walked briskly by the other woman and out the office doors.

Chapter 7

The picnic grounds were crowded and they had to circle the park for almost half an hour before someone pulled out and David found a place to park. By that point, David's mood was less than jocular, Laurie's pout was more prominent, and Jason's stutter more pronounced. Jill shifted the food basket on her lap, hoping that no one would remember that this afternoon's outing had been her idea.

"W-we'll n-never get a f-free barbecue," Jason spit out, as they grudgingly climbed out of the car. "There's a m-million people here this aft-afternoon. There w-won't be any b-barbecues left."

"Then we'll have to share," Jill told him, watching David retrieve the large thermos box from the trunk of the car. "Let's go that way," she said, pointing straight ahead at the crowded campgrounds. "I think the whole city must be here today." She hurried to catch up to David, his two children falling behind. "Do you think we'll be able to find a barbecue?" she whispered once they were out of Jason's earshot.

"We'll find one," he said, forced good will evident in every syllable.

They did. It took twenty minutes, and they had to share, as Jill had predicted, but at least it was already lit and everyone had worked up a considerable appetite in the interim.

"It's so hot," Jason said slowly, as Jill handed him his second hamburger.

"What is? The weather or the hamburger?" Jill asked, feeling that the afternoon might not turn out so badly after all. They had found a comfortable spot which provided a hint of shade, and the people whose space they were sharing seemed pleasant and helpful, although their three-year-old was obviously not happy with the family's latest addition, an infant of only a few months who lay gurgling contentedly on the blanket.

Jason handed back his hamburger in silence, displeased by the amount of blood dripping from the pink meat.

"Hamburgers are better when they're not little black balls of charcoal," David told him.

The boy was instantly apologetic. "B-but I don't like it that way," he protested.

"I do," Jill said, taking it from him. "We'll make you another one," she offered, looking over at Laurie. "What about you, Laurie? Another hamburger?"

"I haven't finished this one yet," Laurie said, watching as the three-year-old ran by his younger sibling, his foot just managing to brush sharply against the baby's side.

"Martin!" the child's mother warned, scooping the infant into her arms and shooting a withering glance in her son's direction.

Jill's attention moved back from the young mother to Laurie's plate, which had barely been touched. She hasn't started, let alone finished, Jill thought.

"More Coke?" Jill asked.

"It's not C-Coke," Jason corrected. "It's P-P-Pepsi."

"More Pepsi, then," Jill stated.

Jason shook his head.

"Laurie?" her father asked. "Some Pepsi for you, sweetie?"

"Nothing," the girl said. Her eyes traveled back to the young family, with whom she would obviously have preferred to be,

Jill thought, watching her, and then she too looked longingly at the baby in her mother's arms.

"How old is she?" Jill asked the young woman.

"Three months," the woman answered proudly.

"It must be a hectic time," Jill said, indicating the small boy watching enviously only several feet away.

"It is, especially with Martin being so jealous," the woman nodded. "He actually peed on little Pamela the other day. Stood over her and peed all over her little tummy. I thought I'd die!"

"Your classic case of piss-on-you," Jill said, and the two women laughed easily while everyone else around them looked vaguely embarrassed.

"How can you talk to a stranger like that?" Laurie admonished.

"Why not?" Jill asked. "I'm old enough." As if to prove her point, she turned back toward the young mother and introduced herself. "You look wonderful," she continued. "You're so nice and skinny."

"I was lucky," the woman said. "I was all baby. And I've been exercising every day like crazy."

Jill patted her stomach. "I have to start," she said. "Actually, I'm going to a class this Wednesday. Rita Carrington's. Have you heard of her?" The woman shook her head.

"Can I come?" Laurie asked suddenly.

"Come where?" Jill asked in return, directing her attention to David's daughter.

"To the exercise class," Laurie answered.

"Sure," Jill said, surprised by Laurie's interest.

"M-Mom's getting one of those b-big gas b-barbecues," Jason ventured timidly at his father.

Jill watched David's face tense. "Is your mother also buying a cook to help her plop the hamburgers down on the grill?" he asked.

"Mom knows how to cook," Jason said immediately in his mother's defense. "She's a great cook. She makes way better hamburgers than these," he added accusingly in Jill's direction. Jill noted the child had not stuttered once.

"So," Jill said, hurriedly trying to change the subject. "Are you looking forward to camp?"

"He better be," David answered, before the boy had a chance. "It's costing enough to send him."

"Mom says it's not costing half enough," Jason said, again with no trace of a stammer, his anger seeming to smooth his tongue.

"She's thinking of having a pool put in for next summer," Laurie contributed.

"What the hell does she want a pool for?" David questioned. "She doesn't swim."

"She says she'll take lessons."

"Private, of course," David added.

"She's entitled," his son shot back. Jill could hear Elaine's voice. I'm entitled, the other woman said.

"Your hamburger's ready," Jill announced, wrapping the well-cooked meat inside a hamburger bun.

"Th-thanks," Jason whispered, looking guiltily away.

David reached over and ruffled his son's dark blond hair. "You're getting to be a good-looking little kid, you know that?" he said with pride.

Jason playfully knocked his father's hand from his head, shaking his head in the same way that David always did to get the hairs back in place. "L-like f-father, like s-son," he stammered shyly.

David laughed and put his arms around the boy's neck, bending over to kiss his forehead. "What do you think of the Moonies or the Hare Krishnas?" he asked, seemingly from out of nowhere. Jill had to stifle a laugh.

"Which one?" Jason asked. "Th-they're two c-completely d-different things."

"Like Coke and Pepsi," David said.

"Yeah," his son concurred. "Exactly."

Laurie nodded in agreement, her plate still untouched.

Jill watched the young family beside them gathering up their now-screaming youngsters and bundling them off toward their car. Little children, little problems, she heard David's voice repeating. Then she looked back at Laurie and Jason.

"And one and two, that's right, ladies, to the right. And one and two. Now switch. To the left. And one and two. And again. To the left. The left, Mrs. Elfer, that's the way. And one and two. Five more times. To the right now, ladies. The right, Mrs. Elfer."

Poor Mrs. Elfer, Jill thought, contorting her body to the right, her hands stretched taut above her head. There's always one in every class who doesn't know her left hand from her right.

"And to the left, now, ladies. And one and two."

The rest of the class of some twenty-five women was already on the second beat when Mrs. Elfer finally found the first.

"Better, Mrs. Elfer," the instructor called out, not missing a beat. She seemed to speak as if every other word represented the clashing together of cymbals. "Okay, one more time. Now, bend forward from the waist and bring your right elbow over to your left heel for two counts, then your left elbow over to your right heel. Got that, everybody?" she yelled above the music (Debbie Harry and Blondie singing "Call Me," which Jill recognized as the theme from *American Gigolo*). The instructor bent forward and peered back between her spread legs at the rest of the group. "Ready? And one and two. Switch. One and two. Switch."

She's trying to kill us, Jill decided, bringing her right elbow to her left heel in time to the blaring disco beat. Whoever said disco was dead obviously had never been to Rita Carrington's exercise class. Jill stared wonderingly at Rita's protruding rear end. The woman was an Amazon, at least six feet tall, with the kind of body that usually found itself in the centerfold of *Playboy* magazine. Indeed, it was said that Rita had once worked as a Bunny and had been prominently featured in the magazine's presentation of "The Girls of Chicago." It gave one something to aspire to, Jill thought. Better than some fat old lady in torn leotard trying to convince them that hers was the way to a better body. At least, with Rita Carrington leading the way, there existed the faint glimmer of hope that it was indeed these exercises—and not an act of God—that had produced those results.

Rita Carrington straightened up and shook her hair free of her face. The hair was a deep auburn color and cut into seductive layers. ("She'd look good wet," Beth had commented when they first saw her.) Almost immediately, Rita Carrington was into the middle of another exercise. "Okay, ladies, up into the jog," she said, lifting her knees rapidly and jogging in place. "Get those legs up. Good. Good. Let's get a little sweat going here, ladies, come on. Let's move."

"She obviously hates women," Beth whispered from beside her.

"Whose idea was this anyway?" Jill breathed heavily in reply.

"Laurie's doing okay," Beth noted, indicating David's daughter in the front row.

Jill looked over at her husband's elder child. She still couldn't fathom why Laurie had expressed an interest in coming along. But since it was the first thing Jill had ever done that Laurie had been even remotely interested in, Jill did not feel it appropriate to turn down her request. Laurie had even called several times since the weekend to make sure the date was still on. And so here she was, all fourteen years of her, in the front row, twisting and turning her already skinny body, working as hard to trim off whatever fat she imagined she had as the rest of the women, who had, unfortunately, a good deal more excess flesh than imagination.

"You're doing pretty good yourself," Jill told Beth sincerely. Beth Weatherby, at forty-five, looked better in her black leotard and pink tights than most of the other women did who were many years her junior.

"No talking, ladies," Rita Carrington cautioned. Jill felt suitably chastised, as if she were a child back in school. Beth made a face and turned her attention back to the instructor. "Okay, ladies. On your backs."

Jill crouched down, watching Beth do the same. When Beth put her hand on the floor, she winced. "Still hurts?" Jill asked.

"I'm not sure if it's really the cut that hurts or just the memory of it," Beth answered.

"Ladies, please, you can talk in the lounge later."

"We can talk in the lounge, later," Jill repeated under her breath.

"Feet up, knees bent. Bend from the waist. And one and two and three and four—"

"Oh, that tastes good," Jill exclaimed, taking a long, slow sip of her Coca-Cola. "There is nothing like the taste of pure sugar after an hour of torture."

"It's better than sex," Ricki Elfer agreed, tossing away her straw and lifting the glass of Coke to her mouth.

"Well, I don't know—" Jill protested.

"Oh, yes, take my word for it," the slightly pudgy blonde protested. "I may not know my left hand from my right, but the two things I do know are sex and Coca-Cola. Coca-Cola's better."

Jill and Beth laughed at the woman who shared their table. Jill wondered if Ricki Elfer made the same distinction between Coke and Pepsi as did her stepson.

"I remember when I was in Rome," Ricki Elfer continued. "This is many years ago, remember. I was twenty. I'm thirty-six now. I was with a girlfriend. We'd been touring Europe all summer. You know, university kids on their summer vacation, and this was in the days of Europe on five dollars a day. And that was like all the money we had, so there was no such thing as little luxuries like a Coke, because we couldn't afford them. And this one day, it must have been a hundred degrees out and we'd been walking around all day looking at the Colosseum or whatever, and we were so thirsty, I thought we were going to die. Suddenly, this car pulls up beside us and these two Italian guys shout, 'Americanas, Americanas.' And my friend, who was getting a little tired of having her ass pinched every two seconds, shouted at them to keep driving. They yelled back that all they wanted to do was talk. So I said, 'Buy us a Coke first, then we'll talk!' And they did. And we did. And later that night we did a little more. And like I said, the Coke was better." She finished her drink. "It always is." She shook her head. "At least you know what you're getting; it doesn't pretend to be something it's not. And it always leaves you satisfied." She smiled. "Oh, youth," she said, still traipsing through the ruins of ancient Rome.

"Speaking of which," Jill interjected, "can you believe Laurie deciding to take another class?!"

"That skinny kid?" Ricki asked.

"My husband's daughter," Jill nodded. "She says her waistline's too thick."

"How old is she?"

"Fourteen."

"She's nuts," Ricki said plainly, and Jill and Beth laughed. "They're all nuts at fourteen. Then they get older, they get worse. Wait till *she* wants to go to Europe."

"You have children?" Beth asked.

"Two boys," Ricki Elfer answered. "Ten and eleven. They live with their father."

"You're divorced?" Jill asked, noting Ricki's wedding band.

"Several times. Paul, my current—I love that word, it makes him sound so impermanent—is my third husband. I'm trying to decide right now whether to have another baby or tie my tubes."

"That's quite a choice," Beth commented.

"Women are always faced with wonderful choices like that. But it's true. Part of me would like to have another child— which part, I'm not sure—and I figure, at thirty-six, if I'm going to do it, I better do it now. The other part of me—the sane part —says I've done my share and what do I need with the aggravation, not to mention the nausea and the discomfort and, lest we forget, the pain." She signaled the waiter for another Coke. "Not to mention what it does to your body. Can you believe that before I married my first husband—his name was Errol, his mother named him after Errol Flynn—anyway, before we got married, I weighed ninety-eight pounds. And I'm five foot four. Not exactly a shrimp."

"You must have been like Laurie," Jill remarked.

"No. I was skinny, all right, but Laurie's almost emaciated. You ever heard of anorexia nervosa?"

"Oh, no," Jill said, dismissing the thought. "She's skinny but I don't think she's deliberately starving herself."

The waiter put a second glass of Coca-Cola in front of Ricki Elfer. "Thank you," she said, then turned her attention back to her new friends. "This place used to be a real dump, but since they put in this lounge and everything, it's picked up a lot. Rita did that. Before she came, there was nothing."

"How long have you been coming here?" Beth asked.

"It's been a second home for the last two years." She looked at her body. "Discouraging, isn't it? Especially when, after all this time, I'm still going one way when everyone else is going the other. Remember when you took ballet and there was always one kid in the class whose arms were going up just when everyone else's were going down? Well, that was me. I'm that kid." She patted her stomach. "I know that somewhere inside here, Jane Fonda is struggling to get out." She shook her head. "After thirty, boy, that's it. The body goes all to hell. Everything drops three inches. What doesn't drop, expands. And your skin dries up and pretty soon you're looking like a big, fat prune." Jill and Beth started laughing again. "Let's get back to sex; it's not quite so depressing."

"How'd you meet your husband?" Jill asked.

"Which one?"

"The latest," Jill smiled.

"I met him while I was married to husband number two. We were thinking of renovating our townhouse and so we called in a few architects to get some ideas. Paul was one of the architects; I took one look at him and got plenty of ideas. Now that I think of it, I probably should have my tubes tied instead of insisting that Paul have a vasectomy. If I tie my tubes, I can still fool around. If Paul has a vasectomy, it's another fifteen years on the Pill."

"Do you fool around?" Jill asked her, amazed she was having such an intimate conversation with a woman who only an hour ago had been a total stranger.

"Not as much as I'd like," the woman answered. "Not as many cars pulling up beside me these days yelling 'Americana, Americana.'" She laughed heartily. "What about you?" she said, turning to Beth.

"Me?" Beth smiled. "Oh, no. I've never even been to Europe." Both Jill and Ricki regarded her expectantly. "No, I've led a very sheltered life. I met Al, my husband, when I was seventeen. I was working in a bank. I was a teller. He used to come to my window all the time. I thought he was cute, not very tall, slight of build, but cute anyway." Jill giggled. She loved stories like this one and she'd always been curious about Al and Beth Weatherby. "He was so full of confidence though, you would have thought he owned the bank," Beth continued. "He used to strut over to my window and deposit his money. After a few months he started talking to me. Told me he was a lawyer. I was very impressed. He said he liked the theatre and lifting weights and that one day he was going to head the city's largest, most successful law firm. I told him that when his bank balance hit ten thousand dollars, he'd have to marry me." It was Beth's turn to giggle. Jill thought that when she did, she looked just like a little girl.

"And he did?" Ricki asked.

"The day after my eighteenth birthday," Beth answered. "My mother wasn't at all happy about that. She thought I was much too young, that Al was too old for me, that he'd always have more dreams than clients."

"What does she think now?" Ricki wondered.

"She died about eleven years ago."

Ricki was appropriately apologetic. "So, you've been married how long?"

"Twenty-seven years."

"My God! Amazing! Any children?"

"Three. Two boys and a girl. The oldest, Brian, is a doctor in New York; Lisa, the middle one, is a singer in L.A.; and Michael," she sighed, "Michael has fallen into the clutches of the Reverend Moon, or someone like that." She looked past Jill into the open space behind her. "It's funny," she said, almost wistfully, "how nothing ever works out quite the way you thought it would."

Jill nodded her head in agreement. Her own life was certainly not what she had expected. "How *is* Lisa?" she asked.

"Oh, fine. She's still not working, but at least she's trying."

"And that married musician—?"

"Married musician?" Beth looked genuinely astonished. "What are you talking about?"

Jill was confused. "Al mentioned that night you cut your hand that you were upset because of Lisa's involvement with a married man, a musician—"

"Did he? I don't remember—" Her voice trailed off. Jill thought it best to drop the subject. There were several seconds where no one said anything at all.

"How about you, Jill?" Ricki asked suddenly, catching Jill by surprise. "How'd you meet your husband?"

"Oh, we met when I was interviewing him for a television show," Jill began.

"You're in television?" Ricki Elfer asked quickly. "What's your last name again? Are you someone I should know?"

Jill laughed. "No, you wouldn't know me. My name was Jill Listerwoll before I got married. Now, it's Jill Plumley." She stopped, thinking that her name had always been full of l's. "And I'm not in television anymore. I'm a teacher at the university."

The door at the far end of the lounge opened, and David's daughter Laurie came inside. For the first time since the three women had sat down, Jill allowed herself the luxury of taking a long, hard look at her surroundings. Rita Carrington had done a good job. The room was restful, almost soothing, with its deep burgundy walls and pink and mauve sofas. Even the bar area, where they were sitting, was well-appointed with attractive white tables and chairs with deep purple cushions. Just the right sort of room in which to pamper yourself after an hour with Rita Carrington. Jill watched as Laurie ambled toward her. The child was still in her pink leotard and leg warmers.

"Hi, Laurie," she said pleasantly. "How you doing? Want a Coke?"

"No, thanks."

"Oh, you gotta have a Coke," Ricki Elfer encouraged. "It's better than—"

"So how was the second class?" Jill interrupted, cutting Rickie Elfer off just in time.

"Great," Laurie said. "Better than the first. It was a different instructor. This one really made you work." Jill and Beth exchanged incredulous glances.

"You better watch that you don't exercise yourself into thin air," Ricki Elfer cautioned.

"No, I really need the exercise," Laurie insisted, then turned back to Jill. "Is it okay if I take a shower before I go home?"

"Of course," Jill said. "I'll wait for you." She paused. "Actually, I thought that since David was working late tonight, you and I could have dinner together, maybe go to a movie—"

"Oh, I can't," Laurie said apologetically. "Ron's taking my mother and me out as soon as I get home."

"Ron?" Jill asked.

"Ron Santini, my mother's new boyfriend."

"Ron Santini, the gangster?" Jill asked, the words popping out of her mouth in astonishment.

"He's not a gangster," Laurie answered indignantly. "He's in fruit."

"Oh," Jill said, nodding. "Sorry. There must be more than one Ron Santini in Chicago."

"I guess so," Laurie pouted. "Ron's in fruit." Jill nodded again. "I'll go take my shower."

"I'll wait for you here," Jill offered. "At least I can drive you home."

"It's not necessary."

"I'll drive you home," Jill insisted. Laurie shrugged and walked away. "I don't know," she muttered, almost to herself. "I try, I really try to be friends with that girl—"

"Shouldn't have called her mother's boyfriend a gangster," Ricki advised.

Jill laughed. "It just slipped out." She watched Laurie make her exit. "I thought everyone knew Ron Santini was a big shot with the Mob. We did a show on the guy a few years ago. Those fruit stores of his are nothing but fronts."

"I bet I know something you don't know," Ricki chimed in a singsong-like refrain.

"What's that?" Beth asked.

"Well," Ricki said, leaning forward, "Ron Santini, reputed Mafioso, is also reputed to have a twelve-inch cock!"

"You're kidding!" Beth exclaimed, looking around her. None of the other women in the room seemed to have overheard, although one woman at the next table was leaning noticeably farther back in her chair.

"I'm serious," Ricki continued. "A girlfriend of mine once had a very brief fling with the guy—he really gets around, you know. Apparently he's Chicago's answer to Warren Beatty."

"It can't be the same guy," Jill said.

"Why not?" asked Beth.

"What would a playboy with a twelve-inch cock be doing with someone who only likes to screw on Christmas and Thanksgiving?"

"Who only likes to screw on Christmas and Thanksgiving?" Ricki asked.

"Elaine, my husband's ex-wife."

"Who told you she only likes to screw on holidays?"

"My husband. He said that in seventeen years of marriage, he doubted they made love more than fifty times."

"Never believe anything a husband tells you about his ex-wife," Ricki advised.

Jill turned to Beth. "You know her, Beth," she said. "What do you think?"

"Who ever really knows about anyone else," Beth answered cryptically.

"True."

"My first husband had a big dick," Ricki said, loudly enough to attract the undivided attention of the women sitting at the next table. They stopped any further pretense at conversation. "A big dick and thirty million dollars," she continued.

"And you left him?!" the woman leaning back in her chair asked, almost falling to the floor.

"He was so boring," Ricki explained, moving her chair in order to accommodate her new listeners. "He was really the most boring person I have ever met. I knew he was boring when I married him, of course, but I thought that with a dick a foot long and thirty million dollars, I could learn to love being bored. Alas, such was not the case," she sighed theatrically. "That plus the fact that he caught me *in flagrante delicto,* or whatever you call it, with his stockbroker. Husband number two, incidentally." She paused. "God has to be a man," she said, thinking out loud. "Only a man could take such wonderful potential and make such a mess!"

Everybody laughed. "They should only know how women talk about them," Jill said, and everyone agreed.

One of the women at the next table stood up. "Well," she began, "it's been a pleasure, and I hate to leave just when things are starting to get interesting, but it's late, and my husband likes his dinner on the table when he walks in the door."

"So, let him put it there," someone else said.

"The only bad thing about marriage," Beth announced, "is that it goes on for so long."

"Not mine, " Ricki exclaimed, standing up as well. "Actually, I should go too."

"We all should," Beth agreed. "Much as I hate to admit it, Al also likes his food on the table as soon as he comes home."

"You go," Jill told her. "I'll wait for Laurie."

"You don't mind waiting alone?" Beth asked her.

"How long can it take to wash seventy-five pounds?"

"Anorexia nervosa," Ricki intoned ominously. "Goodbye, Jill." She extended her hand. "It's been lots of fun. Hope to see you here again."

"Next Wednesday," Jill told her.

"I'll be here," answered the round little woman, bidding a similar farewell to Beth.

"She must be dynamite in bed," Jill whispered under her breath, thinking that it usually took more than a sense of humor to attract three husbands, not to mention thirty million dollars and a twelve-inch cock. She thought immediately of Elaine. What was she doing with a man like Ron Santini? More to the point, what was he doing with a woman like Elaine?

"Jill? Hello, Jill, are you there?" Beth was asking.

"Oh, sorry, Beth. I guess I wasn't. You're leaving."

"Yeah, I really should. You'll be at Don Eliot's on Saturday night?"

Jill looked pleasantly surprised. "Yes. You too?"

Beth nodded. "We'll be there."

"Oh, good. See you then." Beth turned and headed toward the door. "And one," Jill called after her, her voice a dead ringer for Rita Carrington's. "And two. And one—"

Chapter 8

Don Eliot's home was big and old and in as much a state of shambles as one might expect from a place that housed two adults, five children under the age of ten, and three cats. There were also the required number of gerbils and goldfish although they were too prone to unfortunate accidents and flushings to be ever seriously included in the family census. In short, the house looked exactly like the kind of house one would expect Don Eliot to live in—it rambled; it was messy; it was vaguely intimidating; it was very comfortable. Jill tried to reconcile the two final descriptions. How could a house that was intimidating be comfortable? she wondered, yet concluded that those were exactly the right words to use. Don Eliot was exactly the same way.

His wife was only comfortable. There were no airs, no pretenses about her. She was, plainly and simply, a woman with five children and no live-in help. A cleaning lady came twice a week, but both she and her husband had been unhappy with the notion of strangers sharing their house. And so, Adeline Eliot had done it all herself. ("What I really hate," she had confided to Jill, "is these single women who meet you at parties and ask you what you do, and when you tell them you're a mother, they stare and say, 'Yes, but what do you *do?*' ")

"I hope you don't mind, the children are all up," Adeline greeted them at the door. "They wanted to meet you before they went to bed."

"Sounds great," David said enthusiastically, kissing Adeline on the side of the cheek. "Where are they?"

"Upstairs, for the moment—count your blessings," Don Eliot's wife responded, her warm smile etching deep creases at the sides of her mouth. The combination of the lines and the many streaks of gray running through her otherwise dark hair, which she wore pulled back severely into a bun, contributed to the image of a much older woman, although Jill placed her age at somewhere between Beth Weatherby's and her own. "I can't remember whether or not you've been here before," she said to Jill.

"No, I haven't," Jill replied, realizing Elaine obviously had been. "It's lovely."

"Well, it's a mess," Adeline laughed. "But then it always is. I've given up trying to do anything about it. Maybe when all the children are gone—" She ushered them into the large living room where Don Eliot was standing behind a makeshift bar serving drinks. Al and Beth Weatherby, their hands interlocked, sat as close as newlyweds on the tattered print sofa. Everybody rose immediately to say hello.

"Who starred with Richard Burton in *The Spy Who Came In from the Cold?*" Al asked instantly, releasing his wife's hands to take hold of Jill's, and kissing her on both cheeks.

"Claire Bloom," Jill said, returning his kisses.

"Too easy," Al muttered. "I knew it was too easy. Wait, I have another one. Who was the male lead in *Them?*"

"In what?" asked Don Eliot.

"*Them,*" Jill repeated. "It was a horror movie. One of the first about the possible results of nuclear testing, and one of my favorites."

"Naturally," Al sighed, playfully. He looked at Jill. "So, who was the male lead?"

Jill smiled. "Was it James Arness?" she asked.

"It was," Al sighed. "One of these days, I'm going to stump you."

"Many have tried," David laughed, squeezing Jill's arm and going over to Don Eliot.

"We intend to try harder—later on," Don Eliot stated with a mischievous twinkle. "What'll it be?" he asked, indicating the drinks.

"Scotch and water," David said.

"White wine?" Jill asked.

"You got it," Don answered.

"It's quiet," David remarked, looking around.

"That's because we have all the kids locked up in a sound-proof vault until everybody arrives." There were a few chuckles. "Seriously, they must be watching television. We told them if they kept relatively silent until we finished welcoming everyone, they could come in and do their little Von Trapp number."

"Who else is coming?" Beth asked.

Jill suddenly sneezed.

"Catching cold?" Don Eliot asked. Jill shook her head.

"Cats bothering you?" David asked, taking his drink from Don's hand.

"I guess so," Jill said, sneezing again. "I have a slight allergy to cats," she explained. Slight? she questioned herself. She'd be lucky if her eyes didn't swell up and close over by the time the evening was finished. If she was really lucky, she might even be able to breathe by the following morning. She pictured the long night ahead.

"I should have told you about the cats," Adeline whispered. "A lot of people have allergies to cats these days. I could take them outside, if you'd like."

"No, it's the hair," Jill explained, seeing one cat curled up on the sofa and another in a chair by the windowsill. The third was undoubtedly warming her seat in the dining room. "It gets in everything."

"Especially in this house," Don Eliot said, handing Jill her drink. "There you go, Jilly. That'll make you feel better."

"I'll be fine," Jill said, sipping the clear white liquid. "It's probably just the initial contact." She hoped she sounded more confident than she felt.

Don Eliot looked around the room. "Anybody else?"

Beth shook her head. "I'll have a refill," Al Weatherby said. "You didn't answer my wife's question. Who else is coming?"

"Oh," Don Eliot said, returning to the table where the liquor was all set up, "I invited Nicki Clark." Jill sneezed violently. "You all right?" Don asked her. Jill buried her face in the kleenex which Beth thrust suddenly under her nose. "She's been helping me the last few weeks with a case I've been working on. I thought it would be nice to include her. She lives alone, you know. Her father lives in New Hampshire with his wife, who apparently is only a few years older than Nicki. Her mother died of cancer some years back. Kind of sad. She's a real nice kid, but I don't think she has a whole lot of friends."

I wonder why, Jill thought, glancing over at David. He was looking at her as if to explain he was as surprised as she was.

"I'm sure she's given up on the whole thing," he said a few minutes later, walking over to Jill and whispering from behind his drink.

"Oh?" Jill questioned, trying hard not to sneeze again.

"I haven't seen her all week. I think she's been avoiding me. Probably embarrassed."

"Maybe," Jill said. "Don't worry about it. I'm not."

David smiled. "Good girl."

"So, is Nicki coming alone?" Al Weatherby asked in a temporary lull in the conversation.

"No. She phoned Adeline and asked if she could bring a date."

Jill watched David's face. He smiled at her, as if to say, there, you see? Well, maybe he was right. Maybe the game was over. She sneezed again, her eyes beginning to itch.

The doorbell rang again and suddenly everything began happening at once. The third cat appeared and began running through everybody's legs; the five Eliot children exploded into the room, chasing the cats, grabbing at the fresh vegetables and dip Adeline had prepared (God only knew when), playing hide-and-seek behind the liquor table and screaming loudly at no one in particular. "Home sweet home," Don Eliot mused, re-entering the room with Nicole Clark and a young man who looked enough like her to be her brother. "Nicki," Don said, his right arm sweeping across the room as if to bring everyone closer together, "I think you've probably met everyone—at least, the gentlemen. Do you know Al's wife, Beth?"

"I think we've said hello," Beth said graciously. "At the picnic."

"Oh, yes," Nicole said in her deep voice. "Of course."

"And David's wife, Jill?" Don continued.

"We've met," Jill said.

"Nice to see you again," Nicole said, as if she meant it.

"And, of course, my wife you met at the door," Don concluded. Nicole nodded. "And this is Nicki's friend, Chris Bates, right?"

"Very good," the young man smiled, confidently.

"Chris is one of the new lawyers at Benson, McAllister."

Everyone agreed it was nice to meet him. Jill sneezed.

"Do you have a cold?" Chris asked over the general shrieking of the children.

"A slight allergy," Jill said quietly.

"To cats or children?" Nicole asked. Everybody laughed, including David.

"Cats," Jill answered.

"I always thought allergies were psychosomatic," Nicole said cheerfully, before turning her attention back to her date.

"Okay, kids, line up," Don Eliot ordered the children.

It took several minutes but then there they all stood, arranged according to height, before their captive audience. "We'll do this as fast as we can," Don said, starting at the tallest head. "Jamie, Kathy, Rodney, Jeremy, Robin," he said, tapping each head in turn. "Are you going to sing or dance or what?" he asked.

"Or what!" the oldest, Jamie, yelled out, and everyone went wild.

It took almost ten minutes before calm was restored and the children were herded upstairs. "We have a surprise for you," Don said, leading his guests toward the dining room. "It's a game we made up in honor of Jilly. She's our movie buff. I'll explain it at the table."

"Oh, good," said Nicole Clark, looking directly at Jill. "I love games."

The guests sat at the long, heavy oak table and eyed each other warily over their steaming bowls of mock turtle soup.

"This is delicious," Jill said, breaking the silence. Was everyone as nervous as she was? And why was she so nervous? It was just a game, a harmless little parlor game. It didn't matter who won or lost. Jill looked across the table at her husband, who was sandwiched between Beth Weatherby on one side and Nicole Clark on the other. What was making her more nervous —the silly game or her husband's proximity to the woman everyone at the table, except herself, casually, even affectionately, referred to as Nicki? Jill looked over at Nicole's perfect profile. The girl was quietly engaged in a conversation with her host, and except for a smile in David's direction when he'd passed her the bread basket, she had largely ignored the fact that he was seated beside her. Jill tried to reach her husband's feet with her own but the distance between them was too wide. Instead, she collided with one of the table legs. She winced, realizing with some relief that her nose felt less stuffy in this room. We never allow the cats in the dining room, Adeline had told her as they'd crossed the wide center hall.

"Jill?"

Jill's eyes suddenly focused on her husband's. He had been saying something to her. She hadn't heard a word.

"I'm sorry," Jill apologized, realizing everyone was watching her.

"Trying to figure out how to get your line in?" Don Eliot asked gleefully.

"I guess I was," Jill lied, thinking quickly of the game they were supposed to be playing and the line she had been assigned to deliver.

"Adeline asked if you'd like the recipe," David told her, in a suitably subtle admonishment.

"For the soup," Adeline added.

"I'd love it," Jill said enthusiastically. "If it's not too hard—"

"Hard? Are you kidding? Do I have time to make hard?"

"I don't know how you have time to do anything," Beth said, echoing Jill's feelings.

"It's all a fake," Adeline continued proudly. "You just mix Campbell's tomato soup with Campbell's green pea soup, add a little milk and a lot of sherry, and presto, mock turtle soup."

"I'll have to try it," Jill promised.

"I'm hopeless in the kitchen," Nicole Clark interjected. "When I get home, I'm usually so tired, I just call in for a pizza or something."

"She calls in for pizza, and look at her," Beth said innocently. "Jill and I would have to go to exercise class every day for a month before just calling in for a pizza!"

Nicole Clark smiled sweetly at Jill. "Oh," she said, "I think you're exaggerating."

"Has your wife been complaining all week too, David?" Al Weatherby asked. "'This hurts, that hurts. Don't touch me here. Don't touch me there.'" He laughed.

"I've heard the odd complaint," David confessed.

"They go to one exercise class," Al continued. "You'd think they'd been to the wars."

"What exercise class do you go to?" Nicole asked.

"Rita Carrington's," Beth explained. "Over on Warden Street. We joined last week. A humbling experience, wouldn't you agree, Jill?"

Jill nodded, trying to smile.

"I've never been to an exercise class," Nicole said. "I guess I should, though, *before* my body starts to fall apart."

Jill finished off the last of her mock turtle soup quickly before the urge to hurl it across the table completely overwhelmed her.

"Exercise takes a lot of self-discipline," Chris Bates began. "A lot of self-control. I'm not big on control."

Jill's eyes shot directly to his. *"Ordinary People,"* she spat out suddenly. "The psychiatrist, Berger, I think."

"Right you are!" Don Eliot applauded. Everyone else looked vaguely startled.

Chris Bates lowered his head and laughed. "I rushed things," he said. "I shouldn't have been in such a hurry to get the line out."

"It was the perfect time," Adeline said, disagreeing. "But you're up against the master."

"One for Jilly," Don Eliot said and everyone smiled.

The next course was less successful than the first, the salad too wet and lifeless, the roast beef too tough, the potatoes too bland. For a few minutes, Jill felt as if she were back at her parents' home. It was the kind of meal she had grown up on. She was starting to relax more with the game, however, having decided she couldn't be any more clumsy than anyone else. The game consisted of simply being able to identify lines from famous movies. Each person at the table (with the exception of Don and his wife, who had devised the game and therefore knew all the answers) had been assigned a line of dialogue, and it was everyone's responsibility to inject this line into the conversation without detection. It was up to everyone else to do the detecting.

So far, Jill was batting two out of three, having successfully identified Chris's earlier attempt from *Ordinary People* and Beth's subsequent exclamation of "Oh, we're fertile, all right," which Jill recognized instantly as a line from *Rosemary's Baby*. Nicole Clark had guessed the third, Al Weatherby's vain attempt to disguise Faye Dunaway's line from *Bonnie and Clyde* ("We rob banks") in the middle of a long anecdote which Jill had been waiting for him to complete before unmasking him. Nicole, however, chose not to wait. She jumped right in.

The dessert was a soufflé which had fallen somewhere between its removal from the oven and its presentation at the table. It was served without apology and tasted as good as Jill imagined it would have anyway. She finished it all and asked for seconds, realizing that the rest of them had to get their lines in before coffee was concluded.

"How's the Rickerd divorce coming?" Al Weatherby asked David.

"Messy. The stuff of front pages."

"I just want to know who's going to get that gorgeous house," Beth said.

"I've seen it," Nicole Clark stated quickly. "I was at a party there a few years ago. It's just beautiful. All wood paneling, lots of lovely ceilings, some of them twelve feet high. You don't see that anymore."

"Especially not in an apartment," David agreed.

"That's for sure," Chris Bates said, and there followed a long discussion on the housing situation in Chicago.

"How's your sister?" Beth asked David as coffee was being served.

"She's fine," he said, then hesitated. "Well, actually, she's been a little bit depressed lately." Jill tried to figure out what he was talking about. She hadn't heard anything about Renee's being depressed. "A friend of hers committed suicide." He looked directly at Jill. "Julie Hubbard," he said. Jill gasped.

"My God," she said. "When?"

"A few days ago. The family covered it up. I don't know." He paused dramatically, shaking his head. "What can you say about a twenty-five-year-old girl who died?"

"*Love Story!*" Nicole Clark shrieked. "The opening line from *Love Story!*"

"You got me," David confessed, laughing.

"Well done, Nicki," Don Eliot bellowed. "Very good. You're tied up with Jilly now. Two each." He turned toward Jill. "Jill, are you all right?"

Jill felt the color gradually returning to her face. "Julie Hubbard," she repeated slowly, "she's—"

"Alive and well and still living in the West End," David said, his eyes sparkling. "Fooled you. Fooled the champ!"

"Yes, you did," she admitted. "Not exactly fair though. You really had me going. I went to school with the girl," Jill explained to the others.

"I thought she was only twenty-five," Nicole smiled.

Jill looked over at Nicole. "I guess I was too stunned to consider logistics," she said, thinking of how convincing a liar her husband could be.

"Well, you didn't fool Nicole," Al Weatherby chuckled, reaching across the table and patting Nicole's hand. "Good for you," he said.

That left only Nicole and herself, Jill realized. How appropriate. They would face each other like the gunfighters in *High Noon*, shooting their lines, like bullets, straight at each other's hearts. Jill looked around the table, feeling suddenly that it was very important she win this showdown, feeling the symbolism inherent in the situation was too heavy not to be weighted in her favor. She had to win. She had to prove to Nicole that she was still on top of things, even if it wasn't exactly clear what those things were. Neither she nor Nicole had delivered her line. Time was running out. Still, she couldn't rush. What she said had to sound endemic to the conversation. If only someone would provide her with a proper cue.

As if instinctively realizing her role, Beth handed Jill the perfect lead-in. "That's a beautiful dress you're wearing," she said. "I meant to tell you earlier—"

"Oh, thank you," Jill gushed, perhaps a touch too effusively. "I must have changed a hundred times."

"She always does that," David qualified. "But it was even worse tonight. I thought we'd never get out of the apartment."

"Well, you know how it is," Jill explained, feeling her heart beginning to beat faster. Could everyone hear it? Would it give her away? The words tumbled out. "If David doesn't like what I'm wearing, I take it off!"

Nicole's husky whisper was suddenly as loud as any voice Jill had ever heard. "I know that line!" she pounced. "Give me a minute—I know that line, I just have to figure out where it comes from." She threw her head back, her eyes closed. "Just a minute. Just a minute—" Her head straightened up; her eyes opened. Her face was barely big enough to contain her smile. "I've got it! Joan Collins to June Allyson in *The Opposite Sex*. And the exact line was, 'If *Stephen* doesn't like what I'm wearing, I take it off!' "

"Bravo!" shouted Al Weatherby. "How do you like that, Jill?" he said, turning to her. "She got you."

"She certainly did," Jill agreed, good-naturedly. "Actually, I'm relieved. I was so nervous. Am I the only one who gets so nervous?!"

"What's there to be nervous about?" Adeline asked, greatly amused. "It's just a game."

"And so far, Nicki's winning," Chris Bates pointed out proudly.

"Actually," Don Eliot said, "she's already won! Haven't you, Nicki?"

Nicole clapped her hands in delight.

"What about your line?" Al asked her.

"I gave it," Nicole said. "A long time ago. When we were talking about the Rickerd divorce, and Beth wondered who'd get their gorgeous house. I said I'd been in it, which was a lie, of course. I don't even know them. And I said that it was all wood-paneled, with 'lots of lovely ceilings.' That was my line. 'Lots of lovely ceilings.' It's from—"

"*The Carpetbaggers,*" Jill said quietly, recognizing the now familiar line. "Elizabeth Ashley to George Peppard when he asks her what she'd like to see on her honeymoon."

Nicole's already wide smile widened even farther. "Too late," she chirped happily and the party adjourned to the other room.

Jill propped two extra pillows underneath the one she normally used and crawled back into bed beside her husband.

"Is that it?" he asked wearily. "You think you're finally set for the night?"

Jill looked over at the clock. It was almost two in the morning. For what felt like the tenth time in as many seconds, she sneezed. "It's those damn cats," she said, hoping the extra pillows would allow her to breathe easier.

"You're sure it's not something else?" he asked.

"What else could it be?"

"Well, you didn't sneeze at all in the Eliots' dining room."

"They don't allow the cats in the dining room."

"You said yourself their hair gets in everything."

"What are you trying to say, David? That Nicole is right? My allergy is psychosomatic?"

"It just seemed strange that after you lost that stupid game, you started sneezing again."

"We went back into the living room!" she said, her voice rising.

"Oh," he said with infuriating condescension. "Please don't yell." She sneezed again. "Is this going to go on all night?" he asked.

"It might," Jill remarked, coldly. "Why, do you have a heavy date tomorrow?"

"I have to go in to work," he said.

"On Sunday?"

"Oh, let's not start that, Jill," he begged. "I'm swamped. I've told you that. I'm also exhausted. You've been sneezing for the past two hours. Why don't you just close your eyes and forget about the fact that Nicole won. It was just a game, not the goddamn Olympics!"

Jill sat up sharply in bed. "You think I'm upset because Nicole won?" she accused.

"Well, aren't you?" he asked.

"No!" she said, protesting just a shade too strongly. "I *do* think she got a particularly easy line to read," she added. " 'Lots of lovely ceilings' is a much easier line to sneak into a conversation than what I had to say."

"She drew from the hat the same as everyone else," David pointed out. "Come on, don't you think you're making too much of this?"

Jill shrugged, knowing he was right, and knowing also that it wasn't really the fact that she had lost a silly game that was bothering her. What was disturbing her more were the implications her loss had carried to both herself and the other woman. Nicole's victory implied that there would be others; that this was merely the beginning of a long series of titles being snatched away from the reigning heavyweight, that the challenger had won the first round and was on her way to the final count. It seemed particularly ironic that the dialogue Jill had had to deliver had been of such a similar nature to their own situation: June Allyson, knowing of her husband's affair with Joan Collins, confronts the younger woman and says that if the dress Joan is wearing is for Stephen, his tastes run to simpler styles. Joan responds that if Stephen doesn't like what she wears, she— David's voice interrupted her thoughts.

"What?" she asked defensively, the child caught with her pants down.

"I said, you're not upset because you still think she's after me, are you?" His question cried out for a negative response.

"Because if you are," he continued, not waiting for an answer, "you're way out of line."

"*I'm* out of line?" Jill questioned.

"Let's just say you're wrong," he said, retreating. "She hardly looked at me twice all night."

"You sound disappointed."

He turned over in bed. "Let's not get ridiculous."

Jill let out a deep breath. There was obviously no point in pursuing this line of discussion. "Did Beth seem subdued to you tonight?" she asked instead.

"No," he grunted.

Jill looked in his direction, wanting to hug him, to pull him close against her the way they usually slept. She was about to when she felt her stomach cramp.

"Where are you going?" he asked accusingly as she got out of bed.

"My stomach hurts."

"What'd you have two desserts for?" he called after her as she made her way to the bathroom. "Nobody else did."

"I didn't realize you were monitoring what I ate," she said, more to herself than to David as she sat down on the toilet.

She was less surprised than disappointed when she saw the blood. Right on time, she thought, searching through the cupboard for her Tampax. The one thing in my life I can always depend on.

Chapter 9

The staff lounge of the Radio and Television Arts Department of the University of Chicago was a large, rectangular room which always appeared to be a small square, possibly because of the amount of overstuffed furniture squeezed into it. It seemed the college administrators equated mass with comfort and what was shabby with what was artistic, Jill thought, as she came inside and headed toward the coffee machine. The large percolator was already empty, which meant that if she wanted any coffee, she would have to make up a fresh brew herself. Let somebody else do it today, she decided, settling down into the nearest floral print armchair to wait, and trying to get in a suitable position for a two-minute sleep. She felt her muscles tense across her back and wondered idly if the exercise class she'd be attending that afternoon would make her feel better or worse. She also wondered if Beth would show up for this week's class, having missed the last one without notice or explanation. ("Things just got away from me," she had told Jill subsequently, and Jill, sensing a certain reticence on the part of the other woman, had questioned her no further.) When Beth de-

cided she wanted to talk to her—if, indeed, there was anything
to talk about—she would do so.

She shifted uncomfortably on a spring whose time had come
and gone, and deciding sleep was impossible, reached over
across the multi-stained coffee table to pick up the morning
paper. Someone had stolen the Classified section. That did it!
she decided, standing up and going toward the door. No coffee,
no Classified section. No justice. She thought of David. She
wasn't trying hard enough, he had told her. I've been trying my
little heart out, she argued with him silently as she closed the
door behind her and started down the long corridor toward her
class. But honest effort doesn't always change things. And facts
are facts. ("Just stick to the facts, ma'am.") I know it's an hon-
orable profession, possibly even a courageous one. But it's just
not for me!

She stopped in front of the door to her classroom as several
of her students pushed past her, hurrying to make it inside before the bell rang. What am I doing here? she asked herself.
The bell sounded and she stepped inside.

"Documentaries have to do more than simply report the news,"
Jill was saying, hearing several voices speaking just under hers.
"We have news shows that do that; we have newspapers. A
documentary has several functions—one, of course, is to provide the facts. Another more important function is to give those
facts some life—to put images behind the words, to illustrate—
show the people just what the facts are. I've told you all this
before, and it was somewhat edifying to note that your outlines
reflect this. Unfortunately, what most of these outlines lack
is—guts. I don't know how else to put it. You're presenting me
with a lot of facts and figures and telling me how you'd visual-
ize these conceptions, but you're not giving me any *insight* into
these statistics. You're not getting to my emotions."

"You're telling us you want guts and insight and emotion?"
one of her male students asked, incredulously.

"That's exactly what I'm telling you," Jill said.

"In an outline?" he questioned, shaking his head.

"If it's not in the outline," Jill answered, "it won't be there
in the finished product." It seemed as fitting an exit line as any

and she dismissed her students ten minutes early with a nervous wave of her hand. Something Sandy Dennis might do, and probably had, in *Up the Down Staircase.*

Jill sat down behind the desk of indiscriminate wood and undeterminable color and allowed her eyes to drift over to the windows on her right. Outside, it was sunny and hot. Not too humid. Just the right kind of day for sitting in the sun in a bikini and getting the perfect tan.

Whom was she kidding? she wondered, angrily turning from the window with its teasing, almost Kodacolor view of life. When was the last time she had looked good in a bikini? Five, probably ten years ago. If ever. And that was before time and a changing metabolic rate had thickened her waistline and made her aware of just how tightly she was holding in her stomach every time she went out with David. Oh, well, she thought, standing up suddenly and gathering her belongings together, that's what Rita Carrington is for. Ready, ladies? And one and two—

"I don't know, Jill," Beth Weatherby was saying as the two women slipped out of their street clothes and into their tights and leotards. "It seems to me that there are some basic issues you have to resolve."

"I know," Jill sighed in agreement. "The problem is how to resolve them." She watched as Beth Weatherby pulled off her panty hose and slipped into her tights, leaving her skirt firmly in place as she did so. It was strange, Jill thought, she hadn't realized Beth would be so modest. She thought back to two weeks ago, wondering if Beth had undressed in a similar fashion at that time, then remembered that Beth had already been changed when she'd arrived, and that she'd left while Jill was still waiting for Laurie to come out of the shower.

Thoughts of Laurie led to thoughts of the girl's mother. Elaine and her daughter had gone on a sudden holiday to Yellowstone National Park ("Just a little impulse thing," Elaine had claimed when she called to explain to David that Laurie would need a new jacket and some camping equipment for the trip). Jill wondered if Ron Santini would be going along and if he'd be bringing his own infamous equipment.

She sat on the bench in front of the lockers and pulled on her pink tights. "Damn," she said. "I got a run. Look at that. And I just bought the stupid things." Jill looked disgustedly at her legs. The run ran up the inside of her left thigh. She stood up, pulling on her leotard, adjusting it at her shoulders and crotch. "I should really get a new leotard," she said, as Beth pulled her own into place. "I've had this one since my second year at college." Both women sat down on the bench simultaneously, stuffing their belongings into the locker and closing it. "How many minutes do we have?"

"Exactly eight," Beth said, checking her watch.

"So," Jill said, "you have eight minutes to solve all my problems."

"The answer is simple," Beth said. "I know because I'm great at giving advice." Jill laughed. "You get that way after being married to a lawyer for a long time. Seriously," she paused, patting Jill's knee, "you have to talk to David."

"I have talked to him. He knows I hate my job."

"Have you discussed quitting?" Jill nodded. "And?"

"He says it's up to me, but I know he'd be upset. My job was fine until he was married to it, then it didn't seem so glamorous or exciting anymore. It just got in his way." She turned full-face to Beth. "I'm afraid, Beth," she said.

A strange look crossed Beth Weatherby's face. "What do you mean, afraid? What are you afraid of?"

"Of losing David," Jill confessed. "I'm afraid of doing anything that might jeopardize our relationship. Going back into television might do that."

"Then don't do it," Beth advised.

"It's the same thing about having more children," Jill continued. "We used to talk about it. David knows how much I'd like to have a family. But lately, he refuses to discuss it. He even told Don Eliot that he doesn't want more kids. I'm thirty-four years old, Beth. I don't have a whole lot of years left for this sort of thing, but I'm scared stiff to confront him because he's liable to give me a choice I'm not prepared to make."

"Him or children?" Beth asked.

"Some choice," Jill said.

"What would you say?"

Jill shook her head. "I don't know." She paused. "Yes, I do. David," she said. "Always David. I could never lose David."

"Even if it means losing yourself?" Beth asked her. "What's the matter? You look like you've just seen a ghost."

Jill said nothing, feeling the color drain slowly from her face as Nicole Clark bounced into view.

"Well, look who's here," Beth greeted the girl warmly, not connecting Jill's pallor with Nicole's sudden appearance.

"I hope you don't mind," Nicole said, throwing her bag across the bench and proceeding to unbutton her blouse. "But I remembered you talking about this class and I asked Al what time it was you went, and he was good enough to tell me. I finished a little early today, so I decided to join you. I hope you don't mind," she repeated.

"No, of course not," Beth said, turning to Jill for confirmation. Jill made no effort to smile.

What was Nicole doing here? Jill asked herself angrily, turning away as the younger woman unhooked her bra. She is not going to dangle those tits in front of me, she thought, aware of Beth's eyes penetrating her back questioningly. She resolved not to turn around, not to acknowledge this intruder's presence in any way. The game was over whether Nicole liked it or not. There would be no more pretenses, no more ignoring or trying to be nice. This woman had said clearly and succinctly that she was after Jill's husband. She had further said that it was no joke, and more and more, she seemed to be insinuating her wormy little way into Jill's life: in court at David's side, while Jill, herself, sat several rows to the back, an observer only; at dinner at Don Eliot's, again by David's side, while once again Jill merely observed; and now, here, invading Jill's private terrain, strutting her stuff, showing off the competition, intimidating the older models. Make way for this year's pièce de résistance.

Jill turned around angrily. She was going to bring things to a head once and for all.

Nicole spoke before Jill could open her mouth. "I was wondering if we could talk after the class," she said.

"I think that would be a good idea," Jill answered, trying to keep her voice as steady as Nicole's.

"Good." Nicole looked back at Beth. "Excuse me, I'm going to try to find the john," she said, and disappeared as abruptly as she had arrived.

"What was that all about?" Beth asked.

"I'll let you know," Jill answered as Ricki Elfer came waddling hurriedly toward them.

"Whew, almost late," she gasped, pulling off her dress to reveal she was already in costume. "Did you see that gorgeous little thing that just walked out of here? I bet she's one of the new instructors. Now, that's a body to aspire to."

Jill strode quickly toward the exercise room, feeling the knots in her shoulder muscles moving up to surround her neck, threatening to cut off her air supply and leave her breathless and gasping for oxygen, while somewhere behind her, Nicole Clark, in powder-blue leotard and matching tights, was waiting patiently to dance on her grave.

"Do you want to talk here or would you rather go out for a cup of coffee?" Nicole asked, toweling the sweat off her forehead and following Jill out of the exercise class.

"The lounge will be fine," Jill said, wondering why, despite the sweat the younger woman had worked up, her silky black hair remained unaffected. Jill didn't need a mirror to tell her that her own hair must look as if she'd stepped on an electrical current.

"Shower first?"

"No," Jill said, not about to compare nude bodies with the other woman. "Let's just get this over with."

"All right," Nicole agreed. "Lead the way."

Beth Weatherby touched Jill's elbow. "I'll go now," she said.

"Okay. See you next week."

"Call me if you want to talk," Beth added.

"Thanks. I probably will."

"Goodbye, Nicole," Beth called before veering off in another direction. "You did extremely well in there for someone who never exercises."

" 'Bye. Thank you," Nicole answered. "Nice lady."

"Yes. Very."

"Have you been friends long?"

"About four years." Jill turned a corner. "This way," she said coldly.

Nicole followed Jill into the deep purple womb of the lounge. Ricki Elfer was already there, seated at a table with two other women. She waved enthusiastically at Jill. "Come on over and join us," she called. "We're talking about sex."

"Later," Jill laughed, indicating an empty table for two at the far side of the room.

"Now, that's what you call a body," she heard Ricki say as they passed, knowing the body to which Ricki was referring was not her own.

"Do they serve milk shakes here?" Nicole asked, sitting down.

"Do you sit up nights thinking of these things to say?" Jill asked, deciding to eliminate small talk altogether.

"I don't understand."

"Look, I'll admit to a few things right off the top, okay?" Jill told her. "I am thirty-four years old. My hair is too wild, my mouth is too wide, my features in general are far from perfect, as is my body, which I'm sure you've already noticed. It's a nice enough body, but it's thirty-four years old, and milk shakes are a thing of the past." She paused. "You, on the other hand, are what? Twenty-four?"

"Twenty-five."

"Twenty-five," Jill repeated. "So, you're younger, you're better-looking, you're obviously in terrific shape and your innocent little remark about the milk shakes lets me know that you don't have to worry a whole lot about staying in shape. Good for you. You may stay lucky or you might wake up one morning—fat. I don't know. I hope so." She paused. "Anyway, I concede your youth, your beauty, your body. I give you all that. What I won't give you is my husband." Nicole said nothing, listening intently. "You may have it all over me in the looks department; you may even be smarter than I am. I don't know; I don't care. The fact is that *I* am married to the man you say you want and I intend to keep it that way. I was there first," she continued, conveniently overlooking Elaine. "That gives me some rights." Still, Nicole said nothing. "Now, I don't know. Maybe you've changed your mind; maybe you were a little drunk when you said those things; maybe I'm reading more into your remarks than you've intended. David thinks I am. You'll have to straighten me out, I guess. Tell me exactly where things stand. Unlike you, I hate games. They make me very nervous."

Nicole's voice was almost inaudible. "You told David what I said at the picnic?" she asked.

"Wasn't I supposed to? I assumed it was part of the plan."

"What did he say?"

"He thought it was a joke. When I explained it wasn't, he got quite angry."

"He didn't say anything to me."

"I asked him not to."

There was a long silence. Nicole lowered her head. "I'm very embarrassed," she said at last. "And I'm very sorry."

Jill said nothing, waiting for the girl to elaborate. The apology had come so quickly, seemed so genuine, she wasn't sure how to react. She'd been right to level with Nicole, to get things out in the open. Honesty is the best policy, she could hear her mother saying. She waited. When Nicole raised her head again, Jill could see her eyes were cloudy with tears.

"What can I say?" she began. "The whole thing is so stupid. I don't know why I said those things to you at the picnic. Maybe I *was* a little drunk, although that's no excuse." She looked around the room, avoiding Jill's eyes. "I'm from Maine originally. I've been here for four years now. I went to law school here and my family, my father actually—my mother's dead—he stayed back East. He got married again a few years ago and moved to New Hampshire. Anyway, I guess that's my roundabout way of telling you that I don't have many friends here. Girls have always shied away from me." She looked at Jill. "I know you're thinking that's no surprise. Maybe you're right. Whatever the reason, even though I know it's in vogue and all that, I've never had a strong attachment with another woman. There have always been a lot of men around, obviously. But I've never cared much for men my own age." Her eyes froze on Jill's. "Which brings us to David."

Jill held her breath.

"I took one look at your husband and—well, you know. I don't have to tell you." She looked away. "He's quite over-

whelming, isn't he? Everything about him, The way he moves,
the way he talks, the way he thinks—"

"You know what he thinks?" Jill interrupted.

"I know *how* he thinks," Nicole corrected. "He's a brilliant
lawyer. I've watched him a few times since that morning we
were all in court. He's never less than incredible."

Jill hoped her eyes didn't register the surprise she felt at
hearing of Nicole's subsequent trips to observe David in court.
Why hadn't David told her?

"What can I say?" Nicole asked. "I guess it's like a high
school kid with a crush on her teacher. David is everything I
ever wanted." Jill looked away, not sure she wanted to continue
this discussion. She remembered using almost the same phrase
when she had described David to her mother some six years before. "I remember when my mother and I used to talk about
men," Nicole said, as if reading Jill's thoughts, "and she always
said I should find someone whom I really respected. Someone
who respected me. Well, right from the first, David treated me
with respect. There aren't a whole lot of women lawyers at
Weatherby, Ross. Not proportionately, anyway, and when I
first walked in at the end of May, well, I took a lot of kidding.
A lot of the men had trouble reconciling the way I look with
the way I can do my job. Except for David. He treated me like
a lawyer from the start. In fact, it didn't take me long to start
wishing that he'd think of me more as a woman than as an attorney, and once I thought of that, well, fantasies don't need
much room to grow. I knew he was married. I heard from some
of the secretaries that his wife was tall and used to work in television and that David had left his first wife to marry her—you,"
she added, unnecessarily.

Jill said nothing, still pondering the secretaries' description
of her—tall and used to work in television. Did that really sum
her up?

"I guess I've just been watching too many soap operas,"
Nicole said disarmingly. "When I saw you at the picnic, I
thought I might as well be brazen about the whole thing and
come right out with my intentions. I may even have realized
you'd tell David. I guess I thought he'd be intrigued enough to,
I don't know, approach me, maybe. I thought that once I got

him into bed, the rest would fall into place." She stopped talking. Both women looked directly at each other. It was at least a minute before Nicole spoke again. "Anyway, I knew how edgy you were at Don's house the other week and I decided to come today to try and explain, to apologize. I'm sorry that I said those things at the picnic." She waited for Jill to speak, her eyes still fogged with the threat of tears.

Jill felt strangely sorry for the girl despite the open admission of her feelings toward David, or maybe because of them. She felt her shoulders slump with relief. It was over. Nicole Clark—Nicki—was pulling in her long magenta fingernails and backing away. The game was over. She had won.

"That's all right," Jill said, finding her voice. "I guess we all say stupid things occasionally. Things we don't mean—"

Nicole's voice caught Jill by surprise. She wasn't through being magnanimous. It wasn't time for Nicole to interrupt. Her words hit Jill with all the force of a sharp slap across the face. "I didn't say I didn't mean them," Nicole said, her eyes suddenly very dry—("I'm Nicole Clark. I'm going to marry your husband.")—"I just said that I was sorry I said them."

Before Jill had sufficient time to recover, the other woman was gone.

Chapter 10

It was five forty-eight when the phone rang. David reached over and fumbled for the alarm on the clock radio before he realized that the insistent ring wasn't music and that it wasn't time for him to get up yet.

"Well, answer it," Jill said groggily, sitting up beside him. "God, I hope everybody's all right." It was the first thing she thought of whenever the phone rang when it shouldn't.

David picked up the receiver. "Hello?" he demanded.

"Happy birthday to you, happy birthday to you," the voice sang as if through a meat grinder. David looked at his wife in disbelief, holding the phone up so that Jill could hear. "Happy birthday, dear fuckface, happy birthday to you!"

"For Christ's sake, Elaine, it's not even six o'clock."

Jill could hear Elaine's voice clearly on the other end. "Yes, but if I waited another few minutes, you'd be in the shower. You see, I remember all your habits. And I didn't want to miss the opportunity of letting you know how I feel." She paused. "You're getting on, old boy. Forty-five, isn't it?"

"Elaine—"

"No, wait, I have something to say."

"You always do."

"I was thinking about your life insurance policy."

"What about it?" Jill and David, the phone now resting between them, exchanged puzzled glances.

"Is it all paid up?"

David shook his head in disgust. "What are you getting at, Elaine?"

"Well," the woman replied, "when I realized it was your forty-fifth birthday, it occurred to me that you are, after all, only mortal, and that with your workload and your other assorted—appetites, shall we say—that it's just conceivable you might drop dead on all of us one of these days."

David moved the phone to his other ear. "I'm hanging up, Elaine."

"So I think you should change your policy." Jill heard Elaine's voice as clearly as if she were right there in the bed between them.

"You think I should change my policy," David repeated numbly.

"To include me." She paused, giving her ex-husband time to absorb her words. "Because if you should suddenly die, I'd be out in the cold. I mean, the money would just stop, wouldn't it?"

David started to laugh. "It almost gives one something to look forward to," he said.

"Well, as the mother of your children, surely you'll want to make sure they're protected—"

"My children will be looked after, Elaine."

"And me?"

"Goodbye, Elaine." David hung up the phone, allowing his body to fall back against his pillow. "Jesus," he said. "Can you believe that?"

"She never misses an opportunity," Jill said, snuggling up to her husband. "Where does she get her ideas? And at six in the morning—"

"She's been calling the office all week. I haven't answered any of her calls."

Jill ran her hand across her husband's chest, feeling the blond hairs beneath her fingers stand up and rub against her flesh, like a cat brushing up against a pair of bare legs. The thought of cats began tickling at her nose, and she instinctively moved her hand away to block an imaginary sneeze.

"Why'd you move your hand?" he asked.

"I thought I was going to sneeze," she answered, moving her hand back to its previous position.

"Lower," he said.

"Happy birthday," she whispered, stretching over and kissing him, her hand moving down his body.

"I'm getting old," he said, almost to himself.

"Oh, don't let Elaine get to you! Forty-five isn't old. It's barely middle-aged."

"Really?" he asked. "How many ninety-year-olds do you know running around?"

She laughed. "Well, they're not exactly running—" He sighed. "Oh, God," Jill said suddenly, sitting up but leaving her hand where it was, "you're not having a mid-life crisis, are you?"

"If you're not going to show a little respect for my age," he admonished playfully, "at least make yourself useful."

He forced her head down to where her hand was.

Jill moved herself into a more comfortable position, thinking of the man she was ministering to, remembering the first time she had seen him nude, the first time they had made love, when she thought she'd died and gone to heaven. He'd been so over-whelmingly physical. Their first two years together had been so intense. It couldn't have gone on that way forever, she realized, trying to move her head up so they could align their bodies for consummation. But his hand held her head down firmly. He was not interested in consummation this morning. What the hell, she thought, addressing herself to the task at hand (at mouth?) with renewed vigor. It's his birthday!

This thought catapulted her mind ahead to the evening to come. Jason, freshly back from camp, and Laurie, bored after a week back home with nothing to do, would be coming for dinner. As would the rest of David's family and her own parents. The first time she'd had the courage to invite everyone over together. How was she going to get everything ready on time, she wondered, thinking of the menu she'd planned and the shopping she had to do. She was even baking David's birthday cake this year. Luckily, Fridays were a light day at the university. She'd canceled her morning class, which left two in the afternoon. Hopefully, by then she'd have everything under control. She felt herself beginning to worry. Maybe she'd taken on too much. David was always telling her she bit off more than she could chew. David, she thought. My God! Biting, chewing! What was she doing to him? He groaned, his hand still gripping her head. Had she hurt him? This was awful. How could she be doing this? Thinking about menus and classes when she was supposed to be caught up in the throes of passion.

David would know. He always knew what she was thinking. He'd know her mind had been elsewhere. He'd be hurt, angry. He might not even come, she thought with dismay, which would leave him frustrated and unsatisfied, the perfect target for Nicole's subtle advances. Nicole, she thought angrily. The dear thing had been quiet again the last few weeks, no phone calls, no surprise appearances. David hadn't so much as mentioned her name. But then David hadn't mentioned Nicole's visits to court with him either. It made them even, she decided— she hadn't told David about Nicole's visit to Rita Carrington's. What good would it have done? She'd take her cue from David and act as if nothing had happened. It was better to let the whole thing rest. Let it die of boredom— What was she doing? What was she thinking about? Concentrate, for God's sake, concentrate.

She was aware of some faint groaning in the background. David. Had she hurt him? She tried to move her head but the hand held firm. The groans grew louder.

"Jesus, Jill," he gasped, then suddenly exploded. Jill gulped several times, swallowing hard before she felt his hand relax and she was able to sit up. "That was incredible, Jill," he said, kissing her forehead. "Wow. I think that was the best you've ever done."

Wonderful, Jill thought, and I missed it.

David pulled her close against him. Jill thought of that other morning not long ago when her dream had awakened them at a similar hour and David had responded by dragging her into the shower. Perhaps he'd do the same today. She began playing with the hairs on his chest. This time they lay still and soft, a kitten well fed and purring contentedly. Her body longed to be touched, caressed—

She heard a slight click and suddenly sounds of Stevie Wonder filled the room. David reached over and turned down the volume with one hand, while his other arm extricated itself from around Jill's shoulders.

"Time to get up," he said, moving quickly out of bed.

Jill sat up. "Feel like some company in the shower?"

He smiled. "Not this morning, honey, okay? I have a really busy day ahead of me." He paused. "You angry?"

"Just disappointed," she admitted, trying to look brave, the way Ali MacGraw had in *Love Story*.

"I'll make it up to you." He waited until he saw her smile. "Why don't you go back to sleep for a couple of hours?"

"No, I'm too awake for that," she said. "Besides, I have a lot to do, too. It's your birthday party tonight, remember?"

"Oh, shit. I forgot."

"You don't have a meeting, I hope—"

"No," he assured her. "I don't think so. I'm sure there's nothing—"

"Please try not to be late. I have the whole family coming—"

"I'll try," he said, before disappearing down the hall.

Jill sat on the bed, the words of Elaine's caustic birthday greeting filling her head. The woman must still have so much hate inside her, she thought. After all these years. What could make a woman hang on so tightly to that much hate? A man, her thoughts responded in Ricki Elfer's voice. A man could make you hate that much.

"Let's get out of bed and go to Winston's for brunch!" she whooped, jumping out of bed and pulling the covers off his naked body.

"It's two o'clock in the afternoon," he laughed, making no move to cover his nakedness. She could see he was already aroused.

"Well, then, we'll have lunch, or afternoon tea or something." She moved to the window and looked out, saw her landlady and the Doberman out sunning in the backyard.

"The 'or something' sounds good," he said, coming up behind her and covering her breasts with his hands.

"What are you doing?" she squirmed, smiling widely. "Hey—what—" He was lifting her body up, fitting himself into her from behind. "Mrs. Everly's downstairs," she reminded him. "What if she looks up?"

"Then she'll see two very happy people."

"And I'll probably have to start looking for a new apartment."

"That would suit me," he said. "I still don't think this neighborhood is very safe."

"Yeah," she agreed, feeling her breath starting to get shorter. "You never know when someone might sneak up behind you—"

They finally went out for something to eat at around four o'clock. Jill was as happy as she could remember being in a long time. They'd had the whole day—a day of loving and talking and being together. It seemed that there were no problems in their way, no people they had to consider, feelings they had to be mindful of hurting. There was only their love for each other.

"Smile and wave," he was saying, as he drove to the restaurant.

"What?" she asked, cognizant of the change in his tone.

"Smile and wave," he repeated through clenched teeth. Obviously, something was wrong but this was not the time to ask what it was. She turned her head to the right, smiled at the two women in the silver Buick, acknowledging them with a nod of her head instead of a wave of her hand. The women smiled back—had the driver looked vaguely puzzled as well?—and continued driving. No one had said anything.

Jill felt all the joy drain from her body. "Elaine?" she asked, already knowing the answer. He nodded. "Who was that with her?"

"Her sister."

"They're very attractive. She—your wife—is very—attractive." Again he nodded.

"What do you suppose she thought when she saw—"

"She thinks I'm with a client all day. I'll tell her I was just driving you home."

Jill felt the knot in her stomach twist, causing her eyes to sting. "I'm a client," she repeated numbly.

"Well, Jill, what am I supposed to tell her, for God's sake?

That I'll be spending the day screwing my brains out?! I'm sorry. I'm really sorry," he apologized, his voice genuinely contrite and bewildered. "That was a dumb thing to say. Really dumb. I'm just a little shook up, I guess, and embarrassed—"

"And humiliated," she said, adding her feelings to his. "And ashamed."

He pulled the car over to the side of the road. "Oh, Jill, please don't feel humiliated and ashamed. There's no reason for you to feel that way. I love you."

"Then why is it her feelings you're so worried about protecting? What about mine?" He had no answer. "You better take me home. Your wife will be expecting you pretty soon now that she knows you're all finished with your—client."

"What does that mean?"

"Just what I said."

"Don't play games with me, Jill. I haven't got the time or the patience to try and second-guess you. Say what you mean."

"I mean that I want to go home," she said, her voice devoid of expression.

"Is that all you mean?"

"I mean I'm tired and hurt and angry and humiliated and ashamed that I still can't work up enough guts to tell you to get the hell out of my life and stay there. I mean that I still love you more than I hate you and that I still want you." She stopped. "Look, I'm going to take a taxi home. I just don't want to be with you right now." She opened the door and got out of the car. He made no move to stop her.

"You make me feel like such a shit," he said.

"You *are* a shit."

"I'll call you later," he said, watching after her until she found a cab.

Don't bother, she wanted to yell back, but she knew—and he knew—that she couldn't.

"Hello. Is Irving Saunders there, please?" Jill held the phone tight against her ear and waited for some response, looking toward the tiny dining room at the table she had to set for tonight's dinner. How was she going to get nine people around a table which only seated four? "What? I'm sorry, I didn't hear you. Oh, oh, I didn't realize it was still so early." She looked up at the kitchen clock. "What time does he get in? Eleven?" It was only nine-fifteen. "Okay, I'll call back. No, no, wait. Tell him to call Jill Plumley, no, I mean Jill Listerwoll, as soon as he gets a chance. Listerwoll," she repeated, spelling it out slowly as if to confirm that the name was really hers, as much to herself as to the voice on the other end of the receiver. It seemed so long ago, she thought, giving the secretary her phone number. "It's important," she added before hanging up.

She looked around. The cake was in the oven; the salad had already been cut up. She still had the rest of the shopping to do. Maybe now, before Irving called back. No, she couldn't run out and leave the stupid cake—

Her eyes drifted back to the dining room table. Perhaps she should try to figure out the seating arrangement. Jill went to the cutlery drawer, opened it and stared at the assorted forks and knives. "Nine people," she said aloud, looking back out the kitchen doorway toward the tiny end of the L-shaped living room which tried to pass itself off as a dining area. With great effort, you might be able to squeeze six around that little table. But nine? Why hadn't she thought this through before?

Jill stood in the doorway defeated. Where was she going to put nine people? Luckily, her brother and his wife were vacationing in Florida ("Who goes to Florida in the summertime?" her mother had asked repeatedly since they left) or she'd have had eleven to contend with. Maybe they could all go over to Elaine's, she thought. After all, the house had once belonged to David as well. ("Give her anything she wants, for Christ's sake," she had urged. "Let's just get it over with and get on with our lives!") Oh, well, it had sounded like the right thing to say at the time.

Jill left the kitchen and proceeded around the L into the living area. It was reasonably spacious, or at least the floor-to-ceiling windows made it seem so. They faced south toward Grant Park, which provided them with a beautiful view of the magnificent Buckingham Fountain. Well, we should see something for the rent we're paying, she thought. There were two bedrooms, one of which functioned as a den, although she had hoped one day to replace the television and the old, sloppy sofa-bed and leather chair with a baby crib and layette. The thought made her uneasy—she had yet to follow Beth's advice and confront David—and she diverted her attention from it by straightening the pillows of the elegantly patterned chesterfield. I could put them all in here, she thought suddenly, counting the seating capacity. Three on the couch, two on the wing chairs, and she'd bring in the four chairs from around the dining room table. Perfect. She'd set the table for a buffet and let everyone serve themselves. Hopefully, no one would spill any of the beef Stroganoff on the white broadloom. She started back toward the kitchen, absently walking into the side of a square Lucite piece of modern art from which steel sticks dangled musically against horizontal stripes. ("What is it? Some kind of air-conditioner?" her mother had asked.) The steel sticks immediately became tangled and Jill spent the next few minutes trying to extricate them from one another without much success. It would have to wait for David, she decided, straightening up and returning to the kitchen, hoping he wouldn't be late for his own party. It seemed that every time she had her parents over, he was late, causing her father to wonder aloud when it was Jill ever saw her husband. ("He works till ten every night," she could hear him saying. "He works Saturdays and Sundays. When is he home?") Jill always brushed such questions (accusations?) aside by explaining that David's current working hours were only temporary, the same way David had explained it to her. But how long before temporary became permanent? In the first year or two of their marriage, he'd rarely worked past seven in the evening. Of course, she'd been busy herself in those days, often working late hours at the studio, coming home to find him waiting impatiently for her return. They'd order in a pizza; he'd tease her that the only thing she knew how to make for dinner was reservations. So how did she suddenly come to beef Stroganoff and cold blueberry soup?

The phone rang. Jill picked up the receiver. "Hello," she said.

"Jill?" The voice was strong and masculine, bringing immediate traces of the past to Jill's ears.

"Irving?" she yelled gleefully.

"You sound surprised. Didn't you call? I have a message here that you phoned."

"I did. I did phone. But they said you wouldn't be in until around eleven."

"I got tired of staying at home listening to the baby cry," he explained grumpily. "I came in early."

"Baby?! Irving, I didn't know you'd had a baby!"

"Six months ago. A boy."

"Well, that's wonderful. How's Cindy?"

"Fine. She's great. A real little mother."

"And you?"

"Well, I already have the four boys with Janet, so it wasn't exactly new to me."

"And everything else?" she asked. "How's everything else?"

"Wonderful. Couldn't be better. The network is driving me nuts as usual. How about you? How's David? You're still together?"

"Of course we are. He's fine. Great," Jill emphasized, picturing the man on the other end of the phone—fiftyish, tall and muscular, graying hair and pale gray eyes to match. Undoubtedly he was wearing blue jeans and an open-neck shirt and he was leaning against the wall in the control room, televisions blaring all around him, tapes blasting, people racing frantically around. For a moment, she felt she was right in the middle of it. "Irving, can we get together soon? There's something I want to talk over with you. An idea I have."

"Sure," he said. "I'm leaving for Africa on Monday. Africa, of all places, and I'll be there for two weeks. Why don't I call you when I get back?"

Jill felt her shoulders sinking. "Damn, I was hoping I could see you before then. Do you have any time at all today? Lunch? How about I take you to lunch?"

"Sounds important," he said.

"It could be."

"Lunch it is. I'll meet you at Maloney's at one o'clock. How's that?"

"Perfect," Jill said, wondering how on earth she was ever going to get everything done by this evening. "Perfect."

Chapter 11

The restaurant was crowded. Located just across the street from the studio, it was packed with television people, most of whom Jill recognized immediately, and some of whom recognized her in return. She spotted Irving's outstretched arm near the back of the large room and made her way toward it, realizing as she pushed past the stand-up bar that there were a disturbing number of faces that she didn't know at all.

"Jill?! My God, it is! Jill Listerwoll!" the voice bellowed, the arms surrounding her, hugging her close against the prickly tweed of his jacket.

"It has to be Arthur Goldenberg," Jill said, even before she saw his face. "The only man I know who'd wear a winter jacket in the middle of summer."

They kissed each other warmly. "It's almost fall," he reminded her. "Next week is Labor Day." His bright British eyes twinkled at her teasingly. "So, how *are* you? What are you doing here? Are you coming back to us?"

Jill smiled lovingly at one of the station's makeup men. "I

don't know," she said. "I'm here to talk to Irving. See if there's something I might be right for."

"You're right for everything," he said, putting his arm around her shoulders and drawing her conspiratorially closer. "Don't look, but see that woman sitting over at the far end of the bar—don't look!" he chastised as Jill automatically moved her head in the other woman's direction. "She was your replacement. Don't look!"

"Sorry," Jill whispered. "I thought Maya Richards replaced me!"

"She did, but then she didn't work out. This one was brought in from L.A. Susan Timmons. She's a barracuda, let me tell you. With skin to match. Not flesh—scales!"

"Arthur! You're terrible—did you talk like that about me after I left?"

He smiled. "Only a little bit. And that was only because I was so hurt that you left us." He paused. "God, I hope you come back."

"So do I," Jill confessed, only now putting her deepest hope into words. She patted the makeup man on his cheek and pushed past him toward Irving Saunders, who had risen from his chair to greet her. On her way, she managed to get a good look at the woman who had taken over her job at the network. She was younger, Jill estimated, by about five years, and she was attractive in a brittle, blond sort of way. No scales anywhere that she could see.

"How are you, Jill?" Irving asked, kissing her squarely on the mouth. "Still drinking bloody marys?" He signaled for the waiter.

"I haven't had a bloody mary in years," Jill said, sitting down. "It sounds wonderful."

"One bloody mary, one scotch and water," Irving told the waiter, before turning his attention back to Jill, making no attempt to disguise his open perusal of her appearance.

"So?" she asked. "I look okay?"

"You look terrific," he said, and seemed to mean it. "Marriage obviously agrees with you."

"I hope so," Jill said, looking back toward the bar. "I ran into Art Goldenberg—"

"I noticed. How *is* my favorite faggot?"

"He sends his love."

"Yeah, I'll bet he does."

"He pointed out my replacement."

"Did he, now?" Jill nodded. "Yes, well, we're very pleased with Susan. She's bright, ambitious, a hard worker. As a matter of fact, she'll be on this trip to Africa I was telling you about."

Jill tried to look pleased. "You were supposed to say she's not working out at all and that you'll agree to anything to get me back."

Irving looked surprised. The waiter arrived and put their drinks in front of them. Jill raised hers immediately in a toast.

"Cheers."

"Cheers," Irving echoed, clicking his glass against Jill's. "Are you serious?" he asked finally. "Do you really want to come back?"

Jill took a deep breath. "Yes, I am," she sighed. "I do. Although I hadn't intended to let it pop out quite this early in the conversation. I thought we could have a little small talk first." She laughed nervously.

"You were always rotten at small talk," Irving reminded her. "It was one of your charms."

"I was also one of your best producers," she reminded him in return.

"Yes, you were," he admitted easily. "No question about that." There was an uncomfortable silence. "Maybe we better have a few rounds of small talk," Irving said, forcing a laugh.

"Doesn't sound promising," Jill said, feeling slightly embarrassed.

Irving fumbled around for words. "Tell me—uh—you know—how come—" He gave up. "Why?" he asked finally.

"Why what?"

"Why do you want to come back? I mean, I thought that the job was creating all sorts of problems for you. David didn't like your being away so much. He objected to your hours, the danger you always placed yourself in. Has that changed?"

"I've changed," Jill said. She looked directly into Irving Saunders' soft gray eyes. "When David met me," she began, the image of Nicole Clark suddenly as close to her as Irving's face,

"I was an exciting, bright, challenging lady who was always off somewhere chasing bullets or corruption or—something. I had a career! A life! I was an independent, strong woman." She paused, dramatically. "Now, I'm a wife."

"Well, you're more than that," Irving demurred. "You're a teacher—"

"I'm *not* a teacher, Irving, you know that! You told me that when I said I was leaving. You were right. I'm going crazy sitting behind that stupid desk. I need to be *moving* again!"

"And David? You haven't told me how he feels."

"What's important here is how *I* feel!" Jill answered, in tones so strong they surprised her.

"David's feelings were the reason I lost you in the first place," Irving explained patiently. "I couldn't afford to hire you back only to lose you again after a few months."

Jill paused. "I really don't know how David would feel. We've discussed it very briefly. He says it has to be my decision. I know, I *know,*" she repeated, "that he might not be too happy about it at first, but, goddamn it, Irving, I was a producer when he met me! I was a producer when he fell in love with me! That's part of what he fell in love with and now that part is gone!" She shook her head, thinking out loud. "I don't know. A man has a wife who arranges her whole life around him, and yet he gets bored. She's so predictable, after all. Her world is so insular and unexciting. He leaves her for another woman, a woman who has a job of her own, a style of her own, a life of her own. She's everything his wife isn't. So, he divorces the wife and marries the other woman. And before you know it, he starts subtly altering her image until she becomes just like the woman he left behind. Pretty soon, hubby is starting to get bored again. And so the cycle begins all over, the man always searching for what he took away."

Irving stared at her questioningly. "Are you reading from your autobiography?"

"Just an overly familiar scenario. I don't want it to be mine." She took a long sip of her drink. "Am I making any sense?"

Irving polished off the last of his scotch and ordered them each another drink. "I understand exactly what you're saying," he began. "Except that I see it from the male point of view, you understand. You remember Cindy, of course," he continued, not even waiting for her nod. "What is it about marriage anyway that changes people?" Again, no answer was required. "How long was I sneaking around with Cindy before Janet finally gave me my divorce? Four years? Five years? Not only was she the best damn research assistant I ever had, but she was, well, exactly what you said before. She was exciting, challenging, independent, bright. One of the few really effortlessly bright women I have ever met. And now this effortlessly bright lady can spend literally hours discussing the joys of Pampers versus the drudgery of cloth diapers. I *had* all that domestic crap twenty years ago! I lived with it for more years than I like to remember. I left it for a woman who loved picking up on a moment's notice and going out for dinner halfway across the world, who loved all-night parties and last-minute decisions. Now, I have a wife who breast-feeds our new son twenty times a day and wouldn't meet me around the corner for a hamburger without two weeks' notice. I have what I left."

"David has what *he* left," Jill said quietly.

"David has what he says he wants."

"David doesn't know what he wants," Jill scoffed. "And neither, damn it, do I."

Irving laughed emptily. "I don't think *any* of us knows what he wants."

"You want it till you get it," Jill offered. "Then you do your best to change it."

"Or it changes itself," Irving said. "Who was it that said, 'Beware of what you want. You might get it'!?"

Jill smiled. "Grace Metalious," she answered, thinking of the now deceased author of *Peyton Place*. "But I'm sure she wasn't the only one who said it."

Irving was laughing in earnest now.

"What's funny?" Jill asked him.

"You are. You're the only person I know who can actually give me the answer to what was intended as a purely rhetorical question. I hope David appreciates you."

"Do any men ever appreciate their wives?" she asked, then quickly added, "Purely rhetorical, I assure you." The waiter brought them fresh drinks. "Should we order?" Jill asked Irving.

He shook his head. "Not hungry."

"Me neither," Jill told the waiter, who shrugged and went away. "She keeps looking over here," Jill said.

"Who's that?" Irving asked.

"Susan whatever-her-name-is, from L.A."

Irving looked over toward the bar, then back to Jill. "Word's probably reached her about who you are."

"You think she's worried?"

"Well, I guess it's like walking into a restaurant and seeing your husband having lunch with another woman."

"Not all other women are threats."

"Not all other women are after her job."

"I was there first," Jill said playfully, recognizing her words as the same ones she had used when talking to Nicole Clark several weeks earlier, realizing suddenly how childish they sounded.

"Yes, you were," Irving agreed, "but you gave it up. There's always someone waiting in the shadows to grab what somebody leaves behind."

The woman at the end of the bar stood up and came toward them. "Irving," she said pleasantly. "Jill?" she asked, extending her hand. "Someone just told me that you used to have my job."

"Jill Listerwoll," Irving began, introducing the two women, "or would you prefer Jill Plumley?" Jill shook her head as if to say that either one would do. "Anyway, this is Susan Timmons. You all ready for Africa on Monday?"

"All packed and shot full of vaccine," Susan answered cheerfully. "I've never been to Africa before," she said to Jill. "Can't wait to go."

"I always wanted to see Africa," Jill confided.

"Get David to take you," Irving said, a bit too effusively. "A nice rich lawyer has to spend his money somewhere."

"He does," Jill answered, thinking of Elaine.

"Well, I hope we meet again," Susan Timmons said sweetly, almost sincerely. "I'll see you back at the studio, Irving."

"I'll be there in a few minutes," he said, watching her leave.

Jill took a quick swallow of her bloody mary, feeling her head swimming slightly. Liquid lunches were not her specialty and there was still so much she had to do. How on earth was she going to teach two classes on a stomach full of vodka and tomato juice?

"Are you all right?" Irving was asking.

"You're telling me you don't want me back," Jill said plainly.

"I'd love to have you back, Jill," Irving said with obvious sincerity. "But at the moment, there just aren't any jobs available."

"What about on a free-lance basis?"

"You know how the network feels about free-lancers," he told her. "It would have to be a pretty special assignment for us not to use one of our own people."

Jill felt her eyes start to water and immediately lowered her head.

"Hey, I'm sorry, Jill," he said quickly. "I didn't mean to shut you out in the cold that way."

"You can't help it," Jill said, recovering. "I just thought I'd try."

He reached over the table and grabbed her hand. "I'm glad you did. And believe me, I want you back. Look, I tell you what, and this isn't a load of bull I'm feeding you either, you know how quickly everything can change in television." Jill nodded, thinking of the many unfamiliar faces at the bar. "Well, I think you know what I'm trying to say—"

"If anything comes up, you'll call me," Jill answered.

"You'll be the first one I'll call."

Jill smiled, finishing her drink. "Well, I guess that's a start," she said.

"You won't say no when I do," he cautioned.

Her smile grew perceptibly wider. "I won't say no."

The phone was ringing as she fumbled for her key at the apartment door. "Just a minute," Jill called, dropping her parcels and pushing the key into the lock. "I'm coming!" The door clicked open and Jill raced inside just as the phone stopped ringing.

"Why do they always hang up just when you get there?" she asked aloud, retrieving her groceries and closing the door behind her.

She began unpacking the bags, putting aside the present she had bought for David—a silk shirt in shades of blue and black, with big, artist's-style sleeves. It had been expensive, but she'd pictured David wearing it and he'd looked so beautiful that she bought it, knowing he'd love it. She looked forward to his reaction when he unwrapped it.

Jill looked at the clock. It was almost five-thirty. Dinner was one hour away, and being family, everyone would be prompt. Except probably the birthday boy himself.

She was tired already. She'd been running around all afternoon on no lunch and two bloody marys. She needed a few minutes to put her feet up and let her head settle. She decided to relax for a few minutes in the den.

The phone rang.

Naturally, she thought. If they don't get you coming in the door, they get you as you're about to sit down!

"Hello?"

"Aren't we the eager beaver?!"

The sound of Elaine's voice cleared Jill's head instantly.

"Can I do something for you?" she asked impatiently, thinking of Elaine's earlier birthday greetings, in no mood to be pleasant to this woman with whom, it seemed, she was destined to spend the rest of her life. When there were children involved, she realized, there was no such thing as divorce.

"Is my husband around?"

"Your *ex*-husband is still at the office."

"I called there. They said he'd left for the day."

"Oh?" Jill tried not to sound too surprised. Was it possible David had actually been able to finish early and was on his way home?

"Up to his old tricks, is he?" Elaine asked. Jill could picture the smug smile on the other woman's face.

"I'll tell him you called when he gets home," Jill said curtly, hanging up the phone abruptly, hoping to wipe away Elaine's smile. No, she realized, looking over at the dining room table, all set up and waiting for the birthday boy, I'm the one who's not smiling. At this moment, Elaine is grinning from ear to ear in her fully equipped, newly renovated designer kitchen. "How does she do it?" Jill asked aloud, then finished the thought in silence—no matter what the circumstances, Elaine always managed to make her feel as if she weren't worth a plugged nickel.

She picked up the phone impulsively and dialed David's office.

"Weatherby, Ross," answered the crisp tones of the receptionist.

"David Plumley, please," Jill asked, wondering if the woman recognized her voice. She hated wives who always pestered their husbands at work.

"Mr. Plumley is gone for the day."

So Elaine had been telling the truth. "When did he leave?"

"About twenty minutes ago."

"Was he going home, do you know? It's his wife."

"He didn't say, Mrs. Plumley."

"Oh. All right. Fine. Thank you."

Jill replaced the receiver and walked toward the den. Twenty minutes ago meant he should be home. Assuming he was coming home. She angrily picked up the morning paper, which lay in a desultory heap across the brown leather chair, and plopped herself down, determined to read what she hadn't had time for earlier in the day. Determined to relax. Damn Elaine, she thought, flipping immediately to the Birth and Death Notices. Of course David was coming right home. He hadn't wanted to come home when he was married to Elaine precisely *because* he was married to Elaine. Jill Listerwoll Plumley was a different kettle of fish altogether. "Jill Listerwoll or Jill Plumley?" Irving had asked her. Why couldn't she be both?

She looked down the long list of birth announcements. "It's a Boy!" one shouted, immediately followed by "It's a Girl!" Nothing unusual there. She glanced over at the death notices. Just once, she thought, she'd like to flip open the paper and see: "It's a Corpse!"

The phone rang again. She dropped the paper and ran to answer it. She wasn't sure why she was bothering; it was probably Elaine again.

"Hello," Jill said.

The voice on the other end of the line was calm but carried with it unmistakable undertones of anxiety. "Jill? Am I getting you at a bad time?"

Jill was instantly aware that the woman's voice belonged to someone she knew, but she was unable to connect a face to the words. "Who is this?" she asked, feeling clumsy and insensitive.

"It's Beth Weatherby," the voice said quickly. "I'm sorry, I should have said—"

"No, that's all right. I should have known." Why were they so busy apologizing to each other? "Is everything okay? You sound a little—strange."

"I'm fine," Beth assured her, sounding more like herself. "I called a little while ago. I guess you were out—"

"Yes, actually, I was just coming in the door when—"

"I wondered if we could meet somewhere for a cup of coffee—"

"Sure. When?"

There was a slight pause. "I was thinking of now."

"Now?" Jill's eyes went directly to the clock. It was almost six. Her guests would be arriving in half an hour.

"I know it's an awkward time—"

"Oh, Beth, I'm really sorry, but I just can't. I have nine people here for dinner tonight—family—it's David's birthday—"

"Of course, I understand. Please don't feel bad. I didn't think you'd be able to make it—"

"Is something wrong?"

The voice regained its strength and now sounded like the Beth Weatherby Jill was used to. "Oh, no, of course not. I'm sorry, I didn't mean to alarm you. No, no. Al just called and said he'd be late so I thought if David was going to be late too, we could have a cup of coffee. That's all. A little old-fashioned female get-together since I missed the class again on Wednesday. I missed you. But we can do it anytime."

"Well, I'd really like to. How about after class next Wednesday? We could make an evening of it, maybe go to dinner and a movie or something."

"Sounds great."

"Good."

"So, I'll see you Wednesday. Rita Carrington's at four o'clock."

"Perfect. I'll see you then."

" 'Bye, Jill."

"Goodbye, Beth."

Jill hung up the phone, hastily scribbled Beth Weatherby's name in her calendar for the following Wednesday night, and ran toward her bedroom to change into something suitable for dinner.

Chapter 12

She had just finished serving the main course and was wondering what to do about the cake when David arrived home. Without intending to, Jill looked down at her watch.

"It's ten after eight," her father whispered loudly from his place on the sofa.

"Hi, everyone," David said easily, coming into the room to an assortment of grunts and muffled birthday wishes. Jill sat stiffly in one of the transplanted dining room chairs and watched her husband walk toward her, bend over and kiss her on the lips. "Sorry I'm late, sweetie. A few of the guys in the office decided to take me out for a birthday drink."

"I called the office around five-thirty," Jill began, again without meaning to. "That was a long drink, two and a half hours."

"Well, maybe it was more like two or three drinks," he winked. Or four or five, Jill said silently, angry and yet trying to hide her annoyance from everyone else. How dare he be so late! she seethed, ruining her dinner which had dried out waiting for him, embarrassing her in front of her family and his mother (who she knew was thinking that nothing had changed since he'd divorced Elaine). His mother sat between Jill's parents on the sofa. She looked over at Jill as if to advise her to say nothing more. Probably the same advice she gave Elaine. I am not like her, Jill's eyes trumpeted toward her mother-in-law. Our marriage is completely different. Completely. He doesn't treat me at all the same way he treated Elaine.

She heard Elaine's voice suddenly whispering in her ear. "If he treated me the way he treats you," she began before Jill cut her off abruptly with a toss of her head. I didn't invite you to this party, she thought, banishing Elaine's earlier admonishment from her memory and directing her attention to her husband.

"Do you want your dinner now?" Jill asked.

"No," he answered. "I'm not really hungry. I had a huge lunch. I'll just have some cake and coffee." He looked around the room. "If everybody will excuse me for a couple of minutes, I'll go get out of this suit—"

"By all means," Jill replied sarcastically. "We've grown rather fond of waiting for you."

David's eyes narrowed in obvious dismay. Then he smiled boyishly, kissing his daughter and tousling his son's hair before heading toward the bedroom.

Jill sat for several seconds and then stood up abruptly. She was so angry, she felt she was going to cry, which made her angrier still. She didn't want to cry. She wanted to scream and yell and carry on. "Excuse me a minute," she said.

"Uh-oh, f-fireworks," she heard Jason utter as she left the room.

David was tossing off his jacket when Jill came into the bedroom. She didn't wait for him to turn around before speaking. "I don't understand you," she began, watching his shoulders stiffen. "You knew I was having a party for you tonight. You knew I'd invited the whole family, and that I was cooking a special dinner, busting my ass to make everything nice. I even asked you not to be late. And what do you do? You show up at eight o'clock when everyone else has been here since six-thirty and you have the nerve to tell me you've been out for a birthday drink with the guys. Not even a goddamn meeting! Something important, for God's sake, that you could justify yourself with. Something beyond your control. Not a couple of lousy drinks!"

"Are you finished?" he asked icily.

"No," Jill continued. "How dare you eat a big lunch when you knew I was making a big dinner?! Haven't you got any consideration for me at all?" She suddenly dissolved into tears, sinking down on the bed.

David marched over to the bedroom door and closed it. "If you don't mind, I'd rather keep this private."

"What difference does it make?" Jill shot back. "They all know what we're saying in here."

David removed his shirt and threw it beside his jacket on the bed, pulling a fresh, more casual one out of the closet. "Look, Jill, I'm sorry. But I got roped into it. A bunch of the guys came into my office as I was getting ready to leave and they corralled me into having a few drinks. I figured I could still be home in plenty of time but one drink led to another, and I'd had a tough day—that Rickerd woman is driving me nuts about her divorce—and I needed to unwind. It was stupid. It wasn't fair to you, you're absolutely right, but I did it. It's done. Do we have to fight about it? It's my birthday, for Pete's sake." He tried to smile.

"Why do I feel like I should be the one apologizing?" Jill asked, pouting beneath her tears. "You still haven't explained why you had such a big lunch," she said.

"I was hungry," he admitted sheepishly. "God, I was starving!" David lowered his head and sighed. "Jill, could you come here, please, hon." He waited for an instant, then watched her get up off the bed. Jill was vaguely aware of voices coming from the other room, undoubtedly growing more concerned as time passed.

"Come on over here," he continued.

"David—"

"Come on over here."

Reluctantly, she walked into his outstretched arms. They encircled her immediately.

"Oh, Jill, I love you so much," he said, softly kissing her hair. "I'm sorry I'm late. Really I am. I wanted to be on time—

but I just couldn't seem to break away. Please understand. Don't be angry. I love you."

"Your daughter didn't eat a thing," she told him. There was no point in staying angry any longer. She would only succeed in making everyone else uncomfortable and ruining what was left of the evening. She'd made her point; he'd made his apology.

"Elaine probably fed her full of cookies and milk before she got here."

"Oh—she called."

"Don't tell me about it."

Jill smiled. "Your sister and her husband loved the Stroganoff. Apparently, they had some truly superb Stroganoff just the other day at a friend's home."

"Sounds like a typical evening. Come here, you."

"I am here."

"No," he whispered, pointing to his lips. "Here."

He kissed her softly.

"Are you going to change your pants?" Jill asked, moving out of his arms and back to the bed.

"Yeah," he answered. "Jeans okay with you?"

"Sure," she shrugged, lifting his jacket off the bed, about to take it to the closet. "What's this?" she asked, reaching over and picking something off the bedspread.

"A birthday card," David answered, removing one pair of pants and putting on another. "Some of the guys from the office."

"The ones you went drinking with?"

"The same," he smiled.

Jill opened it up. Under the usual Happy Birthday message were written six names. The last one reached her eyes first, staying there and blocking out all the others. *Nicki,* it curved lyrically in black ink.

"You didn't tell me Nicole Clark was with you," Jill said, fresh anger building inside her.

David said nothing for several seconds. "It didn't seem to merit special consideration," he said at last. "I didn't tell you the names of anybody else who was there either."

"You said some of the guys."

David raised his hands in the air as if to say he surrendered.

"Well there, you see, I consider her one of the guys. Come on, Jill, let's not blow this thing out of proportion. It's not like I was alone with the girl." Jill shook her head with dismay. "You don't still believe that garbage about her wanting to marry me, I hope." It was a statement, not a question. "Come on, Jill, jealousy doesn't become you."

"I'm not jealous," Jill shot back. "I'm mad! Can't I be mad?"

"You were over being mad until I mentioned Nicki!"

"You didn't mention her! That's why I'm mad!"

David looked at her. Jill recognized the look—it was his patient parent stare. "Isn't this kind of ridiculous?" he asked. "Come on, I'm home now. Isn't that what you wanted?" He smiled shyly. "I'm not getting any younger, you know."

Once again, Jill allowed herself to be coaxed into his arms.

The rest of the evening was as big a disaster as the first part had been. For starters, Jill's cake hadn't set properly in the middle and everyone seemed compelled to comment on it. Then David's sister, Renee, got into a heated debate with their mother and she and her husband left before the presents were opened. The presents had been uniformly awful—("What on earth possessed you, Jill?" he'd asked, stuffing the silk shirt unceremoniously back inside its box)—and Elaine had called to see if Jason and Laurie could spend the night and the better part of the weekend with their father.

At ten o'clock, Jill's parents had left for home, and at ten-thirty, David left to drive his mother back to her apartment. Jason retreated immediately to the television and the telephone, which he used simultaneously. Laurie helped Jill straighten out the living room and stack the dishes in the dishwasher.

Jill watched the young girl as she worked, her bones protruding sharply underneath her blouse. "You didn't eat much," Jill said.

"The cake wasn't done right," Laurie commented.

Jill sighed. "I know. I meant you didn't eat much in general. Of anything."

"Yes I did."

"No, I watched you. You just shuffled it around on your plate all night."

Laurie shrugged. Jill decided to try again.

"Laurie, is everything all right?"

"How do you mean?"

"I mean, are you feeling all right? Are you happy?"

"Which one?" the girl questioned, putting the last of the dishes in the dishwasher and standing up straight.

"Well, we'll start with the first, I guess," Jill replied. "You're feeling okay?"

"Sure."

"No aches or pains anywhere?"

Laurie shrugged her bony shoulders for the second time in as many minutes. Jill thought she spotted a slight blush in the young girl's cheeks.

"Trouble with your periods?" she asked softly.

Laurie looked away and said nothing.

Sensing this was perhaps the problem, Jill pressed on gently. "I remember when I started my period," she said, feeling Laurie tense noticeably beside her in exactly the same way David's body would tense to any news he didn't care to hear. "I used to get the worst cramps. Sometimes I'd have to stay in bed all day. I didn't like letting something get the better of me that way, but sometimes you have to recognize when you're licked, and just accept it. My mother always used to tell me that the cramps wouldn't be so bad as I got older, and she was right."

"My mother calls it the curse," Laurie said, her back to Jill.

"Oh, no, it's not!" Jill said with great feeling. "It's a wonderful thing, Laurie. It means you're growing up. That you're becoming a woman!"

Laurie turned around abruptly, her eyes suddenly much older than her years. "Who said that's such a wonderful thing?"

Jill wasn't sure how she should respond. "Life is what you make it, Laurie," she said finally.

"Well, I'm fine," Laurie responded. "I don't have any aches or pains and my periods are none of your business."

Jill felt the sharpness of the rebuke all over her body. "How are things at home?" she asked softly.

"My mother's putting in a new swimming pool. It'll be ready the end of next week."

"Just in time for autumn," Jill said, trying to keep her voice light. "Is she still dating Ron Santini?"

"Yes."

Jill shook her head. It *had* to be a different Ron Santini.

"Do you like him?"

"He's all right."

"He treats you nicely?"

Laurie looked perplexed. "He's all right," she repeated.

"Your mother likes him?"

Laurie's answer was swift. "She's not going to marry him, if that's what you're getting at."

"I'm just trying to get at the root of what's bothering you," Jill said, realizing she had raised her voice.

"There's nothing bothering me."

"Then why don't you eat?!"

"I do eat! Why don't you leave me alone?!" She stormed out of the kitchen and back into the living room, plopping herself down in the middle of the sofa, sniffing back the tears Jill could see forming. Jill sat down beside her.

"I don't want you to cry, hon," she said, touching the child's arm. "I want to reach you, touch you—"

"You touch my father. Isn't that enough?"

Jill withdrew her hand. "Wow!" she said, standing up and releasing a deep breath. "Is that what it is? That you still haven't forgiven me for marrying your father?"

"I don't want to talk about it," the girl said.

"One day we're going to have to."

"Why?"

"Because I'd like for us to be friends," Jill said.

"I have enough friends," came the reply. "I don't need any more."

"Do you need any enemies?" Jill asked bluntly. Laurie turned her head away. "Look, Laurie, I don't mean to be tough on you, but facts are facts. And one of those facts is that I'm married to your father. And I intend to stay married to your father." She stopped, suddenly aware of how often lately she'd had to defend that position. Her thoughts refocused on her husband's child. "All I'm trying to say is that if your father's marriage to me is what's making you so unhappy, then you're just going to have to learn to live with it because it's not going to change. I love your father. Believe it or not, he loves me. And he loves you—you know that."

"I never see him," Laurie said, tears starting to fall.

"Who does?!" Jill answered, sitting back down beside the girl. "He's very busy these days," she continued. "What do you expect from a man who's late for his own birthday party!" She reached over and took Laurie's hands in her own. "But it's part of what we were talking about in the kitchen, part of growing up. Recognizing that there are certain things in life that we have to accept, and then making everything else as easy on ourselves as possible. Starving yourself to death isn't going to accomplish anything!"

Laurie tore her hands away from Jill's with such force that Jill was afraid the youngster was going to strike out. Instead, she jumped to her feet and began pacing back and forth in front of her. "Why can't you just shut up and leave me alone?" Laurie yelled, her voice high-pitched and bordering on hysteria. "Why couldn't you leave us all alone? You just messed up everybody's lives when you came butting in. You took my father away. You made my mother unhappy. She cries—I can't tell you how much she cries—and it's all because of you. She's so busy trying to forget about my father that she hardly has any time for me anymore. Nobody has time for me," Laurie cried, sobbing now, her frail body shaking like a scarecrow in a windstorm.

Jill remained seated on the sofa, slowly extending her arms toward the child. "I have time," she said. "Please, Laurie, I have so much time."

Laurie's body swayed in her direction.

"Can you cut out all the noise in there," Jason yelled from the den. "I can't hear the television."

The sound of her brother's voice snapped Laurie back into her shell. Her back straightened; her arms reached up and quickly wiped away her tears. We're back at square one, Jill thought. "Then get off the phone," Jill shouted angrily at Jason. She looked back at Laurie, seeing pieces of Elaine in the young girl's face. It was strange, she realized, but she'd never imagined Elaine crying. The woman is a human being, after all, she suddenly found herself thinking, not just an adding machine. It was a disconcerting thought.

"Do you think that by being my friend you'd be being disloyal to your mother?"

"I already told you," came the reply. "I don't need any more friends."

Jill stood up, about to leave the room. She stopped when she reached the hallway. "I guess it's time I started to take my own advice," she said, her back to Laurie. "About accepting the inevitable and making things as easy on everyone as I can." She turned to face the child. "I won't pester you again, Laurie. I won't ask any more personal questions and I won't comment on what you eat or don't eat. But I want you to know that I will be here if you ever want to talk—about anything—or if you do decide that you can always use another friend. Whatever. The next move has to come from you." She paused. "I'm going to bed. I'm tired. I've had a lousy day. You and Jason can work out who'll get the sofa and who'll get the pull-out bed. I'll leave some sheets and blankets in the hall." She started out of the room, then stopped again. "Tell Jason to get off the goddamn phone," she said, then walked without stopping into her bedroom, shutting the door behind her and bursting into a flood of silent tears.

She heard David's key in the door at just after eleven-thirty. He tiptoed into their room and started undressing in the dark.

"It's all right, I'm awake," Jill said from the bed.

"You startled me," he said, his voice noticeably strained.

"Sorry. I just meant that you didn't have to tiptoe around. You aren't disturbing me. You can even turn on a light if you want."

"No, not necessary," he said, approaching the bed.

"Where were you? It's late."

"My mother doesn't exactly live next door," he answered, crawling in beside her. "And she wanted to talk." He pulled Jill's body close against his.

"About what?"

"About what," he repeated, a short laugh catching in his throat. "About her son who should be more considerate of his wife. God, you women stick together!"

Jill moved her hands down along her husband's body. "Want to make love?" she asked, feeling him squirm away from her touch.

"The kids—"

"Aren't they asleep?"

"I guess so."

"So?"

"So, I just wouldn't feel comfortable making love with them so close—"

"That's ridiculous!"

"Maybe so, but it's how I feel. Come on, Jill, I'm tired. I've had a hard day at the office, I've had a hard time from you—"

"Not hard enough," she said, trying to joke, reaching for him.

"Very funny," he said, pulling farther away. "Look, let's get some sleep tonight, all right?"

"I guess you're not interested in hearing about *my* day," she said, sounding as dejected as she felt.

"To be perfectly honest, you're right," he said. "I'm sorry, Jill, I'm just so tired." He suddenly sat up in bed and pounded his fist against his pillow. "All right, goddamn it, tell me about your day."

"Never mind."

"No, oh no, I'm not going to be the heavy here. I insist you tell me all about your day."

Jill turned over in the bed. "I saw Irving today. He says there's nothing for me at the network."

"Well, you didn't think there would be," he reminded her.

"You don't have to sound so pleased," she chastised.

"Sorry, I didn't mean to. So—what else happened to you today?" he asked testily.

"I had a fight with Laurie."

"What about?"

"The fact that she doesn't eat, the fact that I happen to be married to her father, the fact that she hates my guts."

"Oh, Jill," he said wearily, "leave the kid alone. She's just going through a phase. A few years ago, she was almost pudgy. I remember giving her behind a tap and telling her that there was a bit too much jiggle for my tastes."

Jill became instantly self-conscious. "My God, what do you think about me?" she asked.

"I think that you're a woman and she's a little girl. And I think that as much as I love you, I'm going to throttle you if you don't let me get some sleep."

Jill let her body relax against David's. "All right, I can take a hint," she said, allowing her eyes to close. Things had to be better tomorrow, she thought, suddenly anxiously anticipating sleep.

The phone rang.

"What now?" she demanded, reaching across her husband and grabbing for the phone. "If it's Elaine, she's gone too far, and I'm going to let her have it! Hello?"

She knew the voice immediately, recognizing the dark huskiness. "Can I speak to David, please?"

"It's almost midnight," Jill said, angrily. This was too much —the woman had made him late for dinner and now she was invading the privacy of their bedroom! It was too much.

"I'm very aware what time it is. May I please speak to David?"

"Who is it?" David asked.

Jill said nothing, stretching the receiver over to her husband. "Who is it?" he asked again.

What the hell did she want? And why now?

"Hello?" David asked. "Who is this? Nicki! Is everything all right?" There was a pause. Jill watched David's face change from confusion to concern to outright horror in the space of several minutes. "My God. When did it happen? Why didn't someone call me earlier?" Another pause. He turned angrily to Jill. "Who the hell was on the phone?" he demanded.

Jill stared at her husband, frightened by the tone of his voice. "Jason," she stammered. "Jason was on the phone for a long time—"

He had stopped listening, was back engrossed in his conversation. "I can't believe it. Dead?"

"Who's dead?" Jill asked.

"Where have they taken her?"

"Who?"

"What? All right. What? Yes, I'll be there first thing in the morning. What? Don't be silly. You have no reason to apologize. Of course you were right to call. I'll see you tomorrow." He dropped the phone onto the bed. Jill returned it to its proper position.

"Who's dead?" she asked again.

David's voice was incredulous. "Al Weatherby," he said quietly.

"Al is dead? I don't believe it! How, for God's sake?"

"Murdered."

"What?!"

"Beth is in the hospital. The General. Apparently, whoever killed Al worked her over pretty good."

"Beth! But that can't be—I just spoke to her! My God, no. It can't be!" She jumped out of bed and began circling the room. "What can we do? Should we go to the hospital?"

"The police aren't allowing any visitors until morning." He paused. "It happened around ten o'clock, Nicki said. Don Eliot called her. Apparently, half the firm's been calling here, but the line was busy. She decided to wait and try again now." He shook his head. "It's incredible, the whole thing."

"Has anyone notified their children?"

"I'm sure the police are taking care of that."

Jill sat back down on the bed. "Did—did Nicole say how it happened? Or who?"

"Nothing. We don't know anything. Only that Al Weatherby is dead and that Beth is in the hospital."

Only that Al Weatherby is dead, Jill repeated to herself, and that Beth is in the hospital.

Chapter 13

The hospital corridor was lined with police.

David and Jill stepped off the crowded elevator onto the seventh floor and were promptly directed toward the waiting room, where they were told to do just that. Jill felt her husband's hand at her elbow guiding her toward the designated area. She had to run to keep up with his stride.

They reached the waiting room, and, for an instant, Jill felt as if they had stumbled into one of the staff lounges at Weatherby, Ross. Half the firm was present, most of whom David had spoken to the night before, after Nicki's terrifying phone call. Most stood up to greet David, as if he were the one who could make all the jumbled jigsaw pieces fit together again. Maybe they did that with all the new arrivals, Jill thought absently. Some of the men and almost all of the women were openly weeping. David embraced as many of his cohorts as he could manage before he was approached by a policeman who asked for his name and connection to the deceased and his wife.

Jill became suddenly aware of just how many policemen there were in the reasonably small quarters. Six in uniform, possibly several more in plain clothes. Everyone was talking at once, trying to come to grips with what had happened. The morning paper, several copies of which lay opened on the various tables, had shed no light at all on the matter other than to confirm in large, ugly black lettering that Al Weatherby, one of Chicago's leading legal lights, had been brutally beaten to death, his skull having sustained massive fractures from a blunt instrument. Beth Weatherby was supposedly in deep shock, with multiple injuries to her head and body, apparently lucky to be alive. Who could have done such an awful thing? And why, for God's sake?

"Could I have your name, please?"

Jill turned to stare at the young police officer. He couldn't be more than twenty-one, she thought, quickly looking at the others. They were all about the same age, she realized. Just babies. Or was it that the older she got, the younger everybody else seemed? Right now she felt as old as Methuselah, and probably looked a good deal older than that. Nicole's phone call had made sure she hadn't gotten any sleep, just as the lady, herself, had made sure Jill hadn't had a real rest since their first meeting approximately two months before.

"Jill Plumley," she answered, not sure how much time had elapsed between the question and her response.

"This man is your husband?" the officer asked, indicating David. Jill nodded. "Are you a lawyer too?"

Jill shook her head. "No. I'm in—" She stopped, realizing she had been about to say "in television." "I'm a teacher," she said. "I can't believe this has happened," she muttered, convinced the young man had heard this same remark a hundred times this morning. "I just spoke to Beth last night."

"What?" The policeman's entire posture suddenly changed. He stood up straighter; his back arched; his eyes reflected genuine interest. Jill was immediately aware of his change in attitude.

"I said I just spoke to her last night."

"About what time?"

"About five-thirty. Closer to six, I guess."

The policeman quickly jotted down the information. "Excuse me a minute, please," he said, and went out into the hall. Jill saw him conferring with an older man in street clothes who turned immediately in Jill's direction and then followed the officer back toward her.

David, who had been talking to several of his partners, sensed something was happening that he should be aware of, and returned to his wife's side.

"What's going on?" he asked, as the plainclothes police officer approached and introduced himself.

"I'm Captain Keller," he said pleasantly. "Mrs. Plumley, is it?"

"Yes," Jill answered, aware eyes were beginning to turn in her direction.

"Officer Rogers tells me you spoke to Beth Weatherby last night."

"Between five-thirty and six, yes."

"May I ask please what the gist of that conversation was?"

Jill began to speak. It was silent in the room. Jill realized that she was the center of attention and became instantly uncomfortable, as if she were center-stage and all around her cameras were recording her every move. It was a role she didn't like, much preferring to direct the camera's point of view—okay, Rick, see that tall, skinny policeman over there by the door, see if you can get him to move over closer to the window when we talk to him. Get the tree in the shot if you can. It'll give the scene a little more color. Her cameras had allowed her to get right into the middle of things without having to get directly, personally, involved. Now she was definitely in the center of things, but without her camera she felt naked and vulnerable and a bit foolish. What she had to say, after all, wasn't very important. It didn't matter, she realized, looking at the faces around her. At least she had something new to report. Something they hadn't heard before. That would be enough.

"She called and asked if I could meet her for a cup of coffee," Jill said simply. "I was preparing dinner so I had to say no."

"She wanted to meet you immediately?"

"Yes." Jill took a minute to review the conversation in her own mind. "She sounded very strange," Jill continued, remembering now all the details she had somehow managed to avoid the night before. "In fact, I didn't recognize her voice right away. She sounded—scared," Jill said, putting a word to what she had heard in Beth's voice but ignored because she was too busy to want to recognize it. Oh my God, she thought, had the killer been there when Beth had phoned? No, she decided. Beth had wanted to meet her right away. Surely the killer wouldn't have let her walk out to meet a friend for coffee.

"Did she say she was frightened?" Captain Keller asked.

"No. She just asked if we could meet for coffee. I asked her if something was wrong and she said no, just that Al was going to be late—he was tied up in a meeting—and she thought it would be a good time to get together. She sounded fine then. It was only at the beginning of the conversation that she sounded funny."

"She said her husband would be tied up late in a meeting?"

"Yes. We made arrangements to meet on Wednesday night instead."

"Anything else?"

"Nothing."

"Is Beth Weatherby a close friend of yours, Mrs. Plumley?"

"We're friends," Jill answered. "We play bridge together a bit and we take an exercise class together. I like her a lot." She tried to read some information from his expression but she got nothing. "Is she going to be all right?"

"Thank you, Mrs. Plumley," Captain Keller said. "We may want to speak to you again." He left the room.

"What was all that about?" Jill asked, turning to David.

He shook his head. "Why didn't you tell me Beth sounded frightened when you spoke to her?"

"I just didn't think about it. Do you think there's any connection?" she asked incredulously.

"It seems more than a bit coincidental," he answered, a touch of sarcasm creeping into his voice.

"But how?"

"David." The voice was soft but no less husky than it had sounded the night before. Jill turned toward it in time to watch Nicole dissolve into tears in David's arms. She couldn't believe what she was watching. In front of all these people, her husband was openly embracing another woman. Of course, no

one else present was aware of all the implications—what they
saw was an emotional young woman, not to mention a brilliant
legal mind, who was all broken up at the death of a man everyone had loved, and was turning for comfort to the man so many
of them had similarly embraced. Jill felt embarrassed. How
could she be so petty as to be jealous at a time like this? Her
husband's close associate and friend had been brutally blud-
geoned to death and his wife was who-knew-how-seriously in-
jured, and all she was worrying about was the stiffness of her
husband's cock against Nicole Clark's tight-fitting jeans.

David backed away from the other woman's embrace gently.
"Jill, do you have a kleenex?" he asked.

Jill reached in her purse and pulled out several crumpled tis-
sues. "I hope they're not used," she said, handing them over,
then watching in stunned surprise as David wiped the tears
from under Nicole Clark's eyes. I hope it *is* used, she cursed
silently. Did he have to make such a display of everything? She
didn't remember him wiping the tears away from under *her*
eyes. Then she remembered she hadn't shed any. She'd been
too stunned to cry.

Jill began to feel awkward watching them, as if she were an
intruder in a sacred and beautiful scene. Somehow, she found it
harder to watch her husband touching Nicole than she had
sighting her camera lens on the carnage and severed limbs of
Vietnam. She turned away, aware now of their voices beside
her, Nicole questioning, David having all the answers. A policeman approached and asked the newcomer's name. She heard
him leave again, heard Nicole's whispers and her husband's soft
assurances. Why had they come here? What possible good were
they accomplishing?

"Davey! Nicki! How are you?"

Jill turned to watch Don Eliot approach her husband and
Nicole. Tragedy had not altered his unorthodox style of dressing: He wore tight jeans and sandals along with a white shirt
and green tie. He conferred for several minutes with David and
Nicole before he even took note that Jill was there. "Hi, Jilly,"
he said, grabbing her hand and shaking it.

Hi, Donny, she wanted to respond. "Hello, Don," she
smiled. "Have you heard anything more?"

"Well, I saw Beth last night, of course, after they brought her in, but she was in a state of shock and couldn't say anything. I talked to the police, but it was too early to get much out of them. I just spoke to the doctors and to the officer in charge. Apparently, Beth is awake now and they're going to try and talk to her."

"Are her kids here?"

"The daughter's on her way in from Los Angeles. Her oldest son flew in from New York last night. He's with her now. The youngest son they haven't been able to locate yet."

"You don't think *he* did it, do you?" She thought of the recent tension between father and son since the boy had dropped out of school to don flowing robes and shave his head.

Don Eliot's face grew grim. "It's a thought," he said.

"Oh, God."

The room filled with the sound of fresh rumors. More people crowded into the already overcrowded area. Another policeman returned to recheck Jill's account of her phone conversation with Beth Weatherby. Don Eliot made frequent forays into the hall, conversing with several different officers. David had left Nicole's side and was now giving comfort to one of the other wives. Jill felt vaguely tawdry about her earlier feelings and looked away. Nicole Clark was staring at her from across the room. She looked more like a frightened and confused little girl than a femme fatale, Jill thought, before reminding herself that frightened and confused little girls had a way of being dangerously attractive to other women's husbands.

She turned away, her thoughts suddenly on Beth Weatherby. Yesterday, Beth had had everything. A successful marriage, a wonderful husband, a charmed existence. Today all that was gone. Shattered by several strong blows to the skull. Wasn't it remarkable how everything could change so completely in the space of a single night, and wasn't it strange, she thought, her mind echoing a phrase Beth herself had once uttered, how nothing ever worked out quite the way you thought it would.

"Why won't they let us see her?" Jill was asking angrily. "What are they doing for so long in there? Won't they even tell us how she is?"

No one answered her. Only a handful of people remained, including Nicole Clark, who had gone to bring everyone a cup of coffee and had returned with one cup too few. Jill had declined the girl's offer to make a second trip, claiming she drank too much coffee anyway (although she dearly would have liked a cup), and so she had to content herself with pacing the room and addressing herself to the walls like someone half-crazed and all alone. Of course I'm not alone, she told herself. My husband and his future wife are with me.

"I don't understand what's going on," Jill continued. "Why won't they tell us anything?"

"I'm sure they will as soon as they can," Nicole answered, her voice sweet and soft.

If she doesn't stop being so bloody sweet to me, Jill thought, I'm going to break her bloody sweet little neck.

As if on cue, Don Eliot appeared in the doorway. "Jilly, I'm glad you stayed. We're not getting anywhere. She won't say a thing. She just lies there—"

"Well, she's in shock," Jill protested. "Some lunatic beats her up and murders her husband—"

"She called you last night, is that right?" Don Eliot asked. "Tell me exactly, word for word, what she said."

Jill repeated the conversation to the best of her ability. "Well, she obviously wanted to tell you something," Don Eliot concluded. "It's too bad you couldn't go." He paused long enough to inspire the appropriate guilt. "Look, Jilly, maybe she'll talk to you now. I think I can talk the doctors into giving us a few more minutes. Are you game?"

"Sure," Jill said numbly. "If you think it'll help."

She knew the words out of his mouth before he said them. "It can't hurt," he said, and she walked down the corridor beside him, leaving her husband standing in the doorway beside Nicole Clark.

The woman sitting in the hospital bed had two black and swollen eyes, her skin was severely discolored, and large blotches of maroon, like misplaced rouge, stained her cheeks and chin. There were bandages across her nose and cheek, and one disappeared just inside her hairline. Her lips were cut and twice their normal size, her ears scratched and caked with dried blood. Still, there was something so peaceful about Beth Weatherby as she sat in her hospital bed, the blankets pulled high around her, hiding her other injuries from Jill's sight, that Jill feared in that initial instant that the woman had stopped breathing altogether, that she was being led forward to converse with a corpse.

"My God, Beth," Jill whispered, moving toward her. "Who did this to you?"

Beth Weatherby's eyes remained closed. Jill walked slowly to the woman's side, bent down and kissed her very gently on the forehead, on the only patch of skin which seemed untouched, her tears falling down involuntarily and wetting Beth's skin. "Oh, I'm so sorry," she cried. "I'm so sorry about what's happened." Beth's eyes flickered but stayed shut. Jill realized that perhaps the woman didn't recognize her voice. "It's Jill, Beth. I'm so sorry I couldn't meet you last night." She sniffed loudly, trying to stop the tears. "It's going to be all right, Beth," she continued lamely. "They'll find whoever did this and then this whole nightmare will be over. That's the good thing about nightmares, you know. You get to wake up."

Beth's eyes opened suddenly and focused on Jill. But they did more than stare, Jill realized, careful not to avert her own. They were searching. For what? Jill wondered. For answers? I don't know the question, she admitted silently. For reassurance? All I have are platitudes and empty promises. For support? You have it, Jill tried to communicate. All I have.

"I'm so tired," Beth muttered, barely audible behind her swollen lips.

"I know," Jill said, feeling dumb and inadequate. Just what was it she claimed to know?

"They hurt me," she said, her words slurred.

"They?" Jill asked quickly.

"When they changed the bandages," came the slow reply. "I know they didn't meant to." Her eyes closed briefly, then opened again. "Oh, Jill, I hurt so badly."

Jill tried to speak but couldn't. The words caught in her throat and were lost before they could find her tongue.

"Brian is here," Beth said suddenly.

"Brian?"

Beth smiled, or tried to. "My son, the doctor," she said, and Jill almost smiled in return. "I know he was here before when they were talking to me." She raised her head and began searching the room, a look of mounting panic filling her eyes.

"Your son went out for a cup of coffee," Don Eliot said from his position near the door. "Do you want him?"

Beth lowered her head back to the pillow. "They told me Lisa is on her way in from Los Angeles." She looked toward the window. "They haven't been able to find Michael yet. I think that's what they said. I'm not sure." Her voice was trailing off into a soft whine. "So many people," she said. "So many questions. Something to do with Al." She looked back at Jill. "They keep repeating his name as if they expect more than just its sound in return." She looked puzzled. "Poor Brian. He looks so tired and worried. I know I'm the cause. What did that policeman say to me before?" Jill could see Beth's mind racing to catch up to the scattered debris of her thoughts.

"Why don't you try and sleep, Beth," Jill offered. "We'll talk later."

"Something about Al. He was trying to tell me something about Al. He talked exactly the way they do on television. I didn't say anything. I don't know what he wanted me to say. My God, Jill," she said suddenly. "Al is dead!"

"I know," Jill said, a tear running down her cheek.

"Al's dead," the woman repeated.

"Please try not to worry," Jill pleaded, patting Beth's hand as it rested beneath the covers. "They'll find whoever killed Al. And they'll put him away. He won't be able to hurt you anymore."

"No, he won't," Beth said, her voice suddenly calm, her eyes closing once again, her breath becoming less forced and more even, as she succumbed to sleep.

Jill leaned forward and once again kissed her friend's forehead. "Sleep," she whispered, her eyes staring straight ahead at the white of the hospital pillowcase. Slowly, she allowed her spine to straighten and her shoulders to pull back. Then she turned and walked directly to the door.

"I'm afraid I wasn't much help," she said as she reached Don Eliot.

"You never know," he answered. "She said more to you than she has to anyone. That's a start, anyway."

"The start of what, I wonder," Jill said numbly, then opened the door to the hallway and quickly left the room.

Chapter 14

If and when she ever dropped dead, Jill decided, it would definitely not be in the middle of a heat wave. It just wasn't fair to expect people to crowd into an un-air-conditioned church to mourn your demise when the temperature outside was over 90 degrees and rising. God only knew what heights the thermometer would reach inside the church itself once they were all crowded together inside. Jill wondered if Beth would be present. She had been released from the hospital just yesterday, out of danger yet still strangely silent. In the week since Al's murder, Beth had surrounded herself with silence, speaking to no one, sleeping long hours and allowing only her daughter and sons (the youngest had finally been located) to minister to her needs. According to Don Eliot, she was almost a zombie. He could get no information out of her at all, and the doctors feared the shock might take months, possibly years, to abate. Without Beth, there was little to go on. The police still hadn't located the murder weapon, and there were no signs of forced entry into the Weatherby home, leading the police to suspect that the killer had been known to his victims. Possibly even related. Jill thought of Michael. It would certainly go a long way toward explaining Beth's silence. The shock of watching your own son destroy his father, then turn his rage on you—

Jill felt her breath becoming short and looked down at what she was wearing. David had insisted she wear a black wool turtleneck dress. It was the only black dress she had, and despite her argument that you showed respect at a funeral by your presence and not by what you wore, David had been adamant that she wear black. And so, here she was in the blistering late summer heat wearing a dress she usually saved for only the coldest days of a Chicago winter.

They hadn't even been able to get away over the long Labor Day weekend, the way they always had, Jill fretted, picturing the refreshing lake waters that framed the shore of the Deerhurst Inn, a quaint old country retreat they had stumbled across when their romance was in its infancy. She felt the loss of that weekend hideaway as acutely as a pilgrim denied his annual ablutions at Lourdes. But David had had to work all weekend, Weatherby, Ross having been thrown into an understandable state of chaos. Everyone was waiting anxiously for the police to release Al's body for burial, and the endless tests they were conducting only intensified the outrage, grief and scandal that threatened to swallow up everybody connected with the large firm. The next few weeks could only bring with them more of the same, although possibly the smothering cloak of heat which seemed to have been thrown across the city in the week since Al's death might lift. Jill tugged at the black wool which was sitting at her neck like a sleeping boa constrictor. Someone save me from this heat, she prayed silently, feeling guilty for the overwhelming triviality of her concerns in the face of what she knew Beth must be going through.

She had tried to reach Beth several times during the past week, and had met with polite but insistent refusals from her children. Their mother wasn't speaking to anyone, she was told, a fact with which Don Eliot immediately concurred. Jill repeated to all parties that she was readily available whenever she might be needed, but no one had called. Perhaps today, when she saw Beth—

The sideshow began at the front door with at least ten Hare

Krishnas chanting in cacophonous unison and handing out pamphlets to the stunned mourners. Apparently, Beth had given instructions that they were not to be disturbed, this being her younger son's way of dealing with his grief. Jill and David refused the proffered pamphlets—David muttering something about shooting Jason should he ever don flowing robes—and pushed past the chanters into the interior of the church.

It was even hotter than Jill had been prepared for. The circus at the door had at least provided something of a distraction, but now the body heat of some several hundred mourners, combined with the natural temperature of the outside air, made Jill gasp for breath. For a fleeting second, she thought of the movie *Land of the Pharaohs* with Jack Hawkins and a super-sultry Joan Collins. Joan, having plotted long and laboriously to kill all those who came between her and the throne of Egypt, including her husband, the current monarch, found herself in the great tomb along with the dead Pharaoh and all his favorite slaves, concubines and horses, about to be buried alive. Such were the Pharaoh's wishes. Jill hastily surveyed the large room which was in the process of filling to capacity. Was this Al Weatherby's plan as well? Had he posthumously gathered together the modern-day equivalent of his favorite slaves, concubines and horses? Was he planning on taking them all along? Into which category did she fit? Undoubtedly one of the horses, she decided, as David pushed her toward an aisle where she was forced to climb past several sets of kneecaps, all of which seemed to have been nailed into the floor.

She felt her hair curling into tight little balls around her face —she didn't remember Joan Collins sweating—and wished now that they had accepted one of the pamphlets they had spurned at the door. It would have made a good fan.

"Are you all right?" David asked, suddenly realizing how uncomfortable his wife must be.

"Just very hot," she answered, trying not to think about it.

His voice was soft, apologetic. "I'm sorry I was such an ass about insisting on the black dress and the makeup. I don't know why I was like that. I'm sorry."

"It's okay." She touched his hand, feeling a trickle of perspiration trace a line across her recently applied blush-on.

"You were very sweet about it. I really appreciate the fact that you didn't make an issue of it. I was in no mood for common sense." Jill smiled, trying to concentrate on his words and not the heat, feeling increasingly faint. Just let me get through this and back into an air-conditioned car, she prayed silently, remembering there was still the long drive out to the cemetery. "The makeup suits you though," he said. "You should wear it more often."

It was meant as a compliment, Jill knew, so she said nothing. She'd wash her face as soon as she got home.

The minister took his place behind the podium and began the service. Jill listened as he described the man she had grown so fond of, feeling his loss more acutely now as she was forced to recall details of his life. Poor Beth, Jill thought, brushing aside a tear and straining forward in her seat to try to spot Beth in one of the front rows.

The sight of Nicole Clark just two rows ahead of them caught Jill completely by surprise. For some unaccountable reason, she hadn't expected to see her there, although everyone else from Weatherby, Ross was in attendance, and obviously, where else would the dear thing be? Nicole sat perfectly still, her hair pulled back into a neat French braid, no noticeable perspiration anywhere that Jill could see. She wore a simple black cotton sleeveless dress with just the right amount of white trimming, making it appropriate for all occasions. Naturally, Jill thought, her eyes moving down the rows of mourners, she *would* have just the right dress to wear. My God, there's Elaine, she gasped inwardly.

"What's the matter?" David asked, concerned. She shook her head and shrugged her shoulders. "Relax, honey. We'll be out of here soon," he said, patting her hand.

She smiled, her eyes riveted on her husband's ex-wife. Of course, she should have expected that Elaine would be here. She had known the Weatherbys a long time. It was only right that she show her respect by coming. Jill took a long moment to assess Elaine.

Her features were soft and attractive, not as perfect as Nicole's, not as irregular as her own. She was almost exactly the picture of what one imagines a lawyer would marry just out of college, the childhood sweetheart who grew up without managing to grow in the same direction as her husband, who spent her hours preoccupied with bringing up her children and managing her house, forgetting—or ignoring the fact—that the work world was filling up with lots of bright and interesting ladies. Strangely enough, Jill noted, her eyes instantly taking in the remainder of the room, Elaine was also in black. In fact, they seemed to be the only three women in the entire room in the designated color of bereavement. All the other women—she still hadn't been able to spot Beth—had shunned the darker shades in favor of cooler summer prints. It seemed almost a deliberate display, the black setting them apart from the others, creating a separate entity—David Plumley and his women. It was like John Derek, she thought, conjuring up the magazine picture of the handsome former actor surrounded by his ex-wives, Ursula Andress and Linda Evans, and his current wife, Bo, all smiling, all wearing identical T-shirts, all happy to have had the privilege. My God, get me out of here, she whispered to herself, looking into her lap. Perhaps they should form a receiving line— Past, present— Future?

Her eyes shot to David's.

"What's the matter?" he asked again, becoming alarmed. "Are you going to be sick?" Instinctively, he edged as far as he could away from her. It wasn't very far. The knees beside him held firm.

"It's a thought," she said. "I know, take deep breaths," she continued for him. Following her own instructions, she looked between her knees, concentrating all her energy on the floor, and then returned her attention to the eulogy being delivered. She felt the tears well up inside her and was astonished when instead of crying, she felt the urge to laugh tickling its way up her throat.

The sound escaped her mouth before she could stop it and throw her hand on top of it. How could she do it? How could she laugh out loud at the funeral of her husband's mentor and dear friend? She couldn't stop, almost choking on the effort, doubling her body over to try and suffocate the blasphemous sounds. The tears filled her eyes and she felt David's protective arm around her. "It's all right, sweetheart," he said, soothingly, drawing her up under his arm. He thinks I'm crying, she realized, the knowledge of which was enough to bring on a fresh onslaught of giggles and cause her to bury her face deep against his chest. Around her she heard quiet expressions of sympathy and understanding. They all think I'm crying, she told herself, and for the remainder of the service she kept her head burrowed deep against David's jacket and laughed so hard that she was crying.

Jill stood waiting by the front door of the church while David went around the back to the parking lot to get the car. All around her, members of the Hare Krishna were busy chanting and dancing, shaking their tambourines against the dead air. Jill took in a deep breath of oxygen, hoping it would make her feel less faint, but there was no relief. She looked to the street, eager for the sight of the brown Mercedes. She would turn the cold air on full blast. She leaned her body against the side of the building and closed her eyes. I am walking barefoot in Antarctica, she repeated over and over, inadvertently establishing a silent rhythm with the other chanters.

"I have a bone to pick with you," the voice said from somewhere beside her. Jill opened her eyes and turned in its direction. Elaine stood, cool and controlled, before her. "My God, are you all right? You look like you're going to be sick!"

"Thank you," Jill said. She couldn't think of anything else to say.

"Do you want to sit down?" Elaine asked, indicating the stone steps. "I think we could probably make room between all these Harry and Harriet Krishnas."

Jill shook her head. "I'm just very hot."

Elaine looked Jill over from head to toe. "Well, no wonder, for God's sake. Look what you're wearing! Whatever possessed you to wear a wool turtleneck in the middle of the summer?!"

"It's September."

"It's almost a hundred degrees."

"It's black," Jill told her. Was this the bone Elaine had to pick?

"So what?" Elaine asked.

"Our husband insisted," Jill deadpanned.

Elaine's face broke into a wide grin which made her look years younger and much softer. "You're not supposed to be funny and make me smile," Elaine said, surprising both of them. Was this the woman David had described as humorless and unsympathetic? The whiny and shrill voice on the telephone she had come to despise?

Jill thought back to their first direct confrontation four years earlier. Courtroom C, on the second floor. Plumley versus Plumley. Divorce granted to Elaine Plumley on the grounds of adultery. The other woman: Jill Listerwoll. I know how trite this sounds, she had said to Elaine when they inadvertently came face to face in the hallway, but I really never meant to hurt you. Elaine had been unimpressed, her back rigid. It does sound trite, she had said in reply. And then she had said something else, words Jill had forced into the back of her memory until they had tried unsuccessfully to emerge at David's birthday party, which seemed now so very long ago. If he treated me the way he treats you, she had said, and treated you the way he treats me, this would be a completely different story.

Jill stared wide-eyed at the first Mrs. David Plumley. Perhaps they weren't so different after all. "You said you had a bone to pick with me?" she asked, throwing off the disconcerting thought.

Elaine regarded Jill with a blank expression as if Jill had spoken to her in a foreign language. Then the memory of why she had initially approached her ex-husband's present wife returned and lit up her eyes. "Yes," she said forcefully, her voice gaining strength and purpose with each new word, "I do. How dare you tell my daughter that I'm dating a crook!"

Jill looked helplessly around her. She couldn't believe this was happening. Where was David? Why was he taking so long with the car?

"I'm sorry," she said finally, returning her gaze to Elaine. "It kind of popped out before I could stop it."

"He's in fruit," Elaine said.

"I'm sure he is."

"You must have the wrong Ron Santini."

"I'm sure I do."

"He's in fruit," Elaine repeated, then paused. "Even if he were a crook, it would be no business of yours."

"That's true. Like I said, it just kind of popped out. I don't think Laurie believed me, anyway."

"Oh, those kids believe everything you tell them! It's always 'Jill said this' and 'Jill said that.' It's enough to make you sick."

"I didn't think they ever listened to me," Jill said, genuinely surprised, ignoring Elaine's editorial comment.

"Oh, they listen, all right." She paused again. "For the record, even though it *is* none of your business, Ron Santini is a very nice man, and since I don't propose to ever marry again, I really don't give a damn what he does for a living."

Jill felt the blanket of heat returning to cover her body. "Are you so bitter," she asked, feeling very weary, "that you'll deny yourself happiness just so that David has to keep on paying you monthly support?"

"Ninety thousand dollars a year buys a lot of happiness," Elaine answered. "And yes, I guess I am that bitter. Besides, you're a married woman now! Would you really do it again?" She stopped to let the question take root. "Not me," she answered. "Once was enough, thank you." She looked across the street at her car. "I was lucky—I found a spot right on the street. Well, I'm going to go home and lie in the sun—I guess you heard I had a pool put in."

"I heard."

"I'd invite you over but well, that might seem a little tacky."

"I'd rather go to the cemetery, thank you."

"And, of course, you always get what you want."

"Of course."

Each woman smiled pleasantly at the other, and Jill watched Elaine walk down the church steps and onto the street. A few days ago she would have wished for a car to come barreling down the street and knock the dear lady right out of her two-hundred-dollar shoes. But now, strangely enough, she found she had a grudging respect for Elaine. In a perverse sort of way, she had actually enjoyed their verbal fencing. The woman had more spunk than she'd previously imagined, and she made more sense than Jill had ever thought she would.

The heat must be getting to me, she thought, watching Elaine open her car door and get inside. She's getting a little hippy, Jill thought with no small degree of satisfaction. She leaned back against the church.

"Mrs. Plumley?"

Jill looked over at the young, pale figure who stood before her.

"I'm Lisa Weatherby, Beth's daughter."

Jill straightened up to shake the girl's hand. "I'm so sorry," she began. "If there's anything I can do—I've called several times—"

The girl looked toward her brothers. One had his arm draped protectively around her; the other was busy chanting with his friends. Harry and Harriet Krishnas, Elaine had called them, Jill suddenly recalled, only vaguely having heard Elaine when she had said it before. That was pretty funny. She looked to the street. Elaine's car was gone.

"There *is* something you can do," Lisa Weatherby said. Jill looked back at Lisa.

"Yes?"

"Maybe you could come up to the house one day this week and see my mother. She wasn't well enough to come today, and I know she'd like to see you. We'd hoped that by making sure she got enough rest and not letting anyone bother her she'd be all right, that the shock would start wearing off and she'd be able to tell us what happened that night, but it doesn't seem to be working. She's still not talking to anyone, and—well, you seem to be her only friend."

"What?"

"We'd better go, Lisa," her older brother urged. "The limousine's waiting."

"Will you come?" Lisa asked again.

"Of course," Jill answered. How could she have been Beth Weatherby's only friend? The woman knew everyone; everybody liked her. What was going on? She leaned back against the church edifice. Oh, for a little ice and snow.

"Excuse me, Jill?"

What was it about the front of this building? Every time she leaned against it, someone approached her. For the third time, she straightened up and turned toward the voice, knowing before she looked who was speaking, remembering that the first time the girl had excused herself, she had called her Mrs. Plumley.

"Don't tell me," Jill said before the younger woman had a chance to speak. "Your name is Nicole Clark and you're going to marry my husband."

The girl lowered her head. "I guess I deserved that."

"You're the one who said it."

Nicole Clark nodded. "One of the stupider things I've said."

"I'd have to agree."

"I did apologize," she whispered.

"You have an interesting way of saying you're sorry," Jill told her. She felt fresh streams of perspiration running across her face. "Look, I think we've milked this little subject for all it's worth, don't you?"

"I explained to David how it all happened," Nicole continued.

"Nothing's happened," Jill reminded her.

Nicole ignored the well-timed interruption. "I told him how sorry I was that I'd upset you—"

"You *do* have a way with words," Jill said, feeling her smile stick against her cheeks, held there by the humidity. "But I really think that David has more pressing concerns at the moment than—"

"He's been so wonderful throughout all this," Nicole said, cutting Jill off. "He's really been the one holding the firm together, making sure we don't all crumble and fall apart. Al meant so much to all of us."

"I'm sure he did," Jill acknowledged, wondering suddenly when it was that Nicole had found the time in the midst of all the chaos to explain herself to David, and when her husband had found the time to listen.

"I was trying to get some work done the other day and suddenly I just dissolved into a flood of tears. There were clients around and everything. I was very embarrassed. I could just hear everyone whispering behind my back about how women don't have the emotional makeup to be successful lawyers. All that rot. But suddenly, there was David, and he ushered me out of there and took me downstairs for something to eat, and we talked about it. He really understood how I felt about Al. He felt the same way. It was the first time I'd ever really seen David open up that way. As a man, I mean, not a lawyer."

Jill's voice fairly seethed with fury, each word dripping venom. "How considerate of Al, then, to have passed away so that you might have that opportunity," she said, and waited.

Nicole stared at Jill in obvious shock. Elaine would have had a smart answer, Jill thought, thinking simultaneously of her husband and Nicole Clark out for their cozily revealing lunch. So, the little pilgrim was making progress, she realized with a combination of bitterness and dismay.

The car honking from across the street diverted her attention, and she turned her head around just in time to allow the few tears that had formed in her eyes to fall and mingle with the lines of perspiration which were already streaking her face. In one deft gesture, she wiped her face clear of heat and emotion and turned back to Nicole.

"Excuse me," Jill said, steering away from her young challenger, and heading toward the steps. Please don't let me fall, she whispered silently as she descended them carefully, aware of the girl's eyes on her back, burning a hole into the black wool of her dress. So, her dear husband had taken the sweet little thing to lunch and opened himself up "as a man" to boot. She felt anger and indignation rising inside her. He makes *me* wear a black wool dress in the middle of a heat wave and he takes *her* out to lunch.

Her mind recalled Elaine's past admonition, rearranging it slightly to suit Nicole: If he treated her the way he treats me, she repeated wordlessly, and treated me the way he treats her, this would be a completely different story. Jill walked quickly toward her husband's brown Mercedes and angrily opened the door. Then, taking a last look at Nicole Clark, she got inside.

Chapter 15

"I don't believe this is happening."

"Relax, Jill."

"How am I supposed to relax? I am slowly melting away before your very eyes."

"It should only be a few more minutes."

"You said that ten minutes ago."

"The poor kid's working as fast as he can. He looks terrified."

"So would you if your client was a corpse!"

"Jill, please—"

"If you tell me to relax one more time, I'm going to scream."

"All right. Fine. Don't relax."

"Couldn't we at least turn on the air-conditioner?"

"Sure, if you want to overheat the car. Then we'd really be stuck."

"I just don't believe this is happening."

Jill looked out the window at the other cars lining the side of U.S. Highway 41. Then she looked over at the service station, where a quivering young mechanic was gamely trying to replace the fan belt that had broken on the hearse.

"I didn't think hearses had fan belts," Jill muttered to no one in particular. "If Al Weatherby is anywhere watching this, he must be shaking his head and saying, 'What a fucking mess!'"

"Jill, please, you're not making things any better."

"And if you say *that* again, I'm going to get out and walk."

"Then by all means," he said, reaching across her and opening the door, "get out and walk."

They sat in angry silence for several minutes. Oh, great, Jill thought. We must be playing this scene just the way Nicole Clark wrote it. She reached over and shut the door.

"I don't like ultimatums," he said, not looking at her.

"I know," she said, remembering.

It was late. The room was in darkness. Neither one of them had bothered to turn on a light. Underneath them, on the floor below, Jill knew Mrs. Everly and her monstrous dog were fast asleep. She wished she were in bed too. Asleep. Alone. She didn't want to say what she knew he didn't want to hear.

"I can't do it anymore, David," she began.

"What are you talking about?"

"What we always talk about. Just that this time I mean it."

He sat across from her on the sofa. She sat on the floor, her long legs crossed in a semi-lotus position. She was wearing a long evening gown which made the position most difficult to accomplish, and once mastered, seem singularly out of place; her reddish-brown hair was pulled back into a bun from which thousands of stray hairs threatened at any second to escape; her skin was blotchy and streaked with tears. She looked as miserable and unhappy as he knew she felt. He also knew what she was going to say and he knew he didn't want to hear it. She knew the same thing but was determined to say it anyway.

"I love you, David," she began again, pushing the reluctant words out of her mouth. "I ache, I love you so much. But I'm tired of sneaking around, or waiting up until two in the morning, hoping vainly that you'll show up. And I'm tired of pretending that you sleep in a room all by yourself when you crawl out of my bed to go home." She paused, sniffing loudly.

"Jill—"

"But most of all, I'm tired of having to madly scramble up a date for my cousin's wedding because the only man I've been seeing for the last two years is married and it wouldn't look nice to show up at my cousin's wedding with a married man!" She let out a loud wail, her hand reaching over to push some loose hairs behind her ears. "Oh, shit, it's gone. I lost it."

David looked confused. "What's gone?"

"My flower!" she cried. "I had a blue cloth flower in my hair. Everyone said I looked beautiful."

"I'm sure you did."

"I lost the goddamn flower!"

"I think you're beautiful," he said softly, moving to the floor beside her and putting his arms around her. She laid her head against his shoulder, feeling her mascara forming little black puddles underneath her eyes.

"You must be very horny," she smiled through the tears.

"I am," he said, kissing her neck. "I haven't seen you in three days."

"And whose damn fault is that?" she asked fiercely, pushing him aside and clumsily getting up on her feet. "Damn it, you should have seen me tonight. I really did look beautiful."

"I'm sure you did."

"Leon—I went out with a Leon, if you can believe it—he asked me out again. If you can believe *that!* Friday night. He wants to take me to see Second City."

"What did you tell him?"

"I said that I usually liked to keep my Friday nights open just in case my married lover could make it over for a few hours."

"Jill—"

"I said yes, I'd be delighted. What should I have said?"

David got up off the floor. "What is all this in aid of, Jill?"

She shrugged her shoulder. The strap of her gown fell down across her arm. "You have to make a choice, David."

"Oh, Jill—"

"And I'm sorry I seem to be resorting to clichés. But we happen to be living in a cliché so I choose my words accordingly."

"I don't like ultimatums."

"I don't care what you like!"

They stood for what seemed an eternity in their frozen positions. Then, without another word, he turned and slowly walked toward the door. It was a month before he called to tell her he had asked his wife for a divorce and that Elaine had responded by promising to take him for every cent he had.

Jill turned the small air-conditioning unit so that it blew directly at her throat.

"Feeling better now?"

"I will feel better when I have removed this dress and consigned it to an incinerator."

"At least they got him in the ground."

"That was a relief. The way this day has gone, I was sure they were going to wind up dropping the coffin—as a sort of grand finale."

David laughed. "Quite a day." He shook his head. "I still can't believe any of it's real."

"I know what you mean."

"Al's actually dead," he said, more to himself than to his wife. "We watched him being lowered into the ground."

"Well, we saw a *coffin* being lowered into the ground," Jill corrected. "Al may still be back at that gas station. Maybe he got a job. Even in his condition, he'd have to move faster than that mechanic."

David burst out laughing, pulling the car to a halt at the side of the busy street. They were only a few blocks from their apartment.

"Why are you stopping?" Jill asked, then watched helplessly as her husband's laughter turned abruptly to tears. "Oh, David," she said, her arms encircling him, her head pressed against his shoulders. Tears suddenly filled her own eyes. For several minutes, they cried together, for the man they had both so liked and admired.

David was the first to break away, sitting up straight and drying his eyes. "Sorry," he said.

"Sorry? What for?"

He shook his head. "For everything. For being such a jerk—making you wear that dumb dress—"

"That's all right."

"No, it's not all right. Look at you, for God's sake."

"I'd rather not be reminded about how I must look—"

"See? I did it again. Every time I open my mouth, I make you feel worse."

"No, really. You don't. I feel terrific. Or interesting, anyway. Let's say I feel interesting."

He leaned over and kissed her. "You're so sweet and I'm such a prick."

"Yes, I am and you are. So, what else is new?" She kissed his cheek. "Come on, start the car. We'll go home; I'll burn my dress; we'll take a bubble bath and get into bed. How does that sound?"

He responded without words, nodding his head and turning the key in the ignition. The car started and they drove the two blocks to their apartment in easy silence.

A few minutes later, David pulled the car into their designated parking space in the large underground garage. He stopped, took the key out of the ignition and kept his head lowered, as if he couldn't raise it until he finished whatever thought was in his head. Jill waited accordingly, knowing there was something he wanted to tell her that was more important than getting quickly out of her clothes.

"What is it?" she asked.

Silence. Then finally, "I owe you another apology."

Jill held her breath, thoughts of Nicole Clark filling her mind. Had there been more than just the lunch he hadn't told her about? Don't tell me, she begged silently. I don't want to know. "You've apologized enough already," she said, her voice whispered and strained.

"Not for this."

"David—"

"About your job, the teaching."

"What?"

"About the way I reacted when you told me how unhappy you were."

"How did you react?" Jill questioned.

"That's just the point," he said. "I didn't. I told you to grin and bear it. Some nonsense like that. Legal talk. Practical advice when what you needed was a little support and understanding. Damn it, Jill, if you're unhappy teaching, then you shouldn't be teaching. If Al's death teaches us anything at all, it's that life is too short, too precious to waste it doing something we don't want to do. I love you, Jill. I want you to be happy."

"I will be." Jill smiled through her tears. "Something will come up. Irving will call. You'll see."

David scoffed. "I was really all heart that night you told me about your meeting with Irving," he said, thinking back. "My usual sensitive, sympathetic self."

"All is forgiven," Jill whispered. "Sometimes it's better to be practical than sensitive." She paused, then continued again, her voice soft and quiet. "I just wish I saw more of you, that's all. Maybe then the rest of it wouldn't seem so important."

He nodded. "I'm sorry about that, too. I know it must seem like I'm falling back into old patterns. But believe me, Jill, the work load is extreme at the moment. Everything's gone crazy. I just can't seem to keep on top of things no matter how hard or how late I work. Now, with Al dead, it's even worse. Nobody knows what's going on. It'll be months before things calm down and we get back on a proper course." He looked questioningly at his wife. "Do you think you can be patient for just a little while longer? I promise that after Christmas things should be back to normal. No more working from dawn to dusk every day. I promise. How does that sound to you?"

Jill nodded. "Sounds good."

He leaned over and kissed her gently. Then they each opened their respective car doors and stepped out, closing them again in almost perfect unison. They walked hand in hand to the inside elevator and waited for it to arrive.

"I wonder if Irving *will* call me again," Jill said absently, as the doors to the elevator opened and they stepped inside.

"You were his top producer. Of course he'll call you again."

"He was pretty negative."

"He gets paid to be negative."

"He said the new girl who replaced me is working out very well."

"Nobody could ever replace you," David said, hugging her to him and kissing the side of her face.

Tell that to Nicole Clark, she wanted to say, but she chose instead to say nothing.

"Maybe a new show will come up," David continued.

Jill nodded. "Something based entirely in Chicago," she said. "And here I would stay."

"Until the first opportunity to see China comes along—"

"I've been to China," she reminded him.

"I know," he said, and then they were both silent.

They were pacing the floor, circling each other like two stray cats, their words hissed at each other across the space of their living room, their backs arched, ready to pounce at the slightest provocation.

"Why are you making such a big deal about this trip?"

"I have already given you my reasons. You've been away enough this year."

"No more than last year."

"You were away too much last year."

"Oh, great. We're just going around in circles."

Jill plopped wearily down into the soft fullness of the print sofa. "I'm tired of fighting every time I have to go away."

"Then stop going away."

"I don't go away that often!"

David stopped his pacing and stared at his wife in genuine amazement. "Jill, in the two years we've been married, you've been to London, Paris, Toronto, Los Angeles, Angola and Argentina! Now you're talking about going to China!"

Jill was quiet for several seconds. "We once talked about going there together," she said, emphasizing the final word.

"You know I can't go now."

"Why not?"

"What am I supposed to do, Jill? Put all my clients on hold while I accompany my wife on a jaunt up the Great Wall?"

"Precisely. Why not?"

"Because people in the throes of a divorce don't take too

kindly to their lawyers postponing court dates it's taken months, sometimes years, to set up."

"You have partners, don't you? What are they there for, if not to help out when one of you gets busy elsewhere?"

"You know I don't like to pass off my work—"

"Some people call it delegating responsibility."

"My clients are *my* responsibility."

"Can't you just tell them you're going on holiday for a few weeks? I took my holidays around *your* schedule!"

"Exactly, I've already had my holidays!" David sat down in one of the large wing chairs he and Jill had recently purchased. "What am I going to do in China, anyway? Change the film in your cameras? Be reasonable; I'd only get in everybody's way."

Jill thought of other trips, the spouses of other members of the various crews. David was right. Whenever one of the wives (and it was always the wives, she realized) chose to accompany her husband on any such trip, there was inevitably friction and unhappiness. It was never a good rule to combine pleasure trips with business, she had long ago decided. Somehow all parties managed to feel cheated.

"Besides," David was saying, "we can't afford it."

Jill took a long, deep breath. As a non-working member of the expedition, David would be required to pay his own way. And Elaine had made sure that any of the infrequent holidays David and Jill enjoyed were spent relatively close to home.

"So, where does that leave us?" Jill asked, her voice tired.

"You tell me," David answered, no less fatigued.

"I have to go, David."

He nodded, standing up. "You'll miss the firm party."

"I know. I'm sorry."

"And dinner with the Marriotts."

"We'll have them over when I get back."

"What do I tell everyone?"

"The truth. That I had to go to China. It'll give the old geezers something to talk about other than the fact your first wife was prettier and what does he see in this television lady anyway?" David smiled wearily in her direction. "If you really want to give them something to talk about, you could take a date." A fleeting image of another woman, her legs wrapped around her husband, flashed before her eyes. "On second thought," she said, getting up and slinking over to David, sitting on his lap and wrapping her own legs around him, "let them find their own topics of conversation." She kissed him. "Please don't be angry."

"I'll get over it," he said, returning her kiss.

She had gone to China, filmed the first onslaught of American tourists, and returned some two weeks later to find the apartment unchanged, the weather the same, and her husband as happy to see her as he always was whenever she returned home from an assignment. But something was different. Something intangible, caught only in passing, in a glance that didn't quite connect, or a touch that failed to linger. He'd been with somebody else. She knew it. It was as real to her as if she'd witnessed the act herself, as tangible as if he'd put it into words. He never said anything. She never asked. But it was there. A week after her return she told the network that she would accept no more out-of-Chicago assignments, and soon after, she submitted her resignation and accepted a post teaching TV journalism at the University of Chicago.

"What were you talking to Nicki about?" he asked, as they stepped into their apartment. Jill pulled the black wool dress up over her head and let it drop in a sweaty heap to the floor. "Jesus, Jill, wait till I close the door!"

She heard the door close behind her as she walked, robot-like, toward the bathroom. From the door David heard the bath water running. When he reached the bathroom, Jill was nude and standing beside the tub waiting for it to fill.

"You didn't tell me you took her to lunch," Jill told him by way of a reply.

David didn't require further explanation. "She was upset. She needed someone to talk to."

"And you were the only one she could turn to?"

"I was there."

"Very convenient," Jill said, wishing she hadn't.

"This isn't worth discussing," he said, walking from the room.

Jill debated following him, but decided that the sight of her nude body would compare unfavorably in any discussion of Nicole Clark. She waited until the bath was filled almost to overflowing before she lowered herself into it and closed her eyes. Somehow, in the few minutes between the opening of their apartment door and the running of the bath water, all thoughts of bubbles and making love had been misplaced. David was in one room; Jill was in another. Nicole Clark was somewhere in between.

Chapter 16

The next day, Jill drove out to Lake Forest to see Beth Weatherby.

From the street, the house looked the same as it had the last time she had visited, the green leaves of early summer still filling the trees which surrounded the large gray brick exterior, giving the lie to the silent passage of almost three months. Soon enough, she knew, the green would turn to autumn golds and reds and then, before she was ready, the color would disappear altogether, leaving the branches bare and black against the overwhelming gray of the Chicago sky. Jill stared at the rows of white and red petunias and geraniums which lined the walkway to the front of the house. Despite the fresh flowers and the surrounding heat—the temperature was only slightly down from the day before—she felt suddenly cold. It was going to be a long winter, she thought, taking the first steps up the long path toward the house.

The front door stood before her, a large, heavy oak slab, with a bronze knocker shaped like a dolphin. Tentatively, Jill reached up and grabbed the large fish's tail, feeling a sudden flush of palpable fear race through her body. Why? she wondered, annoyed at her body's reflexes. What was it she was so afraid of? That Al's ghost would materialize to answer her knock, usher her inside with his customary warmth, as he had several months ago when she and David had arrived for that misbegotten night of bridge? She remembered sitting in the comfortable living room, mesmerized by the serenity of its antiques, the room somehow implying a sense of unspoken continuance, feeling David close by her side, looking over at the photograph of the Weatherby children, and then the calm suddenly shattered by a scream in the night. Beth's scream. She saw herself racing toward the kitchen, her eyes freezing momentarily on Al's frightened face, drained white by the sudden gush of red from Beth's outstretched hand. Jill turned her head back toward the road. White and red, she thought, like the flowers.

Jill stood absolutely still, feeling her panic spreading. This is ridiculous, she thought, her self-annoyance building. She was acting like a child afraid of the bogeyman. Was it the aura of death she feared? The knowledge that a man had been murdered inside? She shook her head at her invisible questioner. No, she was not afraid of death even in its most grisly manifestations. She had often trained her cameras on the carnage of global civil wars and inner-city brutality. No, she had no fear of death—she had directed its display.

Yet she had no camera with her now to help her keep her distance. She had only herself—and her fear. For whatever reason, she simply did not want to go inside that house. Without requiring further explanation, she somehow knew that there were secrets in there she didn't wish to hear. That once she set foot on the other side of that massive oak door, her life would never be the same again.

"Oh, stop overdramatizing," she told herself out loud, letting go of the bronze dolphin and listening as it thwacked loudly against its base.

The door opened immediately, as if whoever was behind it had known of her presence and had been patiently waiting for her to make up her mind. Jill felt her heart pumping wildly against her chest. Stop it, she told herself as she came face to

face with the young girl in the doorway. Lisa Weatherby smiled
wanly at her visitor. She looked much younger than her twenty-
three years, Jill decided, younger, in fact, than her seventeen-
year-old brother, and she'd obviously been crying. Her face was
puffy and swollen, a teary mist resting like cataracts over her
hazel eyes. She looked startlingly like her father. Jill quickly
conjured up the image of Lisa's two brothers, both of whom
she had seen at the funeral. Each had much more closely resembled his mother.

"Are you all right?" Jill asked, instantly putting her arms
around the girl.

"I don't know what I am," the girl answered, immediately
bursting into tears. Jill led her quickly inside the house and
closed the door. The hallway looked exactly as it had a scant
few months ago. Had she been expecting blood-splattered
walls? The name of the victim scribbled amid obscene graffiti in
his own blood?

"Are your brothers here?" Jill asked.

"Brian's lying down," the girl said softly. "Michael went
back to his church."

"And your mother?" Jill wondered if Lisa had sensed her
reluctance in asking the last question.

"She's in her room. Can we talk for a minute?" Lisa asked.

"Sure," Jill answered. "That's why I'm here."

The girl allowed Jill to lead her into the large living room.
As it was with the hallway, the room was unchanged. It still
spoke of warmth and permanence, even love.

They walked together like Siamese twins joined at the hip,
sharing a common leg, until they reached the sofa. Slowly,
carefully, they lowered themselves down, sitting side by side,
arms entwined.

"They say everybody in L.A. is crazy," Lisa began without
introduction, sniffing away a tear. "You know, they say that
when God created the world, he tilted it onto its side, and all
the nuts fell into Los Angeles." She tried to laugh but couldn't.
"And it's true, you know. They *are* nuts. There isn't a sane one
in the whole bunch. You can't believe anyone—they lie as easily
as they tell the truth. And all they talk about is money and success. Nobody ever reads or talks about anything that's going on

in the world. They all drive expensive foreign cars and have houses with swimming pools, but nobody is really happy because they're never really sure after a while what lie they've told to whom. They don't even know what's a lie anymore and what isn't. It's like they're living in the middle of a big Hollywood soundstage and they're afraid that, come nighttime, someone's gonna come along and fold it all up. Nobody knows there what's real and what's make-believe." She paused, as if trying to give her thoughts some coherence. "I used to come home to get a sense of balance. Back here, in this house, with my mother and father, I knew there was some sanity left in this world. My parents understood who they were; they accepted each other and the rest of us for ourselves. They never tried to turn us into something different." She shook her head, her mind racing back and forth between her two worlds. "Not like in Hollywood. Everyone's always trying to make you over into somebody else. And everyone's a star, even the ones who've been parking cars for twenty years or waiting on tables. You ask them what they are, they never say I'm a waitress or a parking lot attendant—they're all actors and actresses. They were all up for the lead in *In Cold Blood*. Do you know how many years ago that was?! They were looking for unknowns, they must have auditioned every guy between the ages of sixteen and fifty—but that doesn't make any difference. They were still up for the lead, and one day they're gonna be stars. And it happens, you know, it happens just often enough to make everybody else hang on." She wiped at her eyes with both hands. Jill let her continue uninterrupted. "I've been there close to four years now, trying to make it as a singer. My father didn't want me to go. Not that he didn't trust my talent. He just knew that everybody there was crazy." She laughed a touch too loudly. "I'm one of them. One of the crazies who's busy waiting on tables and waiting for my big break. I've been there almost four years now. Did I tell you that already? And my parents have been extremely supportive of me even though they didn't want me to go. Well, actually, my mother went along with my father when we were all together, but when we were by ourselves, just the two of us, she'd say, 'Go, Lisa. Try for it. You'll never know unless you try,' and I guess that gave me the encouragement I needed because my dad was really against it. But after I made up my mind and went down there, he started sending me money every month, and my mom writes me a couple of times a week. We're very close. We always have been. She tells me everything. She was afraid that things wouldn't work out for me, I think, when I left: I could see it in her eyes. She looked kind of scared. I guess she was afraid she'd be lonely and she knew how much she'd miss me once I was gone, and she knew how crazy they all are there. But she was never one of those mothers who say, 'Stay home and meet a nice guy. What do you want to go running off to Hollywood for? Find yourself a nice lawyer like I did and settle down!' None of that sort of stuff. She thought I had lots of time for all that. I guess eventually she wanted me to meet someone like my father. Someone kind and good and dependable, who made a lot of money and always looked after his family. You don't meet that kind of guy in L.A. They're too busy looking in the mirror." The girl took a deep intake of air. "They were really happy, you know. They were married for twenty-seven years and, do you know something, I never heard them fight. They never even argued. Mom was so supportive of Dad. If we kids ever did anything or said anything to upset him, Mom would get really mad. She said he worked too hard all day to come home and let us upset him. She really protected him. She loved him so much. He was so funny, you know. Funny and warm. All my dates liked him. That's unusual. Guys are usually uncomfortable around fathers. But my dad never made anyone uncomfortable. Everybody liked him—loved him! Especially my mother." A loud sob escaped her lips. "This is killing her—you know that? She misses him so much. She walks around here like she's in a daze except that her eyes are going like crazy. Like she's talking to herself without using words. We try to talk to her but we don't know what to say! We can't reach her—" She was crying almost uncontrollably now. "Talk about crazy," she whispered. "The police found the murder weapon, you know. Yesterday. One of Dad's hammers. It was stuffed into the central vacuuming system. Still covered with blood."

Jill felt her arms tighten around the girl. Lisa cried quietly for several more minutes before straightening up again and wiping her eyes.

"I'm sorry," she said.

"Don't be."

"I feel like such a big baby."

"You're not," Jill assured her. "Your whole life has been turned upside down. You're bound to feel you've lost your balance."

"She seems much more settled today somehow," Lisa continued, standing up and pacing back and forth in front of Jill. "She wouldn't go to the funeral yesterday. She was very adamant. We had hoped that the funeral might finalize things for her, that seeing Dad's coffin being lowered into the ground might—wake her up, I guess, get her to talk about what happened. Tell us who did this awful thing. But she wouldn't go. She just sat on the bed and shook her head."

"The shock, Lisa, of what she went through, what she saw, the beating—"

"I know all that." Lisa stopped pacing. "It just doesn't make it any easier."

"She doesn't talk at all?"

Lisa stared directly into Jill's eyes. "She talks," she said softly. "About the weather, how nice it is to have Brian and me home. She asks questions, lots of questions about what we're doing. She listens. She's a great listener. She even gives advice. She listened to Michael for hours about his faith. But she doesn't say a word about my father. And when you mention anything about him, her eyes get that glazed expression and her face goes blank and that's the end of it."

Jill thought for several seconds, though there was no language to her thoughts, nothing to give them any cohesiveness. "I guess that's the only way she can cope right now."

"Don Eliot said that she spoke to you at the hospital, and we were hoping that maybe seeing you might, I don't know—"

"I'll do whatever I can," Jill offered.

Lisa returned to the sofa and sat down beside Jill, allowing Jill's arms to surround her, resting her head on the other woman's shoulder. Neither woman heard the entrance of the third who stood watching them in silence from the doorway.

"Hello, Jill," Beth's voice called softly, pleasantly.

Jill looked quickly in Beth's direction. The woman she saw was casually dressed in beige slacks and a light cotton shirt. She wore no makeup to hide her many bruises and her sun-streaked hair was short and swept away from her face. The wounds themselves had healed somewhat, their colors slightly muted, less angry, faded by time. Her right wrist was bandaged. As Beth came toward her, Jill detected a slight limp. Beneath the casual clothes, Beth held her body stiffly.

The two women embraced. When they pulled apart, Beth was smiling warmly. "I'm so glad to see you," she said. "You look terrific."

"I look terrible," Jill said automatically. "My hair frizzes up like steel wool in this humidity."

"And mine goes straight as a string," Beth laughed. "Bet you always wanted straight hair," she said conspiratorially. Jill nodded. "Sure," Beth agreed. "And I always wanted lots of curls. That's always the way it is. Let's sit down."

Lisa got quickly out of the way, moving to a chair across the room and letting her mother and Jill occupy the sofa.

"Hi, sweetheart," Beth said, acknowledging her daughter as they crossed paths.

"How do you feel?" Lisa asked.

"I'm fine," Beth said, strongly. "You're the one who doesn't look so hot. Why don't you go upstairs and lie down for a while like your brother?" Jill saw the hesitation in Lisa's eyes. "Go on," her mother urged. "Jill will take good care of me."

"Go ahead," Jill said. "It'll give your mother and me a chance to talk." That's what you want, isn't it? her eyes asked the younger woman, who seemed to suddenly comprehend. Lisa stood up.

"Can I make you some tea or anything?" she offered.

"Not for me," Beth said with a laugh. "They keep filling me up with tea. I've never peed so much in my life."

Jill laughed. "Not for me either," she said, feeling somewhat confused, a trifle disoriented. Far from being quiet and withdrawn, Beth Weatherby was relaxed and gregarious, as animated as Jill had seen her in a long time. It was as though she had totally blocked out any knowledge of her husband's death.

"How's David?" Beth asked after Lisa had left the room and her footsteps could be heard ascending the staircase.

"He's fine. Very busy."

"I'm sure," Beth said cryptically. "The office must be in a terrible state."

Beth's remark caught Jill by surprise. So, Beth *did* know; she *was* aware.

It was as if Beth could read her thoughts. "I don't want you to think I'm crazy, Jill," she began. "I know how upset everyone is around here. I know I'm the cause. But I'm just not ready to talk about it yet. Can you understand?" Jill couldn't but nodded anyway. "I know what happened that night. I know that Al is dead. And there's a lot that I have to say. But not yet. I have to understand it all first before I can talk about it." She paused. "I'm sorry. I know I'm probably being infuriatingly vague about this whole thing, but I'm just not ready yet to talk about what happened. Please bear with me." Again, Jill nodded. "*You* talk," Beth continued. "Tell me about how you always wanted straight hair, you silly lady. You're so gorgeous just the way you are."

Jill laughed out loud. "I thought you didn't want me to think you were crazy," she said, not sure if it was the proper thing to have said. The smile on Beth's face assured her that it was.

"Why do you always put yourself down?" Beth asked.

"I don't think I do," Jill answered. "I'm just realistic."

"What's your idea of a beautiful woman? Go on, I'm curious. Who do you think is gorgeous?"

Jill thought for several seconds. "Candice Bergen," she said finally. "Farrah Fawcett." She paused. "Nicole Clark," she added haltingly.

Beth's eyes registered each new name. "Candice Bergen, yes, lovely face, but the body is kind of ordinary; Farrah Fawcett has a lot of hair and thin lips but I guess she's pretty enough; Nicole Clark—yes, I'd have to say that Nicole is a beautiful girl." She chuckled. "But, who knows, Nicole Clark probably spends as many wasted hours in front of her mirror as the rest of us, wishing her hair was this way, not that, or that her nose were longer or thinner, or that her thighs weren't quite so rounded."

"You saw her thighs," Jill commented. "Did they look too round to you?"

"No," Beth confessed. "They looked perfect to me." She looked around the room at nothing in particular. "Well, maybe Nicole is one of those rare people who is happy with the way she looks. Maybe everything is exactly the way she wants it." Beth turned back to Jill. "She looks like the type of person who gets exactly what she wants, doesn't she?"

Jill held her breath. "She wants David."

"What?"

"I said she wants David."

"What do you mean, she wants him?"

"Exactly what you think."

"Oh, Jill," Beth said, laughing. "What makes you think that?"

"She told me."

"What?!"

"She told me that she wants him, that she intends to marry him, and please don't tell me she must have been joking—she wasn't. She isn't."

Beth digested the information. "So, that's what was going on at our exercise class that afternoon—"

"It's been going on all summer. Since the firm picnic. A real war of nerves. Only I'm afraid her nerves are stronger than mine."

"Does David know?"

Jill nodded. "He knows. I had to tell him."

"Why, for heaven's sake?"

Jill shrugged. "It just happened. If I hadn't, she'd have made sure he found out. Somehow. She always seems to have an alternative course of action ready."

"And? What was David's reaction?"

Again, Jill shrugged. "I don't know. At first I think he was partly annoyed, partly flattered. Now, I think he's mostly flattered. If he's annoyed with anyone, it's with me. And I don't know what to do about it." Jill stood up, and began pacing in the same way Lisa had done. "I've never felt so manipulated in my whole life. I feel like a rat in a maze. Only every path I take is the wrong one. And I'm completely powerless. I don't know.

Maybe I should have let David say something to her in the beginning. He offered to." She turned to Beth. "Except that I know what she would have said if he'd confronted her. She'd have gone all soft and cried, told him how embarrassed and sorry she was, how she was all alone in Chicago, how much she'd admired him, how he was everything she'd ever wanted, the same speech she gave me when *I* confronted her. And David would have stood there looking at this poor, sensitive, terribly vulnerable girl who is not only unquestionably beautiful but who also obviously adores him, and I'd still be standing here not knowing what to do. If I make an issue, I look like a jealous, suspicious wife. If I ignore it and hope that she goes away, she'll take two giant steps forward. Either way, the result will be the same."

"Maybe not," Beth said. "You're forgetting David in all this. He *does* have something to say about the outcome."

Jill stood very still and stared down at Beth Weatherby. "I never forget David," she said, fighting back tears. "Why do you think I'm so worried?" She lowered herself down beside Beth and sat helplessly for several minutes feeling the tears as they ran down her cheeks.

"Oh, Jill—" Beth began, taking Jill's hands in her own.

"I know the kind of man he is, Beth. I was there once myself, remember. He loves women. Lots of women. I knew that when I married him. Hell, I knew it the moment I laid eyes on him. A man who looks like David just has to snap his fingers and half a dozen women come running. I've seen it. We'll be at a party and he's immediately the center of attention. The women are all over him. They stare at him from across the room. Even *I* can read the smoke signals loud and clear. Do you know that sometimes it's like I'm not even there? They ignore me. It's like I don't exist. And if they do acknowledge my presence it's almost worse, because then they get this shocked expression on their faces, like, my God, what is this gorgeous hunk doing with a woman as plain as she is—"

"Jill—"

"No, all right, I'm not plain. I'm not ugly, or even unattractive. I am an attractive woman, a little different, unusual maybe. Certainly nothing that warrants putting a paper bag over my head. But I am definitely not beautiful. I wouldn't appear on anybody's ten-best list, and I know it. And David isn't blind. He knows it. And so here I am, this fairly average-looking female married to a very non-average-looking male, and sometimes I feel so—inadequate, I guess is the best way to describe it. I know that all these women are out there eyeing my husband, wanting him, wanting to make love to him, knowing that he knows it too, and I keep wondering, what is this man doing with me? How long can I keep him? How long before he starts getting restless again? And some nights when we get into bed, I'm just so goddamn grateful that he's there beside me. I feel so lucky—"

"David's the lucky one, Jill."

Jill smiled, wiping away the tears. "You sound like my mother." Beth laughed quietly. "I'm lucky, too," Jill said.

"Yes, you are," Beth agreed. "David is a very charming man. I've always liked him."

"Everybody likes him. That's my problem."

"Everybody isn't his wife," Beth reminded her. "You are."

Jill nodded. "There's a big difference between being a man's wife and being his mistress," she began, "and I feel somewhat qualified to speak on the subject, having been both." She looked away, as if searching for just the right words. "The other woman sees only the virtues. She sees the romantic hideaways and the expensive little dinners for two, and she's so thrilled if he can ever stay the whole night that she doesn't even notice that he snores or his feet smell or he takes up the whole bed. Everything about him is exciting—even his faults—because she's never sure when—or if—she's going to be able to see him again. It's all very—dramatic. Very high tragedy." She paused. "When you're the wife, it's more like a comedy, a very black one." She laughed at her own choice of similes. "Suddenly you're aware of all the unpleasant odors and habits and, well, like that chain letter you gave me at the picnic— God, I broke the chain, do you think this is all a direct result?" The two women laughed quietly. Jill stood up and started pacing again. "The wife doesn't see as many of those expensive little dinners, and when she does, she also gets to see the Visa bill at the end of the month, and she gets to hear all the complaining about how much money they spend, and those dinners are rarely for two anyway. There are children and in-laws and partners. And reality. And suddenly when she looks at her husband, she still loves him, all right, but her eyes have lost that unquestioning adoration they once held. It's gone. And he misses it. And there are all these sweet and lovely little women out there, in the office, on the street, and they're all looking at him with these adoring eyes, and what can you do? How can you fight reality?"

There were several seconds of silence before Beth spoke. "Has David—before—?" She broke off, reluctant to give words to the thought.

"Has he been unfaithful?" Jill asked for her. Beth nodded. Jill took a deep breath. "I think so," she said aloud for the first time. "In my gut, I know of at least one time—" She felt the tears pushing against her eyes again, felt her throat constricting. "But the whole point is that I don't know for sure! And as long as I'm not sure, then I don't have to really confront my feelings or make any decisions. Knowing—to actually know that David was sleeping with another woman—to have to live with that knowledge. Well, there *is* such a thing as too much reality. I don't know what I'd do. And I guess that's what scares me most as far as Nicole Clark is concerned, because there's no way she'll ever be satisfied to just have her one night with him and then quietly disappear. She'll make sure I find out, and then—I don't know." Jill threw her head back in despair, sniffing loudly and then angrily wiping the tears from her face. "Goddamn it," she said, straightening up. "I'm talking like I've lost him already. And I haven't," she stated firmly. "And I won't!"

Beth jumped to her feet. "Now you're talking."

Jill fell into Beth Weatherby's arms. "I feel like such an idiot," Jill said, wiping at her nose with a kleenex she found in her skirt pocket. "Here you are with everything that's happening to you, and here I am complaining about nothing, for God's sake."

Beth Weatherby pushed one of Jill's stray hairs away from her face. "You never complain about anything," she assured her. "And please, don't worry about me, Jill. My problems are all over." Her voice grew very soft. "I did it, Jill," she whispered. "I killed Al. I killed my husband."

Chapter 17

Jill sat behind the wheel of her car and watched her hands shake. She was afraid to turn the key in the ignition, to start the car, unsure how her body would react once in motion. She had to get her feelings under control before she could control anything as potentially lethal as an automobile. Lethal, she thought, choosing to sit and do nothing for several minutes, to allow herself time to think, to calm her trembling fingers, to absorb what she had just been told. "I did it, Jill," she heard Beth repeat. "I killed Al. I killed my husband." As simple as that. As straightforward. No regrets, no hysteria, no tears. Just a calm statement of fact. ("Just the facts, ma'am," she heard Jack Webb mutter at her ear.) Beth had offered no further explanation; Jill had been too stunned to ask for one. And then both Lisa and her brother Brian had suddenly materialized at the foot of the stairs and Beth's eyes had slowly closed and opened again, void of all expression. Jill knew instinctively that what Beth had just told her was not meant to be shared. Too overwhelmed even to speak, she muttered something in Lisa's direction and stumbled out of the house. She had been sitting in her car for close to five minutes, and she still felt too unsure of herself to move.

She stared down at her hands. The nails were all uneven lengths, of no particular shape or design. A few broken chips of polish clung tenuously to several cuticles. She hadn't bothered to remove them. Around the nails, her skin had been picked at and nibbled on, a habit she had often vowed to break, but one she clung to like a child's security blanket. The back of her right hand bore the trace of a small childhood scar, received when she had pulled a hot iron down on top of her. They were strong hands, capable hands. Hands a palmist had once regarded with glee, claiming he barely knew where to begin, there was such an abundance of character to be read, telling her joyfully that she was one of the world's true eccentrics and that insanity no doubt traveled in her family. Could these hands kill, she wondered?

She pictured herself digging through her kitchen drawers for a hammer. (Did they even own a hammer?) She felt herself reach for it, move down the hallway toward the bedroom where David lay sleeping, saw her arm raise the hammer high into the air and watched it fall with sickening speed, stopping just short of David's head. She closed her eyes against the image. No, she thought, she could never do what Beth Weatherby claimed to have done.

Jill looked back toward the gray brick house. It was impossible, she decided, thinking of the gentle woman inside. There was simply no way Beth was capable of such an act unless she had suffered a complete mental collapse, a breakdown for which she could hardly be held accountable. Yet she seemed so rational now, so calm and in control. The whole situation was absurd. Jill simply could not accept Beth's confession as truth. There was no way Beth Weatherby could have murdered her husband.

Feeling the issue resolved inside herself, Jill turned the key in the ignition and started the car, pulling the gray Volvo away from the curb and driving quickly away, watching the exquisite residential streets disappear behind her as she headed toward the highway. For the first time in several years, she regretted that she didn't have school to go to. The fall semester didn't start for several weeks, and even the round of loathsome staff meetings didn't begin until the following Monday, so Jill was left entirely at loose ends, feeling in need of somewhere to go, something to do. Anything to keep Beth's words from replaying in her mind.

She spotted a phone booth and swerved the car into a sweeping U-turn, stopping directly in front of the graffiti-strewn booth and fishing in her purse for change. She noticed her hands were still shaking as she dialed.

"Weatherby, Ross," came the receptionist's familiar voice.

"David Plumley, please," Jill stated, wondering what she was planning to tell him.

"Mr. Plumley's office."

"Diane?"

"Yes. Can I help you?"

"It's Jill."

The secretary sounded surprised. "Oh, I'm sorry. I didn't recognize your voice. You sounded—different."

Jill tried to steady her voice. "Is David around?"

"He's with a client."

"Could you interrupt him, please? It's important." Why did she say that? Was she planning on telling David about Beth's confession?

David's voice came on the phone, concerned, even anxious. "Jill? Are you all right?"

"Oh, yes, I'm fine. I just wondered—whether we could have lunch together. I just noticed it's almost one o'clock."

"I have to be in court at one o'clock," he said, his voice becoming low, losing its quality of concern. "Is that why you had Diane interrupt my meeting?"

"I just came from seeing Beth," Jill ventured.

"And?"

Jill felt her shoulders slump. "Nothing," she said. "I did most of the talking."

"Jill, can't we discuss this later?"

Jill nodded, forgetting that he couldn't see her. "What court will you be in? Maybe I'll come and watch you."

"I don't think that would be a good idea," he said quickly.

"It's not a very interesting case. You'd only be bored. Look—I have to go. I'll speak to you later."

"Will you be home right after court?" she asked, realizing even as the words were leaving her mouth that he had already hung up. "Sure," she said, replacing the receiver. "Call me later."

She wasn't sure how or why she had ended up in front of Rita Carrington's exercise class, but seeing the old rusty brick building suddenly before her, Jill quickly pulled the car into the adjacent parking lot and went inside. Her adrenaline was still pumping wildly, threatening to push itself out through her extremities. Perhaps a little exercise would be a good way to get herself under control.

She was in the locker room before she realized she didn't have her exercise suit with her. "Damn," she said, dejectedly, allowing her body to sink down onto the waiting bench.

"Hi," came the voice from behind her. "Haven't seen you in a few weeks."

Jill looked up to see a sweat-covered Ricki Elfer, nude except for a towel around her neck. "Things have been rather hectic lately," she said quietly, wondering whether Ricki had recognized Beth Weatherby from her picture in the paper and was about to pepper her with questions.

"You're telling me," Ricki concurred. "You taking a class now?"

"Forgot my leotard."

"Great. You can join us for lunch. Me and a couple of the girls. We thought we'd go across the street."

Jill smiled. "Sounds good," she said.

"Great. I'll just grab a quick shower and be right back."

Jill watched Ricki Elfer's expansive derrière disappear around the row of lockers. It was a strange sensation, she realized, to carry on a normal conversation when one of the parties was fully dressed and the other was totally naked. She closed her eyes and tried to rid her mind of all thought except her upcoming lunch. If she couldn't exercise, she decided, the next best thing to do was eat.

"Jill, this is Denise and Terri," Ricki Elfer said, introducing her to the two women who were already seated at the restaurant table. "Wow, that was quite a workout today," Ricki exclaimed, sitting down. Jill took the remaining seat and nodded hello to the other women.

"She gets tougher every day," the short brunette named Denise agreed. "Not even my old dance classes were this tough."

"Well, you have to admit, she looks wonderful," Jill offered.

"Who?" Ricki asked. "Rita Carrington?" Jill nodded. "I should hope so," Ricki smiled, eyeing the salad bar.

Jill agreed. "Yeah, I guess she should if she's teaching exercise classes half the day."

"Exercise? Are you kidding?" Ricki laughed. "You don't get tits like those from exercise. You get them from God or you get them from a surgeon. Last I heard, Rita Carrington doesn't believe in God."

"If you're a surgeon, you think of the two as one and the same," offered Terri, a slim, muscular blonde. "My husband is a doctor," she further explained.

The women laughed. "Rita Carrington's had surgery on her breasts?" Jill asked.

"On her boobs, on her stomach, on her tushy," Ricki Elfer recited. "Everything tucked and tightened and lifted. Haven't you noticed how her boobs never move, even when the rest of her is shaking all over? That's the dead giveaway. She turns right, her boobs still face straight ahead."

"I also heard she had a face-lift," Denise added.

"A face-lift?" Jill asked. "She's so young!"

"She'll never see forty-five again," Ricki told her, as the waiter approached.

The women ordered lunch and a liter of wine. Jill chose a bowl of soup and the salad bar, eventually allowing herself to be talked into ordering dessert.

"This is delicious," Ricki said, devouring the last of her chocolate mousse. "I shouldn't go to these exercise classes. They give me too big an appetite! How's your fruit flan?"

"Good," Jill said. "Would you like some?"

"Just a taste," Ricki nodded, her fork already on Jill's plate. Jill took a long sip of her coffee, feeling the wine dancing

near the base of her neck. Whenever she'd had just the right
amount to drink—not too much or too little—her neck would
begin to feel weightless, as if it were about to separate from the
rest of her body. The lunch had been just what the doctor ordered. This lunch, not lunch with her husband, or watching him
in court. She pictured the crowded courtroom, saw David sitting at his table, Nicole Clark at his side. Was that why he had
been so reluctant for her to come that afternoon? Had Nicole
Clark already made her reservation? Used up the one remaining ticket?

"What's your friend doing these days?" Ricki suddenly asked
her.

"My friend?"

"The lady you usually come with. She hasn't been around
lately."

"She's kind of busy," Jill told her. Maybe Ricki never read
the papers.

"Talk about busy," Terri piped up, pushing her dessert plate
away, and gulping the rest of her coffee. "I have to get home.
I'm interviewing housekeepers this afternoon."

"Good luck," Denise said, her voice filled with frustration
and understanding.

"You know what they say, don't you?" Ricki Elfer asked.
"If she can find the place, hire her."

"What happened to Gunilla?"

"Who?" Jill asked.

"Yes, that's actually her name. Sounds like one of Cin-
derella's nasty stepsisters, I know," Terri agreed. "She's
Swedish. Twenty years old. I got her through an agency six
months ago. She's supposed to help me with the housework and
with looking after Justin and Scotty. A week ago, she informed
me she doesn't want to be a mother's helper, that she doesn't
like having to cater to a two-year-old and a five-year-old. I
reminded her that on her application she specifically requested
two children, aged two and five. You got exactly what you said
you wanted, I told her. She said it wasn't the way she thought it
would be."

"What ever is?" Jill asked.

"Anyway, I decided to try for a housekeeper this time instead of an au pair. The first one is supposedly arriving at three o'clock, and it's almost that now."

"My God," Denise exclaimed, pulling some money out of her purse and dropping it on the table, "I didn't realize it was so late. I have to pick Rodney up at school."

"I guess we should go too," Jill said reluctantly.

"Finish your coffee," Ricki told her. "I still have a few minutes."

The women exchanged their goodbyes and made their exits. When Jill looked back, the waiter had already refilled her coffee cup. "So," she said, addressing her attention to the woman on the other side of the table, "did you make any decisions about tying your tubes or having a baby?"

"Sanity prevailed," Ricki told her. "Paul's going to have a vasectomy."

Jill was genuinely surprised. "I thought you said that if Paul had a vasectomy, you wouldn't be able to fool around—"

"Sounds like something I'd say," Ricki agreed. "I speak a lot of rot sometimes."

"You don't play around?" Jill asked, a little disappointed.

"No," Ricki said, her voice suddenly serious. "Not on Paul. I did—with the others. But when you finally get yourself a good one—and Paul is a good one—you don't take any chances. This is my third marriage, and the first one I'm really proud of. You know what I mean?" Jill nodded. "You don't take silly chances when you finally stumble into a right decision. I like marriage. I believe in it. Christ, I'd have to—I keep doing it." Jill smiled. "No," Ricki Elfer said, shaking her head, "if you're smart—and if I'm not always smart, at least I'm not always stupid—when you grab ahold of something good, you don't fuck up."

Both women finished their coffee and smiled at each other in silence.

That night David moved restlessly beside her in bed.

"Can't you sleep?" Jill asked him, his persistent tossing keeping her awake.

"I'm too sore," he said. "My whole body aches."

Jill sat up and ran her hand down his side. "Do you want me to give you a backrub?"

There was a second's silence, then David turned gingerly onto his stomach. "Okay, yeah, that might be nice."

Jill immediately straddled his back and put her hands on his shoulders.

"Ow, that hurts," he said, his body resisting her touch.

"I haven't done anything yet," Jill protested.

"Not my shoulders," he told her, "my back. Get off me, you weigh a ton."

"Thanks a lot." Jill moved so that she was on her knees beside him. "Where does it hurt?" she asked.

"Where doesn't it?" came his answer.

"Just how many games of squash did you play?"

"Three—and it's racquetball, not squash."

"Well, I think you overdid it for somebody who hasn't played for as long as you haven't."

"You made me feel guilty—ow! Watch it, huh?—about wasting all that money, so I tried to make up for it."

"You're trying to tell me it's my fault?"

"Exactly."

"Figures."

David flipped over suddenly. "God, you give a rotten massage," he said, smiling, putting his arm around her and drawing her to him.

"Who'd you play with?" Jill asked.

"Pete Rogers," David answered. "One of the students. Actually, they won't be students much longer. Another week and they're called to the bar. God, I'm sore." He kissed her cheek. "Sorry I spoiled the little candlelit dinner you had planned. It would have been nice."

"Well, you didn't know," Jill shrugged. "I just decided to do it at the spur of the moment."

"I'm sorry, honey, I just needed to get out and pound something. Al's funeral still has me very shaky." He looked at his wife. "You never did tell me what Beth had to say."

"Nothing really," Jill lied, wondering if, like always, he would see through her. "She didn't say anything. I did most of the talking."

"She's got to start talking soon," David said, almost absently. If he didn't believe her, Jill realized, he wasn't letting on. "What did you do for the rest of the afternoon?"

"I went to my exercise class. There's a woman there I really like—"

"Good," David said. Jill recognized the word and the tone. It meant he wasn't interested. Nevertheless, Jill decided to press ahead.

"She'd been trying to decide whether to tie her tubes or have a baby," Jill ventured. David said nothing. "David," Jill whispered, "I think we have to come to some sort of decision on that subject too."

"What did this woman decide?" David asked, his voice tense.

"Her husband is having a vasectomy," Jill said, now sorry she had brought the issue to light.

"Sounds good to me," David said, almost casually.

"Don't be flip, David. I'm being serious."

"So am I," he said, turning his head in her direction, his eyes searching hers. "I've told you before—I don't want any more children. I have two already I haven't done a very good job with. I'm sorry, Jill," he said, catching the look on her face. "I know you wanted children, but let's face it, I'm not a very good father, and I don't have the energy or the patience—or the desire—to do it again."

"You sound very definite."

"I am very definite."

"Where does that leave me?" Jill asked reluctantly.

"Where do you want to be?"

"With you," she said, after a slight pause, her voice barely audible.

"Then that's where you are," he said, kissing her forehead.

"I love you," she said, feeling her voice growing softer with each fresh remark.

"I love you, too, sweetheart," he answered. "Come on, turn over, get some sleep. Let me hold you."

Jill allowed her body to be turned and held, wishing she could crawl inside him, under his skin where she would be safe. So, it had been decided for her, she thought, feeling the muscles in his legs beginning to twitch. She was not to have children. She closed her eyes. She couldn't blame David. It was something he'd already been through, something he'd already done. He didn't want to do it again. To start over from the beginning. She wasn't even surprised. She'd known this would be his decision.

His arm shifted underneath her. She felt him pulling away, withdrawing. "I'm sorry, honey," he was saying, "I've got to turn over."

Jill moved so that David was free to turn around. Normally, she would have moved her body with his, both of them reversing their positions with neither thought nor effort. Tonight, she clung stubbornly to her side of the bed, her body's posture imitating how she felt—isolated, tied up in knots, and barely hanging on.

Chapter 18

The feeling of déjà vu was almost overwhelming. The long table, the uncomfortable chairs, the smoke and the people responsible for it, their tired voices repeating even more tired speeches, all of which Jill was convinced she had heard in their exact entirety a year before. (Welcome to the start of another school year. The fall semester is perhaps the most important term, setting, as it does, the tone for the rest of the year. We wish to welcome—etc., etc.) Jill looked up and down the old, badly scarred table, the people on either side probably not much different from the network people she used to confront across similar tables during the weekly story conferences of the past. Their interests were similar; many of the teachers had, like herself, come from prior jobs in television and radio. And yet, they were not the same. Something was missing, she thought, searching the other faces, each wearing the same tired and bored expression that her own undoubtedly held. The sense of commitment, she decided, a commitment to something larger than simply getting through the day, was flagrantly absent. Though there were obviously many in the room with a deep dedication to what they were doing, there was simply not the same kind of energy flowing through everyone's veins. It was precisely that missing energy that she missed so much—the constant struggle to get your ideas heard and accepted and ultimately recorded and broadcast.

Jill looked down at the floor. She was in deep trouble, she knew, if she was thinking this way already, on this the first day of this the most important semester of the school year. It didn't bode well.

The phone call came halfway into Jack McCreary's lengthy explanation of the recent budget cuts. Jill had honestly thought she was following the familiar monotone closely, and was somewhat startled to find that the sudden tap on her shoulder brought her abruptly back from a heated story conference at the studio, where she had been bowling them over with the sheer brilliance and audacity of her ideas, to the claustrophobic confines of the crowded campus meeting room, where reality was holding court.

"Phone call for you," one of the office secretaries confided, leaning close, trying not to draw attention. "He said it was important."

Jill looked puzzled, but the secretary's shrug indicated she knew nothing else, and so Jill pushed back her chair and self-consciously followed the tiny woman out into the hallway and toward the office. The secretary barely stretched to five feet and Jill felt like a giant trailing after her. Why do they always send the short ones when they want me? she wondered.

"Line three," the woman indicated before sitting down behind her desk.

Jill picked up the phone and pressed the appropriate extension. "Hello?"

"The shit's hit the fan," David's voice said instead of hello.

"What are you talking about?" Jill asked, startled.

"Beth just confessed."

"What?"

"You heard me. Beth Weatherby just confessed—she says she did it—she murdered Al."

"I don't believe it," Jill muttered, feeling for the chair she knew was somewhere behind her and sitting down. She noticed that all typing and other general office activity had ceased. None of the secretaries was making even the slightest effort to conceal her curiosity. "That's crazy!" she whispered, hearing Beth's voice echo in her other ear. "I did it, Jill," it repeated. "I killed my husband."

"Not as crazy as what else she says," David continued.

"What else does she say?" Jill found herself gripping the side of her chair.

David cleared his throat. "She says it was self-defense."

"Self-defense? You mean, Al was attacking her?"

"No, she admits Al was fast asleep when she started hitting him."

"I don't understand."

"It gets better."

"Tell me."

David gave an abrupt and angry laugh, strangling it in his throat before it could grow. "She claims that he's been beating her for the past twenty-seven years, if you can swallow that one, and that the night she killed him, he'd gone to bed in a drunken rage promising to finish her off once and for all when he woke up." Jill could feel him shaking his head. "Can you imagine her expecting anyone to believe that garbage?"

Jill pictured Al Weatherby dancing romantically with Beth at firm parties, laughing at her jokes, displaying her proudly to his friends and cohorts, holding her hand, sitting close beside her at every opportunity, supporting her when she played badly at bridge. David was right—what Beth was saying was impossible to believe. It couldn't be true. "She must be having some sort of a breakdown," Jill said quietly. "I guess Don will plead temporary insanity."

"I don't know what Don's plans are. He's as confused as the rest of us. She didn't even consult him about her confession. Just called an impromptu press conference. Don heard about it over the radio. Not even her kids knew what she was planning. She just went ahead. The office is in a total shambles—nobody's getting anything done. I'll probably have to work late tonight."

"Jason and Laurie are coming for dinner," she reminded him quickly, surprised she was still capable of remembering such lesser realities.

"Shit," he swore under his breath. "All right, I'll try to be home." He paused. "Good God, what else could happen?" he asked nervously.

"She told me," Jill muttered to herself, "but I didn't believe her."

There was a second's silence, then David spoke. "What do you mean, she told you? Told you what? What are you talking about?"

Jill realized she had spoken out loud, was aware of the growing alarm and even anger in her husband's voice. "When I went to see her last week," she said softly, reluctantly, sensing how David would react to her admission.

"She told you what exactly?" David was demanding.

"Not anything about the self-defense or about Al's beating her," Jill quickly explained. "Just that she'd killed him," she added weakly.

"Just that she'd killed him," David repeated disdainfully. "You didn't think that was important enough to tell me? To tell Don? Or her children? Especially after they begged you to try and help!"

"Please don't be angry, David," Jill pleaded. "I was so startled. I didn't know what to think. I thought, maybe—"

"You didn't think, period," he exclaimed angrily. "How could you not say anything, Jill? You know everyone's been tearing their hair out!"

"I didn't think it was my place to say anything to anyone," she tried to explain. "Beth said she needed time to think it all through. I thought maybe she'd had a breakdown, gone a little crazy—"

"Sure, crazy like a fox," David interrupted. "The only thing she needed to think through is this ridiculous story of hers. You gave her a week to get it down to a science. Now, all she has to do is plead temporary insanity and she'll probably never even see the inside of a jail cell. In the meantime, she'll drag a wonderful man's name and memory through the mud. The goddamn newspapers will have a field day. I mean, it's just the kind of story they love—big-shot lawyer was a wife-beater for a quarter of a century. They'll eat it up!"

"David, calm down—"

"How could you do it, Jill?" She could see the look of disbelief on his face through the phone wires. "If nothing else,
how could you keep it from *me?*"

Jill swallowed hard. "I wanted to tell you," she began. "I
thought about telling you. That afternoon, I called you at the
office. I wanted to see you. But you were busy, and after that, I
just couldn't. I'm sorry. I just knew that Beth had told me what
she did in confidence, and I couldn't bring myself to say anything. I kept hoping you'd figure out I was keeping something
from you, the way you usually do, and press me about it, get it
out of me the way you did about—" She broke off. About
Nicole Clark, she finished in silence. What were you so busy
thinking about that you didn't notice I was holding something
back?

David's voice was angry. "I don't know what you're talking
about, Jill! Are you trying to tell me that it's my fault for not
guessing what Beth told you?! That I should have figured out
you were keeping something from me?"

"No, of course not," she said. Yes, that's it exactly, she
thought. You always did before.

There was a long, uncomfortable pause. "I have to go,"
David said finally. "I only called to tell you about Beth. I didn't
realize it would be old news."

"David—"

The receiver went dead in her ear. She sat for a minute without moving, then she replaced the receiver, stood up and, pointedly ignoring the curious stares of the secretaries, walked from
the room.

The mood at the dinner table wasn't much better. David had
walked in just as Laurie and Jason were beginning an argument
on the merits of a certain musical group and one glance at the
disgusted look on his face told Jill to stay calm and quiet.

"Can't you keep these kids under control?" he had snapped
in her direction, as he took his seat at the table. Jill had said
nothing, noting only the surprised look on his children's faces
as he spoke. He had never talked to her in such an abrupt fashion before—at least not in their presence. Jill had gone quietly

into the kitchen, retrieved his food from the microwave and placed it gingerly in front of him.

"What is it?" he asked, barely looking at it.

"Pork sirloin," she answered.

"How much?"

"What do you mean? How many pounds?"

"How much did it cost?" he asked testily.

Jill looked startled, felt caught off balance. "I don't remember," she said, sitting down. "I've had it in the freezer for a while."

David looked over at his children's plates. "You keep saying they don't eat anything! Why would you cook an expensive piece of meat when you know it'll all go to waste?"

"I'm-m-m eating!" Jason stammered.

"I'm not very hungry," Laurie whispered.

"That's all right," Jill said quickly, feeling her appetite disappearing. "Neither am I."

"Oh, great," David barked. "I have a good idea—next time you kids come to dinner, why don't we just burn some money?"

"Oh, Daddy," Laurie said.

"Don't you 'Oh, Daddy me,' young lady. You look like a walking skeleton and I'm sick of it. You don't leave this table until you finish everything on that plate."

Jill watched as Laurie's eyes welled up with tears. Laurie immediately lowered her head, staring down at her plate. It seemed for several minutes as if no one breathed, and then slowly, Laurie moved her fingers to her fork and stabbed at some of the meat on her plate, bringing a forkful to her mouth. The two never connected, Laurie suddenly dropping the fork to the table and running from the room.

Jill immediately followed the girl into the bedroom despite David's loud protest. Laurie was sitting on the edge of the bed, and while the mirror was located directly in front of her and she was staring straight at it, she didn't appear to be seeing anything at all. Her eyes were stubbornly blank and dry, her lower lip quivering, her upper lip decidedly stiff.

"Laurie," Jill began before she was cut off.

"Could you please leave me alone?" the girl asked.

Jill hesitated. "I just wanted to tell you that you're not the one he's really angry at."

"Could have fooled me," Laurie pouted.

"Well," Jill said gently, "adults are funny people. They don't always say what they mean, and they don't always yell at the person they want to yell at. Sometimes they're not even sure why they're angry and it just comes out at whoever's available, whoever's the easiest target, which tonight happens to be you." Laurie continued to stare straight ahead. "Actually, it's me your father's angry at. Some things are happening now that have everybody more than a little confused—" She tried to read something from the young girl's expression, but got nothing. "I just wanted you to know that it honestly has nothing to do with you." Jill stood for several seconds before moving toward the doorway.

"Thank you," the small voice said quietly from the bed. Jill turned in surprise, saw that the girl was still staring with intense absence at the mirror, wondered briefly whether she had said anything at all, and then returned to the dining room.

Jason and his father were sitting in icy silence at the table. Jason, whether out of hunger or intimidation, had finished everything on his plate. For the first time since she had met the boy, he actually looked glad to see her.

"So, how was the first day of school?" Jill asked him, pointedly ignoring her husband.

Jason's face suddenly looked as disgusted as his father's. "Boring," he said. "R-real boring."

"The word you're looking for is 'really,'" David said sharply. "*Really* boring. It's an adverb, as in *how* boring is it? It's *really* boring. I, for one, am getting *real* tired of all this California slang. *I* find it *real* boring."

Jason regarded his father as if the poor man had lost control of his senses. "Are you all right?" he asked.

"I'm real fine," David answered.

"Good," Jill piped in. "Then we can change the subject. Who's your homeroom teacher?" she asked, smiling at Jason.

"Mr. F-Fraser," the boy answered. "H-He's okay."

"Your command of the English language amazes me," David said sarcastically.

This time Jason lowered his head, obviously dangerously close to tears. Jill put down her fork in disgust and turned sharply to David. "Don't you think you've said enough for tonight? Are you a professor of language all of a sudden? If you're still angry at me, that's fine. Yell at me. But your kids did not come here tonight for you to take it out on them. Now you've ruined a perfectly good dinner with these histrionics; you have one child very upset in the bedroom and another one here at the table. Instead of just one person in a bad mood, you now have four."

"I'm not a child," Jason spat flawlessly.

"Oh, be quiet," David snapped. "Are you so stupid you can't tell when someone's defending you?"

"I don't need her to defend me!" Jason shouted, pushing his chair back from the table, looking in a rage at Jill. "Who asked you, anyway?" he continued, furious. "Why can't you just keep your big mouth out of everything?" He stormed from the room. Jill pictured the two Plumley adolescents sitting side by side at the foot of her queen-size bed. She wasn't sure if she was more surprised by his outburst or by the ferocious ease with which it had been delivered.

"Well," Jill said, starting to clear the table, "a classic case of transference. You're angry at me but you don't want to yell at me in front of the kids, so you transfer your anger directly to them and you yell at them. Then Jason gets angry at you but can't summon the necessary courage to scream at his own father, so he does the next best thing, which is to scream at his nasty stepmother. So—you should be happy. I got yelled at, after all." She took an armload of dishes into the kitchen and piled them inside the dishwasher.

David sat at the dining room table for several minutes without moving, then he brought his plate, largely untouched, into the kitchen.

"I'm not very hungry either," he said, laying his plate down on the counter. Jill said nothing. "I guess I better go and apologize to the kids."

"That's probably a good idea," Jill agreed, wondering if he was about to extend the apology to herself. "I'm sorry," he began. Jill regarded him hopefully, ready to instantly forgive him. "About the dinner," he continued, then turned his back and disappeared down the hallway.

It was a little after eight o'clock when the buzzer sounded. Jill was sitting alone in the den rereading the Classified section of the morning paper ("Wanted—tall, muscular god of the Greek variety who likes dancing through golden showers and understands a little French"). David had left about fifteen minutes before to drive the kids home. He couldn't be back already, Jill thought, heading toward the kitchen. Anyway, he wouldn't buzz from downstairs. He had a key.

She approached the intercom next to the phone and pressed the buzzer to speak. "Yes?"

"Jilly? It's Don Eliot. Is David home?"

Jill felt her heart begin to race, an unwanted cocoon of guilt beginning to wrap its way around her body. "He just went out to drive his kids home," she told the criminal attorney. "He should be back pretty soon, if you'd like to come up and wait."

"Fine," he said. "We're coming up."

Jill pressed the buzzer which allowed the door in the lobby to open and walked to the door of her apartment, opening it slightly and peering out at the long corridor, listening for the sound of the elevator. Had David spoken to Don after their phone conversation that afternoon? Had he told the other lawyer of her alleged deceit, her prior knowledge of Beth's admitted guilt? Would he, too, make her feel like a traitor, an untrustworthy ally who had betrayed all their confidences?

The familiar clicking of the elevator cables interrupted the drama of her thoughts, and she heard elevator doors opening and closing down the hallway, followed immediately by the sound of voices. It was only as they turned the corner and came into view that Jill realized exactly what it was that Don Eliot had said only minutes before. "We're coming up," his words now echoed. We, plural, not I, singular.

"Hello, Don," Jill said pleasantly, shaking his hand as he walked through the door into her apartment.

"Hi, Jilly," he said, obviously upset by the day's developments but not upset enough to have already talked to David.

"You remember Nicki, don't you?" he added, almost as an afterthought.

Jill watched as Nicole Clark, stunning in shades of purple and black, put first one foot and then the other inside her front door. She's in my home, Jill thought, swallowing hard as she watched Nicole's eyes absorb everything that lay before her. She's invading my territory—looking at my belongings, passing silent judgment on my taste, touching, examining, leaving her mark like a dog pissing on the side of a lamppost, Jill thought, relishing the image. Stealing my sense of privacy like a thief in the night. That's what she is, Jill decided, satisfied with the metaphor. A thief in the night.

"I'm sure she remembers me," Nicole said with pleasant confidence, cutting past Jill directly into the living room where she was already sitting down, making herself quite comfortable, when Jill finally summoned up the courage to join them.

Chapter 19

It was almost another half hour before David returned home.

Jill moved from her position on one of the wing chairs (Don sat on the other, with Nicole between them on the sofa) as soon as she heard the key turning in the lock, and went to the door to greet him.

"Don's here," she whispered as he walked inside.

He didn't wait for further explanation, simply moving by her into the living room, laying his wallet and his car keys on top of the stereo as he went. Jill was behind him, unable to see the expression on his face when he saw Nicole. "Don, Nicki," he said easily. "When did you get here?"

Jill watched as David moved to occupy her former position on the large wing chair, feeling very much an outsider in her own quarters, not sure whether to join the three attorneys or leave them alone, retreating to the den or the bedroom like a good little wife.

"Well, what are you going to do, Jill?" asked David, reading her thoughts. "Stand there? Sit down?"

Jill realized that the only place to sit was on the sofa next to

Nicole, affording her husband a fine view for comparison. Jill knew that her jeans-clad body and pink-slippered feet had no chance against the rich silks and high heels of Nicole Clark.

"I'll make some coffee," she said, retreating to the kitchen.

"We got here about thirty minutes ago," she heard Don Eliot say. "Probably just after you left."

"I had to drive the kids home," David explained.

"So Jill was telling us," Nicole offered. Jill didn't like the sound of her name on the other woman's lips.

Jill quickly poured the necessary amount of coffee and water into the coffee machine and waited for it to brew. After half an hour of numbing small talk, she was eager to hear what these two people had come to say.

"So, what's up?" she heard David ask. "Something else happen?"

"I declined to defend Beth Weatherby," Don said solemnly.

"He's feeling very guilty," Nicole quickly explained. "I suggested we come here and talk to you."

Jill felt a sinking sensation at the pit of her stomach. She wasn't sure if it was Don's withdrawal of support for Beth Weatherby or Nicole's subsequent suggestion to see David which was responsible.

"I'm glad you did," she heard David say. "What happened?"

Jill re-entered the room as Don was discussing Beth's confession. "First of all," he was saying, "as an attorney and her friend, I'm appalled that she would do such a thing, make a public confession without even consulting me—"

"She's very confused," Jill interrupted without meaning to, putting a small tray with coffee mugs and bowls of cream and sugar on the square glass coffee table in their midst. "It doesn't sound as if she knows what she's doing."

"I think she knows exactly what she's doing," Jill heard David say, and only a second later realized it had been Nicole who had spoken. Reluctantly, she walked around Don Eliot's chair and sat down only several feet away from Nicole.

"At any rate," Don continued, dismissing Jill's interruption, "it would make it very hard under the circumstances for me to defend her even if I'd never heard of a man named Al Weatherby. As it stands now, the knowledge that she says she did, in fact, murder a man who was one of my closest friends, and that she is making up such a pack of lies to try and cover up her actions—"

"How do you know they're lies?" Jill asked, again without meaning to.

"Oh, come on, Jilly, you can't believe what she's saying about Al?" Don asked in disbelief.

"I find it hard to believe," Jill concurred. "But I also find it hard to believe that Beth would be making all this up. I guess I just don't know at this point what to believe."

"Well, I do," Don Eliot said with defiant certainty. "Take my word for it, Jilly. I've known Al Weatherby—" He stopped, correcting himself. "I *knew* Al Weatherby for almost as long as Beth did. He was one of the kindest, gentlest men I've ever met. He'd take a spider outside in his handkerchief rather than step on it. You're trying to tell me that that kind of man would be capable of abusing his wife for twenty-seven years?"

"You're forgetting that Jill is a close friend of Beth's," David explained quietly. Jill was glad for his soft-spoken support and smiled in his direction, but he wasn't looking at her.

"Well, all right, then!" Don Eliot exclaimed, as if the entire issue had been suddenly resolved. "Did she ever, in all the time you've known her, tell you that Al was beating her? Have you ever seen her with any bruises? Has she ever given you any indication at all that she was a battered wife?"

Jill shook her head. "No."

"Well . . . ?" Don said wearily, leaving her to draw her own conclusions.

"Maybe she's protecting someone," Jill said. "Maybe Michael—"

"Michael has at least a hundred other worshipers who are prepared to swear he was with them all day and night. They never go out alone, you know. They even sleep together on the floor. No, it was Beth's nightgown that was covered with Al's blood, not Michael's flowing robes. It's her fingerprints all over the hammer. She did it, Jilly. She says she did it. I think we have to accept that."

"What seems to be the general consensus?" David asked.

"That the woman's crazy," Nicole answered. "A breakdown

of sorts. Anyway, most people at the office seem to believe that she cracked up and just exploded."

"And you?" David asked her directly. "What do you think?"

"How do you know that's not what I think?" she asked, a curious twinkle suddenly appearing in her eyes. Jill began to squirm uncomfortably.

Her husband looked right past her to stare into Nicole's eyes. "Because it's too facile an explanation. It's too easy," David answered. "I just can't believe that a heretofore perfectly healthy woman would go from sanity to madness overnight. With a breakdown, there are telltale signs along the way, even from the point of view of hindsight. There's nothing here, no evidence at all to indicate a breakdown."

"I agree," echoed Nicole, sipping at her coffee. "I don't think she had a breakdown and I don't think she was battered. I think she's been reading too many novels."

"What's that supposed to mean?" Jill asked sharply.

"Well, you have to admit, it's the current vogue," Nicole said with just a touch of superiority. "You kill your husband, claim he abused you for years, plead temporary insanity and get off scot-free."

"If Al didn't beat her up, who did?" Jill demanded. "How do you explain her injuries?"

"Some were self-inflicted," Nicole stated confidently. "Some were the probable result of Al waking up in mid-attack and fighting for his life."

"You sound like you should be working for the D.A.," Jill told her.

Nicole returned her coffee mug to the glass table. "Well, it would certainly be an interesting case to prosecute," she began, moving her eyes from Jill to David, "since she's rejected a plea of temporary insanity and instructed her lawyers—Bob Markowitz and Tony Bower, incidentally—to plead self-defense."

"What?" David shouted.

"She says she wasn't insane, not even temporarily. She's insisting on pleading not guilty because she says that if she hadn't killed him, he would have killed her."

"Despite the fact that he was sound asleep at the time," Don Eliot sneered.

"Just a minute, what is this?" Jill asked, also returning her coffee mug to the table and watching as some of it spilled onto the glass top. "I don't believe I'm hearing this from a bunch of lawyers." She turned directly to David. "You're always saying that a lawyer has no right to judge his client, that his sole purpose is to defend his client to the best of his abilities, and that if lawyers tried to set themselves up as judges and juries, our whole system of justice would fall apart!"

"This is hardly the same thing," David replied, testily.

"What you're saying is very true, Jilly," Don Eliot added, "and in a curious way we're saying the same thing. A lawyer has no right to be a judge. Whether my client is guilty or innocent is beside the point because my job is simply to provide that client with the best of all possible defenses, which I simply wouldn't be able to do in this instance. Aside from the obvious conflict of interest here—the man she murdered having been a partner and close friend—I believe she's lying through her teeth. The sight of her repulses me."

"Then why do you feel so guilty?" Jill asked.

"He shouldn't," Nicole answered for him. "He's the one who recommended Markowitz and Bower. They were brilliant enough to get Beth out on bail."

"What do her children think?" David asked.

Nicole shrugged. "That she's flipped out. They're hoping, of course, that they can persuade her to plead temporary insanity before the case comes to trial."

"She will," David said with great assurance. "In the meantime, the press will have a field day with this self-defense crap and by the time the case comes up, there won't be a potential juror who can read who won't be convinced she's off her rocker."

"So, you don't think she's crazy at all?" Nicole asked.

"Crazy like a fox," he answered, repeating the phrase he had used to Jill in their earlier phone conversation. "I think she obviously wanted to get rid of Al, who knows why—the money, another man maybe—anyway, he went to sleep early one night.

She saw her chance. Bingo—one dead husband, one instantly battered wife." He started to laugh.

"What's funny?" Nicole asked before Jill had a chance to.

"Well, the damn thing's almost foolproof! Anyone who knew Al knew the man was incapable of the things she's accusing him of. She'd have to be crazy to think people would believe that ridiculous story! Which brings us back to square one—the crazy lady."

"Crazy like a fox," Nicole said, using David's words to separate the two of them from the others in the room. Jill felt as if she had just become invisible, as if the words Nicole had uttered were part of a magic spell and she and Don Eliot had just been made to disappear. The only two people in the room were her husband and Nicole Clark. She had never felt so negligible in all her life.

Jill watched in awe of Nicole's performance. The girl actually managed a tear or two as she lowered her eyes and continued to speak. "And a man like Al Weatherby," Nicole said haltingly, "not only dies, but has his name and memory dragged through every dirty puddle in town. It isn't fair." She looked over at Jill, as if trying to take her into her confidence. "He helped me so much, you know. He was always very supportive, giving me tips on this or that, telling me the best way to make a positive impression, how to be tough. He thought I needed to be tougher." She laughed feebly. Jill fought the urge to join her. "He was the one to suggest I join the firm after I'm called to the bar. He was even going to come to the ceremony this Friday because my own father can't make the trip." Her voice caught in her throat. "How could anyone believe he was the kind of monster who would abuse his wife for over twenty-five years?!"

"No one does," David answered, obviously moved by Nicole's seemingly impromptu speech.

"Even his children are horrified and shocked at their mother's accusations," Don Eliot said, also impressed.

"And you?" Nicole asked, again looking over at Jill.

A neat touch, Jill thought, realizing that her reply was about to place her in absolute isolation. "I just don't know," she answered, opting at the last instant to stick to the truth rather than try to ingratiate herself back into the group by lying. David was always telling her that once a witness started lying, he was doomed. She looked around at the three bewildered faces, taking quick note of her surroundings. What was she thinking about? she asked herself. This was her living room, not a court of law. She was not under oath. She was not on the witness stand.

For a few minutes, nobody said a word.

"Would anyone like a piece of chocolate cake?" Jill asked, trying to break the tension. "I made some for dessert but we never did get around to it."

Her offer was politely declined.

"How old are your children, David?" Nicole asked.

David had to think for a few seconds. "Jason's twelve," he said finally. "Laurie's fourteen. Typical teenagers, I'm afraid." Nicole smiled as if she understood.

"You're too hard on them," Jill said.

"*Somebody* has to be a little tough with them," David answered.

"I guess it's hard to know when to draw the line," Nicole offered.

"Do you have any children?" Jill suddenly asked her.

"Oh no," Nicole laughed. "Not even any younger brothers or sisters. Just one older sister, ten years older, so we were never very close." She laughed again. "No, no children." She looked directly at Jill. "I'm old-fashioned enough to want to have a husband first." She smiled. Your turn, she seemed to be saying.

"Then you *would* like children eventually?" Jill asked, taking up the challenge.

"Oh yes, very definitely," came Nicole's reply. "I don't think a woman is really complete unless she's experienced having a baby."

"One doesn't have a baby just for a new experience," Jill told her.

Nicole's answer was swift. "No, of course not. I didn't mean to imply that at all. I guess I just feel it's something no woman should miss."

Jill said nothing, feeling smugly one-up for the first time all evening.

"Tell me, Jilly," Don Eliot said abruptly, as if no one else had been talking in the interim since he last spoke, "as Beth Weatherby's close friend, didn't you feel a sense of betrayal when you heard her confession over the radio and not from the woman herself? I mean, you tried to help her. You went to see her." Jill felt her face becoming warm, knew she was beginning to blush, and hoped Don Eliot would be too self-absorbed to notice.

"Is something wrong?" Nicole asked quickly, noticing everything.

"She knew," David's voice said softly.

"Knew what?" both Don and Nicole asked as one.

Jill cleared her throat. "Beth told me that she'd killed Al about a week ago when I went out to her house to visit her."

There was a moment of stunned silence. Jill looked nervously at her chewed cuticles. The jury is back, she thought. Their verdict—guilty as charged. Their sentence—death by humiliation.

"I don't understand," Nicole was saying.

"Neither do I," Don Eliot agreed sadly.

"You're not the only ones," David concurred, crossing the invisible line over to their side, leaving Jill alone in a leaky lifeboat.

"It happened right at the end of my visit," Jill tried to explain. "She caught me completely off guard and I was very shaken, to say the least." She searched their faces for a glimmer of understanding, but found none. "She said only that she'd killed Al. She didn't explain the hows or the whys. I didn't ask. I didn't know what to think or what to do. So, I didn't do anything. I didn't feel I had the right to say anything."

Don Eliot was shaking his head. "I don't know, Jill," he said, for the first time since she'd known him leaving out the diminutive at the end of her name, making it sound stiff and formal. "I don't understand. I'm very disappointed in you."

David spoke. "Don, she didn't even tell me," he said.

"I'm sure Jill did what she did out of a misplaced sense of loyalty," Jill heard a voice say and turned quickly to her right, listening to the voice of Nicole Clark speaking eloquently in her defense. "Beth is a close friend of hers, after all, and Jill is a teacher, not a lawyer. She obviously doesn't relate to the issue in the same way that we do. She felt that if she said anything, she would be betraying a friend, a confidence. It's a difficult spot to be in. I'm not sure I would have done it any differently had I been in her shoes."

Don Eliot stood up, pulling at his yellow and black tie. "Well, I guess you women will always find some way to stick together. Now, I really should be getting home."

Jill remained seated, too stunned to speak. Nicole's support of her position had been as surprising as it was articulate. Why then did she feel like jumping over and throttling the young woman? She felt the sofa move beside her and looked up to see Nicole Clark rising and walking with Don Eliot toward the door. She got quickly to her feet, reaching the door just as Nicole was about to make her exit.

"I'm sorry I had to cancel our racquetball game last Friday," Nicole was telling David. "I booked a court for Wednesday at five-thirty. How's that?"

"Should be fine," David acknowledged.

Don Eliot was already halfway down the hall.

"See you tomorrow," Nicole continued. "Goodbye, Jill. Nice to see you again."

Jill said nothing, feeling her bile rising inside her body. If only she could keep her anger from exploding till after she'd heard the elevator depart. She walked back into the living room as David remained by the door. When he finally closed it, she was furiously stacking the coffee mugs inside the dishwasher. He paused by the kitchen doorway, about to proceed to the bedroom, when her voice stopped him.

"Where are you going?" she asked.

"I thought I'd get undressed and take a bath, if that meets with your approval," he said, sarcastically.

"It doesn't," she said.

"Well, you'll have to pardon me then because I intend to do it anyway," he answered.

"I think we better talk," she said, slamming the door of the dishwasher and following him down the hall to the bedroom.

"What's there to say?" he asked.

"There's plenty to say," she told him, hearing her voice level rise. "You didn't have to tell Don that I already knew about Beth! You didn't have to place me in that position!"

"What were you going to do, Jill? Lie to the man?"

"Why shouldn't I? Are you the only one in this family who gets to tell lies?"

He looked appropriately disgusted. "What are you talking about?"

"I'm talking about your little racquetball games with Nicole Clark! Are you forgetting that you told me you were playing racquetball with one of the male students—"

"Don't yell at me, Jill," David warned her. "I've taken enough crap from you today."

"You lied to me!"

He turned to her angrily. "What was I supposed to tell you? I know how paranoid you are about Nicki—"

"I am not paranoid! The woman is after my husband. She told me as much!"

"Oh, Jill, for God's sake. When are you going to stop using that? Didn't you hear her in that living room tonight? She was on your side, for Christ's sake! She actually defended you!"

"I don't need that little bitch to defend me!" Jill shouted, understanding now how Jason felt earlier. "I am perfectly capable of defending myself. I don't need some little undergraduate talking about me like I'm not even in the room, referring to me in the third person, pretending to sympathize with me in order to make herself look generous and fair! She will do anything, David, to make herself look good in your eyes, and if she can make me look bad at the same time, well, then, so much the better."

He pushed past her into the hallway. "I'm not going to listen to this," he said.

Jill was right behind him, shadowing him as he stormed first into the den and then through the dining area back into the living room. "David, for God's sake, do you think it was just a coincidence that she mentioned the racquetball game just as I got to the door? You don't think that was deliberately said so that I would hear?"

"No, I don't," he said with vehemence. "Nicki's mind doesn't work along the same lines as yours."

"Well, at least that much is true! David, can't you see how she's manipulating this whole situation? You and me! Can't you *feel* how you're being manipulated?" She paused, seeing the intractability of his cool green eyes. "Or is it that you just don't care?"

"You're being ridiculous," he said, his voice halfway between anger and sadness. "I'm going out for some fresh air."

"Oh, David, please don't," Jill begged as he opened the door.

"I'll be back later," he told her. And then he was gone.

Chapter 20

Jill looked at the clock for the fourth time in as many minutes. It was exactly eleven forty-five. David had been gone now for almost three hours.

She didn't know what to do. Whether to wait up or go to sleep. Sleep—that was a funny word. She could get into bed; she certainly wouldn't get any rest.

Where was he? Where could he have gone without his car keys or his wallet? An hour after he had left, she'd snuck down to the parking garage to make sure the car was, in fact, still there, and when she was satisfied that it hadn't moved, she returned to the apartment. His wallet and all his cash and credit cards still lay on the stereo where he had discarded them when he'd returned from driving Jason and Laurie home. That meant he had gone walking through the streets of Chicago at night alone. If he were mugged, the thieves would be furious to discover his lack of funds, would undoubtedly rough him up a bit, possibly even kill him. The thought made her panic. She debated whether or not to call the police, but knew they would tell her to wait twenty-four hours and then call them again. Instead she had called David's mother, thinking perhaps he had gone there, but after several minutes of talk about the weather it became obvious that David was not there, and Jill had been trapped into spending the next half hour listening while Mrs. Plumley complained about everything from inflation to the public housing which was threatening to impinge on her neighborhood. When she was finally able to say goodbye, she quickly dialed David's sister, on the off chance Renee and Norman might know where he was. They didn't, or at least his name was never mentioned other than in the casual how-is-your-husband-my-brother category. After that, she kept the phone free in case he was in trouble and had been trying to call. If he had been, he wasn't now.

The last hour had been filled with thoughts of Nicole Clark. Jill wasn't sure which would make her feel worse—the police calling to report they'd found her husband's mutilated body or Nicole calling to announce that David was spending the night with her. It was a discomforting thought. But then, Nicole Clark was a discomforting girl. Maybe she shouldn't have said anything, Jill thought. Maybe she should have just kept her mouth shut and not taken Nicole's bait. Ignored the fact that her husband was now playing racquetball with the girl, ignored the fact that he had lied to her. But she couldn't do that. Once you agreed to accept one lie, you agreed to accept them all, to lend the lies a certain credibility. What was the legal term? To aid and abet?

And yet what had she accomplished by bringing the issue out in the open, forcing it to a head? She had simply succeeded in alienating her husband even further, driving him, tired and disgusted, out of his own apartment. Right into Nicole Clark's waiting arms?

Was that where he was?

Stop it! she told herself. It was ridiculous to torture herself this way. If he had gone to Nicole, there was nothing she could do about it now.

The whole day had been one drawn-out disaster, most of it her own making. If only she'd never confided to him about Beth's admission of guilt. She should have known how he would react to such news. She knew how much David had loved and admired Al Weatherby. He had cried over the man's death, whereas he had never cried when his own father had died. Why did she have to be so insistent about her doubts? Couldn't she simply have agreed that Al was incapable of such monstrous behavior, and then waited until another time to hear what Beth had to say? Of course David was going to take her doubts personally. What else could he be expected to do?

Jill found herself pacing the narrow hallway. She was throwing too much at David at once, bombarding him with disharmony when what he needed was a little peace and quiet. And a lot of support. He had enough problems—his ex-wife, his children, his daily grind at the office, their constant lack of funds. In the last few months, he'd had to contend with Al's death, her unhappiness with her job, and her newly organized jealousy. And now, this. Coming home had to be less than a treat.

She had to do something about it. She had to stop being so suspicious, or at the very least learn to keep her suspicions to herself, to not openly flinch whenever she heard him mention Nicole's name; she had to back away as far as Al and Beth were concerned, learn to keep conflicting opinions to herself, at least for a while. She would refrain from making disparaging comments about Elaine and would continue her efforts to befriend his children. There must be some way to win them over. She could do nothing about what went on at his office all day. She could only concentrate on making home as appealing a prospect as Nicole Clark.

She sighed. That left only the problem about her job, and she'd just have to get used to that too. She was stuck, and there was no point in further complaints. David had to be as tired of hearing about how bored she was as she was of feeling it. But that's the way things were. David was not responsible; there was nothing he could do. The new term had begun and she was going to learn to love it.

If only he would come home—

The phone rang.

She teetered with indecision, knowing she was exactly halfway between either phone, finally racing toward the bedroom. It couldn't be the police, she assured herself, leaping across the bed, because David had left all his I.D. at home. Even if he were lying dead somewhere, the police wouldn't have been able to identify him and call her so quickly. Unless, of course, someone at the police department had recognized him—

"Hello?"

"Jill, I'm sorry."

"David, where are you?"

"At the office. Did I wake you?"

"Wake me? Are you kidding? I've been worried half to death."

"I'm sorry."

"What are you doing at the office?"

She could hear him shrug. "I don't really know. I went walking. Just kept walking. Suddenly, I looked up and here I was. The night watchman let me in. I didn't have a key, of course."

"I know. I was so worried where you could have gone."

"I left the house without a goddamn dime, if you can believe it. That's the trouble with acting like a prima donna, I guess."

"Are you all right?"

"Sure. Just very tired. Actually, I got a lot accomplished tonight. There was no one else around. It was quiet. I managed to take care of all my dockets. You know what a pain they are." There was a quiet pause. "I don't suppose you'd feel like coming down here and picking me up?" he asked sheepishly. "I know it's a hell of a nerve but my legs are killing me and I don't have any money and—"

"And?"

"And I really want to see you."

"I'll be there in five minutes."

Jill hung up the phone, grabbed the car keys and raced to the doorway. Everything was going to be okay from now on. No matter what stunts Nicole tried to pull, Jill would not trip on her own feet. She'd make sure that everything would work out, and that she and David would live happily ever after.

Things started to fall apart the next morning.

For the first time that she could remember, David overslept and consequently was in a big rush to get out, which meant that she would be late because of the time he had to spend in the bathroom. At ten minutes to nine, she called the university and told the office she would be late for the morning's round of meetings because she hadn't been feeling well. She hated using her health as an excuse. Her mother had once told her it was bad luck.

"Can I make you some breakfast?" she asked him when he finally came out of the bathroom.

"Are you kidding? I'm already late."

"That's precisely the point."

He paused. "Sure, why not? Scrambled eggs too much trouble?"

"No trouble at all," she said, grateful to be given the opportunity to do something for him.

She went to the fridge as he reached for the phone.

"Diane Buck," he said briskly into the receiver, then waited while the office receptionist connected him to his secretary. "Diane, I'm going to be another half hour; I'm at a breakfast meeting and it's running a little later than I'd anticipated. Tell Doug Horton I'll be there as soon as I can. Okay? Thanks."

Jill cracked the eggs into the bowl and added some milk, briskly stirring in some salt and pepper. She felt uncomfortable listening to David lie. It seemed so effortless and believable.

"Toast?" she asked, putting the eggs in the fry pan.

"Why not?" he answered. "I've come this far. Might as well go all the way."

A few minutes later, Jill put David's breakfast on the dining room table. David's face was buried inside the business section of the morning paper. "Breakfast is ready," she said, smiling.

He looked over. "Oh, great. Thanks." He laid the paper down beside his plate. "Smells terrific."

"I hope it tastes as good," she said sincerely, surprised how much it meant to her that he be pleased.

He took a bite of his eggs and looked back at her. "It does," he smiled. She sighed with relief. "Aren't you having any?"

Jill looked down at her glass of orange juice. "I've decided to go on a diet," she said.

"Oh? What for?"

"I thought it probably wouldn't hurt to lose five pounds."

David looked back at his paper. "Probably right," he said. "But watch that you don't starve yourself."

Jill laughed nervously. Why was she so nervous? "I don't think that's likely," she said, watching him eat. "David—?"

"Hmm?" He looked up from his paper. "What is it?"

"I just wanted to tell you again how sorry I am about not telling you about Beth—"

"Forget it."

"No, please. I don't want it to come between us—"

"It won't."

"I love you."

"I love you, too."

They stared at each other for several long seconds, Jill desperately seeking some assurance from David's eyes. "I love you so much," she whispered.

"Come here," he said warmly, holding his hands out. Jill got quickly up from her seat and walked into his waiting arms. She felt his hands pressing against her head, squeezing her hair into a tight round ball. "I'm sorry, too," he told her. "I acted like a first-class prick."

She looked at him with tears in her eyes. "As long as it's first-class," she said, sniffing.

He finished the last of his breakfast and Jill took his dishes into the kitchen. "Is today a busy day?" she asked.

"Aren't they all?"

"I thought maybe we could take in a movie tonight."

"Tonight? No chance. I've got too much work."

"I thought you got a lot done last night."

"I did. Unfortunately, there's lots more. I don't think you'll be seeing much of me for the next few weeks. Until I get caught up—"

"What about Friday night?"

"What about it?"

"Dinner," Jill informed him. "At my parents'. They invited us last week—"

"Oh, honey, I'm sorry," he said, putting down the business section and coming into the kitchen. "I *did* forget. I can't make it Friday night."

"Dinner's not till eight o'clock. I could pick you up at the office," she volunteered.

"That's not it," he said, and waited ominously. Jill knew instinctively that she wasn't going to like the next several sentences out of his mouth. "Please don't take this the wrong way," he began. Jill felt her breath becoming short. David felt himself groping for words, a fact which made Jill all the more uncomfortable, knowing her husband was rarely at such a loss. "I don't know quite how to say this because I know how you feel about her already—"

"Feel about who?" Jill asked, already knowing the answer.

"Nicole Clark," he said.

"What about her?" Jill asked, her voice cold, flat.

"She's being called to the bar on Friday."

"She asked you to come?"

"Her father can't be there. She has no one."

"What about her friend, Chris whatever-his-name-was, the one she brought to Don Eliot's that night for dinner—"

"He's just a casual friend. He doesn't mean anything to her."

"And you do?"

Jill held her breath.

"I guess I do," he said, softly. "Jill, please listen to me. This is the last time that I'll ever put myself in this position. I promise you that. Now, I think you're wrong about Nicki's intentions and I don't think she's the calculating, manipulative woman that you believe her to be. But I'd have to be an idiot or a blind man not to have realized by now that she *is* in love with me, and I'm neither an idiot nor blind. Nor do I regard her in any light other than that of a brilliant young attorney who's also a very sweet and lonely little girl. But that's all there is—and there'll never be anything more to it than that. I promise you." He looked around. "But I'm not being fair to Nicki, and I'm certainly not being fair to you, if I allow her fantasies to continue. It's flattering having a beautiful young girl like Nicki in love with me, but that's *all* it is. There's no more. There never will be. So—" He took a deep breath. "From now on, there will be no more courtroom observances, no more lunches, no more racquetball games. I will go to her graduation this Friday because I promised that I would be there. I committed myself. But that will be the end of it." He stared into Jill's eyes. "All right?"

Jill turned away, wanting to tell him the answer she knew he was waiting for but unable to find the words. "I didn't realize the ceremony was at night," she said.

"It isn't," he answered. "It's in the afternoon."

"You're taking her to dinner?" Jill asked.

There was a slight pause before he answered. "Not just me. About five or six of us. To congratulate her, welcome her into the firm."

"That's very nice of you," Jill said, her voice empty of feeling.

"Jill, please understand. It's nothing. It's never been anything. After Friday, it'll be even less."

"How can there be less than nothing?" she asked.

David looked at the floor. "Well, what can I say? I've been completely honest with you. I've told you all there is to tell. I can't do more than that. The rest is up to you. Maybe it's too much to expect you to understand—"

"It *is* too much," Jill said, feeling very old inside. "But I'll try," she added.

David's arms went quickly around her, hugging her tightly to him. "I love you," he said.

"I love you, too," she repeated.

"And I'm very late," he said, checking his watch. "Doug Horton must be shitting bricks by now, I've kept him waiting so long."

"Tell him it's my fault," Jill said, watching David bound toward the door.

"I might do that," he said, opening it. "Call me later." The door closed behind him.

Jill stood for several minutes in the middle of the tiny box that was their kitchen and contemplated all that had transpired in the last hour. She replayed David's apologies several times as if she were listening to a tape recorder. Push to start and listen, press down to reverse and rewind, push back down to start again. His voice was rich and soothing, filled with deep understanding for what she must be going through. I realize that she *is* in love with me, he was saying, or words to that effect. When was it, Jill found herself asking, that David had come to this enlightened realization? Last night in her living room? Before— over a quiet lunch perhaps? She shook her head. It didn't make

any difference when, she tried to tell herself. What was important was that David was about to put an end to Nicole's little
game of cat and mouse. After Friday, the weight of the world
could go rest on somebody else's shoulders. After Friday, she
repeated, almost aloud. It was going to be a long week, she decided, impulsively reaching for the phone.

It was answered after three rings.

"Hello?"

"Beth?"

"No, it's Lisa. Is this Jill?"

"Yes. How are you, Lisa? How's your mother?"

"My mother's just fine, thank you. It's the rest of us that are
falling apart."

"Oh, Lisa—"

"I take it you heard the news about her confession."

"Yes."

"And what she's saying about my father."

"Yes."

"Well—what do you think?" There was a slight tinge of hysteria beneath the young woman's voice.

"I—I don't know what to think."

The girl's voice went suddenly very low and quiet, as if she
did not want to be overheard. "She's saying that he beat her,
hurt her, abused her, ever since they got married. She's saying
that my father was a maniac. A monster that had her in constant fear of her life. Jill," she pleaded impassionately, "it's impossible! I lived here in this house for nineteen years. How
could I possibly live under the same roof as a monster and not
recognize him for what he was? How could any of us grow up
here and not have been aware of what was going on, if even a
tenth of what she's saying is true? It's impossible. Three kids
were brought up here. None of us witnessed anything she's
claiming took place! I never heard one cry in the night, never
saw my mother covered with bruises. Nothing. All I saw was a
warm and loving husband and father who never even spanked
us when we were bad. And let me tell you, there were times
when we were really rotten. He never even lost his temper with
us! God, Jill, what she's saying is absolutely impossible!"

"Is it easier for you to accept that your mother is lying?" Jill asked.

The cry was one of pure anguish. "No!" the girl despaired. "I don't know why she's saying these things unless—"

"Unless she's crazy," Jill said quietly.

"She has to be crazy," Lisa pressed. "There's no other explanation. I know my parents. My father was no more capable of beating my mother than—" She broke off abruptly.

"Than she was of killing him," Jill said, finishing the sentence.

"Unless she was crazy," Lisa concluded tearfully. "And I just can't believe that she's crazy! I don't know. You live with people, you think you know them, think that you know everything about them, and then you find out that you don't know a goddamn thing! Nothing! Zero! Zilch! And what does that say about you? About your life?"

"What does your mother say?" Jill asked.

"Why don't you ask her?" Lisa said numbly. "She just walked in the room."

Jill heard the phone being transferred. "Jill?" Beth's voice inquired.

"I didn't realize before how much you sound like Lisa," Jill told her.

"I guess we do." Jill could feel Beth smiling. "How are you?"

Jill laughed. "Me? I'm all right. How are you?"

"Never better," Beth answered. "But the fur's really flying, I'll bet."

"You *do* have a way about you."

"At least I gave you some advance warning."

"Thanks a lot."

Both women chuckled ruefully. "Well," Beth began, "what do you think? Am I crazy? Or am I lying?"

Jill could feel Beth's eyes directly on hers. "Why does my gut tell me you're neither?" she asked.

Beth's answer was immediate. "Because you're my friend," she said.

"I'd like to listen if you feel like talking," Jill offered.

"How about tonight?" The swiftness of the invitation caught

Jill by surprise. "If you're busy, of course, we can make it some other time. It doesn't have to be tonight."

Jill took a second to sift through her thoughts. David would be working late. He wouldn't be home before ten. There was no reason to stay home except for her fear. And what was she so afraid of? Whatever Beth had to say couldn't hurt her. "Tonight's fine," Jill said.

Chapter 21

The front door of the Weatherby house was already open when Jill pulled her gray Volvo into the driveway. She climbed out of the car, pulling her sweater around her shoulders. In the last week, a chill had abruptly descended on the city like an unwanted house guest, suitcase firmly in hand, prepared for a lengthy visit. Jill ran up the walkway to the front entrance. Beth stood waiting for her just inside the doorway.

"God, I'm glad to see you," Beth said, her arms reaching out to surround Jill.

Jill kissed Beth's cheek. "You look fine," she told her.

"Every time I tell someone I *feel* fine, they get that peculiar look in their eyes like that's definitely not what I'm supposed to say. Anyway, come on in." Jill entered the front hallway as Beth closed the door behind her. "Lisa's in the living room waiting. She's made some tea." Beth winked conspiratorially. "Tea must be the Wasp answer to chicken soup. One sip and all your problems go away."

"Wouldn't that be nice?"

"How's David?" Beth asked, leading Jill to the living room, where Lisa immediately rose to greet her.

"He's working late. Hi, Lisa. How are you doing?"

"Okay," the girl shuffled.

"I understand you made us some tea." Lisa nodded. "I'd love a cup."

Lisa moved immediately to the antique coffee table where she'd set up the tea service. "How do you take it?"

"Black. I'm trying to diet."

"Good God, what for?" Beth asked.

"Oh, you *are* a friend," Jill laughed. Lisa handed her a cup of tea.

"Mom?"

"Sure. Milk and sugar, sweetie."

A minute later, they were all sitting down in much the same positions they had occupied the previous week—Jill and Beth on the sofa, Lisa on the chair across from them. Do I look as nervous as Lisa does? Jill wondered, trying to concentrate on Beth.

"I told Lisa that you were coming over tonight to listen to my version of Life with Father. She's heard most of it before but she insists she wants to hear it again. Certainly she hasn't heard it in the kind of detail I'm about to tell you. I wanted to spare her." She paused. "But I've been doing that all her life. And she keeps telling me that she's a big girl now, so I guess it's time she heard the whole gruesome story." She looked around. "Brian is upstairs. He doesn't want to listen to any of this. He prefers to believe I'm crazy." She looked back at Jill. "You're sure about this now?" she asked. "You really want to know?"

"I want to know," Jill replied.

"I'll start right at the beginning, twenty-eight years ago when I first met Al," Beth Weatherby began. "Some of this you've already heard, Jill. You'll have to excuse me if I repeat myself, but I find it helps to keep things in pretty strict order, to incorporate all the little trivial details." She paused, taking a sip of her tea and then returning the cup to her lap.

"I was very young when we got married, as you already

know. I had just turned eighteen. Al was twelve years older. We met at a bank. I was a teller. He was a customer. He used to come in once or twice a week, always very nattily attired. I thought so anyway. I noticed him right away. He was so friendly to everybody. Always smiling. Everybody liked him. That never changed. Everybody always liked Al." She stopped, taking a deep breath. "I liked him, too. I used to sneak smiles over in his direction when I thought he wasn't looking, but one day he turned around and caught me at it, and from that time on, he always came to my window.

"I was crazy about him. Right from the beginning. He was just so appealing, I thought. And, of course, he was older. And a lawyer. God, I was so impressed when he told me that. And he seemed to be interested in me, that was the really amazing part of the whole thing. Me—who'd never even finished high school. Al was always ashamed of my education, or lack of it, but my family needed the money and working seemed more important than school at the time. After we got married, I thought I could go back to school, but the babies came along so fast and Al—well, we told everyone that I'd gone to school part-time when the children were very small, till I finally got my B.A. It was what Al wanted. He didn't want anyone to think I was stupid, and I wanted him to be happy, and since it seemed so important to him, I went along with it. But I always worried about it. I was afraid somebody would ask one too many questions that I wouldn't be able to answer, and I'd be uncovered—a fraud with barely a high school education. So, I made it a point to read just about every book that I could get my hands on, and I kept myself well informed about current affairs. Anyway—" She paused, knowing she had jumped too far ahead of herself. "We started going out together," she began again, returning to the beginning of her story. "I couldn't believe I was so lucky. The only one who wasn't happy about any of it was my mother. When we got married, she was very upset. When she died, Al wouldn't even let me go to her funeral! My brothers haven't spoken to me since. Not even now.

"I don't know. Maybe she knew. Maybe she sensed the violence, the cruelty inside him. Me—all I saw was this cute guy, full of confidence, always happy, even-tempered and easygoing. Wow! So much for first impressions.

"We got married. It was a small wedding. My family didn't come. Al had no family left. A few of his old school friends were our witnesses. Afterward, we went out for dinner. Nowhere fancy. I remember I was surprised because I'd figured Al would go all out. But it didn't matter because I was Mrs. Alan Weatherby and I was thrilled. It didn't matter about my family or the restaurant or even that we weren't going to have a honeymoon. I was married to the man of my dreams, as we used to say, and that's all that was important.

"The violence started on our wedding night.

"I was a virgin, of course. I'd hardly even dated before Al. But he was the one who kept insisting we wait until after we got married. I didn't care. I would've done anything he asked. He wanted to wait, so we waited. I don't know what I was expecting, but I guess I was like any other young girl. I thought it might hurt a little, but that mostly it would be wonderful. We'd hug and kiss a lot and he'd be gentle and understanding, and very loving. But he wasn't any of those things. And there was no hugging or kissing or even the slightest show of tenderness. It was awful. It was like I was in bed with a complete stranger. He was so different than he'd been even an hour before. He didn't smile. He wasn't tender. He was rough, even mean. He kept pinching me, hurting me, and when I'd try to squirm out of his grasp, he'd just do it some more. Harder. There was no tenderness. He just pushed into me until he was finished, and then when he was through, he turned me over and spanked me like a little girl. Hard, ugly slaps. They hurt and I cried, trying to get away from him. That made him angrier, so he twisted my arm until I thought he'd break it. When I pleaded with him to tell me why he was doing these things, he screamed that I'd lied to him, that it was obvious I'd been with a lot of guys. I tried to reason with him. His answer was a slap across the face. I didn't know what to do! I felt—I really felt—like it was all my fault that it was happening. That somehow I had brought it on myself. I started to apologize. I was always the one who apologized. It got to be something of a ritual.

"Every time we made love—funny term—he would strike me.

At first it always took the form of a spanking. He'd use his hands. Gradually, he advanced to hairbrushes and then belts. After we had the children and they were old enough to recognize their mother's cries, he'd put a gag in my mouth, tie my hands behind me. He was always very careful to make sure he'd hit me where the bruises wouldn't show. Unless he could make it seem like an accident, of course. He was very good at arranging accidents. I became 'accident-prone,' as they say. I was forever walking into things, burning myself. I was usually sporting one bruise or another somewhere, but people don't remember that now. I mean, everyone has an occasional bruise. Most of them, you can cover with clothing. If you have to be somewhere, like an exercise class," she said, looking directly at Jill, "you show up already properly uniformed. That way there are no questions asked that you can't answer. Anyway, I did such a good job of joking away any mysterious bruises that did turn up, that I got to be a bit of a joke around Weatherby, Ross for a while. What happened to your leg? someone would ask. Oh, you know me, I'd answer merrrily. I tripped again.

"I tripped over Al's outstretched foot; I burned my fingers when he held my hand down over the toaster; I cut my hand when my husband ran a knife across it after I missed a grand slam one night at bridge—"

Jill gasped, lowering her head in shame. Somehow, she had always known. Her fear had been that she would hear these exact words and know them to be true.

"When I found out I was pregnant with Brian," Beth continued, "I got very excited. God knows why. Maybe I thought it would calm Al down, give him the son I assumed he wanted. I guess I also thought the beatings would stop. He wouldn't hurt a pregnant woman. He wouldn't hurt his baby.

"The worst beating I ever got was the night I told him I was pregnant. He went into a rage. I don't even remember the things he said. Just the blows. Most of them to my stomach. He even threw me down a flight of stairs as a sort of grand finale. I really thought he was going to kill me that night. I think I hoped he would.

"I don't know how Brian survived that pregnancy. Somehow, we both did, even though the beatings kept up as fierce as ever.

A few years later, Lisa was born. Five years after that, Michael came along. I lost a few in between. Altogether I had four miscarriages.

"Now the story gets a little monotonous. Twenty-seven years of abuse is twenty-seven years of it, and what you've heard is pretty much how it continues. Al's business began to grow. He became extremely successful, just the way he always said he would. We moved into increasingly bigger homes each year. Everyone thought he was some sort of miracle worker; they thought I was the luckiest woman alive.

"That part always amazed me about him. That he could be Dr. Jekyll one minute and Mr. Hyde the next. The nicest man you'd ever want to meet in public. I knew how much everybody adored him; I remember how much *I'd* adored him. He was so strong—you wouldn't have believed how strong he was, being so slight. But he lifted weights, you know. It made him very strong." She stopped short, and laughed abruptly. "That's what it all boils down to. The root of all our problems, all our fears. The fact that men are simply physically more powerful than we are. Even the weakest man has little trouble pinning down the strongest of women. And that's where all the injustices start and where they lie. Equal pay, better jobs, equal rights—all of it, everything women are fighting for—what we're really fighting against is sheer masculine strength. Everything else springs from that." Beth cleared her throat and returned without further digression to her original train of thought.

"It got so that I always dreaded whenever Al would be nice to me in public. The nicer he was, the worse the beating would be when I got home. The more solicitous he was, the meaner he would be later on. You remember how he laughed about that chain letter I sent out? Well, he didn't think it was so funny in private. No, not funny at all.

"I got a real working over for that one. He wouldn't let me have any friends—you were the only real friend I had, Jill. I could relate to you instantly. It wasn't like we had to see each other a lot or speak to each other every day; we always seemed to pick up where we left off. Al couldn't do anything to stop that. And I think he sensed it would be dangerous to try.

"I can't begin to tell you what it was like all those years the kids were at home, the kind of fear I lived in that they'd find out what was going on, that he'd stop being satisfied with just beating me and turn on them. I never uttered a word against him all those years. I was desperate to protect them. I never so much as disagreed with Al in front of them. If I ever did, you can just imagine how I would have paid for it later. I centered my life around my husband, and so, of course, that's what they remember now. Why Lisa and Brian are having such a hard time believing the truth." She stared at her daughter's tear-streaked face. "I'm sure Lisa told you, Jill—her parents never disagreed, let alone had the kind of normal fights all married couples have. And she's right. I never dared disagree—our fights were never normal." Beth paused, for an instant lost in thought. "Except Michael," she said. "I've always suspected Michael knew something about what went on. I don't know what. I'm not sure I'm right. But I always wondered if that wasn't at least part of the reason he left school and joined that group—" She cut herself off abruptly.

"It was a mixed blessing when all the kids were finally gone. I'd encouraged them all to get out of Chicago, quietly, of course, without Al's knowledge. He'd have killed me if he'd found out. But I wanted them as far away from him as possible. I wanted them out of this house. At least I didn't have to worry about them anymore. Of course, it gave Al a freer hand, so to speak. He didn't have to time his outbursts anymore. He was like a teenager who'd had his curfew lifted. It was open season at the Weatherbys'."

Jill opened her mouth to speak. Her words came out of Beth's mouth instead. "You're going to ask me why I didn't leave him, I know," she said. Jill nodded. "Everyone asks that. It's a perfectly natural question. God knows I asked myself that a hundred times. Maybe only another woman who's lived through that kind of terror can understand. But you have to remember a few things—first, I was so young when we got married, and so confused. I thought the sun rose and set around that man. In the beginning, I thought maybe that's how all marriages were. That women accepted abuse as a natural course of events. I thought sex was like that for everyone. And I had so much pride! How could I admit my mother had been right?

How could I go home after all the fuss I'd made? He swore he'd find me anyway, if I ever tried to leave. Find me and kill me. By that time, I was absolutely terrified of the man!

"And then, of course, I thought it was all my fault. I saw this wonderful man whom everybody liked and who was terrific with everybody else but me, and so I naturally assumed I had to be to blame. God knows I tried to improve. I became a wonderful cook. I waited on Al hand and foot. But things were never done right—at least not right enough for Al. And the children—Al couldn't tell me often enough how unfit a mother I was. He threatened to take them away from me if I ever tried to leave him. He said I wouldn't have a chance in court against him, that no one would believe my story." She looked around the room though her eyes settled on nothing. "And, of course, he was right. No one does believe it."

Jill swallowed hard. "I believe it," she said softly.

There was a long moment of silence.

"So do I," whispered Lisa, moving immediately to her mother's side and collapsing into her arms. Beth Weatherby's eyes filled instantly with tears and she hugged her daughter closely to her, rocking her silently back and forth like a baby. Without shifting her position, she moved her free arm toward Jill. Jill's hand reached out and grabbed it tightly. The three women sat without words for several minutes. When Beth finally began to speak again, her voice was stronger, more assured. The desperation that had been clinging to each word had disappeared. "The night that I killed Al," she began again, "wasn't any different really from any of the other nights, except that Al had had a few drinks, something he didn't usually do. God knows he didn't need liquor to make him mean.

"It was a Friday night; I was getting dinner ready. He phoned from a bar and started yelling at me that I was a useless drain on his existence, a rotten mother, a terrible bridge player. Anything you can think of. That's what I was. Then he said he was coming home. I knew he was going to beat me. He'd been getting bolder since Michael had left; the abuse was becoming more exotic. He was becoming careless, telling lies that could easily trip him up. Like when he told you that I was upset because Lisa had a married lover. He didn't seem to care as much if anyone were to find out. It was like he was almost daring people to discover his secret. I was terrified he was going to kill me!

"I phoned you."

Again, Jill lowered her head in shame. Beth gently disengaged her daughter and turned to face Jill.

"No, please. Don't blame yourself. How could you know? That was my mistake for years. I blamed myself! Instead of the man responsible. That's what abuse does to you. And why I don't think I'll ever be able to forgive Al. *Why* I killed him that night.

"Not for the years of being physically abused. But for what he did to my soul. For the sheer terror I lived in all those years. For the degradation. For almost destroying the human being inside the flesh—for making me feel guilty and of no more worth than yesterday's newspaper. I had no value to anyone— especially to myself. I actually felt I deserved whatever he dished out. And I'm not talking about just in the beginning now. I'm talking about later, after I became more aware, knew that things were not as they were supposed to be, that it *wasn't* my fault, that something was wrong with Al, not me— By that time, it was too late. It didn't matter anymore, which is why I never left—not even after Michael was gone. It wasn't just that I was terrified, that I knew Al would find me and kill me. It's more that there just wasn't anything left of me to go anywhere. Can you understand that? My soul was dead.

"When Al did come home that night, I was just sitting there waiting for him. He didn't waste any time. Started right in hitting me. Only this time was worse than the others. I know he was going to kill me. He had his hands around my throat and he was choking me. He obviously didn't care who saw his handiwork this time. I panicked. And for the first time, I started fighting back. Well, he thought that was the biggest joke of all. He said I was ridiculous. That's when he started scratching at me. I finally collapsed on the floor. He was kicking at my sides like I was so much dirty laundry. Then suddenly, he just stopped—he said he was tired; he was going to bed and he'd finish me off when he got up.

"He went upstairs. I lay on the floor for a long time. My

whole body was sore. Finally, I decided to go upstairs and try to get some sleep. Maybe I already knew I was going to kill him. At the time, I remember thinking he probably wouldn't wake up until the morning, and by then he'd forget about it, at least for a while. So, I went upstairs, got undressed, put on my nightgown. Actually got in bed beside Al, ready to die if that's what he wanted.

"But a strange thing started to happen to me as I lay there. I realized that I didn't want to die after all. And that I didn't have to take his beatings anymore. That I didn't care whether or not anyone would believe the truth. I knew that if I left him, he'd make good his threat to find me and kill me. Accidents happen, he used to say. I knew that the only way I could survive was to get out of bed and kill him first. In self-defense.

"That's what I did.

"I don't remember too many of the details from that point on. I got the hammer. I hit him with it. I remember looking down at my nightgown, seeing Al's blood, knowing he was dead. I remember feeling—relief. I don't remember stuffing the hammer into the central vacuuming system, but I guess I did. Or going outside, where the police found me. I just remember being there."

Beth Weatherby shook her head. "The lawyers want me to plead temporary insanity. They say I was crazy the night I killed my husband. Maybe I was." She paused, looking from Jill to Lisa and then back at Jill again. "But I really don't think so. To tell you the truth, Jill," she said earnestly, "and please forgive me, my darling Lisa, but I really believe that the night I murdered Al was the sanest I've been in twenty-seven years."

Chapter 22

The phone rang just as Jill was leaving her apartment for the university.

"Naturally," she muttered, returning to the kitchen and picking up the phone, sneaking a look at the clock. It was already ten-thirty. Her first class was in half an hour and unless she left the apartment in the next five minutes, she would be late. Since it was only the second day of regular classes, Jill didn't think such tardiness would be appreciated, and she had resolved to start this year right—with the proper enthusiasm and dedication. "Hello?" she asked, rather than stated. Probably a survey or somebody trying to sell her a magazine subscription.

"Jill?"

"Yes. Who's this?"

"It's Irving. Irving Saunders. I hardly recognized your voice. You sounded so tentative."

"I'm always tentative on Tuesdays. How are you? How was Africa?"

"Fraught with its customary turmoil and hot as hell. I have some great news for you."

"Oh?" Jill found herself clutching the telephone as tightly as if she had just been told the floor was about to disappear from underneath her feet.

"Aren't you going to ask me what it is?"

"What is it?" Jill repeated numbly.

"We're doing a new show," he began. Jill took a deep intake of breath and held it. "It's a sixty-minute news show," he continued, "kind of like 'Sixty Minutes,' in fact. A bit of muckraking and exposés, along with some issues that are concerning the people of this city. We're calling it 'Hour Chicago'—Hour with an H, which I think is a great title, because it sounds like *Our* Chicago, without the H—which, of course, is what it's supposed to do. Anyway, are you still with me?"

"Right here."

"Good. We want you."

"What?!"

"Well, there's a slight hitch. A couple, in fact."

"You want me?"

"Yes."

"You've got me."

Irving Saunders laughed loudly. "I like you, Jill. You're so easy!"

"When do I start?"

There was a pause. "Hold on a minute. We have to discuss the slight hitches I was talking about. They're important."

Jill felt the beginnings of unease curling around her toes. She felt her heart thumping, and wanted only to seize the happiness of the previous moment and fly with it. He wanted her! He was offering her a job! She swallowed. With several slight hitches. Important ones.

"What are they?" she asked.

"Well, first, it's only a pilot. So, we shoot one show, we see how the network likes it, how it goes over with the public. I don't have to tell you. If everything clicks, we start mid-season. So, at the moment, what I'm offering you is a one-shot deal with the potential for more, but no promises."

"I understand."

"We go into pre-production in two weeks, which means I need a definite answer soon."

"You've got your answer already," Jill told him, decisively.

"What about the university?"

"They'll consider it invaluable practical experience. I can't see why they'd object. We're only talking about a few weeks. But that's my problem, and I'll deal with it." She took a breath, her eyes returning warily to the clock. "Why do I get the uncomfortable feeling there's more?"

"Probably because there is."

"And you've been saving the best for last?"

"As always. You ready?"

"They can't pay my usual rates?"

"No, that's not it. The money I'm sure can be negotiated."

"As always," Jill said, parroting his earlier expression. "Okay, what?"

"It's the subject matter."

"The subject matter?"

"Of the segment you'd be producing."

"Which is?"

There was a pause. "Wife-beating," Irving answered.

Jill felt her voice fall several octaves. "Wife-beating?"

"The state of the art in Chicago," he said dryly. "Statistics. Reasons. The legal ramifications." Another pause. "Examples." Another silence. "Jill, it's no coincidence that I want you for this particular assignment. In fact, it's the raison d'être for this whole conversation. I'll be frank. The network wasn't interested in free-lancers. Things are tight here, as everywhere. But I went a bit out on a limb. I know how much you want to come back. I know how much I want you back. So, when the idea for this show came up, I thought about you right away. And then when this Weatherby murder thing happened and the guy's wife started yelling foul, well, it's a natural. It's your husband's firm! You knew the man! I assume you've met his wife. Now, that might get you in places an outsider couldn't; it might not. But it was an interesting hook to sell to the network. I convinced them that with your inside connections both to the Weatherbys and to the legal profession, you were the only person who could do this job. And they've agreed."

There was another silence. "Beth Weatherby is my friend," Jill whispered.

"Don't get me wrong, Jill," Irving said quickly. "The episode doesn't have to be just about Beth Weatherby. I'm more interested in the legal ramifications. But there's no question that the Weatherbys would have to be mentioned, either as a jumping-off point, or possibly as a frame for the whole segment. That could be worked out during story conferences. But it's the Weatherbys that give this story its relevance—Beth Weatherby's claim of self-defense, not temporary insanity. Is self-defense a legitimate argument for what she did? For that matter, is temporary insanity any more legitimate? Would freeing Beth Weatherby be granting all women in her position a license to kill?"

"Is a marriage certificate a man's license to kill?" Jill asked in response.

There was a satisfied pause. "I knew you were the right person for this job," Irving smiled. "Think you can handle it?"

"I don't know," Jill said quietly. "David wouldn't be very happy under the circumstances."

"I realize that. That's why I'm giving you a few days to think it over." Jill said nothing. "I don't know when I'd be able to call you again, Jill, if your answer is no," he added, unnecessarily.

"I understand."

"Call me Thursday afternoon."

"I will."

" 'Bye."

"Goodbye." Jill replaced the receiver and stood staring at the tile on the kitchen floor. How did she get in messes like this? It was almost as if they deliberately sought her out. (There's Jill Plumley and, my God, it looks like she's had two peaceful days in a row! General alert! Messes—attack!) David wouldn't like it at all. He would want her miles away from any public involvement in the Weatherby case and any of its attendant legal ramifications! And Beth herself? How would she feel?

And if she said no? Irving had made the outcome of her refusal pretty clear. There'd be no further offers, at least for some time. This was her chance, her opportunity knocking. She could take it and run, or she could run and hide. She hadn't spoken to

Beth Weatherby since that extraordinary night the week before. She hadn't had time to discuss with David what Beth had told her. He'd been working late every night—the earliest evening being the Friday night he'd returned from taking Nicole Clark out for her celebration dinner—and the weekend had been lost to his work as well.

She'd needed the first few days to simply sort out all that she had heard, to come to terms with what Beth had confided. Only when it was clear in her own mind exactly how she felt would she feel free to discuss it with David. If they ever had the opportunity to really sit down and talk.

She needed to talk to both David and Beth, she realized. Irving had given her till Thursday afternoon, which meant she had to speak to both of them as soon as possible.

Jill looked up at the clock with a sudden shock. It was twenty minutes after eleven! How long had she been on the phone? How long had she been staring down at the floor?

She quickly headed for the door. If she was lucky, and the traffic was with her, she'd make it to the campus just in time for the end of her first class.

She was as surprised as he was by the way she looked.

"What did you do to your face?" he asked, getting up from behind his desk.

"I went to Saks. They were having a special today on makeup. Mr. Claridge himself was there. He told me personally what makeup was right for me," Jill laughed, finding herself embarrassed in front of her husband, "and well, they do it for you right there in the store. What do you think? Too much?"

David walked around his wife, examining her face as if it were a rare object. "No, not too much. You know I like you with makeup. I'm just not used to seeing you with so much of it on."

"You *do* think it's too much?"

"No," he laughed, "I think it's just right. I think Mr.—"

"Claridge."

"Mr. Claridge did a first-rate job. But it's a shock, that's all, considering that you never usually wear any. But I like it."

"He showed me how to put it on."

"Good." He leaned forward and kissed her. "So, is that why you dropped by the office?"

"Well," Jill hesitated, "it was one of the reasons. I finished classes at four o'clock and I dropped by Saks, and then I thought, well, I'm in the neighborhood, why don't I come up and show you how glamorous I've become while you've been so busy working and see if I can't persuade my always-gorgeous husband to take his newly renovated wife to dinner."

"Oh, Jill—"

"Please don't say no, David. We could go across the street to Winston's. It wouldn't take long."

"Look at my desk, Jill. Can you see over that pile of paperwork?"

"Your desk was always a mess," she reminded him.

"I can't, honey. I'm sorry."

"David, it's important. I need to talk to you."

There was a tap on the door and then it opened. Nicole Clark stood, regal and beautiful, in the doorway. "Oh, sorry," she said quickly to David. "I didn't realize anyone was with you. How are you, Jill?"

Jill felt the makeup burning acid-like holes into her skin, feeling like the clown in a circus when his time has been usurped to make way for the main attraction. Mr. Claridge, Jill decided in the second between Nicole's greeting and her own response, could take a few lessons from her husband's newest junior associate.

"I'm fine," Jill answered with pleasant briskness. "I want to congratulate you on your being called to the bar, and on becoming a member of the firm."

"Oh, thank you very much," Nicole said graciously. "It was very exciting. And wonderful having your husband at the ceremony. I needed the support."

"We all like support," Jill said, smiling at David.

David's voice caught her slightly off guard. "I'm taking my wife out for a quick dinner," he explained to the younger woman. "No more than an hour. Is there something you needed to discuss now or can it wait until tomorrow? Unless you'll be around later—"

Jill waited for Nicole's inevitable "I'll be around," but instead she heard, "No, I'm going home now. I'm tired and this can wait. Nice to see you again, Jill. Good night."

So, David had spoken to her as promised. And this was the result. I should have let him talk to her in the beginning, Jill thought, as David took her by the elbow and led her out of his office. It would have saved months of worry.

They sat across from each other and nibbled at their salads.

"So," David said firmly, "we have exhausted the weather and Mr. Claridge and your new crop of students. Are you going to tell me now why we're here? I mean, your day was interesting, I'll give you that," he continued, smiling. "But so far, I haven't heard anything I would describe as important." He reached over the table and grabbed her hand. "Not that seeing you isn't important. It is. And I'm glad I was coerced into this dinner."

Jill smiled widely. The makeup had been a good idea. Even if it did feel like she was wearing someone else's face. It was obviously a face that David liked.

"Irving called," she said, swallowing the last of her lettuce.

"Oh?" Definite interest.

"The network is producing a new show. Just a pilot. If everyone likes it, it would get its own time slot mid-season."

"What kind of show?"

"Chicago's answer to 'Sixty Minutes.' They're calling it 'Hour Chicago.' Hour with an H."

"Very clever."

"Yes," Jill agreed. "It would be based entirely in Chicago, I think. At least that's the impression I got, since it's supposed to be a show about Chicago and what's concerning the citizens and everything. And—"

"And what are you so nervous about telling me?" he asked, almost laughing. "It sounds wonderful! You'd be doing exactly what you want without a lot of traveling. I think it's fantastic!" He looked at her worried expression. "Did I jump the gun? They do want you, don't they?"

Jill nodded. "They want me."

"Well, that's great. Why the long face?"

Jill reached for her glass of water while the attentive waiter removed their salad plates and replaced them with the main course. She stared at her plate of ginger chicken on a bed of green noodles and immediately lifted her fork, absently twirling the green noodles, cooked, she knew, to *al dente* perfection, around and around the sterling silver utensil. "I love this restaurant," she said. "Remember when we used to come here a lot?"

"I remember. Did you forget my question?"

"No," she said. "I'm just not sure I want to answer it."

"What is it that they want you to do on this show, Jill? Work nights?"

"No," she answered quickly, wishing she could have said yes.

"You want to write it down on the napkin and slip it to me under the table?" he asked boyishly.

She laughed, her fork now fat with pasta. "I don't know how to say this except to just say it," she said. "I've made too much of it already. I'm sure you won't have any objections. I'm just being silly."

"Jill—" he said, with growing exasperation.

"The episode that they want me to produce is about wife-beating." Immediately, she saw his eyes narrow. "To be more specific, they're interested in not just the general phenomenon, but in Beth Weatherby. They feel her desire to plead self-defense opens up a lot of interesting legal possibilities that might make for an equally interesting television show."

"I bet they do," David scoffed. "And they just happened to pick you."

"No, they picked me quite deliberately. Irving made that very clear."

"Well, what did he say when you told him no?"

Jill laid down her fork but continued to stare at it. "I didn't tell him no," she said. "I told him I'd think about it."

"What is there to think about?" he demanded.

"It's not so simple, David. This might be the last chance I get."

"Baloney! There's always another chance. You know that as well as I do."

"What would be so wrong in my doing it?"

"Everything!" he almost shouted, surprising Jill by the vehemence in his voice. "You'd use your friendship with Beth; you'd use Al's memory; you'd use me, for God's sake."

"How would I be using you?"

"If it weren't for me, you'd never have even met Al Weatherby!"

"You forget," Jill reminded him, "that I met Al Weatherby the same way I met you. Doing my job!"

"And that's all that's important to you, isn't it?" he said, angrily. "Not me, not Beth, not Al. It doesn't matter who you hurt!"

"Who says I'd be hurting anybody?"

"Jill, for Christ's sake, you're not a child. You know that someone's going to be hurt if you do this story. Why else would you need time to think about it?"

"Because I felt I should discuss it first with you and with Beth."

"Well, you have my reaction. I think it stinks! I think that anything that lends any credence to Beth's disgusting allegations is a disgrace and I would object very strenuously to my wife having anything to do with it. And as for Beth, how do you think she'd feel knowing you'd exploit her friendship to get yourself back into television?"

"I didn't go seeking this job, David. It came to me."

"If you accept it, that's hardly relevant, is it?"

"I don't think Beth would view it as exploitation," Jill ventured.

David shook his head. "No, probably not. It might play right into her hands. You realize, of course," he continued, after a slight pause, "that no lawyer in the world would allow her to appear on the program."

"Oh, obviously," Jill quickly concurred, delighted they could agree on something. "I would never ask that. The angle of the show, from the way I read Irving, would hinge much more on the moral and legal aspects of what Beth did and her reasons for doing it."

"Great," David muttered, sarcastically. Jill noticed that neither of them had touched their food. "So, your mind's made up." Jill started to shake her head in protest. "Who are you kidding, Jill?" David asked her quickly. "Your mind was made up before you walked into my office. If you think anything else, then the only person you're fooling is yourself." He shoved his plate away. "You don't want my opinion. You want absolution. You want me to say, sure, go ahead, destroy what's left of a fine man's reputation. Use me and my firm and everyone around you. I'm right behind you. Well, I'm not, and I can't say it. I think it's wrong, and I don't want you to do it."

They stared at each other across the table. When Jill spoke, her voice came from deep inside her chest. "And if I decide to do it anyway?" she asked. "I mean, I really think I could do a good job of being fair to everyone, not blackening anyone's memory—"

"Wake up, Jill," David snapped. "Stop lying to yourself!"

"I don't think I am," she protested.

"Well then maybe you're too naive for television." He stood up. "At any rate, the answer to your question, which I believe was 'and if I decide to do it anyway?' is that it's a decision with which we will both have to learn to live."

"What does that mean?" she asked.

"Exactly what it says," he answered, putting thirty dollars on the table. "Look, I have to get back to work now. There's no point in running this thing into the ground. Finish up, take your time. I'll be home later." He bent over and kissed her forehead. "Don't wait up," he said.

Jill remained seated, staring down at her plate. Her appetite was gone.

"The food is not to your liking?" asked the waiter, several minutes later.

"The food is fine," Jill told him. "I'm just not feeling very well."

"I'm sorry to hear that," the waiter said with sincerity. "Some tea, perhaps?"

Jill shook her head. "No, thank you," she said. "Nothing."

Chapter 23

Jill wasn't sure at what precise moment she realized her husband was having an affair with Nicole Clark. She was sure only that it was a fact that was now a part of her life.

She sat in the staff room between the periods of her two morning classes and tried to focus her attention on the morning paper. Two men and three women had been found in a rooming house stabbed to death. Probably drug-related, the police surmised. Another man had murdered his wife and two children because he claimed that Christ had told him to do so in a dream the night before; yet another woman had been shot to death by her insanely jealous husband because he felt she'd smiled too long at the mailman. Jill flipped the page. A woman had been given a jail sentence of two years less a day for crushing the skull of her infant son; another couple, three of whose children had already died under suspicious circumstances, was telling the courts that they considered themselves excellent parents and that they intended to keep having children until God decided otherwise. Jill folded the paper in disgust, tossing it to the low table in front of her. She had no interest in the Classified section today. Companions Wanted didn't interest her. Her husband was sleeping with another woman.

She had felt him crawling into bed beside her the night before, accepting her feigned sleep as if it were real, not bothering to try to rouse her, to snuggle against her, to warm his body against hers. She felt him moving restlessly, trying to find a comfortable position, finding it after several minutes and drifting quickly off to sleep. She heard his breathing become slow and deep. Sitting up, she looked over at the clock. It was almost 1 A.M. She'd heard his key turn in the door not more than ten minutes before. He'd come straight into the bedroom, undressed quickly and gotten into bed. And yet he smelled so clean, so absolutely odorless that she knew with certainty he had taken great pains to rid himself of any unwanted body smells. Like the smells of lovemaking, she had thought, lying back down beside him, remembering that the last time he had smelled this nondescript, this sanitary, was the night several weeks ago when he had called her at night from his office and asked her so lovingly to pick him up. She remembered her nervousness the following morning, running around trying to please him, to disguise the smell of his deceit with the odor of scrambled eggs and toast, hiding from her conscious self the knowledge that he had been with Nicole.

And so the last few weeks had all been a lie. The little scene she had witnessed the two of them play out in his office the day before—("Is there something that you needed to discuss now or can it wait until tomorrow? Unless, you'll be around later . . ." "No, I'm going home now. I'm tired and this can wait.")—had been played strictly for her benefit and all in code. He was working late the same way he had done with Elaine. The work was the same. Only the names had been changed, she thought idly, surprised by how unsurprised she felt.

She yawned and stood up, walking over to the phone at the far end of the staff room. She dialed slowly and waited as it rang. It was picked up on the third ring.

"Hello."

"Mom?"

"Jill? Is everything okay?"

She smiled. "Come on, Mom. You can't tell me you knew something was wrong just from the way I said 'Mom.'"

"Of course I could. A mother knows. Tell me. Where are you?"

"At school. In the staff room."

"Now I know something's wrong. You never call me from work. What is it? Something with David?"

"Maybe I should just let you tell me," Jill sighed.

"No, you tell me. What is it, darling?"

Jill looked around the room, trying not to cry. "I'm just a little depressed, Mom, that's all. I don't know why."

"You want to talk about it?"

"I don't know."

"Why don't you come for dinner tonight? Your father is going to play duplicate over at the club and I'll be alone. I'd appreciate the company. I take it David's working late again."

"Yes," Jill whispered.

"Good. Then you'll come?"

"What time?"

"Six-thirty?"

"Fine."

"See you later, darling."

"Thanks."

"'Bye, sweetie."

Jill hung up the phone and wondered what precisely she was going to tell her mother. That she'd been right all along? That David, having had no trouble cheating on one woman, was having no more trouble cheating on another? That everything was happening exactly as her mother had predicted it would so many years ago? God, were men really so predictable? Had someone taken out a patent on the situation? Were they all reacting in accordance with some divine plan, like the man who said Christ had directed him to murder his family? Was the whole world nuts? Jill looked around the room, seeking out the strange in each familiar face. Or is it just me? she wondered, leaving the staff room and walking toward her next class.

"Did you hear what happened to Sarah Welles?" her mother asked as she opened the front door and ushered Jill inside.

"No, what happened to Sarah Welles?" Jill asked, conjuring up the image of the young movie queen, Hollywood's latest attempt to duplicate the magic that was Marilyn Monroe.

"She's dead! Weren't you listening to the radio? They've been talking about nothing else."

"I didn't have it on. What happened? Suicide? Murder?"

"Neither. A stupid accident. She was washing her hair in her sink and apparently she lifted her head and hit it against one of her solid gold faucets and it knocked her unconscious."

"And she died?"

"Not from that. She drowned! Can you imagine? In her own sink! Her face fell into the sink full of water and she drowned! Only twenty-six years old! I don't know! You'd think that with solid gold faucets, she could afford to go to the hairdresser's."

"That's awful," Jill said, following her mother into the kitchen, slowly organizing her thoughts. "The implications are so scary," she began. "It means that we don't have any control at all over what happens to us. Here's this young woman with everything going for her, and one minute she's washing her hair and the next minute she's dead. Like Janet Leigh in the shower in *Psycho*."

Her mother looked closely at Jill. "Except that if Janet Leigh hadn't stolen that money to begin with, she'd have never ended up in that cheap motel. So—we do have some control over our lives, my darling. Accidents happen, sure. Tragic accidents. But that's all part of life. End of motherly lecture. You hungry?"

"Yes," Jill smiled.

"Good. I have a nice stew ready. Sit down."

Jill sat down at the round table in the comfortably wide kitchen of her childhood. "Are you ever going to change this wallpaper?" she asked, looking at the green and brown print of clocks and country flowers that covered the room. It had been there as long as she could remember. It was still in remarkable condition.

"We did change it," her mother said, putting a plateful of steaming stew in front of her. "Last year."

"You got the same paper?" Jill asked, incredulously.

"Can you imagine? They still had it in stock! I guess it's a classic." Her mother laughed, sitting next to Jill with her own plate of stew. "Take some bread," she said, pointing to the bread basket in the middle of the table.

"How come you got the same one?" Jill asked, amazed.

"Your father likes it," her mother answered simply.

"And that's why?"

"It's a good reason," her mother said.

Jill sighed, putting down her fork and looking at her mother. "You've been married how long?" she asked.

"Thirty-eight years this January," her mother answered.

"Thirty-eight years," Jill repeated. "That's a long time."

"It's all relative," her mother said. "It goes by so fast."

"You're happy?" Jill asked, knowing her question was simplistic, not knowing how else to ask it.

Her mother shrugged. "Well, they say that the first twenty-five years are the hardest." Both women smiled. "How can I answer you? You know what else they say—that one couple's perfect marriage is something no one else in his right mind would want. You know—you pick what peculiarities you're going to put up with, and you learn to live with them. Sometimes you're happy; sometimes you're not so happy. In fact, sometimes you're miserable. But what usually keeps you going during those miserable times is the knowledge that it was good before, it'll be good again. Everything goes in cycles. Some years are better than others. But you have to have faith in your instincts—you say to yourself, there must have been some reason why I married him!—and usually you can remember what it was, even if it takes a little doing. You say to yourself, I loved the man enough to marry him. Surely, there's some of that love still around. You look hard enough, you can usually find it."

"And love is all you need?" Jill asked with the proper amount of musical irony.

"Of course not," her mother answered. "You've been around long enough to know that besides love, you also need a high degree of tolerance, and respect and acceptance. And luck," her mother added. "Look at your brother. He married Emily when he was twenty and she was seventeen. They've been married for sixteen years and they still can't keep their hands off each other. They're planning a ski trip to Aspen this winter. I don't know," she said, shaking her head, "they go where it's hot in the summer and where it's cold in the winter. Beats me. What was I saying?"

"How Stephen and Emily can't keep their hands off each other," Jill reminded her.

"That's right. It's embarrassing sometimes." She looked directly at Jill. "But physical attraction isn't the main thing. It may be part of the reason two people get married, but it shouldn't be the whole reason. There has to be more. So what if a man is good-looking? There are lots of good-looking men around. So what if he's good in bed? A lot of men are good in bed. Don't tell your father I said that." She smiled. "A good marriage is made up of so many things. And even good marriages are made up of a lot of very bad times. You have to decide what's most important to you, what you're willing to give to keep it going, what you're willing to give up. Sometimes people ask too much." She paused, almost reluctant to ask the next question. "Is David asking too much, Jill?" she said, taking Jill's head in her arms and pressing it against her breasts.

"I don't know," Jill moaned against the warmth of her mother's body. "I don't know."

Jill called Beth Weatherby from her mother's house and asked if she could drive up and speak to her. Beth readily agreed and at nine o'clock, Jill found herself in front of the now familiar gray-brick exterior. She sat inside her car, her head swimming with words her mother had spoken. ("Stop talking like you're some little nobody who miraculously landed herself such a prize! You're bright; you're beautiful; you can do anything. You're the prize! Don't laugh. This is not just a mother speaking. Take a good look at this prize you've got. It might look good and it probably moves well, but what else has it done for you? I'll use your words—are you happy?") Jill closed her eyes and was immediately surrounded by images of her husband and Nicole Clark dancing around her head, their legs catching in her hair yet not tripping, still dancing, pulling her hair out by the roots with their careless feet, unaware or unfeeling of the pain they were inflicting.

Jill opened her eyes and pushed open the car door, sitting

with her feet touching the sidewalk for several long seconds. How had everything gotten so turned around? She wasn't stupid. She wasn't weak. She wasn't some blithering little bubblehead whose happiness depended on having a man in her life. Or at least, she hadn't started out that way. She had begun life as a bright, secure little girl who had grown into a bright, secure young woman, independent, talented, full of natural resources. She had married at a time when she was supposedly very much her own person, someone who certainly knew the ropes and was not about to fall into all the familiar traps. And yet that's precisely where she had ended up—in the most familiar trap of all.

What was it about women that made them so eager to put themselves in this kind of position? Or worse, she thought, looking over at Beth Weatherby's house, thinking of all that Beth had endured over the years. Why are we such willing victims? Was Beth Weatherby right—did everything stem from man's superior physical strength? Did the socialization process start in the cradle? "Damn," she said, shaking the weight of rational thought off her shoulders. She could sit and intellectualize till dawn; she could rationalize and analyze and theorize and it would still boil down to one thing—she wanted David. She would do anything to keep him. She would make herself over, even turn herself inside out to keep him. She could outwit Nicole Clark, and if that proved impossible she could simply outwait her. And any others who came along. If David was unhappy at home, then she was at least partly responsible. She would change.

Jill stepped out of the car and slammed the door, hoping the night air would empty her head, clear away the unwanted pictures that seemed intent on driving her half-crazy. Sarah Welles had died while washing her hair. Nothing made any sense. Everything in this world was at least vaguely absurd. Why should her life be any different?

Beth had agreed instantly to the idea of her doing the show. ("Do it, Jill," she had said. "It's important. Tell people what I told you. Do the show. Maybe it'll wake some people up.")

Beth's easy acceptance had made the problem all the more

acute. Jill had convinced herself in the time it took to walk from her car to the front door that if Beth's reaction was as negative as David's had been, she would tell Irving no. David was probably right—Irving would call her again, if not this year, maybe the next. ("Do it, Jill," Beth had said, without any questions. "It's important. Do the show.")

Jill pulled her Volvo into the space beside the empty parking place that was reserved for David's Mercedes. She got quickly out of the car and headed toward the elevator, her keys held firmly between each finger, like a set of brass knuckles, to fend off attackers. Not that she expected anyone to be lurking around, but then, hell, Sarah Welles hadn't expected to drown in her bathroom sink either.

She reached her apartment, and despite her knowledge that David was not home, was disappointed to find the place empty. She quickly moved from room to room, turning on every light and leaving them on as she entered her bedroom and plopped down on her bed.

She picked up the phone and called David's private office number. It was just past ten-thirty. What was she going to tell him? Come home—I've decided not to do the show? Just please, stay away from Nicole and come back home.

There was no answer. Jill let the phone ring ten times, hung up and dialed again. After ten more rings she gave up. Perhaps he was already on his way home, she thought, kicking off her shoes and lying back on the bed. Maybe the whole thing was part of her imagination, something she had invented to get the old adrenaline pumping because things were starting to move too smoothly. She had no proof her husband was having an affair with Nicole Clark. Indeed, she had no hard evidence, as David would call it, that he wasn't doing exactly as he claimed to be doing each night. The firm was undoubtedly in a state of chaos because of Al Weatherby's death; the work load she had seen on David's desk was indeed prodigious. It was understandable, laudable even, that he felt he had to work this hard, this late, and this often to catch up. She had nothing but a lot of overhasty assumptions and conclusions to back up her unwarranted suspicions. David had done nothing. Was doing nothing. She was the only one who was making herself miserable.

The phone rang beside her and Jill picked it up, feeling strangely groggy.

"Hello."

David's voice was soft and mellow. "Hi, sweetheart. Did I wake you up?"

"I must have dozed off," she said, clearing her throat, her eyes turning away from the bright glare of the overhead light.

"I'm sorry, hon. I just wanted you to know that I'm on my way home."

"Where are you?" she asked.

"Where do you think?" he said, surprised. "At the office."

"I called you," she said, looking at the clock. "About half an hour ago." She sat up.

"You did?" he asked. "Not here."

"I let it ring ten times. Then I hung up and called again."

"Well, it didn't ring—oh, shit, just a minute. I've got the phone turned down. There, I just fixed it. Stupid thing. I turned it off this afternoon so I wouldn't be distracted. Then I forgot about it. Sorry about that, honey."

"No harm done," she said, a tear falling the length of her cheek. "See you soon."

She replaced the receiver and sat on the side of the bed for several minutes in absolute silence. She saw David sitting in a strange room filled with nondescript furniture, Nicole Clark moving languorously in the background. She pictured Nicole as she moved to stand beside David, whose hand remained poised over the telephone, a look of doubt trimmed with a slight tinge of guilt falling over his beautiful face. She felt Nicole's hand come down gently, encouragingly, on David's shoulder. Saw him reach up and gently stroke that hand, looking back and smiling sadly in her direction. The same way he had done approximately six years ago when she had stood in Nicole's position and heard him say virtually the same words to Elaine.

Chapter 24

She checked her makeup in the mirror and then checked it again and then a third time, trying to remember everything that Mr. Claridge had told her. Light under the eyes, a little high-lighting at the sides, just a hint of mascara, a liberal stroke of blush-on and a finishing gloss over her lips. Why did she feel like she needed to wash her face?

She heard his key turn in the door and rushed to the mirror again to check her appearance. The negligee was new, expensive and completely out of character. Soft pink lace had been discarded with her diapers. It hadn't felt right then and it felt less right now, but David had once expressed a liking for things frilly and feminine, and despite the fact that her arms and feet were freezing and she knew she'd feel much better wearing a heavy sweater and a pair of socks, she persisted, pulling her shoulders back and trying to fill out the delicate trim of the low-cut bodice.

She took a deep breath as she heard David close the door behind him, and walked from the bedroom into the hall. David Plumley meets Total Woman, she thought as she moved, feeling like an inept understudy for an ailing Raquel Welch. What am I doing, she wondered, wearing these clothes and this face and carrying on in this ridiculous fashion? I am trying to get my husband back, her inner voice responded. And if this approach can't help, well, then, at least it can't hurt.

"Hi," he said when he saw her. "What are you doing up? It's late."

"Just midnight," she replied, throatily.

"You didn't have to wait up," he said, moving into the kitchen to check on the day's mail.

"Just a lot of bills," she told him, coming up behind him and encircling him with her arms.

He patted her hands gently. "What do I smell?" he asked.

"Oh," she said, her heart beginning to race, "I just took a bath. I used a new bath oil—"

"No, that's not it. Smells like chocolate."

"Oh, I made a cake," she said quickly.

"Sounds good," he said, moving to the dining room and sitting down. "Can I have a piece?"

"Sure," she said, wondering why instead of rushing her into the bedroom, he was suddenly hungry for chocolate cake. What she was wearing couldn't have totally escaped him; he had to have noticed the way she was made up, the way she smelled. He had to realize why she had waited up. It had been several weeks since they'd last made love. He had to know what she was trying to tell him.

She took the cake from its dish and cut two substantial pieces.

"Would you like some coffee?" she asked.

"No," he said, his back to her. "Coffee'll keep me awake, and all I want to do is sleep. I'll have a glass of milk."

All I want to do is sleep, she heard his voice repeat. Well, he noticed all right, your face, your negligee, your whole ridiculous get-up. And this is his reply. Jill felt cold with humiliation and strode purposefully into the bathroom, turning on the hot water and scrubbing her face until it squeaked. Then she marched briskly into her bedroom, retrieved a warm sweater from her closet and threw it over her shoulders while she fished in her top drawer for a pair of heavy socks and pulled them on.

Pushing her now wool-stockinged feet into a pair of tattered pink slippers and thrusting her arms inside the sweater sleeves, she headed back to the kitchen and poured her husband his glass of milk, putting the food in front of him on the table.

"Thanks," he said absently as Jill sat down across from him and took a bite of her cake. "Thought you were on a diet," he said, half managing a smile. If he noticed that her appearance was in any way changed, he said nothing.

Jill shrugged. She'd been wrong when she thought disguising herself behind makeup and soft frills wouldn't hurt. It hurt plenty. She took another bite of chocolate cake.

"This is good," he said, joining her.

"Thanks," she said. The way to a man's heart, she thought. "So, how come you waited up?"

"I wanted to see you," she said, truthfully, staring into his deep green eyes, his face as beautiful to her as ever, as refreshing to her sight as a cool glass of lemonade. Would she always feel this, she wondered, this rush of pure pleasure every time she looked at him?

"Well, that's sweet, honey. But you shouldn't have. You look tired, and God knows I'm in no condition to be much company."

Jill looked down at the table, trying to ignore his remark about her looking tired. "Do you have any idea," she asked quietly, "how much longer all this is going to go on?"

"Not much longer, I hope."

"It seems to be getting worse."

"I don't like it any better than you do. Christ, I'm so tired all the time."

"Too tired to make love?" she asked, trying to sound as appealing as she could. He said nothing. "It's been a while," she continued softly.

"Oh, Jill, please don't start," he interrupted. "Can't you see I can barely stand up these days?!"

That's not my fault, buster, she wanted to yell. Instead she said, "I'm sorry. It's just that I miss you."

His face softened again. "I miss you, too, honey."

Jill finished off the rest of her cake.

"So," he said, "what did you tell Irving? Today was the day you had to decide, wasn't it?"

"Yes."

"And?"

Jill said nothing, wishing now she had gone to bed early.

"You told him you'd do it," he said for her after a pause.

"Yes," Jill answered.

David brought his hands to rest behind his head. "Well, what can I say?"

"I spoke to Beth," Jill explained. "She was very supportive."

"I'll bet she was."

"She wants me to do it. She feels it's an important issue."

"I'm sure she does."

"So do I, David."

"That's obvious." He stood up.

"I'd like to talk to you about it, now that we're on the subject."

"I've said all I have to say about it, Jill."

"I haven't," she reminded him.

He sat back down. "Go ahead."

"I want you to understand why I'm doing the show."

"No," he interrupted. "You want yourself to understand."

"Please don't put words in my mouth! I know what it is I want to say. I'm quite capable of expressing myself."

"Look, Jill, I'm really tired. Just say what you feel you have to say and let me get to sleep. You know that I'm never going to understand."

Jill swallowed. "I've seen Beth several times in the last few weeks. She's looking much better. Most of the bruises are gone. Her ribs are still a bit sore, but generally, she's looking pretty good."

"Better than Al," David said, his voice overflowing with sarcasm.

"I believe her, David," Jill said finally.

There was silence. His look was quizzical, verging on the defensive. He would not like what she was going to say.

"You believe what?" David asked without moving.

"I believe Beth's story." Another silence. "I've talked to her. I really listened to her. And I believe her."

"Believe what?! That Al was beating her?! That she was a battered wife who suddenly flipped out?"

"She didn't flip out. She says she's not crazy, not even temporarily. I agree. I don't think she's the slightest bit crazy. I think she did what she had to do. She had no choice. She was fighting for her life!"

David stood up with such sudden force that his chair fell over backward and crashed to the floor. "What?!" he demanded. "I can't believe I'm hearing this!"

Jill stood up, torn between comforting her husband and standing her ground. "David, I don't want to fight about this—"

"What is it with you lately? Maybe you're the one who's gone temporarily insane!"

"David—"

"What do you mean exactly when you say that you believe her?" he demanded.

"I believe that Al did all the things she says he did."

"What things *exactly?*" he repeated, stressing the final word.

"What do you want me to say? I'm trying to answer your questions but all you're doing is shouting at me." She began pacing nervously back and forth.

"Jill, for God's sake, you knew Al! And not just casually. We played cards with the man, had him here for dinner, how many times? You saw the way he was with Beth—"

"In public."

"You're saying he was a tender, loving husband in public and a monster in private?"

"That's what Beth is saying. I am saying only that I believe her."

"A few weeks ago you didn't know what to believe."

"I didn't understand then."

"Understand what?"

"About Al! David, what good is this doing? We're just going around in circles."

"You said you wanted me to understand! Okay. Go ahead. This is your big chance. Make me understand. Make me understand how Al could fool the whole world for over twenty-five years. Make me understand why my wife would believe the word of a cunning, conniving murderess and not her own eyes and ears."

Jill stopped her pacing and lowered her voice, trying to restore calm. "I listened to her, David. I really listened to her. She wasn't making it up. She wasn't lying. No one could be that good an actress."

"Everyone can when their life is at stake." David walked around the table to face his wife. "Has it occurred to you that if what she's saying is true, that for as long as you've known her, everything else about her has been a lie?" Jill said nothing, allowing his words to find meaning in her mind. "If she could fool you for four years, why couldn't she fool you now?" Jill was about to protest, but her thoughts were too confused. "Why didn't she confide in you sooner? Why didn't she just leave him, for God's sake?"

Jill sank back into her chair. "She was terrified he'd kill her. She was too beaten down—"

"Did she ever seem frightened to you? Ever seem beaten down?"

Jill's mind traveled quickly through four years of friendship. "The night we played bridge," she answered at last.

David's eyes reflected his confusion, then cleared, indicating he had the answer. "She was upset about Lisa's involvement with a married man. Al explained—"

"Yes, Al explained. He always had an explanation. But it was a lie. There was no married boyfriend. There was only Al. David, Beth didn't cut herself that night—Al did it!" David was about to shout his protest; Jill kept talking. "And now that I think about it, so much of it makes sense. At the picnic, Beth gave me some stomach pills, told me she'd had ulcers for years—"

"Oh, Christ, you're fishing at straws!"

"I believe her, David."

"Her own children don't believe her!"

"Lisa does."

David paused. "If Lisa's decided to believe her mother, it's because she can't deal with what's happened in any other way."

"Maybe she believes her because she knows it's true."

"Oh, hogwash, Jill! I'm not listening to any more of this!"

"Why are you taking it so personally? It has nothing to do with you."

"It has everything to do with me! Al Weatherby was my friend, my mentor, my colleague. I loved the man, damn it, and my wife, who also knew and liked the man, is suddenly willing to believe every horrible little tidbit she hears about him. Not only that, but from what you're telling me, you actually believe he deserved to die."

"No, I—"

"If you believe Al was the kind of monster his wife says he was—do you or don't you?"

"I believe—"

"Just a simple yes or no."

"David, stop it. I am not on the witness stand."

"Answer the question."

"I believe what Beth says."

"That Al was a monster?"

"You're putting words in my mouth again!"

"You feel Beth was justified in what she did?"

"I don't feel she had any choice."

"She couldn't pick up the phone and call the police?"

"David, you know how ineffectual the police are about things like that—"

"You feel she was right to take the law into her own hands?"

"Please lower your voice."

"Answer my question! Do you feel she was right in taking the law into her own hands?"

"It was self-defense!"

David stared at his wife in dumb amazement. "I just can't believe what I'm hearing."

"David, when a man murders his wife, more often than not, his only weapon is his fists."

"The man was asleep!"

"She had no chance against him when he was awake! He would have killed her. She had no choice."

"We all have choices. It's part of what being an adult is all about."

He turned from her and stared out the window at the wide

expanse of the city. Jill stood for several minutes before coming up behind him and running her hand across his back.

"Please don't," he said, without looking at her.

"David, we don't have to be angry at each other—"

He turned sharply toward her. "Can't you see what you're doing?"

She backed off several paces. "What am I doing?"

"You're making a mockery of my whole way of life."

Jill was genuinely confused. "I don't understand. How am I doing that?"

"I'm a lawyer! You're telling me that all I believe in, all I've worked for is just a big joke. That it's okay for people to take the law into their own hands—"

"What I'm saying is that I believe Beth's story. David, how can you be so damn sure that there isn't the slightest possibility that what Beth is saying is true?"

"Because I knew the man!"

"You didn't live with him."

"I didn't have to!"

"You won't admit to even a tiny speck of doubt?"

"Not one speck! Al was a kind and decent man. There is simply no question in my mind about that. But even if there was some doubt, even if I was willing to accept these ridiculous lies as truth, it would all be strictly beside the point."

"The point being?"

"The point being that Beth Weatherby murdered her husband in cold blood!"

"Not if it was self-defense!"

David looked back out the window, then without looking at Jill, turned and walked past her to the door. Jill's eyes followed him silently. He stopped. "I'm going out for a while."

"Oh, David, please don't—"

"I'm sorry, Jill, I can't stay here. My head is reeling. I'm tired and angry—very angry—and I need some time to myself. Actually," he said, suddenly laughing, "what I really need are a few stiff drinks."

Jill tried to keep her voice from betraying her inner hysteria. "Please don't go out, David. Just get into bed. I won't bother you."

"I can't, Jill. I can't lie down. I have to get out. Walk around or something."

"Where will you go? You can't walk around the streets of Chicago after midnight."

"Then I'll drive," he said simply, heading for the door.

"Can I come?"

"No."

"David, please, you can't keep walking out on me every time we have an argument! Can't we just agree to disagree?"

He opened the door. "Tell your good friend the next time you're talking to her that she'll stand a much better chance in court pleading temporary insanity."

Without turning back, he shut the door behind him.

Jill felt the urge to cry and forced the tears down into her throat, returning to the dining room and righting the overturned chair, then sinking into it. Why did everything lately have to end in a fight? Why couldn't she just learn to keep her big mouth shut? Absently, she reached over and finished off the remainder of David's piece of cake. Then she walked into the kitchen and polished off the rest.

Chapter 25

Jill rolled over in bed, determined to find a comfortable position. It was useless. She'd never get comfortable. She sat up and turned on the light, looking at the clock. It was after 2 A.M. David still wasn't home.

She felt small tinglings of panic begin to spread across her body, the start of what she recognized as an anxiety attack. Calm down, she told herself, wishing she had one of Beth's chalky white tablets. Lie back. It'll be all right.

She did as her inner voice demanded, laying her head against her pillow and taking several deep breaths, telling her body to relax. Relax. David would surely come home, probably quite drunk, very apologetic. He wouldn't stay out all night. Oh please, don't let him stay out all night.

Her body immediately tensed, the tingling in the tips of her fingers and in the pit of her stomach returning. Relax, she repeated. He'll be home. He wouldn't be so obvious; he wouldn't hurt her in this way. He was just going through a very difficult time and she wasn't making things any easier for him. But he'd get over it. They'd both get over it. He wouldn't stay out all night. He had to know she'd be thinking of a night so long ago when he'd left another house after another fight and turned up drunk and searching at another door. Her door.

She opened her eyes wide, feeling her breathing becoming short and choppy. There was no point in trying to relax—she knew she'd never sleep.

Jill got out of bed and marched into the den, flipping on the television with the remote control unit. Cary Grant's youthful face filled the large screen. She recognized the movie immediately—*I Was a Male War Bride*. A wonderful, funny movie. Running quickly back to her room, she seized her heavy sweater and returned, plopping herself down inside the big leather chair and giving the TV her undivided attention, losing herself in a world where even armies were filled with innocents, and the colors of reality were not permitted to disturb the simple blacks and whites of the land of make-believe.

She tried hard to concentrate on Cary Grant and Ann Sheridan, struggled against the image of the shadowy figure who was emerging in the background, getting clearer, until she came strongly into focus, throwing everything else into the background, as if the cameraman had readjusted his lens, superimposing her face over all the others. Jill watched the image become real, powerless to move or change the channel.

She saw Nicole Clark in bed, asleep. Watched her turn over, earlier smells of David still lingering against her pillow. Felt her dreaming, as she herself had been dreaming on that distant night, dreaming about a parade, a marching band. The drummers banging loudly on their drums. So loudly that she had felt her eyes open against the noise in protest. Aware now that she was awake and yet the drumming was continuing.

Now the image shifted again. Nicole getting out of bed, moving to the door, became Jill stumbling toward the window. What was going on? Who was out there on the street? It was cold. It was the middle of the night!

And now, not only banging but other sounds as well. Angry, barking noises. The great Doberman awake and alarmed, his owner's voice shrill and demanding—"What's going on here? Get away or I'll call the police!"

David was shouting her name. "Where's Jill?" he was demanding.

"Get out of here or I'm calling the cops, do you hear me?!" her landlady shouted through the door.

"No, wait, please!" Jill called, running down the steps. "It's for me."

"Not at three o'clock in the morning, it isn't."

"Please, Mrs. Everly, he's obviously drunk. We can't let him go anywhere in that condition."

"He got here, didn't he?"

"Yes, he did," Jill said with surprising strength. "And he's staying here. In my apartment. Now I'm sorry he woke you up. It won't happen again. But he *is* coming inside."

The landlady had retreated, with her dog still snarling. Only as she closed the door behind her did Jill notice that Mrs. Everly's right hand firmly clutched a large, unfriendly shotgun.

"She could have killed you," Jill exclaimed, ushering David quickly inside and closing the door, only now thinking how she must look to him, her hair greasy, her skin sweaty with a newly broken fever, her body wrapped in flannel. Why, of all nights, did he have to pick this one?

"I came to see how you were feeling," he said as his arms reached out for her. She let herself be surrounded by his body, smelled the liquor that permeated his skin, felt his blond hair softly whip against her damp forehead. He's in my arms, she thought.

"I look such a mess," she whispered.

"You look so pretty," he said simultaneously.

It was cold in the hallway despite the warmth of his body. "Can you make it up the stairs?" she asked, reluctant to loosen her grip. He said nothing and she realized she was holding him up. "Can you walk?" she asked. Again he said nothing, allowing her to lead him. They walked slowly, stumbling against the walls, clutching at the railing, finally reaching the top of the stairs and getting inside Jill's apartment. David collapsed onto the floor. "David?"

He looked up at her. Jill felt like a giant. "You're so pretty," he said.

"Let me get you a cup of coffee," she pleaded. He nodded.

"I'll go put the kettle on. I only have instant. Is that all right?" He smiled. She ran into the kitchen and poured cold water in the kettle, setting it down on the electric burner. Then she measured some coffee into a mug and put it on the counter. He was here; David was really here. And it didn't matter that she hadn't seen him all week or that she'd been sick with a cold and he hadn't come over; that they'd been trying to cool things and she'd been miserable; he was here now. It didn't matter that it was the middle of the night and her landlady would probably throw her out in the street come morning or that his wife was probably frantic with worry, wondering where he was so late. All that mattered was that he was here, that this wasn't a dream. He probably doesn't know *where* he is, she thought, hurrying back into the main room. "David, are you awake?" she asked, kneeling in front of him. His eyes were closed. He opened them.

"Yes," he said.

"Do you know where you are?" she asked.

"In your apartment," he said simply.

"Do you know who I am?" she asked, holding her breath.

"You're the prettiest girl I've ever seen," he answered.

She smiled, running a hand through her hair. Why did she have to look so awful? "Do you know my name?"

His smile grew very wide. "I may be drunk," he said, "but I'm not an idiot! You're the woman I love! You're Jill," he said softly.

"Well, I had to make sure," she cried happily. "You keep telling me how pretty I am. I thought you might not be seeing too straight!"

"I'm not, but you're still pretty."

"You shouldn't be sitting on the floor," she said, suddenly. "You'll get a chill. Come on, let me move you over to the bed."

She put her hands under his armpits, trying to lift him up. It was like trying to move a cement statue. "David, do you think you could help me a bit—"

He smiled at her innocently. "What would you like me to do?" he asked.

"Just lift your butt a little," she said. "Try and get up on your feet."

"I'm very good at lifting my butt," he said. Jill laughed.

"That's right," she told him as he tried to follow her instructions. She managed to get him to his feet and together they stumbled toward the bed. "Okay," she said, "let go."

"Not a chance," he said, pulling them both down.

Jill lay breathless in David's arms. This isn't a dream, she kept repeating. Please don't let this be another dream. They lay completely still, David too drunk to move, Jill too afraid he might.

It was a few minutes before she realized that she couldn't breathe. Her nasal passages were completely blocked; her head was swimming. They made a fine pair, she thought, and the thought made her laugh. He opened his eyes and rolled over, his hand moving without plan to cover her mouth. Oh great, she thought, he's covered the only breathing apparatus I have that still works.

Gently, with great care, she tried to remove his arm. She touched his fingers, felt the soft hairs on the back of his hand, and very slowly pushed the hand aside. He took no notice. Jill sat up slowly in bed, careful not to make any sudden movements that might disturb him. Why had he come here now? she wondered. And why so drunk?

Possibly a fight with Elaine, she decided. Over what? She grabbed a kleenex from the side of the bed and blew her nose as quietly as she could manage. It didn't seem to help. Her nose remained as stubbornly plugged as ever. And probably fire engine red, she thought, and flaky. Why did you have to come tonight? she demanded of him without asking. Maybe it's better that you're so drunk, she decided. But what had happened that made him that way? Was it all over with Elaine? The thought made her feel light-headed. She stood up too quickly and he sat up abruptly. Oh no, she thought. Please don't get up; please don't go home.

"Where are you going?" he asked. It was obvious from his tone that he wasn't planning on going anywhere.

"The water's boiling," she said, her voice a hoarse whisper. "I'm so mixed up I can't remember if you take cream or sugar."

"Beats me," he said, smiling.

"I think black would be best," she told him, shuffling toward the kitchen, looking back in his direction to make sure he was still there. She poured his coffee and made herself a cup of tea, slowly adding the boiling water, feeling the steam reach up into her nose, momentarily clearing her sinuses, allowing her the luxury of breathing again, if only for the moment.

She heard him moving, the sound of his feet on the floor. Grabbing a mug in each hand she hurried into the other room.

"Where are you going?" she asked. He was almost at the front door, although he'd left his jacket in a crumpled heap on the bed.

"The bathroom," he muttered.

"The bathroom is over there!" Both hands being full, she used her chin to indicate direction. He smiled and came toward her, kissing her full on the lips. She felt a sinking sensation in her legs, knew that if she didn't put down the mugs, her hands would simply drop them. He pulled away from her as if in slow motion.

"God, you're sweet," he said, then looked totally confused. "The bathroom?" he asked again.

"Over there," she told him, following behind and lowering both mugs to the floor by the bed. "Are you all right? Can you make it by yourself?"

"I've been going to the bathroom by myself since I was three years old," he said.

"Drunk?" she asked.

He laughed and lurched forward, out of her sight. She heard the light switch on and the door close behind him. He's going to stay, she thought. He's really going to stay. Jill reached down and brought the mug of tea to her lips, sipping slowly, allowing the steam to seep into her pores. It made her perspire more, and soon she felt trickles of sweat running across her face. She finished her tea and decided on another cup, returning quickly to the kitchen. This was crazy, she thought. It was almost three-thirty in the morning and she should be asleep in bed, not walking around her apartment, not contemplating the things her mind couldn't stop thinking about. About the possibility that he had left his wife for good. Elaine had to know he was with another woman. How could she live with that knowledge and not confront him? Staying all night meant more than just a casual affair. It meant that he no longer put Elaine's feelings ahead of hers, that he could no longer hide her existence from his wife. That he no longer cared to try.

She looked toward the bathroom. David had been there a long time. She hoped he wasn't being sick but imagined he probably was. She poured herself another cup of tea, catching her reflection in the toaster. My God, she looked absolutely awful. She ran for her purse in the front closet, searching through it and pulling out her brush. Taking another fast glance at the bathroom, she ran back into the kitchen and tried to brush her hair. The frenzied brushes only made it look more greasy, and her eyes were all puffy and as swollen as her nose. There was nothing she could do that would make her look any better short of cutting off her head. She looked down, saw the sweaty flannel nightgown and heavy wool socks and winced almost audibly. Thank God he's so drunk, she told herself, wondering if perhaps she shouldn't see if he was okay.

"David?" she called quietly, knocking gently on the bathroom door. "David, are you okay?" There was no response. "David? Can you hear me?" She put her hand on the doorknob and felt it turn. It wasn't locked. "David, can I come in?" There was nothing, no sound at all. "I'm opening the door, David," she called, her voice as loud and strong as she could manage. She tried to push the door open but nothing happened; it wouldn't budge. There was something blocking it. Jill felt herself becoming frightened. She pushed frantically at the door, felt it give a few inches, saw David's blond hair on the floor on the other side. "My God," she cried. "David, are you all right?" Had he fallen? she wondered, or simply lain down? Had he hurt himself? Had he passed out? "David, please, can you sit up?" She pushed the door farther open, saw his eyes closed with sleep. She couldn't see any bruises or bumps; there didn't seem to be any blood. She reached her hands inside the door and awkwardly tried to pry his body loose from the other side. She succeeded in getting enough of her own body inside to give the door the extra push it needed. David rolled over lifelessly as the bathroom door opened against him.

Jill crouched down, turning him onto his back, looking over

his face and head for signs of a bad fall. There weren't any. She lifted his head, examining the back of his skull. It didn't look like he'd fallen.

Jill looked hopelessly around the small room, trying to decide on a course of action. She could throw him in the bathtub, try to sober him up. No, he could drown that way, she decided, choosing instead to stick him under the shower. She couldn't just leave him on the bathroom floor all night.

She stood up, having laid his head gently back on the floor, and turned on the shower. Just warm enough to wake him up a little. To be able to get some coffee into him. The first problem, of course, was getting him in the shower.

She looked at him, asleep on the floor, the most glorious-looking man she'd ever seen. Pale and blond and perfect. This is all I will ever want, she thought. She kissed him, felt his body instinctively stir. Her eyes traveled the length of his body. She'd have to undress him.

The room was starting to get warm. The noise of the water was echoing in her ears. She started to unbutton his pale blue shirt, the fair hairs on his chest coming immediately into view. She couldn't believe she was doing this, couldn't believe the excitement she was starting to feel, despite how sick she was. She finished undoing the last of the buttons and pushed the shirt aside, bending down without thinking and kissing his exposed chest. Again he stirred, his hands moving automatically to her back and then falling to the floor again, lifeless. She undid the buttons at his cuffs and pulled one arm slowly free of his sleeve and then the other. The combination of the water and her effort brought a further onslaught of perspiration. She felt tired and weak and positively elated.

She moved down to his feet and quickly discarded his shoes and socks. See Mom, she thought, his feet don't even smell. There isn't a thing about this man that isn't beautiful. She heard her mother's voice—except his wedding ring, it said. Jill found herself looking at the thin gold band. It doesn't look very substantial, she told herself, moving on to the belt buckle of his trousers and undoing it before she could persuade herself otherwise. Then she unzipped the front zipper and yanked the pants down past his knees. Underneath he wore regular Fruit-of-the-Looms.

He groaned and opened his eyes though they were still mere slits.

"You have to take a shower," Jill told him. "Do you understand?"

He grunted but made no move to get up.

"I'm trying to get you undressed. Can you help me? Try to stand up." Once again, she grabbed him under his arms. He took hold of her with one hand and the door handle with the other, and pulled himself up. His shirt remained on the floor; his slacks bunched up at his feet. He stepped out of them.

Jill looked at his body, clad only in his shorts. He looked even better than she remembered, his man's body youthful but yet not boyish. Slim, tight, sensual. She wanted him so badly she could barely move. "Can you get out of your shorts?" she asked, not trusting herself to touch him further. He looked sleepily down at his torso and pulled down his shorts in one surprisingly smooth motion, stepping out and away from them, kicking his clothing aside. Jill tried not to look at him, coming around him instead to lead him toward the shower's spray. "Step up," she said, as they reached the bathtub. He did, though not far enough, and hit his leg, causing him to cry out. "Try again," she advised, guiding his legs with her hands, feeling the water hitting the side of her shoulder. Once inside, she pushed him toward the wall and directly under the water. He gasped, opening his mouth, at first hugging the wall with his back, then moving back toward the spray, tossing his head back, opening his eyes wide.

She watched him, worried he might fall, feeling herself weak with fatigue and desire. He caught her watching him out of the corner of his eye and suddenly reached over and grabbed her arms, pulling her toward him. Her legs caught against the side of the bathtub and she fell forward at the knees, feeling her hair and face hit by the sudden force of the water, feeling her nightgown grow damp and then wet. He pulled her up and inside the tub, surprising her with his sudden strength. The water pounded against her nose and mouth. She closed her eyes against the downpour, feeling his hands all over her body, on the buttons at her neck, fumbling with them, ultimately ripping them open and pulling the wet flannel up over her head.

"You're so beautiful," he said, his words slurred, his eyes not quite focused.

"I look ridiculous," she cried, tears suddenly mixing with the water from the shower. "I have these dumb socks on and I'm all wet!" Suddenly, she was laughing and crying at the same time, seeing them suddenly the way an impartial camera might —David, drunk and barely able to stand, soaking wet in the shower, herself, feverish, stuffed up with a cold, her hair drenched by sweat and the downpour, nude now except for white wool knee socks hugging against her feet.

David knelt down and pulled at her socks. Jill grabbed hold of the side of the wall as he tugged the wet wool off her feet, discarding the heavy material by the side of the tub. Suddenly, she felt his hands on her buttocks and his face buried inside the wet hair between her legs. The water continued to pour down on them. This isn't happening, she thought, digging her nails into his shoulders, unconscious now of the water's steady beat. David slowly worked his way up her body, moving his hands to her breasts, catching the water in his mouth as it dropped off her nipples. He reached her lips and kissed her ferociously, as if he wanted to swallow her, make her disappear inside him. They stumbled over—she wasn't aware if she had lost her balance or he had pushed her down, but there they were on the bottom of the bathtub and he was pushing into her, sitting up and wrapping his legs around her, reaching over and wrapping her legs around him, pounding into her as the water poured hot all around them. Jill wondered for an instant if they would drown before they climaxed, then stopped caring, surrendering herself to the absurdity of the situation. Nothing in her wildest imaginings could have prepared her for this, and if she wasn't quite as comfortable as she might have chosen to be, it would certainly make for a hell of a story to tell their grandchildren. Finally they dried one another with her blue towel, moved to her bed and fell asleep.

He awoke in the morning before she did, sitting up suddenly, coming wide awake instantly, looking down at Jill, just now opening her eyes, aware of her hair damp across her face. Automatically, she covered her face with her hands. "Oh God, I look awful," she said.

He pushed her hands aside and kissed her. "No," he said, "you look beautiful." He looked toward the drawn curtains. The sun was shining on the other side. "What time is it?" he wondered out loud.

Jill sat up and pulled the clock radio on the bedside table toward them. "A little after seven o'clock," she said.

He rubbed his head, obviously mulling over his alternatives. "I better go," he said, standing up and looking around. "Do you happen to remember where I left my clothes?" he smiled.

"I think they're in the bathroom," she said, deciding to let him make all the moves. Did he even remember what happened last night? she wondered, arching her back carefully and rolling her neck around in an effort to relieve the stiffness. She debated what she should do, get up and make coffee or stay where she was. She decided to stay longer. What would he say to Elaine? Would he try to explain? To lie? Would Elaine believe him? She'll believe anything she wants to badly enough, Jill said to herself, realizing for the first time since early that morning that essentially nothing had changed. There would be a few more lies, that's all. Bigger ones, perhaps a little harder to deliver, a little tougher to swallow but swallowed nonetheless. Last night had been no more a declaration of independence than any other night. It had simply started later and therefore ended later. It didn't matter that Elaine had slept next to an empty space. Her eyes were closed. They were undoubtedly prepared to remain so.

David walked back into the room. He was fully dressed and ready to go.

"Do you want a cup of coffee?" she asked him.

"I better not," he said. She nodded. He sat down on the bed beside her. "How are you feeling?" he asked, running his hand across her cheek.

"Pretty good," she lied.

He tucked the blankets around her. "Stay in bed today. I don't think I let you get a lot of rest last night."

She looked at him questioningly. "Do you remember anything?" she asked.

He smiled, leaning forward and kissing her. "I just remember how pretty you are," he said, and then he kissed her again. A minute later, he was gone.

Jill opened her eyes. He was gone. Cary Grant had disappeared along with the night. David was reaching over and turning off the television.

"I'm sorry," he said, freshly changed into a new suit. "I went to a hotel. Slept there. It was a dumb thing to do. I hope you didn't worry too much."

"Not too much," she said, her voice as dead as the gray morning sky.

"I have to go to work," he told her.

"Fine," she answered, not looking at him.

"I'll try to be home early tonight."

"That would be nice."

Jill heard the door close behind him. So the lie had been fairly easy to deliver after all. Jill swallowed hard. Then, like Elaine had done before her, she closed her eyes.

Chapter 26

She saw Laurie as soon as she entered the restaurant, and rushed past the bar of familiar faces toward the table where the young girl sat waiting. "Hi, Laurie," she said breathlessly. "I'm sorry I'm late. These meetings can go on forever. I was afraid I'd never get out. Everyone gets so caught up in what they have to say they forget there are still a few of us around who like to eat lunch now and again. Were you waiting long?"

"Just a few minutes," Laurie said. Jill knew from the sudden blush that appeared on the girl's cheek that she was lying. She threw off her coat and hung it over the back of her chair, sitting down and taking a long, deep breath.

"I'm really glad you could meet me for lunch," Jill said, taking in the teenager's careless posture with a quick, subtle glance. Her arms seemed only flesh-covered sticks as they projected out from under the red-and-white-striped sweatshirt that hung, as if on a hanger, from her shoulders. "No school today?"

"It's a P.D. day."

"A P.D. day? What's that?"

"Professional development, supposedly. The teachers get about one a month. Mom says they just want another day off. She doesn't believe they have meetings and stuff. She says it's all an excuse."

Jill laughed in spite of herself. She could hear Elaine's voice as she launched into her tirade against the teaching profession. "Did you have any trouble finding the place?"

Laurie shook her head. "My mom drove me. She said it looked suitably shady."

"Shady?" Jill asked, looking around the crowded room, waving at one of the network script assistants. "No, it's just kind of a hangout for television people, because it's so close. You know, right across the road. I never thought of it as being particularly shady."

"I like it," Laurie offered.

"Good. So do I. Has a waiter been around yet?"

"He came. I told him to wait till you got here."

Jill looked around, trying vainly to attract the waiter's attention. "I think they go to a special school," she said after several futile attempts. "They major in lack of peripheral vision." She smiled at David's daughter, who was obviously enjoying herself. "So, how are you finding school so far?"

"It's okay."

"What's your favorite subject?"

The girl paused. "English, I guess," she answered, unexpectedly.

"Really?" Jill asked, genuinely surprised. "That was always my favorite subject. I used to love writing compositions—"

"Oh, I hate that part."

"Oh."

"It's a drag. I never know what to write about. I like to read."

"What sort of things are you reading?"

Laurie reached for her glass of water, taking a long sip before answering Jill's question. "I like the Nancy Drew books," she said.

The waiter suddenly approached with the menus. "May I get you anything from the bar?"

"A bloody mary," Jill said, turning her attention back to

Laurie. "What about you, Laurie? Would you like a Coke or something?"

"No thanks," she said. "Water's fine."

Jill picked up her menu and pretended to glance over its contents. There was no need. She knew it by heart. She hoped Laurie would eat something—it was one of the reasons she had decided that they should meet for lunch. Actually, their getting together had been Laurie's idea. In the last month, as Jill and David seemed to be pulling farther apart, she and David's daughter had begun to grow inexplicably closer to one another, and although they had yet to really trust each other with anything remotely resembling a serious conversation, there was now a certain degree of warmth replacing their customary cool. Especially in the weeks since Jill had begun her job at the network, Laurie, and to a lesser extent, Jason, had been less overtly hostile, occasionally even friendly. When David had abruptly canceled plans to take them all to a movie because of a last-minute meeting, they had willingly gone ahead with Jill and had spent several hours at its conclusion arguing about what it all really meant. It was ironic, Jill thought, lowering the menu, to be losing David just as she was winning over his children.

She cleared her throat. "Can I recommend something for you or do you know what you want?" Jill asked.

Laurie shook her head. "You order."

"How does steak on a kaiser bun sound?" Jill asked, picking out what sounded the most fattening. "It comes with a big plate of french fries."

"Sounds good," Laurie answered, the bones across the top of her chest protruding ominously through her sweatshirt. Jill tried not to look too surprised at Laurie's easy acceptance of her suggestion.

"Some soup to start? They make a wonderful homemade vegetable soup," she suggested, afraid she might be pushing her luck. Laurie smiled, her face, once pretty and full, now stretching gaunt and sallow, her eyes almost sunken. Couldn't Elaine see the changes in her daughter? Why wasn't she doing anything about it? Jill remembered Ricki Elfer's solemn proclamation: anorexia nervosa. Was that it? Was Laurie really trying to starve herself to death?

"That's fine. Soup sounds great."

"And a salad?" Jill ventured. Laurie nodded. "Good. I'll have the same," Jill concurred, counting up the mountain of invisible calories. "We can order dessert later if you like."

Laurie looked around the room, quite taken with all the network types, as Jill gave the waiter their order. God, let her eat this, she hoped, looking back at Laurie. And if she doesn't, if she just pushes the food around her plate the way she usually does, what then? Another lecture? Another bitter scene? Or another meal of looking the other way and pretending the problem doesn't exist? What was the matter with the girl's mother? Jill asked herself angrily. Or her father, for that matter. They were the ones who should be insisting that the child get some good professional advice. And where were the girl's teachers? Why hadn't one of them said anything? Jill smiled over at David's daughter. Her teachers were away being professionally developed, she remembered, thinking that it might make for an interesting target of investigation if 'Hour Chicago' got beyond the pilot stage.

"Did you ever read Nancy Drew?" the girl was asking.

"Did I read Nancy Drew?!" Jill laughed. "Every single one. *The Hidden Staircase* was my favorite."

Laurie's eyes grew big and wide, a smile creasing their edges. "Mine too," she said. "And I love Judy Blume."

"Who?"

"Judy Blume. She writes books for teenagers. I read all her books."

"I don't know her work," Jill said, feeling the name was vaguely familiar.

"Well, you're not exactly a kid," came the reply.

"That's true," Jill said, as the waiter put her bloody mary on the table. "And I'm not getting any younger! Cheers!"

"Cheers," Laurie mimicked, raising her water glass. "Tell me about your new job," she said eagerly.

Jill returned her drink to the table. "Well, I'm not sure it *is* a new job yet. It's still pretty temporary. We have to see how the pilot goes first. I'll just be another few weeks here and then it's back to the university until I know one way or the other."

"What do you do *exactly?*" Laurie pressed, obviously interested.

"Well, let's see," Jill began, "that's what we're having all these story conferences about right now, to try to figure out exactly what it is that we *are* doing."

"What's a story conference?"

Jill was pleased at Laurie's questions, realizing that David hadn't asked her anything about her work since she had begun. "It's a meeting where all the producers and researchers are present," she explained. "That's where you sit down and fight for your ideas. And let me tell you, there's always a good fight. You present your idea for something you'd like to see done, and then you have to pitch the fact that it's not only a good idea but a good idea *for television*. You have to show that it would appeal to a wide audience, that you can present it in such a way that it would be suitable viewing for an entire family, and that it would *look* good on television. That sounds kind of dopey, but you have to remember that television is primarily a visual medium. You with me so far?" Laurie nodded. "Okay," Jill continued, "so, assuming the producer—that's me—sells her idea to the group, then she usually gets about three weeks to put the whole thing together.

"The first thing that gets decided is who's going to be your research assistant, and you can pretty well bet that whoever you dislike the most, or have the most trouble with, is who you're going to wind up being assigned. The researcher spends most of his or her time on the phone. They're the ones responsible for getting you all the necessary information. Then you have to decide, which is what we've been doing a lot of lately, just what the 'breaking point' of the story is. In other words, what do you want to say and how do you want to say it?" She paused, thinking of Beth Weatherby. "Say you're doing an exposé on people who place those ads in the Companions Wanted columns of the newspapers," she said, abruptly shifting the focus of her thinking. "Well, you decide your angle, maybe it's that these people aren't perverted or oversexed or any of those things, but are really just a bunch of poor, unhappy people who are desperately looking for someone to love, and you pick as your breaking point a happily married couple who met through one of these ads, and you build your show around them. You might start by contacting the various dating services, going to singles' bars and discos, maybe even cruising the park benches for some lonely people. You might even answer one of the ads yourself. You have to be *specific*. You need one example to focus on and you always have to be thinking about visualizing your story concept. You never shoot in the studio. You're always on location and you have to pray that whoever you finally do sit down to interview doesn't have a criminal record because that would blow your credibility right out the window."

The waiter approached with two bowls of steaming hot soup. "Thank you," Jill said, watching in amazement as Laurie lifted her spoon and dug right in. "Is it good?" she asked a minute later.

"Delicious," Laurie answered. "Go on, tell me more about your job. What happens after you finish shooting?"

"It goes to editing," Jill said, tasting a spoonful of the hot liquid and then continuing. "In some ways, the editing is the most rewarding part of the whole thing. But it's also the most frustrating. That's where you see all your mistakes. You know, like the camera was out of sync or the film's defective or the best part is happening just out of range. There's a separate editor," Jill explained, taking another spoonful of soup, noticing with great satisfaction that Laurie was already finishing hers. "You work with the editor. Tell him what you want to keep and what you want to throw away. Anyway, what you're looking for are the sequences that flow. You're looking for moments that—how can I say it without sounding trite? You're looking for moments that illuminate. You're in a black room with no air, and you spend hours just staring at a tiny screen. You're recutting constantly. One day you're happy; you think you've done a terrific job. The next day you see it again and you hate it. It's an exhausting, exhilarating time, usually taking two days *and* two nights. It's like you're up for forty-eight solid hours."

The waiter waited to remove their soup bowls until Jill quickly gulped down the last of hers. "Two steaks on kaisers and fries," he said, putting the overflowing plates in front of

them, along with their salads. Again, Laurie barely waited until
the plate was on the table before picking up her fork and popping a monstrous french-fried potato into her mouth.

"This is great," she said, enthusiastically. "So, go on. Do you
keep everything you shoot?"

Jill laughed. "Oh, no! That would be a real miracle. It's usually a six to one ratio of what's discarded to what's retained.
Three to one if you're really expert, which I'm not."

"But you are good," Laurie said.

"Yes," Jill answered, "I *am* good." She smiled widely, feeling almost smug about the successful direction that this meal
had taken. Maybe this was what had been needed all along—
someone to show an interest in the child, and to show that interest by not only asking the right questions but by caring
enough about her to share some of *their* lives with her. By talking to her as if she were a person and not just an unruly adoles-
cent. Jill took a large bite of her steak. "Anyway," she continued, almost cockily, "at this stage, you usually have to write
the script. Then you have to do the mixing, which is a real
drag. I hate it."

"What is it?"

"Well, you have to get a narrator to read what you've written. And then you need music and other sounds for ambiance.
You know what ambiance means?" The girl shook her head,
stuffing a forkful of salad into her mouth. "Atmosphere," Jill
explained. "And then you also have your interviews. They're
all on separate tracks. You have a three channel audio mix, and
what you do basically is to marry the picture and the sound."
She stopped, watching Laurie eat. "Kind of a neat phrase," she
said, repeating it in her mind. "And that's it. Then it's
finished."

"Sounds really exciting," Laurie said, chewing.

Jill laughed happily. "No, not exciting, really. Exciting isn't
the word," she said, groping for what the right word would be.
"It has more to do with movement," she said finally. "Producers of this kind of format move around a lot. We like to go
around with the crew, gathering up all the news and stuff.
That's what I like. I feel like for the first time in a very long
while, I'm moving again! Does that make any sense?"

Laurie scooped up the last of her gravy with the remainder of her kaiser. "I think so," she said, pushing away her empty plate.

"Do you want some dessert?" Jill asked.

"Do they make hot fudge sundaes?"

"Is that what you'd like?" Laurie nodded enthusiastically. Jill signaled for the waiter. "One hot fudge sundae," she said, returning her attention to her plate as the waiter removed Laurie's.

"You met my father on one of your shows, didn't you?" Laurie asked suddenly, catching Jill off guard.

"Yes," Jill answered, quietly.

"And you decided you liked what you saw," Laurie paused, "and so you went after it?"

Jill put down her fork, not happy with the sudden shift in the conversation.

"Laurie," she began cautiously, "I did not break up your parents' marriage. Your father was unhappy for a long time before I came along—"

"That's not what my mother says. She says everything was fine until you—"

"If everything had been fine," Jill said, trying to defend herself, "your father wouldn't have—" She cut herself short. She had been about to say that David wouldn't have looked at her twice. But it wasn't true and she knew it. David always looked twice. More, given the chance. And if it hadn't been for her, he might very well have stayed married to Elaine, continuing on in his already established pattern of affairs and casual couplings. "You're right. Or at least, you're right enough," she said. The waiter deposited the giant hot fudge sundae in front of David's daughter and left.

Laurie stared at Jill in genuine surprise. Without speaking, she raised the spoon to her lips and began to eat. She finished off the entire sundae before either one spoke again.

"You liked the ice cream?" Jill asked incredulously.

"It was delicious."

"I'm glad." Jill wasn't sure what to say, aware that the youngster was expecting her to continue. "Laurie, I—when I

met your father, I didn't know he was married. I thought he
was separated from your mother—"

"Why'd you think that?"

She couldn't say "because that's what your father told me."
Honesty was one thing. But a fourteen-year-old girl didn't de-
serve that much truth. "I don't know. Anyway, it doesn't really
matter because I found out quickly anyway—"

"How?"

"He told me. Your father told me. But by then it was too
late, I was crazy mad in love with him, and I just couldn't give
him up. I tried. We both tried. We didn't want to hurt you or
your brother or your mother—"

The waiter retrieved the empty sundae dish and Jill's half-
empty dinner plate. "But you did, didn't you?" the girl asked.
"You hurt all of us."

"Yes we did," Jill quietly agreed. "And I'm sorry."

Laurie shrugged. "My mom is going to re-cover the living
room furniture," she said, unaware of the non sequitur.

Jill smiled. "Why not?" she said, wistfully.

Jill checked her watch. It was almost two o'clock. If she waited
any longer for Laurie to come out of the restaurant bathroom,
she'd be late getting back to work. She left an oversized tip for
the waiter—perhaps he had in some way contributed to the
meal's success—and pushed back her chair, striding purposefully past the stand-up bar, exchanging several quick greetings
as she made her way toward the ladies' room into which Laurie
had disappeared some ten minutes ago.

The smell hit her as soon as she opened the door.

"My God, Laurie, are you all right?" she called, rushing to
the open stall where Laurie knelt, her arms curled around the
toilet seat, her face deathly pale.

"I guess I ate too much," she said, holding back the tears.

"It's my fault," Jill said, kneeling beside her and running her
hand gently through the child's hair. She felt that if she applied
even the slightest amount of pressure, the girl's head would
crack open, come apart. "I'm always after you about how you
don't eat enough." She went to the sink and pulled a paper

towel from its box, soaking it in cold water and taking it back
to press against Laurie's forehead.

"I'm sorry, Jill. It was really delicious."

"Don't talk about it. It's okay."

She knelt beside the fragile girl and held her against her own
body until Laurie felt well enough to stand. Then they slowly
left the restaurant and stumbled out into the fresh air. They
were immediately surrounded by the definite October chill, and
they hugged their coats around them.

"Are you okay for a few minutes alone?" Jill asked her.
Laurie nodded. "I'll be right back. Wait right here."

Jill promptly disappeared into a book store at the corner and
came back several minutes later with a book under her arm.
"For you," she said.

Laurie looked at the paperback novel. *"Wifey,"* she said
aloud.

"Do you have it already?" Jill asked. Laurie shook her head,
quickly rifling through the pages. "I asked the book clerk for
the best of Judy Blume. This is what he gave me."

"Looks great," Laurie said, still very pale.

"Are you going to be all right in a taxi?" Jill asked.

"Yeah," Laurie nodded, looking not at all convinced.

"Laurie," Jill broached, signaling at a passing cab which
promptly pulled to the curb beside them. Laurie looked search-
ingly into Jill's eyes. "You need help," Jill said simply. "You
need to see someone who can help you—"

"A psychiatrist?" Laurie asked quietly.

"Yes," Jill answered. "Starving yourself for months and then
stuffing yourself until you throw up is not healthy behavior and
you're smart and sensitive enough to know it. I want to help
you, Laurie, but I don't know how, except to tell you that you
need more help than I can offer." The cab driver opened his
door and looked at them expectantly. Neither one moved.
"There's a name for your condition, Laurie," Jill continued.
"And believe me, you're not alone. There are a lot of mixed-up
girls out there doing the same thing to themselves as you are.
I've been doing some research on it lately—"

"Maybe you'll do a show on it," Laurie said with a smile.

Jill reached over and hugged the young girl, surprised by the strength with which her hug was reciprocated. "Maybe," Jill said. "Will you think about what I said?"

Laurie nodded and broke from their embrace, getting quickly into the taxi. Jill watched as the car moved into the traffic and disappeared into the general maze. Then she turned around and headed toward the studio, a feeling of curious elation spreading through her. "I'm moving again," she said aloud. "I'm really moving."

Chapter 27

She was aware of the noise for several minutes before she realized she wasn't still asleep.

"What's that?" David asked groggily from beside her.

Jill opened her eyes, focusing them on the clock. It was 8 A.M. on what she knew instantly was a Saturday morning. The noise had stopped, and for a second Jill contemplated dismissing whatever it had been as a collective dream until it began again: an incoherent Morse code repeating itself in short, staccato gasps.

"It's the buzzer," Jill said, recognizing the sound only as she began to speak.

"The buzzer? Who the hell—?" David started, but Jill was already out of bed and on her way to the kitchen. She returned to the bedroom less than a minute later, going instantly to the closet.

"You better throw something on," she told her startled husband. "Elaine is here. She's on her way up. She doesn't sound very happy."

Jill pulled a long terry-cloth robe over her head and threw David's blue velour bathrobe in his direction.

"Oh, shit," David muttered. "What does she want?"

"She didn't say," Jill told him. "Maybe she can't get the top off her bottle of orange juice."

"Very funny," David said, running an exasperated hand through his tousled hair. He stood up, draping the bathrobe over his naked body. Jill noticed he had an erection, and felt an instant of longing sweep over her. They had made love exactly twice in the last month.

There was a loud banging at the door.

"I think she's here," Jill said wryly.

David stood still at the side of the bed. He made no effort to move.

"We could pretend we both died," Jill offered, hoping to produce a smile on David's sullen face. She got none. "I'll let her in," Jill said at last. David said nothing.

Jill went quickly toward the door, debated asking who it was, decided Elaine's humor would probably be in the same state as the man's they once shared, and decided to open the door without further preamble.

Elaine brushed angrily past her straight into the living room. "How dare you!" she began, almost instantly, turning abruptly on Jill as Jill followed her into the room.

"Hello, Elaine," Jill said, calmly. "Why don't you come inside?"

"Don't get smart with me," Elaine shot back bitterly. "How dare you?!" she repeated, fairly seething with rage.

Jill fought with all her strength to keep her own temper under control. There was no point in confronting David with the sight of two hysterical women. Where the hell *was* David anyway? "Just what am I being accused of?" Jill asked.

"Please stop playing Little Miss Innocent," Elaine snapped, waving something around in her hand. "I thought we passed through that stage years ago when you admitted your adultery!"

"Oh, wow!" Jill said, resurrecting an old favorite expression as she sank into one of the large wing chairs. As long as they were traveling that far back, it seemed a most appropriate turn of phrase. Elaine moved without pattern back and forth before her, her right hand flailing out sporadically, waving what Jill now recognized as a paperback book under Jill's nose. "If you don't mind keeping that thing away from my face," Jill pointed out, hearing her voice rise.

"You didn't mind rubbing my daughter's nose in it!" Elaine yelled.

"What are you talking about?" Jill demanded.

Elaine hurled the book onto the glass coffee table. It bounced, then landed face up. *Wifey,* it proclaimed innocently. By Judy Blume.

"That's the book I bought for Laurie," Jill said.

"I know goddamn well what it is! It's a piece of pure filth that even adults shouldn't be reading, let alone a fourteen-year-old girl—"

"What's the matter with you?" Jill asked, reaching over for the book and picking it up. "Laurie told me that Judy Blume is her favorite author. She writes books for teenagers." Jill flipped through the opening pages while Elaine turned her attention to David, who had just entered the room.

"What's going on here?" he asked in the quiet voice of extreme agitation that both women recognized.

"Your current wife," Elaine began, bringing the same sense of impermanence to the word that Ricki Elfer had once said she loved, "is filling our daughter's mind with filth." Each word was spat out with special significance.

"It's all a misunderstanding," Jill said, standing up and unable to conceal a smile. "I didn't realize—"

"What are you smiling about?" Elaine demanded.

"I'm sorry," Jill apologized, lowering her head when the smile refused to budge, "but I didn't realize— It was a mistake." She turned to David. "I thought all Judy Blume books were for kids. This one is obviously not." Her smile grew wider.

"Why are you smiling?" David asked, accusingly.

Jill's smile immediately disappeared. She turned back to Elaine. "Forgive me, Elaine," she said, generously. "It's my fault, of course, but it was unintentional, believe me."

"Was it also unintentional when you advised my daughter to see a psychiatrist?!" Elaine retorted, immediately switching tracks when she reached one dead end.

"What?!" David asked, astonished.

Jill's eyes traveled back and forth between the two angry faces.

"What the hell is she talking about, Jill?" David asked impatiently. "What's this nonsense about Laurie seeing a psychiatrist?"

"I don't think it is nonsense," Jill said quietly.

David was too surprised to speak.

"So, you admit it!" Elaine shouted.

"Yes, I admit it," Jill shouted back, startling the other woman. "It's time somebody took an interest in what's happening to that girl."

"How dare you—" Elaine seethed, repeating her opening line.

"Look," Jill retreated somewhat, "I don't mean to say that you don't love her or that you don't care what happens to her. That's certainly not the case. But I also care about what happens to her and I think I have the right to speak up when I feel something is terribly wrong."

"You have no rights where my daughter is concerned," Elaine announced.

"Just what do you feel is so terribly wrong?" David asked.

Jill spoke directly to her husband. "David, all you have to do is look at her. She weighs half of what she weighed when I first met her." She watched David's eyes cloud over, a mixture of boredom and disbelief filling his face.

"Oh come on, Jill, we've been through this. She's a typical teenager, for heaven's sake."

"A typical anorexic," Jill said.

"What?" Elaine demanded.

"An anorexic," Jill repeated, about to explain before Elaine cut her off. "It's a person, usually a teenage girl, who—"

"I don't want to know what it is! I want you to stop saying it! And to stop filling my daughter's head with filth and a lot of crazy ideas!" Jill listened without trying to interrupt as Elaine became more hysterical. "What is it you want from my life?!" Elaine continued. "What more can you take? I gave you my husband! Now you want my child too? Why? Can't you have any of your own? Is that the problem? That you're barren and you can't produce a child of your own so you have to try and grab somebody else's? Maybe if you had your own children you'd understand what being a mother is all about. But as long as Laurie and Jason are *my* children, you are to keep your hands off them and your filth and your crazy ideas away from them. Do you understand me?"

Jill turned to David, feeling numbed from head to toe, Elaine's words having been sprayed from her mouth as if from a can of Novocain, covering Jill's body, leaving her immune to the pain of the attack yet fully cognizant of its presence. I gave you my husband, she heard echoing in her frozen brain, colliding with words like barren and filth, words from the Middle Ages, she thought, or maybe just the words of middle age. Help me, David, she thought, recognizing there was no point in trying to talk sense to Elaine. Give me some support. I'm your wife.

"Elaine's right," he said, instead. "This really isn't any of your concern. Laurie is *our* child," he continued, looking over at his ex-wife. "We'll deal with her."

His words had the effect of a carefully aimed blow behind the knees. Jill felt herself buckling forward and grabbed hold of one of the wing chairs, allowing her body to sink into it.

"You'll also deal with all her psychiatrist bills," Elaine said, heading toward the door. "Laurie's decided she rather likes the idea of a psychiatrist. It'll probably give her some extra prestige at school or something. Anyway, we'll send all the bills over as soon as they start arriving." She opened the door. "Goodbye, Jill. Nice talking to you."

Jill heard the door close and Elaine's footsteps retreating down the hall. She was aware that David was standing not more than two feet away from her. Still, she stared resolutely at the white carpet. She was afraid that if she looked up at her husband, she might want to kill him. It was a feeling she didn't want to know.

"Well, that was smart, wasn't it?" he was saying. "As if we don't have enough to worry about financially—"

"I'd say our financial problems are the least of our worries," Jill said, quietly.

"Christ, Jill," David continued, unmindful or uncaring of the fact that she had spoken. "A psychiatrist! Don't you think you overreacted a bit?"

"Just what is my status in this family, David?" she asked, barely audible.

"What?" he asked, testily. "What are you talking about?"

"I'm talking about what happened in this room a few minutes ago, when I was reduced to a non-person."

"Oh, hell, Jill, make sense."

Jill raised her eyes to him for the first time since he had taken Elaine's side against hers.

"You don't see what you've done at all," she marveled.

"What *I've* done?" he asked. "I'm not the one who gave my daughter a pornographic book and told her to see a psychiatrist."

"It's hardly a pornographic book. It's maybe mildly risqué, at best, but, at any rate, that was a misunderstanding and I have no intention of apologizing for it again. What's more important here, *all* that's important really, is your attitude."

"My attitude?"

"Yes." She stood up, feeling the strength returning to her legs. "What am I doing here, David?" she asked sincerely. "I'm your wife. I assumed that meant I was part of a family that also included your two children. It's not what I would have originally chosen for myself but I have always accepted your children because they're a part of you, and the three of you belong to the same package. I assumed I'd become part of that package. God knows, I've always been included when it meant picking them up from somewhere, or cooking them dinner or looking after them for a weekend, or spending time with them when you've been busy—working late." She stopped. "Now, I find out that my status is no better than a housekeeper's. I can provide for certain of their physical needs but I sure as hell better not interfere in anything important."

"Jill, you're exaggerating—"

"I am *not* exaggerating! I have just been shot down by an expert marksman while my husband stood by and passed her the ammunition. Elaine said some very vicious things to me, things one doesn't exactly expect to see one's spouse stand still for, and what does my husband say? He says 'Elaine's right.'

Elaine's right," she repeated in disbelief. "I have been thoroughly humiliated and my husband was too busy being inconvenienced to notice." She paused. "I guess there's nothing more to say. I've been put in my place in no uncertain terms, and so, now that I know what that place is, I can get on with my life, and start making the master of the house his breakfast." She turned to leave.

David grabbed her arm. "Jill, you're acting like a child! No one says you're a servant here!"

"Well, what am I?" Jill shouted, as loud now as Elaine had been earlier. "I'm not a mother, step or otherwise, as I have been told very clearly this morning. I'm not even a wife anymore."

"Jill—"

"Am I? Well, am I? We don't make love anymore; we don't talk anymore. Christ, how can we be expected to make love or talk when we don't even see each other anymore."

"It's that damn TV show," he began.

"The hell it is!" she countered angrily. "How dare you try to blame it on that?!" she demanded, suddenly self-conscious about having used Elaine's phrase. "Do you realize that you haven't once asked me how the show is progressing, if I like what I'm doing."

"You know how I feel about this show."

"Yes, I know how *you* feel. What I'm asking is if you have any idea of how *I* feel!"

David said nothing for several minutes. "I can't fake interest where none exists," he said, finally. "I hate the whole idea of this show, Jill. If you want to know the truth, I think you only agreed to do it to get back at me."

Jill stared hard into David's beautiful green eyes, their lashes fluttering nervously before her. She felt her heart sink, knowing that the moment of truth could be ignored no longer. "Get back at you for what?" she asked slowly.

The question caught David off guard, the implications of what he had said only now reaching his conscious self. He turned away.

"Is there any point in more lies, David?" she asked, trying to grab at the retreating numbness. The next few minutes seemed to happen in slow motion. Her mind spoke each word before her ears replayed them with the actual voices attached, and then again without the sound.

She watched as David sat down on the sofa, carefully avoiding her eyes. I'm sorry, Jill. I thought it would be all over by now. "I'm sorry, Jill," he said with great emotion. "I thought it would be all over by now." I'm sorry, Jill. I thought it would be all over by now.

Jill's eyes immediately filled with tears. "It's not?" she asked, knowing the answer. It's not. It's not. It's not.

"No," he said, still not looking at her. No. No. No. No. No. No. No. "God, Jill, I'm so sorry. I feel like such a bastard, but I just don't know what to do. I love you. I don't want to lose you. I'm sure that all it is with Nicki is an infatuation. She's young; she's beautiful. She makes me feel like I'm King of the Mountain—"

"I'm not interested in how she makes you feel!" Jill yelled, hurling herself at her husband and pounding him with both fists. "Goddamn you, you son-of-a-bitch!"

She struck him one carefully aimed blow across the face before he was able to restrain her hands and force her away from him, his one hand gripping tightly to both her wrists, rendering her powerless, while her tears took away her voice and reduced her to a frenzied helplessness. She felt her nose beginning to run, tried to extricate one hand from David's grasp but was unable to, feeling him suddenly surrounding her body with his own, trying to comfort her, to quiet her. To stop her.

"Jill, Jill," he whispered against her ear. "Please don't cry."

Slowly, he released her hands, leaning over her and burying his head against her breasts. She lifted her arms to strike out at his back, to pummel his flesh. Instead, her hands moved like those of a drowning woman to grasp at a life preserver just tossed out, gripping it tightly, pulling it close against her. In a minute, he had pushed up her terry-cloth robe and discarded his own, and soon they were making the kind of urgent love that only comes from desperation, where tears replace sweat, and guilt and fear take the place of genuine passion. Both recognized it for what it was. Neither had any illusions when it was over.

"What now?" she asked, as he was pulling back on his robe. "What happens now?"

"I don't know," he said truthfully.

"What do you want to happen?" she pressed. "Do you know that much?"

"I'd like things to go back to the way they were before," he said quietly, after a pause.

"Before?"

"Before all this mess started," he began. "Before Beth murdered Al. Before you took on that stupid job—"

Jill couldn't believe her ears. "Before Beth murdered Al! Before I went back to TV! David, listen to yourself. You have just absolved yourself of any and all responsibility in this matter. What about Nicole?! What about the part that each of you played in all this?"

"I'm not saying I'm not responsible. I'm just trying to explain the extenuating circumstances, what made me particularly susceptible to Nicole at this point in my life—"

"Damn it, there are always going to be extenuating circumstances! You talk about wanting to go back to the way things were before. When Al was alive, when I was still teaching. May I remind you that your whole infatuation with Nicole started when things were exactly the way they were before! When the interesting career woman you married became the boring little wife at home—"

"No one said you were boring!"

"I bored myself half to death. How could I not bore you?!"

He began pacing. "I'm sorry, Jill. I can't help but feel that it's only since you started talking about this whole television thing that our troubles started."

Jill closed her eyes. "I can't even talk about it now," she said, as if from another room.

"I didn't say that. You know that's not what I meant."

"Yes, I know," she acknowledged. "But you *are* saying that you want me to give it up."

David stopped. "I don't know," he said. "I don't know anymore what I'm saying. I don't mind your working in television. You know I don't. It's just this show about Beth Weatherby—"

"The show is not about Beth Weatherby," she reminded him, "but that's kind of beside the point, isn't it?"

"The point being—?"

"The point being that my working in television doesn't bother you as long as you control my hours, my location, and now my content. That's the bottom line, isn't it, David? I stay in Chicago, work from nine to five and be careful to keep away from issues you find offensive or inconvenient—"

"Jill—"

"All right." Jill stared wordlessly at David for several seconds before speaking. "Okay. You win. I'll do it. I'll give it up. Now what? I've just agreed to the first of your demands. What else?"

"Else?" he asked, puzzled by the sudden turn of events.

"Well, I think we should know exactly where we stand, don't you? Children—what about children?"

Jill watched David's head sink. "Jill, please, you know the answer to that. You know how I feel—"

"Fine, then. Okay, no children. Settled." She stopped, biting off her next word and spitting it into the air between them. "Nicole."

Silence. "What is it that you want me to say, Jill?"

"What do you think I want you to say?"

"That I'll stop seeing her," he answered, after a pause.

"Bull's-eye." She waited.

"I can't," he said, finally.

Jill felt her feet burying into the thick, white carpeting the same way they had sunk into the grass at last summer's annual Weatherby, Ross picnic, holding her a prisoner then as they did now. "You can't," she repeated, numbly. Her eyes shot him a look of real fury. "You expect me to give up goddamn everything—my career, a family of my own, even my husband whenever he feels the overwhelming urge of extenuating circumstances, and while I'm at it, you also expect me to keep my mouth shut about your children although I'm still expected to help take care of them, and put up with your ex-wife and all her cockamamy demands and insults and keep paying the rent on this apartment, while you divide your time and money between your ex-wife and your current mistress. Of course she thinks you're King of the Mountain! Does she realize that the mountain is made up of a stack of unpaid bills?!"

"I don't think this is getting us anywhere," he said with infuriating calm.

"Oh, you don't?" Jill questioned. "Well, that's just too damn bad. Because I do! I think it's helping to put this relationship into its proper perspective." She thought over the past five minutes. "I have just accepted all your terms. I am willing to live with your hours, your debts, your children, even your ex-wife. I am willing to live without my chosen profession or children of my own. I'm willing to do whatever you want, to be whatever you want, to turn myself inside out if necessary to keep you. I'm asking you, in return, to give up only one thing. Nicole Clark. And you're telling me you can't do it!" She shook her head in disbelief.

"I can't lie to you, Jill," he said sadly. "Would you rather I lied?"

"Why not?" she snapped. "Why can't you lie all of a sudden? You've done it often enough before!" She started to cry. "Why the sudden pangs of conscience now?" she sobbed, desperately.

"I'm so sorry," he said, reaching for her, only to be brushed aside. "I wish I could say the things you want to hear. I wish I could tell you that she doesn't mean anything to me, that I can just walk out of her life. But I can't. All I know is that despite the fact that I love you, and I do love you, Jill, I just can't let Nicki go. Not yet."

"How long?" she asked.

"What do you mean?"

Jill choked back her tears. "Not yet implies a future. A time when you will be able to let her go. How much time?"

He shook his head. "I don't know," he said.

"You expect me to sit here and wait for you?" she asked, feeling as she imagined Sybil Burton must have felt when confronting Richard with the years of casual infidelities.

The truthfulness of his answer surprised her. "It's what I'd like," he said. "I know I have no right to expect it."

"You're damn right, you don't!" she shouted, suddenly furious again at his complacency. "I could really fix you, you know," she continued, surprising herself possibly even more than her husband. "I could take you for everything Elaine hasn't, which I'll admit isn't a hell of a lot, but it would sure teach little Nicole a thing or two about reality!" She stopped, amazed by the force of her own bitterness.

There was a long silence. Neither party moved.

"You have to do whatever you think is right," David whispered, at last. "It's your life. You have to live it the way you see fit. If you want a divorce, then that's what you'll get. If you want to take me for everything I've got, well, you'll do that too. I won't stop you. I'll give you whatever you want."

"I want you," she said, her voice cracking.

"No," he said, his voice resonantly clear, "the woman I just listened to wants a lot of things, but I'm not one of them." He started to leave the room.

"Oh no, David, please," she begged, running after him. "I didn't mean it about taking you for everything. You know I'd never do that. Please, David, I'm sorry." He retreated into the bathroom and closed the door behind him. Jill sank to her knees on the other side, her tears falling like drops of wet paint down the length of the door. "I'm sorry," she repeated over and over again as she heard the shower beginning to run. "I'm so sorry."

Chapter 28

"Brother, it's cold out there!" Irving's voice bellowed as he came inside the small screening room and took off his coat. "How's everybody?"

The room, which Jill noticed had become quiet with expectation, was suddenly full of noise again. All the old, familiar grumbles about Chicago in November were brought forth and given new life. Jill listened for a few minutes while Irving explained to the dozen people present that the client had been delayed and so the screening would be held off until the sponsors could arrive. "Can you imagine, it's actually starting to snow out there," she heard him utter in disbelief before she allowed her eyes to drift back toward the giant, empty screen.

She heard the door opening and closing several times behind her, knew more people had arrived, and was aware that soon every seat would be filled with not just people like herself, the drones, but by the Queen Bees themselves, the people from the network, the sponsor's representatives—the people who would be deciding whether "Hour Chicago" would be allowed more than its initial sixty-minute run.

I should be nervous, she thought. Happy. Scared. Angry. Confused. Something. But she felt nothing, in the same way that she was only slightly more aware of the outdoor cold than she was of the indoor heat, only marginally more aware of sound than she was of stillness, of day as opposed to night. For the past three or four weeks, she had walked through her life as if she were occupying someone else's body, a body that, like the now extinct leaves of autumn, had been drained of all its former color, shriveled up against itself, a brittle shadow of its former vibrancy, waiting only for the wheels of traffic to crush it into obscurity or for the winds to scatter its dried-up pieces into oblivion. The dried-up pieces of her soul, she thought eerily.

"So, what did you think of that?" he was asking her.

"What?" Jill asked, looking behind her to Irving, who was leaning up against the back of her comfortable chair. "I'm sorry, were you talking to me?" she asked.

"I said," he repeated, "November hit Chicago with the force of a hard snowball against a car window. What do you think?"

"What do I think about what?" Jill asked, aware she was smiling, aware that it had been a long time since she had smiled.

"I made that up as I was walking over here, about November hitting like a snowball. I thought it was rather poetic." Jill's smile widened. "You all right?" he asked her.

"Sure," she answered.

"They giving you trouble at school?"

Jill shook her head. "No. I explained that this screening was important. That I had to be here."

"What's it like to be back there?" he asked.

"All right," she said, without inflection.

He patted her shoulder. "Well, don't let it get too all right. I have a feeling the powers-that-be are going to like what they see today and that you can dump those hallowed halls for good and get back to the world where sex and violence still have a good name. What's the matter, Jill?" he continued, without missing a beat.

"Nothing," she said. "Just tired, I guess."

"Well," he said, patting her shoulder again, "tell that good-looking husband of yours to let you get some sleep."

Jill turned back toward the empty screen and saw it filled with David's face. He occupied it easily and well, the warmth of his eyes and his smile only magnified by the increased size of her imaginary projection. Suddenly, Jill knew that no matter what changes time wrought, physical or otherwise, to their lives, that he would always have this effect on her, that just looking at him would make her feel weak-kneed and awkward, the nervous wallflower opening her front door to greet her blind date and coming face to face with the campus hero.

The image of her husband was like a magnet drawing her closer toward him. She wanted to run to it, throw herself into it, disappear inside it, yet she knew now that the slightest pressure would force the image to crack and break. That she would collapse empty-handed and bruised on the other side, that behind the screen—the face?—there was nothing.

The sudden intrusion of rational thought caught Jill off guard. In the past month, she had managed to keep all semblance of reality a good arm's length away. It was as if everything had stopped. Like the princess on her fifteenth birthday who pricks her finger on a spindle and becomes the Sleeping Beauty, Jill had simply waved her magic wand and suspended all time and emotion, choosing the blind path of the somnambulist, waiting for the kiss of the handsome prince to wake her up. Between pricking her finger and kissing the prince, there was nothing. The Prick and the Prince, Jill thought suddenly, surprised to find herself laughing.

She pretended to be stifling a cough, taking a surreptitious look around the room and seeing all but four of the seats now filled. The room was starting to feel stuffy, especially now that cigarettes were appearing with greater frequency than before. Years ago, when she and David had first married, he would complain that the stale odor of cigarettes clung to her clothes and hair for days after these smoke-filled meetings. Now, she doubted he would notice at all.

He was rarely home these days, his time divided between herself and Nicole, and when he chose to sleep at Jill's side it was only when he was overwhelmed with fatigue. There was no passion. Even desperation had slipped away into something more abstract. She was like a buoy in the water, conveniently

marking off a familiar spot. What was it he had said? I can't
fake interest where none exists? Jill closed her eyes, forcing her
mind to go as blank as the screen. It was all her fault, she
thought, sinking down into her seat, and laying her head back.
She had forced the issue, forced everything. Now she had to
wait in limbo like the sleeping princess to see if David could cut
his way back through the thorns to find her.

A phone rang from somewhere beside her. She opened her
eyes to see Irving picking up the red receiver and saw his lips
moving, although she deliberately avoided hearing any sounds
and only snapped fully to attention when she realized the room
was emptying of people.

"Come on," he was saying, leaning over her, "I'll buy you
some dinner."

"What happened?" she asked.

"Damn winter," Irving answered, grabbing his coat. "People
forget how to drive as soon as they see a flake of snow. The client's been in some kind of a minor highway mishap. He's all
right. But he won't be here till seven o'clock."

Jill grabbed her coat and allowed Irving to usher her into the
hallway and then into the cold outside air.

"How's that stepkid of yours doing?" he asked as they
crossed the road, heading toward Maloney's.

"Laurie?" Jill asked, stopping at the door to the restaurant,
feeling the wind slapping against her face, as if it had been told
that she was suffering from a drug overdose and needed to be
revived. "She's doing fine," Jill told him. "She still weighs as
much as a green bean but she's seeing a doctor twice a week
—her mother is actually going with her—and I think she'll be all
right. I really do."

"Sounds like it might make for an interesting show," Irving
said slyly.

Jill laughed. "Laurie said the same thing," she said, recalling
Laurie in almost the same spot approximately a month ago,
thinking simultaneously of the girl's father and how he would
undoubtedly react to this fresh idea. "Listen," Jill said suddenly, "would you mind if I begged off supper? I just feel like
walking for a while."

"Walking? It'll get dark pretty soon, and it's freezing out!"

"It's not that cold," she protested good-naturedly. "And I'll stick to the main streets."

"As long as I don't have to walk with you," he said. Jill moved to the restaurant door and held it open for him. "See you at seven," Irving added, disappearing into the inner warmth. "Be careful."

Jill stood for several seconds alone in the cold air. It *was* cold, she realized as she started to walk. Why had she been so oblivious to it before?

She crossed back across the street, not at all sure where she wanted to go. She felt the wind pushing against her cheeks, and moved her collar up to hug against her neck. She faced directly into the bitter onslaught of cold air, feeling her eyes sting and her nose automatically beginning to run. Naturally, she thought, wiping at her nose with the back of her gloved hand. Keep walking, she told herself, her hands now thrust deep inside her pockets. Keep moving.

What was she doing at this screening anyway? She had told David she would quit television. No, that wasn't entirely correct. She had agreed not to go back only if he agreed to give up Nicole. He had not agreed. She was still in limbo. Therefore, she was at the screening.

And if the clients, the sponsors, the people from the network liked the show? What then? If she was offered a regular position? What would her answer be—I can't tell you, I have to wait until my husband makes up his mind about his mistress?

And if he did make up his mind, if he walked in the front door that evening and announced that he had chosen her over Nicole, over all the fairest maidens in the land, what then? What would her answer be? God, could she really give everything up? Could she remain buried up to her neck in frustrations and recriminations, knowing the branch that could have saved her had been within her grasp, only to have been tossed carelessly aside? Could she really allow herself to be shut up in some ivory tower for one hundred years because she had allowed herself to be kissed by a Prince?

She turned onto shop-lined State Street and continued.

"Hour Chicago" was good. She knew it was good. Her segment was probably the best thing she had ever done. She had

torn the issue of battered women who kill their husbands inside
out and upside down, and while ultimately she was providing
no easy answers, she would certainly be filling the airwaves
with disturbing and thought-provoking questions. "This program is about fear," she heard her narrator's voice intone. "The
fears of thousands of abused wives and the men who abuse
them, who now see their women fighting back with often lethal
results. And about the fears of many who feel that this latest
trend will give new meaning to the old phrase that women get
away with murder."

Jill drew a deep breath of satisfaction and felt something
falling wet against her cheeks. Opening her eyes directly into
the cold of the clear sky, she saw bits of snow falling. On a sudden childlike impulse, she opened her mouth and caught several
snowflakes on her tongue, feeling them disappear instantly. She
was looking forward to winter, she realized with no small
amount of surprise, since it had always been her least favorite
season. Maybe this winter she'd buy herself a pair of skates, a
thought that alarmed her, as her only two previous excursions
on skates (the last time twenty years ago) had resulted in two
broken wrists. ("Someone should have told you not to skate on
your hands," she remembered Beth Weatherby once telling
her.)

She headed north on Michigan, thinking of Beth. She'd been
so preoccupied of late, she'd neglected her good friend. Spot-
ting a phone booth across the street, she ran, without looking,
to the other side, aware of cars honking angrily behind her. She
chose not to look back, preferring not to see how narrowly she
might have missed death, knowing that in recent weeks she'd
become almost purposely careless, as if she were leaving this
aspect of her life (with all other aspects) to the will of others.
She rummaged in her purse for the necessary change, fought
with her memory for Beth's telephone number, and dialed.
Beth's voice answered after two rings.

"Beth, how are you?"

"Jill?"

Jill nodded, then realized Beth couldn't hear a nod. "Yes,"
she answered, possibly too loudly. "I'm so sorry I haven't
called lately. I've just had so much on my mind."

"I know," Beth said, tangibly warm. "How's the show going?"

"Good. Really good. There's a screening in about an hour for the people at the network, possible sponsors. My segment is the last of the three, right after welfare fraud and the Second City troupe."

Beth laughed. "You're pleased?"

"Yes," Jill said. "Your name is never mentioned. You're alluded to only as a 'recent event,'" she explained with invisible quotes.

"How quickly we become recent events," Beth remarked with a smile. "I'm sure that makes David rest easier," she added.

Jill said nothing. Beth said nothing further.

"How are you holding up?" Jill asked her.

"Well, I've held up this long. I don't intend to fall apart just as I'm entering the home stretch."

"Have the courts set a definite date?"

"Three weeks this Thursday," Beth announced, audibly exhaling.

"Are you nervous?"

"No," Beth answered. "Well, maybe a little. My lawyer's the one who's a nervous wreck. He's still trying to persuade me to change my plea. I'm still clinging to my right to self-defense. Actually, I've become quite a cause célèbre in the women's movement. All sorts of money has been coming in, offers of support, letters from prominent people." She paused. "And Michael's come home."

"Oh?"

"I'm not sure if he's here to stay," Beth added quickly. "He's still wearing his robes and there are a lot of funny-looking people hanging around outside, but—I was right, Jill. He did see something. Apparently, several times over the last few years, he'd seen Al attacking me. Of course, with my hands bound and my mouth gagged, he assumed it was some sort of kinky sex thing and was too embarrassed and ashamed to say anything about it. My mother the pervert, that sort of thing." She laughed nervously. "Poor baby, no wonder he prefers his chanting." She paused. "He's going to testify for me in court. The prosecution will undoubtedly claim I was a consenting adult, out for a little fun and games. Anyway, be prepared, I'm liable to be a hot topic of conversation for some time."

"Does that upset you?"

"No," Beth answered simply. "There's nothing anybody can say about me now that can hurt me. The worst time I had since all this started was that week I was trying to come to terms with myself and with what I'd done, with what I had to do, what I had to say, knowing how many people the truth would hurt, knowing I wouldn't be believed, that I might have to spend the rest of my life in prison. But it's funny," she continued, "once you finally do make up your mind, the rest is relatively easy. When you finally make the decisions, and just get on with your life, well—you just get on with it." She paused dramatically. "It's when you don't know what to do that the panic sets in. The minute you make those decisions, it stops."

"It's that easy?" Jill asked, knowing Beth had intended the words for her.

"No," Beth laughed. "But it sounds good."

Jill joined in the laughter. "I better go," she smiled.

"Call me later."

"I will. Bye-bye." Jill replaced the receiver and headed toward the elegant shops of the "Magnificent Mile," glancing into the windows, crossing and re-crossing the street, continuing this random pattern for some while, aware of time's passage only by the increased presence of snow on her red coat and by the growing darkness around her. The sound of traffic seemed to be following her, and the farther she traveled the more impatient the drivers became, pushing against their horns, gunning their engines uselessly against the encroaching night. She had gone another two blocks before she realized that the persistent honking she was hearing was intended for her. She turned toward the shiny beige and brown Seville, failing at first to recognize either the car or its driver.

"It's me, you fitness freak," the driver yelled, lowering the tinted glass window as Jill approached and squinted inside. "I've been following you for blocks. Where the hell are you going? Don't you know it's dangerous out here at night?"

Jill recognized the voice of Ricki Elfer before she was able to make out the face. She smiled widely. "What are you doing downtown?"

"Put it this way," Ricki told her. "When I'm not at Rita Carrington's, I'm out exercising my wallet. Do you have time for a coffee?"

"What time is it?" Jill asked.

"Ten to seven," Ricki answered.

"Oh my God, no," Jill said. "I have to be at the studio at seven o'clock! I didn't realize I'd been walking for so long."

"Well, hop in, I'll give you a lift," Ricki offered.

"Great," Jill agreed, coming around to the other side of the car and giving Ricki directions, then briefly describing the show she was working on.

"Oh," Ricki smiled knowledgeably, "like that lawyer who got himself killed." Jill nodded silently. "How's your friend holding up?" Ricki asked, catching Jill by surprise.

Jill felt a slow grin spreading across her face. "She's fine," Jill said quietly.

"Wish her luck," Ricki offered.

"I will," Jill answered, looking around. "This is some car," she exclaimed, changing the subject.

"Like it?"

"It's gorgeous."

"Paul gave it to me."

"Wow! Birthday? Anniversary?"

"Guilt," answered Ricki with a smile. "I'd been complaining a lot lately. The usual wifely complaints. Finally, Paul got fed up and he said in that special tone they all get, you know the tone, 'What do you *want?*' And I said, 'I want you to be more affectionate, I want you to be more loving, I want you to spend more time with me.' And he said, 'Couldn't I just buy you something?' " She laughed, indicating the car's plush interior with her hands. "How can you not love a guy like that?"

The car pulled to a halt in front of the studio. "That didn't take long," Jill commented, opening the car door. "Thanks a lot, Ricki."

"Listen," Ricki said, leaning over, "maybe you and your husband could come for dinner one night soon. Or the four of us could take in a movie some time—"

"Sounds good," Jill lied, slamming the door. "I'll see you at class soon."

Ricki honked her horn several times as she drove off. Jill watched until the new Seville disappeared from sight, and then she turned toward the building and went inside.

"This program is about fear," she heard the narrator begin, watching the photographs of bruised and beaten women fall one on top of the other like lifeless corpses. After that, the soundtrack became blurred, the images unfocused, and Jill wondered for a fleeting instant if something had gone wrong in the editing process, if another sound track had been improperly substituted for the correct one. She hadn't interviewed Beth Weatherby; she hadn't questioned her mother or Ricki Elfer or Elaine. Or Laurie. And yet here were all these women up there on the large screen, exchanging profiles, their lips moving in unison, their voices superimposed on top of one another, blending into each other, speaking as if from one voice, speaking as if one. So what if he's good in bed, the voice asked, as all around her heads nodded eagerly. Lots of men are good in bed. One couple's perfect marriage is something no one else would want. There are certain things in life that we just have to accept. Sarah Welles had drowned in her bathroom sink. Life is too short. The faces, blown up and expansive, registered shock, amusement and concern at the various remarks, moving easily from one emotion to the next. They separated, argued, came together again, agreed. Suddenly, a shadowy figure approached, his image growing until he all but overwhelmed everything around him. You're going to ask me why I didn't leave him, the women began as Jill felt her eyes drawn to the new presence. You have to remember that for a long time, I blamed myself. (I'm sorry, David, Jill heard herself plead under the other voices.) I kept thinking that it was my fault. (I didn't mean to say those things, David. Please, I'm so sorry.) Your pride goes first—then your common sense. (I'm so sorry, David. Please forgive me.) Soon, even your soul is dead. He killed my soul. (Jill saw the torn pieces of her soul floating, like leaves, up past David's head.) What is there to forgive? the voices

asked angrily. "What the hell am I so sorry about?!" Jill demanded of herself.

Immediately, everyone disappeared, leaving a screen filled
only with the powerful photographs of a more powerful hate.
My God, what we do to one another, Jill thought, realizing that
she was as bruised as any of the photographs. It was just that
her bruises didn't show.

What do I want? she asked herself in silent annoyance. What
is it that I want? She fidgeted in her seat, crossing one leg over
the other and then returning it to the way it was before. I know
what I *don't* want, she realized abruptly, sitting up very straight
in her chair.

I don't want to be like Elaine, consumed by bitterness and an
overriding need for revenge. I don't want to end up like Beth,
driven beyond all endurance, forced ultimately to kill in order
to survive. I do not want to destroy what good there *was* in my
marriage, and thereby destroy both my husband and myself. I
never want to hate my husband—or myself—as much as either
of these women. I still believe in marriage, despite everything
that's happened, but I can no longer just sit by and be a passive
observer of my own life. I know what I want. I want to stop
feeling guilty and unsure. I want my pride back. I want my
soul.

Jill watched in silent confirmation as the episode ran to its
conclusion, saw her name flash as the credits rolled quickly by,
failing to note whether they had read Jill Listerwoll or Jill
Plumley, discovering she didn't really care. She accepted the
congratulations of the people around her, recognized in the
noncommittal smiles of the prospective sponsors that it would
be several weeks before the final verdict was in, and realized
that that was all right too. Everything in its own good time. She
hugged Irving warmly and left the studio.

Nicole Clark lived in a relatively modern apartment in a nondescript part of the city. It took Jill only ten minutes to drive
there and half that time to find a place to park. Then she pulled
the two suitcases she had spent several hours packing from out
of the back seat and carried them to Nicole's apartment. It was
late. There was no doorman, only an elaborate buzzer system

which Jill was in the process of deciphering when an elderly couple returned home and held the door open for her. She picked up the luggage and stumbled through the doorway. Apartment 815, she repeated to herself as they rode up together in the elevator, watching as the old couple departed at the fourth floor. The doors closed after them, taking her up to the eighth floor in silence before depositing her at her destination.

She promptly turned right, realizing after following several of the numbers on the apartment doors that she should have turned the other way, and doubled back. The suitcases were starting to feel heavy, as if for the first time she was conscious of their weight. She released them, letting them fall gently to the floor, feeling a sudden twinge of panic. "It's when you don't know what to do," she heard Beth's voice repeat, "that the panic sets in. The minute you make those decisions, it stops." It wasn't that easy, she knew, projecting ahead to later that evening when she would re-enter an empty apartment and know for certain that David would not be coming back—but it wasn't any easier now.

She grabbed the suitcases and proceeded with renewed determination to Apartment 815, stopping when she saw the appropriate number, lowering the bags once more, wondering what she was going to say to whoever opened the door. Perhaps she wouldn't have to say anything. The sight of the luggage would undoubtedly speak for itself.

She could try humor, she thought, feeling strangely lightheaded. Hi, everyone. Since all the fun seems to be happening over at your place, I've decided to move in.

What if David had already left to return home? Suppose he'd just broken it off with Nicole and he and Jill had crossed, unknown to each other, in traffic. Strangers in the night, she said to herself.

The door opened.

Nicole Clark stood in the doorway draped in a white velour bathrobe, her skin dotted with moisture, a towel wrapped around her neck. A Siamese cat hovered shyly around her legs. "David's in the shower," she said, after a pause, disengaging the cat with one foot and pushing it back inside.

M48

Jill felt her throat constrict, her nose begin to twitch. ("Hi, I'm Nicole Clark. I'm going to marry your husband.") "These are most of David's clothes," she said softly, forcing back the itch. "He can come by for the rest of his things tomorrow. I'll be out all day. My lawyer will get in touch with him in a day or two," she continued, wondering who the hell her lawyer was. "I'd rather David didn't try to call me personally."

The two women exchanged long, probing glances.

She even looks good with no makeup on, Jill thought, allowing her glance to drop down to the other woman's bare legs. The cat had returned and was licking greedily at Nicole's damp feet. The second toe of each foot is longer than her big toe and she has a rather large corn just below one nail, Jill realized, joyously. She has ugly feet! She looked back up into Nicole's puzzled face and smiled, noticing for the first time a slight blemish just beneath the younger woman's lower lip. Perhaps it had been there all along. Or maybe it had merely been biding its time, waiting for just the right moment to pop up and announce its host's mortality.

"I don't understand," Nicole stammered. "You're giving up?" She paused, mentally moving the suitcases inside her apartment. "I win?"

Jill straightened her shoulders, feeling her throat return to normal. The constriction was gone, as was any urge to sneeze. "I guess that depends on just what you think you've won," she answered, and knowing that Nicole's eyes were watching her, turned and strode quickly back toward the elevators, confident for the first time in many months that she was not about to trip and fall.